Praise for *The Flames*

'Magnificent. Feels destined to be a classic – exquisitely crafted and so absorbing. I loved it and refuse to accept it is a debut. It's simply too good.'
Katie Lowe, author of *The Furies*

'Completely convincing and utterly compelling, *The Flames* gives vivid voice to four muses who refuse to be remembered as just that. Haydock is a writer to watch.'
Kiran Millwood Hargrave, author of *The Mercies*

'I knew nothing of Egon Schiele. I'm now obsessed, and heartbroken for all four women. An unforgettable book about wanting more for ourselves than we are told we are allowed.'
Ericka Waller, author of *Dog Days*

'*The Flames* paints a history so detailed and vivid that we feel we were there in the flesh. A book to get lost in, a great feat of a debut.'
DBC Pierre, winner of the Booker Prize for Fiction

'Thought-provoking and illuminating – I so enjoyed discovering the world and the women behind works of art I adore.'
Kate Sawyer, author of *The Stranding*

'The four women who loved Schiele come back to life, combining an exquisite sense of place and era with a passion and sensuality that transcend time altogether.'
Isabel Costello, author of *Scent*

'Readers are going to fall very hard for this one.'
Sue Rainsford, author of *Redder Days*

'In *The Flames*, Haydock turns a forensic eye on the loves, fears, hopes, and heartbreaks of four extraordinary women who might otherwise have been swallowed by history . . . a beautiful and timely narrative.'
Rebecca F. John, author of *The Haunting of Henry Twist*

www.penguin.co.uk

The Flames

Sophie Haydock

doubleday

TRANSWORLD PUBLISHERS
Penguin Random House, One Embassy Gardens,
8 Viaduct Gardens, London SW11 7BW
www.penguin.co.uk

Transworld is part of the Penguin Random House group of companies
whose addresses can be found at global.penguinrandomhouse.com

First published in Great Britain in 2022 by Doubleday
an imprint of Transworld Publishers

Illustrations by Egon Schiele: p. 9 Leemage/UIG via Getty Images;
p. 111 photo by Imagno/Getty Images; p. 225 Universal History Archive/Universal Images Group
via Getty Images; p. 329 and p. 423 photos by V. C. G. Wilson/Corbis via Getty Images.

Extract from 'Ariel' by Sylvia Plath on p.vii reproduced by permission of Faber and Faber Ltd.

Every effort has been made to obtain the necessary permissions with
reference to copyright material, both illustrative and quoted. We apologize
for any omissions in this respect and will be pleased to make the
appropriate acknowledgements in any future edition.

A CIP catalogue record for this book
is available from the British Library.

ISBNS 9780857527622 (hb)
9780857527639 (tpb)

Typeset in 12/16pt Minion Pro by Jouve (UK), Milton Keynes
Printed and bound in Great Britain by Clays Ltd, Elcograf S.p.A.

The authorized representative in the EEA is Penguin Random House Ireland,
Morrison Chambers, 32 Nassau Street, Dublin DO2 YH68.

Penguin Random House is committed to a sustainable
future for our business, our readers and our planet. This book
is made from Forest Stewardship Council® certified paper.

For Ali Schofield, my friend

Bodies have their own light, which they consume to live:
they burn, they are not lit from the outside.

Egon Schiele, 1912

Is it the sea you hear in me,
Its dissatisfactions?
Or the voice of nothing,
that was your madness?

Sylvia Plath, 1960

Prologue

T he women crash together, a blur of twisted limbs and contorted faces. Eva opens her eyes to the lilac sky. There's blood in her mouth, on her knuckles, and her corduroy dress is ripped. She curls in, wheezing, one hand on her stomach, then straightens her glasses, cursing the crack in one lens. She watches the wheel of her bicycle spinning its slow, ticking orbit. A form comes into focus, a few metres away – an old woman on the ground, her mouth ajar, misaligned teeth poking from behind flaccid lips.

It all comes back. The last thing Eva had seen in the seconds before the collision was a pair of watery eyes, widened. Hands raised to a mouth. The white-haired woman had appeared out of nowhere, dashing through a gap between parked cars, barging into her.

Eva had been distracted as she'd cycled home along this residential backstreet in Vienna's leafy Hietzing district. She'd argued at lunchtime with the man she'd made a tentative life with. They'd met in a coffee shop near where she worked as an assistant at a store selling second-hand books in a tourist-crammed area of the Innere Stadt. But what should have been a moment for intimate revelation had become fraught with recrimination. Eva had run from the café and her lover had let her go. She'd been rehashing the day's argument, reliving the

1

things she'd said, thinking about the things she should have disclosed. The next thing she remembered was the blurred flash of a figure running into her path.

She'd gripped the brakes, tried to swerve, but their momentum was unstoppable.

'Oh, no, are you hurt? Can you hear me?' Eva asks now, lowering herself to the woman's wounded frame. 'I'm so sorry! I didn't see you until it was too late,' she adds.

The woman doesn't move. Her silence is numbing.

Eva stares into the face of her victim, with its high cheekbones and sunken sockets. Blood oozes from the woman's forehead, vivid against pale hair. Her skin is cool to the touch, a sickly mauve, and a pungent smell, like old soil, radiates off her. Eva notices the ragged clothes and black-rimmed fingernails. A thin-soled shoe, lined with newspaper, has fallen off and the toe of the bared foot is ugly, its bunion oversized and ruby.

'I don't know what to do,' Eva whispers, rubbing her dark hair from her eyes, willing herself to concentrate. She searches for a passer-by, anyone who might help them. A light appears in the window of one of the grand apartment buildings overlooking the street, but nobody appears. She staggers over and presses the dozen brass buzzers.

'Call for an ambulance, please!' she says into the intercom, but hears only static.

The skies are darkening and threaten rain.

Eva returns to the woman and leans in, her heart pounding, listening for any signs of life. She shakes her, gentle but insistent. Silvery moths loosen from the seams of the woman's coat, startled by the light.

The bag the woman had been carrying is ripped, its contents scattered across the road. Eva searches for a clue to the woman's identity. There's a bundle of letters, tied in a ribbon, the ink faded, but nothing else by way of identification.

Please, I beg of you, write to me, any response will do . . . Eva deciphers the old-fashioned handwriting on almost translucent paper. *It's unbearable to have this rift between us. I need forgiveness. Eternally, your loving sister . . .*

'Edith?' Eva says, pocketing the letters, her eyes on the old woman once more.

It's then that the muscles at the edge of the old woman's lips flicker. Eva starts, encouraged by the movement. She grasps the old hands, which are rough like bark.

The woman's eyelids flash open, revealing dilated pupils. A violent rasp comes from her mouth as she bares her gums. For an unspeakable moment, Eva believes this shrunken, injured stranger might be capable of sinking teeth into her flesh.

'Get your filthy hands *off* me!' the woman barks. 'I'm not dead yet, you know! Even if you've damn well given it your best shot.'

Eva backs away as the victim struggles to her feet and brushes herself down, rubbing her elbow, then her lower back.

'I was only trying to help,' Eva tries, by way of apology.

'You call this helping, do you?' The old woman tests her frame like a bird before flight. She puts a hand to her head and winces as she sees the blood on her fingertips. 'You didn't see me, did you?'

'You just appeared out of nowhere,' Eva replies.

'Oh, invisible, am I?'

'But you ran into me!'

'Fifty years I've been searching.' The white-haired woman fixes her with a razor-sharp glare. 'Since before you were even born!' Her arthritic fingers move in a flourish. 'And then you come along and knock me down, almost kill me, just as I lay eyes on her again.'

Eva feels as if they're being watched and turns, but nobody's there – only a tree with loose bark beside a poster for an art exhibition, pasted to a whitewashed wall.

'You've no idea!' the older woman continues. 'No idea at all. All the sacrifices I've made, everything I've suffered, the heartbreak, every day, searching for a single glimpse of her. Then finally, here she is, after all this time. Look, goddamn it! There she is, exactly as she has always

3

been.' Her breathing is ragged and a sob punctuates her words. 'I'm seventy-eight, with nothing to call my own. I've lost it all, ruined. If I were to lose her, too, on top of everything . . .'

'Please, let me help you. What is it that you've lost?' Eva asks, disorientated by the weft of the stranger's sentences, the peculiar desperation of her words.

Panic streaks across the old woman's face as she dips her fingers down the front of her blouse. She fumbles for a moment, then the fear fades as she pulls out a chain. On it is a gold band. She clasps it, her eyes closed, pressing it to her lips.

The rain begins. Crows, cawing from the roof of Schönbrunn Palace, rise and circle in flight.

'Edith?' Eva asks gently, touching the woman's arm.

The old woman's lip quivers. 'Whatever would you call me that for?'

'I saw your name on these letters.' Eva holds out the bundle and they are snatched away.

'You have no right to look at those!'

Eva is hurt and unsettled. She hears the unmistakable sound of an ambulance siren.

'With any luck, that's coming for you,' Eva says, to reassure the woman, and herself. 'Somebody must have called for help.' She looks up at the windows of the apartment building. 'They'll want to take you to the hospital, just to check you over,' she adds. 'You'll get all the help you need there.'

'*Genug*! *Nein*!' the old woman shouts, jumping back and trembling. 'I won't go! You can't make me!'

The blue light of the *rettungswagen* reflects off the cobblestones as it turns into the street. Eva hurries over to the vehicle, as a driver and his assistant step out of it.

'There was an accident,' she explains to the two men. 'I'm not hurt, at least I don't think so.' She glances at her shoulder. 'But I cycled into her.' She gestures to the white-haired woman, who has hobbled over to the poster. 'I knocked her to the ground. She wasn't responding at first, she was out cold for a few minutes. I tried to help, but she's not the type to accept it. She seems confused.'

'You've done all you can. We'll see to her from here,' the driver replies.

The injured woman is pressing her hands against the exhibition poster. It depicts a young model, her cheeks flushed, an intense, uncertain look in her eyes.

'*Junge Dame*? Hello?' the man tries as he approaches. 'How are you feeling? We can see that you're hurt. Your head is bleeding. We need to take you to hospital. Let's get you out of this rain, shall we?'

'*Nein! Nein!*' the woman says fearfully, recoiling.

'This is for your own good, *meine Dame*.' He places a hand on her shoulder.

'Get off me! Don't you dare. You can't make me go back there.'

'Come now, let's not be like that. You must be in a lot of pain. We only want to help.'

'I've done without anyone's help for long enough,' she snaps.

The two men flank her, their shoulders above her head, their feet planted, mouths set.

'We'll take care of things from here,' they reassure Eva. 'If you're feeling well enough, you can go on home.'

They take the older woman by the arms and lead her towards the rear of the ambulance. They're gentle but firm. But she is ferocious. She fights and twists, kicks and squirms. Her eyes lock on to Eva's. 'You, girl! Help me!' she shrieks as she's forced through the vehicle's doors. 'Do something, please! I've nothing left! No one will help me! I didn't make it up.' She thrusts a fist in the direction of the poster. 'This proves it. I'm not mad! We existed. You can't—'

The doors slam and that haunting glare is gone.

Eva is ashamed that she feels relieved. She has enough to deal with, without all this. Still, her heart is racing and she can't shake a gnawing feeling of guilt. She tells herself she has helped this strange woman, but perhaps she has only succeeded in making things worse for her. Eva swallows and turns to the uncertain smile of the figure on the poster.

The driver starts the engine. 'Wait! Stop!' Eva shouts. She runs over to the ambulance, banging a fist on the back.

But the vehicle is moving, the siren starting up as it speeds away.

She has no name to go on.

Eva is exhausted, utterly spent, aware that the rain has soaked her to her bones. Her stomach aches in a new way. She considers her bicycle – another thing, along with her glasses, she can't afford to repair. She will have to walk the broken frame home, a journey that'll now be much longer than expected. She'll find no words of reassurance there.

Then she sees it.

There, on the ground, between the cobbles, is a glint of gold. Eva bends to pick the object up. It's a long, antique necklace. The clasp has been pulled apart but the chain is twisted around the scuffed metal of a round-edged band. It is still warm to the touch. Eva holds it up between her thumb and finger. Inscribed inside, in elegant cursive, are two initials: E & E.

Or is it E & A? The second letter isn't clear. It looks as if it could have been scratched over, or reshaped, by the tip of something sharp.

The ring belongs to the old woman who ran into her. Eva only wants to forget her and get on with the rest of her life, as best she can, but she's haunted by the rapture that had lit up the woman's face as she held this item to her lips only moments before – and the terrified look in her eyes as she was locked away. Eva grips the band. The weight of it in her palm offers strange comfort. She knows how it feels to lose something, for a piece of you to be missing.

Eva accepts what she must do: somehow, soon, return the ring to its rightful owner.

⤙

Inside the ambulance, the old woman is strapped quickly and grace-lessly on to a stretcher and secured in place. She aches with new-found knowledge. She was *there*, before her very eyes, after years of searching.

There's a dull pain in her breast. And suddenly, a loud, insistent banging on the rear door of the ambulance. Above all the racket, that blasted plain-faced girl, the one who'd been dashing along on the bicycle, is demanding to know her name. But it's too late for such things. As they speed towards the hospital, the siren continues its unholy wail, promising to part the traffic, carrying her away from the only thing that matters.

What does *her* name matter now? I could be anyone in this world for all people care, she thinks. It has been decades since anyone wanted to know who she was. The last time a person spoke her name, the word was delivered as a bullet – an order, an insult, disgust stitched between its letters. Then it was forgotten entirely.

Did she ever really exist? Yes. She knows that now. And her life before . . .

As the stretcher is pulled from the ambulance, she can't help but hear a dreamy echo of her name's three lilting syllables, like champagne bubbles popping on her tongue.

She remembers it the way *he* said it. The thrill of it being whispered, the promise once carried within it, the desire she knows it provoked. The phantom sound touches a space that has long been numb: the part of her that holds the capacity for joy.

'Adele?' she remembers, in a wave of wonder, as a face peers down at her. '*A-dé-le*,' she repeats and her consciousness begins to drift, a smile across her bloodied, torn face. 'Why, yes, that's it. My name, if you must know, is Adele. Adele Harms. And don't you damn well ever forget it.'

ADELE

1

October 1912

'Adele, I swear, if we're late again, I will disown you,' Edith complains. She's red in the face, hot with the effort of trying to pull her sister from the gold chaise longue positioned by the window in the parlour of the Harms family's apartment. Adele makes herself heavy upon the velvet cushions. She knows her infuriating little sister won't leave without her.

'Don't rush me!' she says. 'You know how I hate to be rushed.' Adele shakes her sister off and stretches both arms above her head, wriggling her fingertips.

She is lingering in the hope of a final sighting of the man she has been watching from her vantage point all afternoon. She'd spotted him immediately as he walked down the street earlier in the day. Adele can't help but notice the comings and goings of the building opposite the one in which the sisters live with their parents, Hietzinger Hauptstrasse 114 – on the wide, tree-lined main street of Vienna's wealthy and aristocratic thirteenth district. She enjoys observing the signs of life behind the dozen windows which, on this last day of October, are covered with the lacy imprint of dead ivy. Mostly, she spies thickset men with elaborate facial hair, mothers, maids. This young man is a welcome novelty.

He can be no older than Adele – in his early twenties, if she were to hazard a guess. And what's more, he has spent many hours moving his belongings into the building: cases, heavy furniture and a huge mirror that for the briefest second was angled in her direction and reflected back an image of herself, framed by the window.

'I simply don't understand how you're not ready,' Edith continues. 'The curtains go up in less than half an hour and you've barely moved an eyelid all afternoon.' Adele's sister scans the room for evidence. With pursed lips, she notices the unopened French novel abandoned on the floor, a silver tray laden with crumbs from a slice of that after-noon's freshly baked chocolate *guglhupf*, alongside an empty cup, its rim marked by the residue of coffee and frothed milk. She follows her sister's eyes to the street below. 'Oh, I see. You've lost yourself in other people's business again.'

Edith takes a step towards the window for a closer look. She places her fingers to the glass and her touch and breath leave visible blooms on the cool pane.

'Ssshh, he's coming back again,' Adele says.

Below, the dark-haired man, slim and unkempt, is labouring under the weight of an easel that's taller than him. He's pale and seems hol-lowed out in places Adele cannot properly determine.

'My, my, that confirms it!' Edith turns abruptly and snaps her fingers in Adele's face. 'Off to the asylum, dear sister, for madness has over-come you. The only thing that dishevelled specimen has going for him, the only thing that could possibly have attracted your attention, is that his hair isn't thoroughly grey.'

Adele throws a fringed cushion that hits her sister square on the chest.

'A little excitement wouldn't kill you,' she counters.

'And who do you suppose *she* is,' Edith asks, raising her eyebrows and pointing to a young woman who has left the building by the same door to pick up a valise. 'His maid?'

The woman in question, who looks to Adele as if she could be a gut-tersnipe, here to sell her wares, pauses to loosen her fingers.

'Well, she *could* be his maid?' Adele pouts, and narrows her eyes. 'It's impossible she's his wife. His sister, perhaps?'

The woman below them is hardly a great beauty. Her clothes are unflattering and dull, with none of the tailoring the sisters take for granted. But the longer Adele has observed the waif, the more she must grudgingly admit that there is something appealing there: peachy skin, wide eyes, a tender, exaggerated mouth, and masses of thick burnt-red hair.

'Come, now! We mustn't dally any longer,' Edith warns. 'Papa will be furious. Young ladies must never operate below their station,' she says in a low tone, mimicking their father's repeated instructions. 'And this, this shameless spying, is far below your station.'

'One cannot forever embroider a handkerchief, you know,' Adele sniffs. She pulls her long boots on to her feet and laces them up her calves as slowly as she can manage. She stands. Even without her shoes, she's taller than her sister, and she enjoys the sensation of being able to look down at her. Adele instinctively checks her reflection in the mirror above the fireplace. All very satisfactory indeed, she decides, turning her face first to the left, then the right, smoothing her eyebrows with the tip of her little finger and tidying the silky auburn hair around her ears. The peaks of her upper lip are diabolical, she concludes, even if her teeth are somewhat misaligned – but not unappealingly so. She breathes out, smiles, then draws her furs around her, angles her feathered hat, and experiences a tingle of anticipation for the evening ahead.

'How do I look?' she demands of her sister.

'Simply wonderful, as you well know. And me? What flaws can you find this time?'

Adele inspects her. Edith's cheeks are round and rosy, as if she were a farmer's daughter, and her hair is an unfortunate shade of dirty straw. Even dressed in her finest gown for the opera, she looks as if she'd be happier in a barn full of cattle. Adele has tried to encourage her sister to take more care of her appearance, but it has proved a fruitless endeavour.

'Exquisite, *as always*,' she offers. 'I've never thought otherwise. Why, if you weren't my sister, I'd envy you. Luckily for me, the traits I admire in you I possess in abundance.'

Edith looks at her suspiciously, shaking her head.

Their old maid, Hanna, is waiting in the hallway and holds the apartment door open in anticipation of their departure. In starched apron and flat shoes, she bids the sisters a pleasant evening, succumbing to a modest curtsey, despite Mutti, ever the pedant for the appropriate way of behaving, not being there to appreciate the gesture.

'See to it that you open the parlour window after we've gone,' Adele commands. 'We need fresh air in this dusty old space. Now, if you please.'

'Yes, *gnä' Frau*,' Hanna replies, with another brief dip of the knee.

'Goodnight, Hanna,' Edith says as she leaves, giving the old woman a kiss on the cheek and clasping her hands warmly. 'No need to work too hard on our account.'

Adele sighs loudly. Her sister has always been needlessly kind to the help.

⤿

Outside, the air is even more biting than Adele had expected. It will ruin her complexion, making her as ruddy as a country barmaid. But with a little luck – and before she loses her glow entirely – she might orchestrate an encounter with the man who has so fully captured her attention this afternoon. 'Hurry, now, Edith, do come along!' she encourages.

Adele deliberately steers her sister away from the spot where the carriage their parents have arranged is waiting to pick them up.

'You're leading us astray!' Edith grumbles. 'Mutti and Papa will be waiting for us.' Still, she hooks her arm inside her sister's, as is their habit, while they cross the street, stepping under a tall tree and heading towards the building that the mysterious man will surely soon be leaving in order to collect the last of his belongings.

The streetlamps cast a pearly glow through the darkness. With the quality of an apparition, the stranger moves suddenly into their pool of light. Adele's step falters, her heel meeting the ground a moment out of time. She takes in the young man's heavy brows and high hairline, the artful curl of his thick, wild hair. He's tall, mesmerizing, almost demanding to be touched.

The trio walk towards each other, Adele pulling Edith to an even slower pace. She rushes to absorb every detail – the firmly pressed knot of his blue woollen tie, the delicate pinpoint detail on his shirt, the place where his neck rubs against his collar. His nostrils are quite large and there's a depression at the tip of his nose. She watches him cough in the cold air: observes the mechanics of his throat, the judder of muscle, the hard angles.

He's so close now that even in this shadowed light, Adele can see the velvet hairs of his earlobe and the clean line a razor has taken down his cheek, the skin matte on the lower half of his face. The man looks up – his eyebrows rising at the sight of them. Adele's eyes quickly meet his. A falling twist of shadow prevents her from distinguishing blue from hazel.

He's staring too, and her throat has tightened, her heart radiating blooms of heat. Her step, miraculously, does not falter this time.

Everything outside this nucleus is hazy and hollow, everything except for him, this man, who is in perfect, precise focus. He sparks with the wild rebelliousness that Adele has been craving every second of the day for longer than she can remember.

She puts her fingers to her mouth, angling to present him with her best side, and holds his gaze. He's heading straight towards them but neither he nor Adele – arm still linked with a bristling Edith – will step aside to let the other pass. It's a small test, a teasing, trivial game.

Then, at the last possible moment, he veers away, putting his palm on the trunk of the tree and spinning around it. As he returns, he brushes up against Adele's arm and she pulls away, her eyes wide, as if his touch has burned her.

The man turns back and smiles at them, entertained by the encounter. A bolt of victorious energy surges through Adele. She marvels at it, her head rushing. She can almost taste it.

This man is her future, she will make sure of it.

2

October 1912

Adele and Edith dash into the grand foyer of the Hofoper – the Vienna Court Opera – feathers and furs flapping, then stop in their tracks. The space is laden with marble, mosaics and Vienna's fashionable *beau monde*. Adele runs a hand up the gleaming banister as they ascend to the upper echelons. She has an urge to spin on her heels and bow to an imagined crowd, accepting their rapturous applause. Instead, she steals glances at the other society women who have yet to take their seats. They wear silk dresses, pleated and draped, adorned with tulle and lace; their hats plumed with feathers and pearls, their gems refracting the light of the chandeliers.

Adele loosens her mink from her shoulders and manages to step ahead of Edith as they head towards the box where their parents are waiting, along with their close family friends, the Brons. As they enter, she can see Papa's shoulders are hunched and he is pulling a hand along his beard, sharp eyes reading the time on his pocket watch.

'It's a record,' he says, shaking his head. 'You've arrived with a single second to spare.'

Adele leans in to him as she passes to take her seat.

'I tried to hurry Edith,' she whispers. 'You know how she dallies.'

Mutti, preened to high heaven, the air around her scented with lilac, offers her daughters a withering look, a small tut escaping her lips. Edith takes their mother's hands and kisses her warmly, soothing her irritation at their late arrival. It is fortunate they are in a private box, not the stalls below, for Mutti has piled her silver hair into a towering nest, past which not even the tallest usher would be able to see tonight's performance. Herr and Frau Bron take the seats at the front, due to Frau Bron's weakening eyesight. Adele sees her holding a pair of opera glasses by the long stem, peering through them not at the orchestra or stage, but at the glittering audience below and around her. She turns to Mutti to crow at some point of indiscretion. The Brons' daughter, Emilia, smiles conspiratorially as Adele takes her place, the fabric of her dress rustling.

Then the lights dim, the audience falls silent, and the velvet curtains swing open.

Adele prepares herself, as always, to be awestruck. Without doubt, she'd attend the opera three hundred nights a year if she were left to arrange her own social calendar. The flamboyance of the musical performance, the poetry of the human voice, the elegance of choreographed movement, the extravagant costumes, all speak to her very core. She lives for this passionate world, and especially for Mozart, who ignites her soul with joy, tenderness, despair and indifference in a way that no other composer can; and for the work of Johann Strauss II, whose lightness of touch delights her. She soaks up the theatrical melodrama, the stories of intense longing, revenge and forbidden love – unlike poor, sensible Edith. Her little sister claims to love the opera, too, but seems to fear the excess of passion it brings. It's at times like this Adele most feels the difference of the three years between them.

During the interval, there's an opportunity to talk. Papa and his business partner, Herr Bron, share a rich history – they joined forces years ago when her father established a fine furniture shop in the Innere Stadt and needed an investor. Their daughter, Emilia, is only a few months older than Adele and a longstanding friendship developed between the two families. They take annual sojourns to the Austrian countryside together, share the cost of a box here at the Hofoper, as well as at the Burgtheater, and dine weekly in each other's homes.

Now the men talk of business, the fluctuations of the Wiener Börse, Emperor Franz Joseph's latest decree. Frau Bron talks to Mutti about an upcoming religious service at which the Emperor will be present, and suggests they attend also. 'Everyone who's anyone will be there,' she adds.

Both families are still adjusting to the news, announced at the start of the month, that Emilia is soon to be married. The revelation, somewhat ahead of the usual schedule of things, has unbalanced the dynamics of the friendship. Mutti in particular holds it against Adele. Her daughter's fault, earlier this year, was to break off her own engagement to Heinrich, a transgression which her mother cannot overlook, and which is made all the more unbearable now that Frau Bron is planning the wedding of the season.

'She's rubbing my nose in it,' Mutti frequently mutters.

Adele is not jealous of Emilia. She's prepared to wait, amid this pressure from her mother, for a man who sets her heart ablaze, rather than marry in a hurry just to get the job done – a tactic Emilia seems to have employed, with the wedding scheduled for the new year. Adele believes she has all the time in the world, so refuses to pay heed to her mother's warnings that she'll end up an old maid.

The relationship between Emilia and the man who is to become her husband has gained pace at such speed that the Harms family has yet to meet him. For Mutti, it makes the reality that much harder to swallow; she cannot legitimately point out this suitor's flaws until she has made his acquaintance, identified them all, and thrown in a few more for good measure. She suggests again that he must attend the next supper at the Harms residence.

'I've told you before, Josefa, he's terribly busy, he travels extensively for his apprenticeship,' Frau Bron replies. 'You'll meet him soon enough. He's a fine man in the making.'

'Alwin has a brother, you know?' Emilia nudges Adele. 'Albert is a very sweet young man, just slightly older than you. He has excellent prospects. We could be sisters-in-law!'

'Sweet?' Adele retorts. 'I don't intend to marry until it's for love rather than convenience,' she says to her friend.

'A suffragette are we now, Adele?' Emilia teases.

'Enough of that kind of talk,' Mutti interrupts, one ear always listening.

'I'm not sure I can be counted among the reform rabble just yet,' Adele replies.

Emilia makes a polite movement with her shoulders. 'You and Edith will both have your pick, I have no doubt. I've every expectation that all three of us will be married within the year.'

'I'll make sure of it,' Mutti declares.

Edith whispers that marriage sounds like a thing best avoided, like the plague.

Three chimes announce that the interval is over and they return to their seats. Adele's mind is full of the young man she saw earlier. The truth is, she does want to marry, to have a love story of her own.

⌒

The lights go up. The audience is revealed. They applaud those on stage, the exquisite performers, the orchestra and conductor, but mostly, they applaud themselves. For this is Vienna, and is it not they who are forging a path of progress and change into this new, promising, unblemished century? No other audience is more deserving.

'That was splendid,' Adele sighs. 'But can we go home now? Please, Papa?'

Papa loosens his tie and clasps his hands. 'You girls usually beg me to let you stay out just a little longer.' He looks sideways at his eldest daughter, his lips twitching under the grey bristles of his moustache.

'Oh, but we're exhausted,' Adele complains.

'Some of us have had a lot of excitement for one day,' Edith teases.

Outside, a mist has fallen, a woven veil of spider silk that masks Vienna's magnificence. Papa hails a *fiaker* with a flick of his wrist and gives the bowler-hatted coachman their address in Hietzing. With any luck, they'll be home before midnight.

The horses' nostrils flare against the cold air. Edith rubs her hand down the neck of the one closest to her, whispering in its ear. She'll carry that rough animal smell with her all the way home to the bedroom they share, Adele thinks, watching her with disdain.

Mutti bustles her sculpted hair and voluptuous skirts into the carriage first, taking up almost all the space inside. Adele squeezes in beside her, followed by their father and Edith. During the journey, she endures her mother's prattling about the latest society gossip. This is precisely the petty existence Adele is desperate to escape. She may wish to be married, but she doesn't want some lawyer or banker for a husband, certainly not one of the specimens Mutti has been trying to force upon her.

The coachman pulls up in front of their elegant apartment block. Papa pays, counting out the *kronen* precisely. A few windows glow in the building opposite. Adele searches for movement and spots the dark silhouette of a man in one at the top, in the attic space, with its large bay window overlooking the street. Edith follows her sister's gaze and rolls her eyes.

'Destined for the asylum,' she whispers, loud enough for their parents to hear.

Adele kicks Edith's shins, holding a finger to her lips, as Mutti turns to the pair with a questioning look.

∽

'What do you think of our mystery neighbour?' Adele says to her sister when they're alone.

She drapes her dress across the back of the chair, while Edith hangs hers, carefully.

Pulling the blankets to her neck, Adele watches Edith at the dresser, her face reflected several times in the three-way mirror as she brushes her fair hair over and over.

Thick shadows fall across the walls.

'He is rather handsome,' Edith admits.

'Aha!' Adele kicks her feet beneath the coverlet. 'So you're not blind, after all?'

Edith turns a shade of beetroot. 'I'm just making an observation, that's all.'

Adele plumps her pillow. She pulls the shaft of an otherwise downy goose feather through the pillowcase, so it won't bother her during the night. Her sister won't have a single nice thing to say about their new neighbour now, after that little slip. Perhaps she shouldn't say anything at all. Isn't that what girls are taught? To be seen and not heard?

Adele turns and brings her fingertips to the wallpaper's flowers while Edith slips into her bed, nightdress buttoned to her chin and hair neatly tucked away.

'Don't lose your mind over a man that Papa will never agree to,' her sister adds.

'Who said I've lost my mind? I'm simply intrigued.'

Edith snorts and turns off the lamp. 'I know you better than that, dear sister. Remember Herr Färber.'

It hadn't mattered that Herr Färber was the same age as the students' fathers, that he was in no way handsome, with his bulbous ears and coarse hairy hands – or that he was married. Those things were overlooked. It had begun as a way to inject a little excitement, a little fun, into their otherwise endlessly dreary lives. Each Wednesday, the dozen or so older girls in his religious studies class would vie to outdo each other, passionately absorbing his tropes, elbowing one another to be the first to recite them, eager to impress.

Adele, then aged seventeen, had worked steadily, but there was heat in her eyes. She quietly demanded his attention, and felt a tremble of power when he bestowed it upon her. Before long, the other girls came to believe that he paid her a fraction more consideration: it was an exaggeration, but one that she encouraged.

On the final day of term, Adele had stayed back as the others filed out of the room and sent withering looks her way. Edith, still needy, at only fourteen, had wanted to leave together.

'Give me a minute or two,' Adele had insisted.

Edith pulled a face. 'You don't have anything to prove,' her little sister whispered as she edged beyond the door. Then Adele and her teacher were alone. She wiped the blackboard of its chalk and helped gather the books, stacking them together.

'Thank you,' Herr Färber said, straightening the pile so the spines aligned. 'It has been a pleasure to teach you this year,' he continued. 'You've worked hard and applied yourself. I've seen much less of the daydreaming that characterized your attendance last year.' He smiled.

'I've learnt lessons that I'll carry with me for a lifetime,' Adele had replied. 'Is there anything else I may need, do you believe, to help me on my way?' She'd waited a few seconds, then moved her fingers on to his hand. She blinked. She had expected a jolt, but there was nothing at all.

Herr Färber had gently removed her hand, then walked her to the door.

Outside, Edith was waiting.

'What happened?' she asked, taking in her sister's hot cheeks when she finally appeared.

'Nothing. Nothing at all.'

It was the truth.

'You're lying.'

'No,' Adele replied, almost haughtily. 'I am not.'

But Edith would not leave the question alone. 'Something happened in there.'

'Fine. If you must know,' Adele said, flustered, 'Herr Färber' – she hesitated – 'kissed me.' She tried to look nonchalant. 'His bristles were quite unpleasant.'

Even Adele was surprised at how easily she had managed to rewrite her experience. The power she'd lost was restored and that burning sensation behind her ears lifted almost entirely. 'But you must promise not to breathe a word. It's our secret.'

'But he's married,' Edith protested.

'It was one small kiss,' Adele replied, taken aback. 'It's not as if it'll happen again.'

'You shouldn't have. You know it's wrong.'

'It wasn't my fault he kissed me.' Adele didn't have to feign her indignation.

'Don't deny that this was your plan all along. You wanted this.' Adele could feel Edith's disapproval, and it shifted the balance. She couldn't tell Edith the real truth: that she'd made a fool of herself.

Over the following week, Adele had expected that Edith's stance would soften, that they'd laugh about it together. But a few days later, after a wearisome hour of piano practice, Papa had barged in and grabbed Adele's arm.

'Come with me,' he snapped. He prided himself on being a man of logic, of reason, and rarely raised his voice. 'Is it true?' His features were altered, his lips pulled back. 'Don't make this worse for yourself,' he continued. 'Your teacher has been summoned. Tell the truth so there's no confusion when I see him. I don't want to accuse an upstanding man of doing a thing such as this, if . . .' He stopped. 'If you lie to me now, Adele, you'll regret it.'

'It's not true, whatever Edith has said.' Adele twisted away. 'She always wants you to think the worst of me.'

Her father weighed her words, then released his grip as the bell rang.

'This will be him. We'll get to the truth, whatever that may be.'

Herr Färber, with sickening solemnity, tapping his fingers in a steady sequence on the dining table, had denied all knowledge of anything improper.

The walls seemed to shrink in upon Adele.

'Categorically untrue.' His whiskers jostled above his lip as he presented his side of events with distinction. 'The girls were caught in a period of extreme silliness, I'm afraid, and Adele's behaviour was the most extreme. She simply got carried away. I cannot say why she acted as she did, but I can say with certainty that I did nothing to encourage her. I assure you, there was nothing resembling a kiss.'

'I didn't lie, I didn't.' Adele had cried real tears. 'He kissed me, you have to believe me. Why does nobody ever believe me? I didn't make it up.'

Papa had shot her a withering look. 'We've heard enough from you, young lady. It's about time you took on board, once and for all, the notion that actions have consequences. Lies ruin lives.'

Adele continued to cry – and her anguish lasted for weeks.

After everything, she could no longer remember what was real and what wasn't.

3

Winter 1912–13

A dele Harms is a busy young woman. She and her sister Edith have barely a minute to spare – each hour of the day is filled, often months in advance, with an array of classes, cabarets, recitals and receptions. From an early age, the girls have engaged in all the pursuits deemed suitable for women of their standing. They study English, French, Greek and Latin and both continue to advance each week, with lessons in conversation and literature. Adele also enjoys classical history, learning about the myths and mishaps of the past, but her true passion lies in music. She receives twice-weekly tutorials in piano, and plays with flair. She adores Mozart, Mahler, and Maria Theresia von Paradis. Adele and Edith are also fine dancers.

Edith's other pastimes are more sedate: she spends hours on embroidery, card playing or craft. Adele has never been able to master the bullion knot and her ruby roses unravel.

Aside from the formalities of education and musical pursuits, their mother curates a packed social calendar. She's an attendee of every salon and society event on the Viennese circuit – galas, gallery shows and grand openings – and her daughters are brought along, to be seen in the right places by the right people. The sisters are popular among their peers, young women who inhabit the same sphere, and the only reason they don't rely more heavily on these friendships is that they have each other. Their loyalty to one another always comes first.

'What's the point of all this education?' their father sometimes quips. 'Men don't appreciate overly intelligent wives.' He chuckles, and his wife and daughters shake their heads. Papa, for all his teasing, is proud of his girls. Adele knows he values his family, and is grateful for the security he can pull around them all, with his wealth and experience. Her mother, Josefa, is a decade younger than Johann – they didn't meet until an advanced stage in their lives. After a whirlwind romance, Adele's parents had married within months, days before Mutti turned thirty-five. Adele had arrived promptly, nine months later. Johann was forty-five and a first-time father. Edith was born three years later.

Papa's work always keeps him busy. He collects fine furniture, buys at favourable prices, dabbles in a little repair – mostly of the gentle wear-and-tear variety – and sells the items on for a tidy profit to the noble patrons of the city. Adele loves spending time in his shop, among the curiosities. Now, at sixty-seven years old, Johann Harms has not yet retired and has no plans to do so – he's as engaged and energetic as ever.

The income, over the years, has allowed the Harmses to enjoy a modest upper-middle-class lifestyle. It's a delicate balance, of course, and Johann jokes that his family's tastes don't get any cheaper, but Adele knows that Papa also has his investments, pots tucked away here and there. Adele has every certainty they'll fare well in the coming years, and she imagines the ease of her existence unfurling into the future like ribbons of silk.

⌒

Plans for Emilia's wedding continue apace and Mutti becomes frigid with annoyance every time she glances at Adele. The situation comes to a head when a heavy envelope arrives, inviting the Harms family to the wedding of Heinrich – the man to whom Adele was previously engaged.

Since her girlhood, Adele had admired Heinrich from afar. She'd been the one, at the age of twenty, to push for an introduction and Mutti had been only too happy to oblige. They'd courted for close to eighteen months, Adele enjoying the tickle of anticipation as she stoked his hopes and desires. On Boxing Day 1911, Heinrich had proposed with an emerald and Adele had agreed, with her mother's explicit encouragement, to accept his hand in marriage. The New Year edition of Vienna's most esteemed newspaper had reported their engagement. But, as fantasy moved closer to reality, the sheen came off. Adele found herself looking at her husband-to-be and noticed that he was twenty-six, already balding, soft around the edges. Yes, he came from a good family, yes, his prospects were unimpeachable, but his shoulders were hunched from years of his father slapping him on the back, proud of what a fine, upstanding fellow he'd produced. Heinrich's obliging nature often left Adele wanting to scratch him. Frankly, he was insipid, and by the end of January, she could no longer tolerate a shred of him. So she broke off the engagement. Heinrich had taken the news with equanimity; it was Mutti who threw a priceless vase at her head.

Within three months, he began courting Lina, the parish mouse. And now they are getting married.

'Don't pity me!' Adele rebukes Edith when she offers condolences. 'I don't envy that woman, with her ever-expanding stomach.'

But Adele feels a hard sentiment gnawing inside, a desire to prove her true worth.

⌣

Adele increasingly spends her spare moments watching for her mysterious neighbour. She can't stop scanning the street for a glimpse of him, losing herself more and more in dreams of a chance encounter.

Exhausted by some social event or another, a shopping trip to the boutiques of Vienna's finest district, or fresh from a piano recital, her fingers tingling from overexertion, Adele settles herself on the chaise longue – a book plucked from the shelves as a ruse – to watch the door of the building opposite. She requests that Hanna serve refreshments here from now on. In the late afternoons, Adele brushes crumbs of pistachio from her dress as she continues her vigil. She sucks icing from her fingers, cursing the other men who pass by.

Where is he? What is he doing? With whom? The taste of marzipan lingers.

Adele might be rewarded once or twice a week. The man flashes with a seductive energy as he moves, a cigarette or paintbrush tucked behind his ear. He's often late, dashing so fast he barely has time to close the door behind him. Sometimes he's with a friend, a well-dressed man who enters the building empty-handed and leaves with a neat parcel or two under his arm, wrapped in brown paper and tied with string. More often than not, the man is accompanied by that red-haired guttersnipe, whom Adele has never seen smile. Occasionally, she sees the woman entering the building by herself, opening the front door with a key she slips back into her pocket. The woman must surely be his maid, Adele decides – hired help and nothing more.

She puts out feelers on the Viennese gossip circuit, and salacious rumours make their way back to her ears. And, to her chagrin, also to the ears of her parents.

'Did you know we're living opposite an *artist*!' Mutti exclaims.

'They say he's a disciple of Gustav Klimt,' Papa adds, tugging on his beard.

'That doesn't make it any better,' she reprimands him.

Adele tries to quell her excitement; the man is an *enfant terrible*, defying convention, ripping up the rulebook. There's a frisson of scandal, that much she can glean, although the details are withheld from a woman of her position. Instead of repelling her, as it should, this reputation only deepens her desire. She knew he would be the kind of man who'd shuck off tradition, embrace the future.

Her senses heightened by this knowledge, Adele continues to watch. The man seems to have no routine – he'll be gone for days at a time, then he'll be back, not leaving his position near the window in his front room. Adele assumes he must be working. A stream of pretty girls comes and goes and Adele is racked with envy. If only she could orchestrate a meeting.

She has no doubt that when he finally meets the formidable Adele Harms, the attraction will be mutual and all other women will be forgotten. Even in the darkness, Adele can conjure his features clearly. She imagines pushing a hand through his hair, nestling her lips against his jaw. He runs a thumb across her neck. Fine, so perhaps she is losing her mind, as Edith so often remarks. But what can Adele do? She is feeling, has felt for some time, an emotion that she cannot put into words, certainly not in a way that her simple-minded sister would comprehend – but here it is, an uneasy fluttering in her chest. It's an intense impatience, as if something were meant to happen, were on the brink of taking place, but day after day, the revolution she desires fails to materialize. Does everyone not harbour this overwhelming urge for action, momentum, change? Do they not pray for something to come along and alter the path of their life?

4

Spring 1913

T he day has finally arrived. Adele and Edith stand on the precipice of the grandest evening in Vienna's carnival season, *Fasching*. The spring society ball draws archdukes and princes in pristine medallioned tuxedos, princesses and grandes dames draped in silks and dripping with diamonds and sapphires. Masks conceal the identity of Vienna's powerful elite – from politicians to royalty, foreign diplomats to distinguished artists, musicians to actors. Couples waltz in the grand hall, heels turning on the polished parquet, crystal and gold glinting from the chandeliers above. Adele and Edith have attended every year since they came of age and this year will be no exception. Emilia would usually be in attendance, too, but she is enjoying her honeymoon in the countryside.

Tonight, Adele is the one to be ready ahead of the carriage that will take them to Vienna's Innere Stadt, to the sprawling Hofburg Palace, travelling along the Ringstrasse – a magnificent boulevard in the city centre – passing the opera house and the pair of imposing court museums, with the lights of the neo-Gothic town hall glittering just beyond. The sisters have spent the entire day preparing themselves, bathing in water scented with rose petals, rubbing lotion into their skin, as if they were the reincarnations of the Empress Elisabeth herself. Their hair was set the previous evening and both have had elaborate ballgowns made – Edith's in the finest pale-green silk, with oozing underskirts laden with lace. Adele's is silver brocade with a midnight-blue velvet bodice; it pulls in at the waist, showing off her height and slender frame. The dresses were purchased from Vienna's most exclusive boutique, the designs straight from famous Parisian couturiers. The sisters have attended several fittings over the past months and the fabric is cut to perfection, nipping in at all the right places, drawing the eye.

Adele places her mask upon her face, covering her eyes, and dances over to Edith.

'You'd never know it was me, would you?' she asks, spinning.

'I'd know that neck anywhere,' Edith replies.

'But I could be anyone, for a short while, at least.'

'I don't believe you have a preference for anonymity.'

'I like to be known,' Adele agrees, removing the mask.

'You like to be *seen*,' Edith says.

'I do wish to be noticed,' Adele admits. 'But a little mystery can be a good thing, can't it? After all, don't all mysteries demand to be unravelled?'

∽

As the sisters step into the Kleiner Redoutensaal ballroom, Adele looks around at the enormous chandeliers and candelabra, the glittering crystal and precious porcelain. A band on the upper balcony strikes up the 'Fledermaus Quadrille' by Johann Strauss. The sisters know that the dancing will linger long into the night, peaking at midnight with a waltz led by a distinguished *tanzmeister*. The women will curtsey, the men bow, and for that witching hour, the thousand partygoers will be transformed into a mass of elaborate motion. The last revellers can often be found rubbing sore feet at four in the morning, but the Harms sisters will not be permitted to stay out so late. Adele looks around and imagines the faces of all the men behind their masks – it's a disorientating procession, and she feels dizzy for a moment. She can't help but hold on to the hope that her neighbour might be one of them, although she can't imagine he'd feel at home in a place such as this. He's the opposite of men like Heinrich, men who represent order and sobriety, who shape themselves within the bounds of convention and grow dull with respectability. Even though she hasn't yet met the man across the street, to Adele he represents passion, freedom, independent thought – a different life altogether. He's the antithesis of the stuffy men who vie to entrap Adele in a life of sewing and society, precisely the kind of dreary existence led by her mother.

'May I?' A man with medals pinned to the chest of his dinner jacket approaches.

Adele looks the man up and down, represses a smile, then offers him her gloved hand. The musicians coax notes from their instruments, producing a powerful, persuasive sound, and Adele and her partner spin off on to the dance floor.

As she dances, Adele watches her sister over the man's shoulder. Edith steps away to the edge of the ballroom, where a waiter hands her a glass of something sparkling, segments of fruit visible in the long flute. Her sister smiles at nobody in particular, looking aloof but guileless. Edith loses all her awkwardness when she dances and can waltz as well as anyone in the room, with her impeccable posture and innate sense of timing, but the elegance she radiates on the dance floor is rarely seen, as she is rarely asked.

The rousing score draws to a close, and the orchestra rest their instruments for a moment, before they launch into the next piece. In the pause, Adele's dance partner takes hold of her arm and walks her to the balcony, which overlooks gardens, immaculately tended.

The light has mostly faded from the sky; pinks and purples remain, and the stars are becoming visible through the veil of darkness. The man leans on the balustrade, taking in Adele, his eyes roving along the contours of her figure.

Adele keeps her eyes on the topiary, determined not to give him the satisfaction of her attention. He touches her elbow. She ignores him.

He becomes more insistent. She turns to him, her eyes on his, a challenge shining through the cut of her mask.

'Remove it,' he says, touching the side of her face.

'Why?'

'I want the pleasure of seeing you.'

A waiter walks past, a silver tray balanced on his hand. The man takes two flutes and passes one to Adele.

She takes a long, slow sip, then removes her mask, looking the man directly in the eye. He whistles softly.

They converse for a while, Adele dancing the delicate line between withhold and reveal. Other revellers drift over to the balcony to admire the view, but soon they are alone again.

Adele hears the band start playing Edith's favourite waltz.

'Excuse me,' she says. 'My sister will be looking for me.'

'But you're not excused,' he teases, stretching out a hand to stroke her bare arm.

Adele turns to leave but now he holds her back and won't let go.

'You're hurting me,' she says angrily, pulling away. He has ripped a small seam on her dress.

Suddenly Edith is by her side. 'Get your hands off her,' she warns.

The man laughs, his arrogance flaring. 'Don't delude yourself. There are plenty more like you here.'

He struts away and the sisters retreat, Edith pulling Adele through the main ballroom and out into the garden on the other side. They sit on a bench, their backs to the palace.

'I don't suppose you want to share this?' Adele asks, her hand trembling slightly. She produces a long, thin cigarette from her clutch bag.

'Where did that come from?' Edith asks.

'What you don't know can't hurt you,' Adele laughs. She takes out a box of matches, and draws the matchstick across the strike paper. With a flick of the wrist, it sparks to life and dances in the darkness between them. Adele smiles, triumphant, and inhales. 'Let me be a bad influence,' she says, passing the ebony cigarette holder to Edith, kicking off her shoes as she does so, and feeling the coolness of the ground through her stockings.

Edith puts the cigarette to her lips, attempts to breathe in a little smoke, then splutters and passes it back. She smiles at her sister, resting her head on Adele's shoulder.

'I'll leave all the risqué pursuits to you from now on,' she says.

'Thank you for stepping in earlier,' Adele says. 'My heroine,' she laughs, hugging Edith to her, and kissing her little sister's cheek. 'What on earth would become of me without you?'

5

Autumn 1913

I n the second week of September, Mutti receives an invitation to the opening of a new exhibition at a gallery in Hietzing, and the girls' presence is required. Adele feigns protest at first, in her usual way, but she also can't ignore the possibility that her artist might frequent such a place, so prepares herself accordingly.

The gallery is well lit, the doors open to the street, letting in the last of a late-summer breeze. A dozen young men, seemingly attendees of Vienna's Academy of Fine Arts, congregate around a table laden with flutes of sparkling wine. Adele circles them, trying to distinguish if her artist is among them. They disperse to view the framed paintings and Adele follows, staring at the artworks without enthusiasm.

In the adjoining gallery room, Edith appears to be talking to a man who has his back to Adele. But she'd know that silhouette anywhere! Her sister is engaged in conversation with the artist. Edith keeps looking away, as if begging to be rescued.

'I can't get over the beauty of the art,' Adele says, approaching. 'Doesn't it move you, Edith?' She steps in close to her sister. 'Oh, I'm terribly sorry to interrupt,' she adds, as if she has only just noticed the artist. This is as close as she has ever been to the object of her desire. The room seems to palpitate with his presence. The bones of his knuckles are so prominent they show up whitened through his skin. There's ink on his shirt, by the pocket, and his teeth are tobacco-stained. It is clear he has smoked a cigarette recently; Adele inhales a long drag of its residue, leaning in closer.

'I should introduce myself. I'm your neighbour,' he says, bowing.

This is the first time Adele has heard him speak.

'Neighbour? Are you new to the area? I've not seen you around,' Adele fibs.

'Well, I've certainly spotted you.'

Edith stands, prim and proper, by her side.

'You have?' Adele says.

'You're the girls in the window. I can see into your apartment from my attic. The angle between us is perfectly aligned. But don't be concerned!' he laughs. 'I can only see into the front room, so there's little to incriminate you.'

'Such comments could get you into trouble,' Adele says, feeling emboldened.

'Oh, they already have.' The artist smiles, but she notices his expression tighten. 'Do you have a name? I can't refer to you as the "sisters across the street" for the rest of my life,' he says, turning playful again.

'My name? Why, yes, if you must know, it's Adele. Adele Harms,' she says with all the confidence in the world, holding her hand in his direction. 'I hope you won't forget it.' Edith fidgets next to her. 'Oh, yes, and this is Edith.' She rolls her eyes a little at him.

'The Harms sisters,' the artist muses, taking Adele's fingers and squeezing them, pressing his thumb into the back of her ring finger. She has the urge to let him waltz her round the gallery; how she manages to remain standing on her own two feet is a mystery. 'How delightful,' he continues. 'It's a pleasure to meet you. Finally.'

'And do you have a name?' Adele asks.

'I certainly do. One that follows me everywhere I go. I simply can't get away from it, and believe me, I've tried. Egon Schiele.' He drops her hand to perform an elaborately deep bow. Adele feels his phantom touch lingering on her skin. She weighs the name on her tongue and decides she admires it very much. It suits him.

'You're an artist, I presume?'

'Many have called my chosen profession much worse,' he concedes. 'But yes, I have a solo exhibition, my very first, at the Galerie Hans Goltz.'

'Perhaps we might attend?' Adele says. 'To see your work for ourselves.'

'You'd have a long way to go. It's in Munich.'

'Goodness!' says Adele. 'You must be rather good.'

'You'll have to sit for me sometime. The pair of you.'

'Our father wouldn't allow it,' Edith says. 'He's very strict.'

'We'd be delighted,' Adele replies.

Suddenly, from the edge of the gallery, she catches sight of their mother heaving into view.

'My apologies, please excuse me,' he sighs, checking his pocket watch. 'I'm due to meet my patron, Herr Roessler, here any minute now. He's the one running late, for a change. He keeps the wheels in motion, my name on the lips of the city's art dealers and gallerists, so I'm forced to be attentive to his every whim.'

The artist holds Adele's gaze. His eyelashes are long for a man, his lips pleasingly pink.

'Aha, there's the old dog. Arthur!' Schiele catches the man's attention and steps away.

'Pay us a visit soon,' Adele says after him, their mother fast approaching but still out of earshot. Edith turns on her. 'What?' Adele hisses. 'A little fun won't kill us, will it? Now, ssshh, here's Mutti.'

'Who was *that*?' Mutti says sourly, her nose turned up in distaste.

'Nobody,' Adele replies.

'It was our neighbour, wasn't it?' She peers over her shoulder at the man's departing figure. 'The artist . . . My goodness!' She fans herself. 'You weren't encouraging him, were you?'

She looks around, to check who might have seen her girls talking to such a depraved individual. Mutti draws in a sharp breath as she takes in the flush on Adele's cheeks. 'Stay away from that man, he's an absolute disgrace,' she instructs. 'I've warned you before. Artists are the very worst of society. And, Adele, don't be indulging any of your silly ideas, young lady.'

'I've no clue what you're talking about,' Adele protests.

Mutti narrows her eyes. 'Come with me. There's an eligible banker you must meet. His mother is one of Vienna's most esteemed ladies.'

Adele lets herself be led away; but her eyes, all the time, remain on the artist.

⁓

'A toast,' Herr Bron announces. 'To my dearest acquaintance, Johann. A man I've known and admired for almost thirty years. In that time, I'm happy to report we've seen much by way of growth – our friendship, which has gone from strength to strength, our business prospects, which fail to falter, and of course, our darling daughters, who've done us proud by developing into the most beautiful and sensitive young women.' He tips his glass in Adele and Edith's direction, then to the other side of the table, where Emilia is seated beside her new husband, who has brought along his puffy-faced younger brother, Albert. They each smile, politely. He turns his attention back to Papa, who's sitting at the head of the table, his hands clasped together, as the waiter in a tuxedo fills his glass with the restaurant's finest Grüner Veltliner. 'We're all here,' Herr Bron continues, looking around at the dozen gathered guests, 'to celebrate the occasion of your birthday, Johann, to toast your continued good health, and to pay thanks for your presence in our lives.' Mutti nods, reaching out a hand to her husband in a rare display of affection. 'We'll be especially grateful,' Herr Bron continues, 'when you pay the bill at the end of the evening!' The party erupts into cheers, knocking glasses together and clapping.

Her father is pleased with the display, Adele can tell.

Platters of food arrive – sizzling veal schnitzel; whole roast fish, the skin scored and crisp; vast bowls of potato salad. Adele's mouth waters at the scent of freshly chopped herbs. Everyone eats, mindful of their manners, and talks about the usual topics, the older men sticking to the realm of business, the deals they hope to broker, the latest news of the Habsburgs, and the fate of the Empire, on which the sun will never set. The women swap notes on courtships, engagements, marriages and newly arrived babies – Vienna, despite its sprawling size, is small when it comes to society gossip and everybody knows everybody else's business. Heinrich and his new wife are pregnant with their first, Adele overhears – she ignores an icy glare from her mother – and there are hints that Emilia will be next. Alwin's brother, Albert, has taken a shine to Edith, and every time Adele glances over he's trying to engage her in conversation. So Adele turns her attention to the rest of the guests. Among the younger generation, talk jumps from advances in photography and the latest cinematic releases, to a discussion of dreams, the unconscious and a man named Freud, the psychoanalyst who has published a new collection of essays on the subject of taboo. She tries to follow the discussion, but everyone is talking at once, the young men the loudest of all, and she can find no opportunity to express her opinion. Her ears pick up words of interest: repression, fantasy, sacrifice. She would like to know more of Charles Darwin, of Oedipus . . .

'Klimt's been at it again,' says Herr Nathansohn, an art dealer, to Papa.

Adele chews carefully, her lips closed, and leans in closer, not want-ing to miss a word.

'What's our esteemed national artist done this time?'

'*The Virgins*,' Herr Nathansohn says with a raised brow.

'Good Lord! Is it as gaudy and oozing depravity as the last one?'

'The word on the street is that Gustav's golden period is well and truly over.'

'He's gambling with our affections after the popularity of *The Kiss*,'

Papa says. 'I'm not a fan of this Art Nouveau style. Why mess with centuries of perfectly good tradition?'

'Then you won't like the young chap they're calling his natural heir.'

'You're talking about that Schiele fellow?' Papa says, sipping his wine thoughtfully.

'That's the one. That young man has ruffled the feathers of the bourgeoisie, that's for certain.'

'You'll never believe it, but he lives just across the street from us.'

'No!' the man says, piercing the air with his fork. 'He had to face a judge last year, in a county courtroom. Guilty, they found him. You're living opposite a convicted criminal!'

Adele splutters into her napkin, earning an alarmed glare from Mutti.

'Heavens! Was that him? I hadn't made the connection. Quite the scandal,' Papa agrees, his eyes wide. He turns to Mutti. 'It's worse than we dared imagine,' he whispers.

'They're calling him the pornographer of Vienna,' Herr Nathansohn continues.

'That man better keep his distance, for all our sakes,' Mutti says, her eyes on Adele.

When Adele is alone that evening, she conjures herself into her neighbour's attic room. The talk at dinner has only kindled her desire further. She visualizes the stance she will strike for the artist – shoulders back, wrists crossed over her knees – and enjoys his admiration of her elegant pose, the sensation of his eyes on her skin as he paints. But it's not long before she tires of this static fantasy, and her imagination pushes her further, from the drapes on the floor over to the makeshift bed. She beckons to the artist and he succumbs. She licks the bristles of his brush, lets it cover her lips, then takes his fingers in her mouth. She tastes chalky pigment at the back of her throat. She knows she should not do this – good girls never partake in such wicked thoughts – but she's swollen with the dream of his forbidden touch. In her mind, her lips, cheeks, chest, the inside of her thighs, the soles of her feet, are smeared with his palette. There's an addictive tingling in her hot, hollow space as she imagines him searching her body with his paintbrush. She's surprised by the urge she has to feel him inside her: the need to push against him and fight for release. Adele wants more and more and more. She's greedy. She replays it over and over – a close-up of his face, the sensation of his long fingers running all over her body. She experiences a quickening throb. A rush. From the unknown erupts an explosion of colour and a furious beat. She is alight.

6

June 1914

O ver the following months, Adele manages to orchestrate more chance encounters with the artist, although usually on the street and always too fleeting for her liking. Their social circles are worlds apart and, fuelled by more tales of the artist's misdemeanours, Mutti has redoubled both her vigilance and her efforts to find Adele a suitor. Only in her imagination can Adele truly lose herself to the artist, the only snag being that other woman – she still doesn't know exactly who she is – and Edith. Her silly little sister can see that she's love-lost and has no patience or sympathy. Edith has her own distractions – after the dinner with the Brons, Albert has called at the apartment a couple of times, enquiring after her, keen to begin a courtship, no doubt. But what does Edith know of the heart? She has always been so good, so pure; scared of offending others, of being cast adrift to possibilities. She's far too sweet to survive this modern world.

Adele remembers one occasion when the Harmses were coming home from a trip to the countryside. Edith, aged five at the time, saw an injured animal through the window of the carriage, its fur dusted with blood.

'A fox.' She pointed. Its small body juddered with short breaths, and its eyes were open. Edith, who was sitting on Papa's knee, put her hand to his dark, perfectly groomed beard. 'Stop the horses. Please, Papa.'

'Darling. Don't bother yourself over such things,' he said. 'It's vermin. And death is natural,' he added, pulling her face into his shoulder so she wouldn't be able to see it as they passed.

'We can take it home, make it better,' she pleaded.

'No,' Papa replied, sterner this time. 'The thing's probably infested with fleas. And think of what a mess it would make of this lovely carriage. You don't want to dirty your dress, do you?' he asked, smoothing the green folds of fabric. Adele said nothing, but as the carriage continued on its journey, Edith's distress turned into a full-blown tantrum.

'She should know better than to behave like this,' Mutti complained, wiping away her daughter's tears.

Papa later told Adele that he was proud of her, for she'd retained her composure. He rewarded her with a truffle, rolled in cocoa and coconut. The chocolate had melted on her tongue. It was the crowning moment of her childhood. She could still taste the unfettered sweetness of conquest over her little sister.

Later that evening, in their beds, Edith whispered to Adele that she could not banish the fox from her thoughts – its eyes kept searching out hers, saying, 'My friend, help me.'

When she'd finally fallen asleep, Adele, with childish malice, had whispered those words in Edith's ear, slow and deep, with as much throaty essence of fox as she could muster.

Edith woke later that night crying out, incoherent, sobbing.

'She's an over-privileged child,' Mutti said, when alerted by Hanna.

By the morning, however, Edith could not be moved from her bed and her neck was swollen. Mutti sent urgent word for the physician.

'I'm burning,' Edith moaned. In the next moment, she became dull-eyed and floppy.

'It's tuberculosis,' the doctor confided, his face etched with concern. Mutti began to pray and even Papa had a tear in his eye. Adele had never seen him express such emotion. The household went to great lengths to keep Edith alive. But Adele never believed that she'd die. It wasn't blind faith. She simply could not imagine a world without her sister in it.

For long months afterwards, Edith was weak. She coughed and wheezed and spent most of her time in bed. Even today, at twenty, Edith still seems to be surprised she exists. Adele sees her confusion when people recognize her or remember her name. Edith believes she's forgettable, impermanent. The two of them have witnessed how photographs are processed – the subject's features coming into focus, slowly; a body, head, hands, eyes. Edith does not believe she is solid. She thinks she changes from one light to the next and is soon eclipsed.

Edith will not read Papa's broadsheet for fear of not being able to sleep, of that toxicity that had touched her soul returning. She cannot tolerate news of deaths or disasters. Adele, on the other hand, seizes upon every opportunity to read the *Wiener Zeitung*. And so she is horrified to learn, one day in late June, that Archduke Franz Ferdinand, nephew of the elderly Emperor and the man expected to take over rule of the Austro-Hungarian Empire, has been assassinated.

AUSTRIAN ARCHDUKE AND DUCHESS DEAD

Archduke Franz Ferdinand and his wife died from gunshot wounds, an official confirmed.

The news sends shockwaves through Vienna. The city's music halts. Flags are lowered to half-mast. In Sarajevo, riots break out. Mobs go on a demolition spree. Serbs are targeted, beaten, many killed. Troops and police fill the streets. Martial law is declared.

The world seems to tremble.

Adele lingers over the words. The Archduke's wife, Sophie, Duchess of Hohenberg, was sitting beside him as they toured the streets of Sarajevo in an open carriage. They'd made quite the impression when they married in 1900 – the Archduke chose love over duty by marrying a woman who was, at the time, lady-in-waiting to the wife of the Duke of Teschen. As a member of the royal House of Habsburg-Lorraine, the expectation had been that he would choose a bride from a royal family. The marriage was only permitted on the condition that their children be barred from succession. Now it has ended with her being shot in the abdomen.

The funeral is to take place the following day.

'The man who fired the weapon,' Adele reads to Edith, who has her hands over her ears, 'then turned the gun on himself.' She crumples the printed sheets and leans forward, kicking Edith's card table as she does so.

'It's appalling, an outrage,' Papa says, warning that the assassination of the heir to the imperial throne could spell serious trouble. He says this is a declaration of war by Serbia, which can only be followed by another declaration of war. Adele tries not to think about the repercussions and tells herself they won't reach Vienna, even though she already senses a tension in the city, as if it is waiting.

⏝

Later that day Adele spots the artist and the woman leaving his building. He is carrying a closed umbrella, even though it's a bright, cloudless day, swinging it with careless ease. Adele decides she must find out where they are heading. She launches herself up and grabs what she needs, which is very little – a small bag, her coat, her hat.

'Where are you off to in such a hurry?' Edith asks, clutching at her hand.

'Nowhere,' she says. The less she can incriminate herself at this stage, the better. She pulls away from Edith's grasp and hurries out of the apartment, flushed with determination. Her footsteps echo as she rushes down the stairs and across the tiled hallway to the main door.

In less than a minute, Adele has caught up with the artist and the woman as they walk along the main street. She follows at a safe distance and steadies her breathing, which is out of kilter, smoothing her outfit back into place. The artist and the woman walk and talk with balanced ease. She's dressed in cheap material in the plainest style, and has tried to hide the fact with a brick-red sash around her waist and an amber brooch on her lapel. Her hair is uncared for, her boots as thick-soled as a man's, and her skirts smudged with dirt.

After a few minutes, they come to a stop at the entrance to the gardens of Schönbrunn Palace. The two stand at the gates, dappled in light and shadow from the overhanging trees, about to go their separate ways. The artist has one hand on the curve of the umbrella handle, the other in his pocket. The woman is talking, her hands animated, a coquettish slant to her shoulders and hips. Adele holds back, just out of sight, clasping her handbag in both hands, her knuckles whitening. The woman laughs at something Adele cannot hear. Her joy is jolting. Adele takes a step closer, eyes narrow, determined not to miss a thing.

'Please? *Fräulein*?'

A beggar approaches – an old woman, haggard, with a missing tooth and greasy hair.

'Go away,' Adele hisses. 'I've nothing for you.' She turns her face away from the woman's odour and directs her attention once more to the artist.

He has now placed a hand, with those long, delicate fingers, on his companion's shoulder.

'A *heller* for the destitute,' the beggar implores, reaching out her gnarled hand to Adele.

'Not now!' Adele steps past her. She watches as the woman with the red sash smiles at the artist. He smiles back. Adele holds her breath. She is his maid, that is all, Adele keeps assuring herself.

'Please, spare some *kleingeld*, or at least a thought, for the unfortunate souls of this world.'

'Leave me alone!' She cannot take it any more. 'How dare you loiter in the shadows, seeking sympathy?' she demands. Adele turns her head just in time to see the artist lean in towards his companion. His lips are a deep pink bud, and she watches, aghast, as he lands them, not on the woman's cheek, but directly, discreetly, on her lips – lingering for a moment, full of intent. Adele stares, open-mouthed, as the artist pulls away. It's then that she sees the tenderness in his eyes. The woman brushes her fingertips across his forehead with exquisite gentleness.

'A little kindness is all I'm after,' the beggar pipes up again, seizing Adele's arm.

'Leave me alone! Your misfortunes mean nothing to me.'

'It could happen to any of us. It could happen to you,' the beggar sneers.

Adele's anger is ripped from her and she pushes the woman away, her fingers digging into the chicken-carcass bones around her shoulders.

'Your downfall is of your own making,' she says. 'You've made your stinking bed, so now you must damn well lie in it.' As she speaks, Adele looks, for the first time, into the woman's fearful, chalky-blue eyes, and sees herself reflected there.

7

August 1914

There, in plain daylight, is a woman in a wedding dress. Adele stops in front of the window, her cup clatters to the rug. She cannot believe her eyes and kicks the cup out of the way to get as close as she can to the pane. The young woman is utterly luminous, tall and lithe with a halo of copper hair, tendrils of it framing her features. The dress is beautiful, everything Adele dreams of wearing on her own wedding day. The bride carries a bouquet of lilies, holding them in front of her, waiting, but her face betrays her impatience. She looks around.

Adele's heart hammers.

As the figure in the wedding dress raises her eyes to the window, Adele experiences a skipped heartbeat of recognition. She has seen this woman on this very street. In fact, she has seen her outside that very building – the artist's apartment block – coming and going with increasing regularity over the course of the past year. She is one of the artist's models! And now she's wearing a white dress, outside his home . . .

The main door to the building opens, and the artist steps out. He's dressed impeccably in a smart suit, his shoes polished, his hair combed. He could be a lawyer off to court, or a banker with a prestigious position. But no. He's striding up to the woman with a look of annoyance, as if there's somewhere else he'd rather be.

'Do drag yourself away!' Edith says as she enters the room, sipping camomile tea.

'Ssshh!' Adele orders.

The woman in the wedding dress fusses with the artist, straightening his tie, smoothing a lick of hair, placing her grand mass of flowers on the ground to do so. Adele sees it then: a swelling beneath the silken material of the dress – a neat but unmistakable bump.

'Oh, my Lord,' Adele whimpers.

'What? Is it the Emperor himself?' Edith asks, approaching the window.

'It's the artist. And one of his models. She's . . . she's pregnant.'

'But he never said he was married!' Edith frowns.

'They're off to the church, it seems. To make it official.'

The woman in the wedding dress retrieves her bouquet, then spins on the spot, looking, no doubt, for words of appreciation from the artist. His reply cannot be heard, but he does not smile and can be seen only to shrug gently, his eyes looking at the ground. Then he and the young woman set off together, she half a step ahead of him, as if he has said something unpleasant and she wants to put some distance between herself and his words.

'I was blind, so caught up with the thought that he was in a relationship with that awful guttersnipe,' Adele says, her nostrils flaring, taking in the magnitude of what is unfolding, 'that I failed to see *another* woman right under my nose. The whole time, this dalliance has been going on and I was looking the other way. Now, it seems, the consequences must be taken care of.'

'Come! There's no time to lose!' Edith grabs her sister's hand. Surprised by her reaction, Adele needs no further encouragement. Together, they run on to the street, slowing their pace when they catch sight of the couple so as not to bring attention to themselves.

'Thank you for coming to my rescue like this . . .' Adele says.

'I know how much it means to you. Besides, it'll be weeks before we get the full story through the grapevine.'

Within a matter of minutes, the artist and his bride stop outside the local church.

Adele's heart feels crushed, the whole future she has conjured for herself collapsing. She and Edith sink on to a bench.

'The artist, married. He's doing the decent thing, at least,' Edith comments, squeezing Adele's hand.

Adele is touched by the concern that her sister is showing for this devastating unravelling of her expectations.

'I appreciate this, you know,' Adele says. 'You're here, at my darkest hour.'

Edith turns to her sister, kisses her hand, and wipes away a tear. 'What a wrench it must be to see him marrying another woman.'

The sisters watch as their neighbour talks to the other guests gathered outside the church. A portly man in a waistcoat shakes the artist's hand, and he smiles, a little bashfully. The man offers the artist a red chequered handkerchief and he takes it, dabbing his brow. A tight-faced woman approaches; she has similar features to the artist, the same deep-set eyes and thin nose. She looks tired. She says something, then nods in the bride's direction. The artist frowns.

The woman shakes her head, purses her lips, then walks away with a limp.

The guests enter the church, to take their seats for the ceremony.

It's just the artist and the bride left outside. The notes of an organ can be heard.

Now that nobody is watching, he takes the bride's face in his hands and kisses her tenderly, sadness etched on his face. Adele has been to enough society weddings to know this is not standard procedure. What is going on?

The bride waits for a moment on the threshold, smoothing her dress, running a hand across her stomach in a fluid motion, her nerves visible. Then the artist takes a breath, hooks his arm through hers, and they enter the church.

Adele watches her dreams disappear into the shadows of the holy space. Edith suggests they wait in a nearby café, as Adele can't bring herself to leave, not yet. They order two coffees and position themselves by the window.

Forty minutes later, the guests gather once more outside the church, the women's hats lifting in the breeze as they await the bride and groom. They appear to be holding handfuls of what could be rice or confetti, to welcome the happy couple.

The bride steps out first, blinking in the light, a wide smile on her face, her eyes sparkling. A band glints on her finger. Adele's heart contracts.

The groom follows her a moment later, grinning broadly.

'Who's *that*?!' Adele asks, leaning across the table to get a better look.

This man is tall, with pink-tinged cheeks, a heavy moustache, and sandy-brown hair. He's the one now holding the bride's hand, there's no doubt about that.

'The groom!' Edith exclaims.

'Whoever he is, he's not our man!' Adele says, her spirits soaring once more.

Their neighbour finally emerges through the arch of the church doorway, the last to leave.

Egon shakes the groom's hand, and claps him on the shoulder.

Adele and Edith look at each other, then burst into laughter. They clink their coffee cups, and take a celebratory sip.

'Hope is not lost!' Adele announces, beaming. 'But I now realize I must double my efforts if I'm to achieve my mission.' She smiles. Edith shakes her head and wipes a splash of coffee from the side of her lip.

8

January 1915

'*Je suis contente. Tu es contente. Il est content. Elle est contente. Nous sommes contentes.*'

The sisters are returning from language tuition. Adele holds Edith's arm, her younger sister singing her French verb conjugations into her ear.

'What have you to be so cheerful about?' Adele comments sullenly.

There's been little by way of joy in the capital since war was declared over the summer of 1914. Thirty days after the assassination of Arch-duke Franz Ferdinand, the Austro-Hungarian Empire announced it would go to war with Serbia. Austrian men have been conscripted, drafted to fight, and are dying in their thousands. Vienna has lost its soul.

Adele is dabbing her eyes when the artist appears. He takes a few steps towards them, his shoulders hunched. There's something about him – he appears nervous.

He reaches into his bag and pulls out an envelope, which looks offi-cial and weighty. 'This is for you, the Harms sisters.' He hands the letter to Adele. 'Read it in the privacy of your own home,' he advises. 'I can't stay, but please, consider your response. Good evening to you both,' he adds. The warmth of his breath lingers.

They wait, in silence, for a second, two, three, before Adele holds the envelope aloft, then cracks the seal and removes the creamy paper folded inside. It's covered in elaborate handwriting, with a maroon border outlined in crayon. The language is archaic. There are no ink-blots or crossings out. She reads it greedily, hoping for a charm in it she can call her own.

'It's an invitation,' Adele says, turning it over in case there's more on the reverse.

'He told us to read it at home.'

'How can you even contemplate waiting?' Adele pulls a face. She imagines a drawn-out afternoon, sitting with their parents in the salon, discussing the weather – it would burn a hole in her pocket. 'Why, my goodness,' she says, tracing the signature. 'He's inviting us to the Park-Kino to see a moving picture there. Surely we'll be allowed to attend a screening? Oh, and he says we will be accompanied. His friend is going to join us, *Vally* – do you suppose she's *that* woman? She'll be our *chaperone!*' Adele raises an eyebrow. 'Our only hurdle now is to convince Mutti and Papa.'

⌒

'Out of the question!' is Papa's reply when he hears the name and the nature of the request.

Mutti almost faints in horror.

'The artist!' she mutters, glancing at her daughter. 'Over my dead body!'

'It's an outing to the cinema, Mother,' Adele says.

'I've heard the gossip. My daughter, drawn to a man like that. I knew it!' she gasps. 'You'd both do better to pay more attention to someone suitable like Albert – what a polite young man he is.'

'Herr Schiele is thoroughly pleasant. His manners are impeccable.'

'We can imagine what his intentions will be,' Mutti declares, her eyes flashing.

'He'll be coming to my door wanting to paint you, next,' Papa says.

'It's not like he'll force us to undress in the stalls of the cinema,' Adele snorts.

'Johann! *See!* What did I tell you? She's growing more vulgar by the day.'

Adele throws up her hands, walks to the window. She feels her chance slipping away.

'It's a moving picture,' Edith says calmly, eyeing her sister. 'We'll be surrounded by upstanding people.'

'You'll be surrounded by rabble,' Papa says.

'What harm can it do?' Adele jumps in. She is flushed and her tone is taut.

Edith darts her a look, a warning not to lose her temper. 'We'll be chaperoned the whole time,' she continues. 'It says so in the letter.'

Father holds the artist's invitation in his hand. He reads it once more, his glasses perched on the end of his nose.

'Edith wouldn't let anything untoward happen. She's far too sensible for that,' Adele adds.

'And who knows, it might put paid to Adele's infatuation, if she spends some time with him,' her sister retorts.

'Edith!' Adele feels betrayed, but she also sees how her sister's logic has opened something in Mutti.

Their mother looks at her husband sideways. 'I suppose the letter does display some eloquence, at least. It shows the young man isn't a complete delinquent.'

Adele pounces on this concession. 'I promise to meet whoever you deem eligible if you'll let us go. I'll even spend an afternoon with the Admiral's son.'

'Aha! I'll hold you to that!' Mutti says, a satisfied smile spreading across her face.

Adele wonders with a start if it is she who has successfully manipulated her mother, or the other way around.

'So, it is agreed?' Edith asks. 'We may say yes to the artist?'

Papa removes his glasses, dismayed at the scene that has unfolded around him.

'Agreed. But don't expect us to allow this to become a regular occurrence,' Mutti warns, glancing at her husband.

'You won't regret it,' Adele says, kissing her parents on each cheek.

'Not so fast, young lady. It goes without saying that your father and I will expect an introduction,' Mutti says. Adele wonders if this, perhaps, is what her mother has been angling for all along: a close encounter with the artist, to unpick him, to be better equipped to assassinate his character for her ladies. That would be the crowning moment of her next salon. 'It's just that we want to draw our own conclusions before sending our darling daughters out into the world in the company of Egon Schiele,' Mutti adds, as if guessing Adele's thoughts.

⸺

Adele watches the hand on the grandfather clock creep towards the hour. She's keen to make Papa see that Egon Schiele is a respectable man with prospects. Her hopes are pinned upon it.

'Please, don't be late. Do not confirm all Papa's prejudices,' she wills her neighbour. She cannot bear the thought of her chances being ruined before they've begun. She fidgets with a button on her sleeve, spinning it until the threads are ready to break.

The clock strikes seven, chiming a hammer to her heart.

What if the artist has forgotten that he invited the sisters out for the evening? He may have become engrossed in his work. Or what if Adele misread the invitation and made a mistake about the date?

She runs to their bedroom and pulls the letter from beneath her pillow. She knows it by heart, but she must read it again. Yes, it's there in black and white. She is not mistaken. Then a thought enters her mind. What if this has been nothing more than an elaborate joke between Egon and that damned woman? Wouldn't they find it riotous to torment Adele and Edith, the bourgeois sisters from across the street, pretending they wanted to spend time with them? Vally would have orchestrated the whole thing, of course. Adele had thought it strange that the woman had agreed to the outing, when it's so clearly to her disadvantage.

'Edith!' she calls out. There's no reply. Her sister has made it clear that she's only attending for Adele's sake – and has kept herself otherwise occupied all afternoon.

Back in the salon, Papa checks his watch, rubbing his thumb over its face as if to read it more plainly. Adele's ribs ache with apprehension. It is almost ten past the hour.

'Our guest is quite late,' Papa says.

'It's not as though he has far to come,' Mutti adds drily, inspecting her rings.

'It's a clear indication that he believes his time is more valuable than our own.'

Adele jumps as the doorbell rings. Papa and Mutti exchange a glance as Hanna enters the lounge with the artist and his common little friend. Adele feels scant relief at his arrival.

'*Grüss Gott*, Frau Harms, Herr Harms. My sincerest apologies,' Egon says, hurriedly. His hair is slicked back. 'My companion delayed us.' He looks at the woman, who won't meet his eyes. Her face is thunderous. 'It was never my intention to keep you waiting.' Mutti offers her hand and he takes it, bending to move his mouth to just above it, as is the tradition in polite society, before turning to Papa and shaking his hand firmly.

'Herr Harms, I'm honoured to meet you and delighted that you're entrusting me with your delightful daughters,' he says, as if the words have been rehearsed.

Even the artist's shoes are freshly polished.

'I hope we'll be able to say the same of you, young man.' Papa looks him up and down. Adele recognizes a flare of disappointment that there isn't more to criticize him for.

'And may I introduce Fräulein Neuzil. Walburga, to be precise,' the artist adds.

'My name's Vally,' the woman says, her voice thick with defiance.

'Vally is one of my models,' Egon explains.

The woman's hands appear to shake as she looks around the Harmses' parlour. With new eyes, Adele sees the embossed wallpaper, marble fireplace and chintzy ornaments. Adele catches their guest as she turns a lip up at what the woman no doubt considers to be a fusty series of landscape paintings. It is abundantly clear that Vally is unimpressed by her role in this scenario. Adele notices patches of dust across the young woman's knees, a gleam of sweat on her forehead.

Mutti is intently examining Egon, compiling her inventory.

He adjusts his tie, places his hands in his pockets, then pulls them back out again.

'Well, I've heard much about you, through the grapevine. You're an artist, so they say,' Papa states.

'Yes, sir, I trained at the *Akademie* – I was their youngest student. It was a great honour, but I was troubled there. I found the environment stifling, so I left and formed the *Neukunstgruppe* with my fellow students. We've exhibited in Prague, Budapest and Munich.'

'And your subject matter is a little . . . controversial?'

'I paint life, sir, in all its forms. Men, women, children.'

'Frequently in the nude, I believe? Isn't that so?'

Vally shuffles as Papa's eyes rest fully on her for the first time.

'Johann!' Mutti chides, but she narrows her eyes and waits for the artist's response.

'There has been a long and healthy tradition of figurative art in Austria and beyond.'

'So you deny that you're a pornographer?'

Adele cannot breathe. The dust settles in the spaces between them.

'I'm not the first to depict a woman in a state of undress,' he says. 'And I won't be the last.'

'I can see why such a pastime would postpone your fighting

alongside your fellow countrymen for the honour of Austria and the Empire,' Papa retorts.

Only now does Egon redden. 'I've been exempted from the draft, sir. My heart, it's not strong enough. I have a doctor's certificate to prove it.'

'What is the world coming to? I can't fathom it any more,' Papa says, removing his glasses and polishing them. 'Well, you'd better be on your way, we won't hold you back any longer,' he adds, glancing at Adele. 'But where has your sister got to?'

Edith comes into the room, as if beckoned, half running, her cheeks flushed.

'I promise to return your daughters to your care before midnight,' Egon says.

'Make that ten o'clock, young man.'

'Papa!' Adele pouts. 'The film won't even be finished by then.'

They frown at each other, but then Egon breaks the silence with his laughter and, in a fit of good nature, Papa claps him on the back.

The lights go down, and Adele grips Edith's hand on her right. The projector clacks and hisses as the film is fed through the reel, the sound changing as the opening images appear on the screen, grainy and unsteady. The artist is seated to her left – Adele had carefully manoeuvred her position as they entered the auditorium so that she would be seated next to him. The proximity is dizzying, and she barely knows how she will follow the plot. She glances at him, but his eyes are on the screen, light and shadow flickering across his face. Vally, on the other side of Egon, sighs loudly as the piano plays accompanying music. On the screen, an elegantly impoverished woman appears. To be an actress would be a wonderful thing, Adele muses. Egon catches her eye and smiles.

They watch the story unfolding, the characters developing, and

Adele enjoys herself greatly. Edith, too, is transfixed. But less than halfway through the film, there's a snapping sound, the characters fade, and the scene is cut through with a heavy black line, before the images halt altogether. For a moment they are all plunged into darkness, the screen blank, the music stopped. They hold their breath and wait, but there's no release. After a few moments of hushed silence, the lights go up and voices rise again as questions are whispered among the audience. What has happened? Why has it all ended so abruptly? An acrid, waxy smell filters to the stalls.

'Apologies!' the grey-haired projectionist calls, appearing through the curtain from high in the rafters. 'The show's over, I'm afraid. There's a fault and it can't be fixed. The celluloid has melted. I'm sorry to say we can't continue. But rest assured, you can ask for your money back.'

A wave of protest and disappointment sweeps through the crowd.

'That was a rather unexpected ending,' Egon says.

'I was growing quite fond of that poor woman,' Adele adds.

'We'll never know what happened next,' Edith agrees.

'Well, we should go our separate ways,' Vally says, yawning, pulling on her threadbare coat.

'Edith, can you fetch our garments from the cloakroom?' Adele orders, trying to mask her disappointment. 'Here's our ticket.'

'What's the rush?' Egon says. 'We've more than an hour before your father expects you home. Why waste such a golden opportunity? I know the perfect place.'

'Your well-to-do neighbours won't appreciate some back-alley bar, Egon!' Vally says. 'I'm sure they'd rather be tucked up in bed.'

'Nonsense, we'd love to go,' Adele says, glaring at Vally. 'Please, lead the way.'

⁓

They walk to a bar – one that Egon says he frequented when he was a student at the *Akademie*. They pass the windows of elegant boutiques the girls have shopped in along the main road. Egon keeps walking. 'This way,' he says, and Adele notes the look of apprehension on Edith's face as she steps over a greasy puddle, and disdain on Vally's as Adele hitches up her hems. The shortcut takes them through a narrow alley, where rotting rubbish is piled against crumbling brick. Matted rats dive into gutters as they pass, and women, their eyes ringed in black, wait in doorways, reaching out a hand. 'Pay no heed to them,' Egon says, tipping his hat to a particularly emaciated figure as they pass. The woman spits crude words after them.

After a few moments, they reach a door, and Egon knocks confidently.

'Are we in the right place?' Edith whispers to Adele.

A man wearing an apron, his ears red, opens it and looks them up and down.

Adele hears Egon mention his name, and reference the owner, and the man lets them pass, squeezing close to Adele as she moves by, his hand stroking her hip. Inside, they push themselves through the throng of people, a layer of smoke swirling above the gathered heads, the air thickened further with sweat and the sour smell of fermentation from the kegs lining the back wall. Egon sees a gap at a bench, and gestures for Adele and Edith to take a seat. The men around them stare. The women smirk. Adele holds her clutch bag off the table, which is wet with foam. Egon disappears, then returns after a few minutes with four tankards of pale-brown beer. They are filled to the rim, froth oozing over the edge of the glass.

'Quite the experience, is it not?' he says, raising his eyebrows and taking a large sip. 'For women used to the finer things in life.'

'We like it.' Adele nudges her sister, who's busy pushing away a mutt that has approached under the table and is nuzzling her thigh. 'Don't we, Edith?'

'Charmed, I'm sure,' Edith says, moving her legs away from the flea-ridden animal.

Vally scratches the dog behind the ears, before it heads off in search of scraps.

Egon smiles at the three of them. 'Don't you want the drink?' he asks.

Adele picks hers up gingerly by the handle and moves it to her lips.

'Delicious,' she says, after a small sip. She puts it down and rubs her fingertips.

'I don't like the taste of alcohol,' Edith says, leaving hers untouched.

Vally takes a long drink of her beer, swallowing again and again, until she reaches the bottom. She places the empty tankard on the table and smiles, giving a small hiccup as she does. Egon laughs and empties his own in the same way.

Adele takes another polite sip of the vulgar liquid.

A group of men at the bar is singing loudly, shoulders swaying against each other, while a mime artist performs in one corner, doffing his hat and sweeping it around for coins.

Adele could never have guessed that such a world existed.

Then there's the sound of broken glass, an angry jibe, the thump of flesh on wood.

A fight breaks out and the crowd parts as a young man takes an older one by the scruff of his neck and flings him across the room. He comes to a skidding halt, before he's flung again, crashing into their table. Egon leaps up and stands in front of Adele and Edith, his arms spread to prevent them from being hurt in the altercation.

'Enough!' he shouts. 'There are ladies present.'

Vally, exposed and alone, stands slowly. She looks down, her hands raised. In all the commotion, Edith's untouched drink has been knocked straight off the upended table, tipping over into Vally's lap. The liquid has soaked through her layers of skirts. Her eyes are on Egon, his shoulders squared, protecting Adele and Edith, but he hasn't noticed and doesn't glance her way. She kicks the dripping table, then curses, before dashing from the bar.

9

May 1915

M utti bustles into the lounge, her steps fast and determined as she throws open the window, allowing a breeze to swirl in, and stands directly in front of Adele, effectively disrupting her peaceful plan to watch for the artist.

'Rouse yourself, young lady,' Mutti announces. She's dressed and powdered, her best jewels on display. 'Hanna's leaving for the market, and I want you to accompany her.'

'What? But why?' Adele demands. This is a rare unplanned hour in her schedule, and she's been looking forward to settling into her thoughts and fantasies uninterrupted.

'I need this room for my meeting with the local ladies. It's my turn to host. We've district matters to attend to, and Frau Weissmann lost her husband last month, so I expect there'll be tears. I don't need you under my feet.'

'And what about Edith? Must she accompany the maid on her errands as well?'

'Your sister is poorly, she's in bed with a cough, as well you know. Please don't disturb her.'

'But, Mutti, what will people think?' Adele can hear the ugly, pleading note in her voice, and knows it will carry no weight with her mother.

'It'll do you no harm to have some fresh air and physical activity. You're welcome to return after midday – that's little more than an hour to pass in Hanna's company.'

Adele heaves herself from the chaise longue, pouting with a childish look of disappointment, which her mother does her the honour of noticing. She takes Adele by the shoulders, smooths her hair. 'I'm only thinking of you, darling. These women are all angling for a beautiful, spirited daughter-in-law from a good family, so it's best you are out of the way.'

Adele sighs dramatically, then laughs despite herself. 'You always know the right thing to say to get your own way, Mutti,' she says, rolling her eyes, as Hanna appears at the door, a basket in each hand.

⌒

Adele makes polite conversation with Hanna during the twenty-minute walk through the Schönbrunn Palace gardens. It's a warm day. The rains of the previous week have passed, giving way to fresh blooms of leaf growth, and buds bursting forth from soil and stem. Adele and Hanna pass the entrance to the zoo with its menagerie of animals, the grunts of some unknown beast making itself heard over the walls. They continue, crossing in front of the Palmenhaus, the elegant greenhouse filled with exotic plants. A blaze of colour is visible through the great glass panels, which are moist with condensation from the fetid heat within.

Hanna asks after Edith, showing great concern over her sister's health.

'Nothing suggests it is anything more than a cough,' Adele replies.

'I'm sure she'll recover quickly enough,' Hanna says.

The market, when they arrive, ripples with energy. Adele carefully skirts thick puddles of mud – one could pick up all kinds of disease in a place such as this. Its workers – hard-nosed women as well as men with dirty forearms – shout coarse words, calling out prices, holding up bunches of radishes, mud clinging to the roots, or the creamy heads of cauliflowers, trying to distract customers at a rival stall with all kinds of promises and slander. They wink in amusement when they catch Adele's eye. She holds a handkerchief to her nose, trying to block the smell of manure, sweat and spoiled vegetables.

Adele hangs back, watching Hanna barter. She's surprised at the warm repartee that passes between the maid and the market traders. Hanna returns the banter as she negotiates a better price for a cut of meat, which is wrapped and placed in her basket.

'Just a few more items on your mother's list,' Hanna says.

Adele thrums with impatience as they add butter, eggs and sugar to the basket, for Mutti wants cake, but Hanna refuses to be hurried. Adele rolls her eyes as Hanna insists on picking up every piece of fruit to test its freshness, but finally, they have everything they need.

They walk home, the young woman a step or two ahead of the maid, who insists her hips are slowing her down. She stops to toss crumbs from a stale leftover crust, carried from the Harms family home, to feed the birds in the park. The church bells toll midday as they walk down the tree-lined street of Hietzinger Hauptstrasse.

'Is that Edith?' Adele asks, stopping Hanna with a hand on her arm, peering at a young woman two dozen steps ahead of them. 'Edith!' she calls, but the sound is drowned out by the rhythmic clatter of passing horses. Edith is wearing an overcoat, despite the sunshine, but Adele's first thought is how beautiful her sister looks. Sunlight glints off her hair as she waits for the horse-drawn cart to pass. Edith steps into the road, before crossing to the other side, heading in the direction of the main door to their building.

Adele takes a few eager strides to catch up with Edith, but then she sees the artist. He's hurrying after her sister, a hand raised in Edith's direction, clearly trying to engage her in conversation. They talk briefly and Adele's heart skips a beat.

'Feeling unwell, Fräulein Adele?' Hanna asks.

'Take the shopping back, Hanna, if you please. I'll just be a moment.'

The maid lumbers off, carrying both baskets, as Edith turns and spots Adele. The artist sees her also and waves a friendly greeting.

'Fräulein Harms, how delightful to see you once more.'

Adele thinks he looks slightly flushed.

'Herr Schiele. I trust you're not bothering my poor sister?'

Egon laughs. 'I hope not,' he replies. 'We bumped into each other and were passing a few minutes of the day in conversation. It's unfortunate you couldn't join us,' he says.

'I don't have anything to get back to, if you have a little more time?' she suggests.

He looks pained. 'Nothing would bring me more pleasure,' he says. 'But I must tear myself away before I'm late for a very important appointment with my mentor. He hates to be kept waiting.'

The artist smiles, gives them both a quick bow, then heads off down the street.

Edith turns to Adele, smiling brightly.

'How was it at the market? You survived?' Edith asks.

'You're the one I should be worried about! What on earth are you doing outside?'

'I just needed a little air.'

'Does Mutti know you're out?'

'Please don't mention it, she's been preoccupied with her ladies. You know what it's like; I couldn't bear to hear Frau Weissmann's sobs a moment longer.' Edith shakes her head, looking at her with clear blue eyes.

Adele smiles sympathetically, and takes her sister's arm in her own.

'Enough about Mutti! Tell me, what did the artist want? Recount precisely everything he said. Should I anticipate any further invitations?' She looks at her sister expectantly.

'Actually, he was enquiring about personal matters. He asked what age we both are, and wanted to know your birthday. Perhaps he intends to send a gift?' Edith replies.

'My birthday?' Adele is overcome. 'Do you really think so?'

Edith's words add to a certainty that Adele has felt growing in her recently. She's sure the artist is preparing for a grand gesture, perhaps the grandest of all . . . He busies himself with tasks that require him to leave his building with increasing frequency, always waving when he sees Adele in the window. It's as if he wants to be seen, as if he wants to see *her*. He regularly bumps into the sisters on their outings and he's always gazing at her, she can feel it. Of course he'd accost Edith for information, wanting to know more about her.

Adele lets the thought soar inside her, forgetting everything: the stench of the market, the grunts from the zoo, Edith's wretched cough, Hanna's aching hips. Could it be, finally, that her dream will come true – is marriage on the cards?

10

June 1915

I t's a warm, wet day, with a muggy intensity, the kind that brings on headaches. Adele, only moments ago, heard the low rumble of thunder in the distance. But her good mood cannot be deterred by the weather. She feels she's poised on the cusp of everything she has longed for.

Papa enters her room, straightening his tie. His grey whiskers are twitching. He turns to her and opens his arms wide.

'Come! We've reason to celebrate at long last.'

'What's the news?' Adele almost whispers, her knees weak, her mind instantly on Egon. Could this be it?

'It's Edith,' he says. 'A brave man has asked your sister for her hand in marriage.'

'But who'd be foolish enough to do such a thing?' Adele demands, only half joking. 'Tell me it's not Albert?' Surely that limpet hasn't finally steeled himself to make a proposal? Usually, Adele would have intimate knowledge of this kind of news before any other soul, but she has been distracted and has not given her sister the attention she deserves in recent weeks. She realizes now that Edith has been attempting to broach a conversation with her, approaching her at quiet intervals, sitting on the edge of the bed, twisting her fingers. But Adele has been too wrapped up in her own dreams, her hopes sky-high, thinking of nothing but Egon Schiele. She feels mortified that she has failed to notice that Edith also has a suitor – if not Albert, then one of Mutti's other eligible young men, someone equally boring and predictable.

In response to her question, Papa takes her by the hand and leads her to the parlour. His hand feels smooth and cool, as if the blood doesn't reach his fingertips.

'Come, let her tell you,' he says. 'Edith is also shocked by the turn of events. She wasn't expecting this.'

Adele is overjoyed. Perhaps she and Edith can have a double wedding! Wouldn't that be a wonderful state of affairs? They'd both, finally, make Mutti proud.

Edith is waiting in the parlour. Mutti is fussing at her, straightening her dress. Adele goes to embrace her sister, but Mutti steps between them. Edith looks over her mother's shoulder with large, pathetic eyes. Why isn't her sister happy, today of all days?

Champagne is chilling. It's in short supply, with the war still dragging on, but Papa has saved one bottle for a special occasion. He heaves it from the silver bucket and water drips on to the antique rug. Adele sees Hanna weighing up the mess.

'So, who is the lucky suitor?' Adele's question goes unanswered.

Papa releases the cork with a flourish. Fizz shoots over the lip and pools on the rug before anyone can proffer a receptacle. He pours Edith's glass first. She looks sad, almost in pain, as she watches the bubbles rise to the rim.

'I feel awfully dizzy,' is all she says. She does look terribly pale.

'A toast,' Papa says. 'To our delightful daughter. Soon to be a beautiful bride.'

Adele clinks glasses with Edith and her parents, then pushes on with the only question worth asking: 'So, who is my sweet, silly sister to marry?' She takes a sip. Sparkling bubbles pop on her tongue.

'Why, the *artist*, darling,' Mutti says. 'Have you not seen the way he has been making a nuisance of himself these past few weeks? You clearly haven't been paying much attention.'

The long-stemmed flute Adele is holding becomes enormous in her hand. Everything else shrinks away. She grips the back of a chair to stop herself from falling. Blood pulses behind her eyes, her jaw aches and the taste of the champagne in her mouth turns sour.

There has been a momentous mistake. She has to remedy this error and save Edith and their parents from any further embarrassment.

'Oh, but you're all very much mistaken!' Adele says, giddy to the point of laughter, her arms flailing. 'It's *me* he wants to marry.' She puts a hand to her chest, to make it clear how ridiculous it is to imagine the artist choosing Edith over her. She feels her heart beating wildly.

Papa looks surprised. But how do they not understand?

'Adele, my dear.' Papa holds her arm, trying to contain her.

'Tell me, what did he say? Which sister did he ask for?'

All eyes are on Adele. Edith sets down her glass and shares a look with Mutti.

How bloody dare she.

'You must tell me.' Adele's desperation rises a notch. 'Did he ask for *her*? Or did he only say "your daughter"? You've just assumed, have you not, that he meant Edith' – she wrinkles her brow while speaking her sister's name – 'when, in fact, I'm the one he wants to marry.'

'Darling, calm yourself. Your mother and I had no idea you felt this strongly, but I can assure you, there has been no error. None whatsoever. The artist made himself extremely clear. It's Edith he wants to marry,' Papa says. 'I'm sorry if that is disappointing for you.'

'You've made a mistake. A terrible mistake. You don't even *like* him,' Adele howls.

'We were as surprised as you.' His jowls shake. 'As you know, that young man would certainly never be my first choice of husband for either of my daughters. But look at what the world is coming to. The Empire is crumbling beneath our feet. The war has ravaged us. Our finances . . .' He grimaces. 'We did suggest that, as the elder daughter, you'd be more suitable, but he held his ground. Young men these days don't care for tradition or the correct way of doing things. And I had no choice but to accept. He was unwavering in his request for Edith.'

Papa raises a hand to pat Adele on the shoulder and she comes very close to biting it.

'I'm sorry,' Edith says now. She's grey in the face, her cheeks tear-blotched.

'Herr Schiele wants to marry your sister,' Papa repeats, slowly. He walks over to his youngest daughter and puts his arm around her. The traitor. 'And she has agreed. We had a long chat this morning, to weigh up our options. She initially opposed the proposal, on your behalf. Your sister loves you very much and has your best interests at heart. But this is how it has turned out. You must accept this, Adele. The wedding will take place, and soon – in little over a week. The war has added a layer of urgency to these proceedings. So, please, just be happy for your sister, as she always is for you.'

The world rushes in once more, and Adele pulls a ragged breath into her lungs.

'I will *not!*' she says, spitting the final word, rage overtaking her. She cannot bear to look at them, at their pitying, mocking faces. 'This is all your fault!' She launches her flute at Edith. 'I will never, ever forgive you.' The glass hits her sister full on the chest and then smashes on the floor at her feet.

Edith breaks into loud sobs, clutching at herself as if she has been shot.

Adele runs from the room and slams the door.

She'll burn this house down before she is happy for her sister.

She'll do whatever it takes to ruin things. For ever.

11

T here's nothing to numb it – the pain that Adele endures. It has rattled and ricocheted through her mind every second since the engagement was announced. The pure burning shock of that moment still singes her soul. Adele hasn't left her bed for ten days. She hasn't been able to move from this darkened pit of a room. Her muscles are weakened. Her vital energy sapped. The word 'betrayal' rings through her mind on an endless loop, like the tune on a merry-go-round she heard as a child – always there, repeating, endless, as she drifts in and out of sleep. In the very worst moments, on that first day, Adele had wanted to murder. Her sister. The artist. Herself. In those hours of boiling rage, she'd have rammed a knife through his heart, suffocated Edith as she slept, or sipped poison straight from the bottle. She wanted to inflict pain, in an attempt to rub out the great injustice that had been inflicted upon her.

Now that initial violent rage has subsided and left in its place a hollow, dazed comprehension: the person Adele loved most in this world, her own sister, has entirely discarded her, in pursuit of her own future. Adele's most tender feelings, her passionate desires, her very existence, have all been rejected. The knowledge leaves her empty.

But in the past days, behind the anger, there has also been confusion.

72

How could she have been so wrong; how had she misread all the signs? Had she really lost her mind to such an extent that she hadn't been able to see what was right in front of her? And what of Edith – what is her part in all of this? Adele realizes, with a squeeze of the heart, that Edith may be scared to be setting out on this path, especially without the support of her elder sister to guide her. What kind of life will timid Edith have as Frau Schiele? It's hardly conceivable that her little sister will marry, that she will marry first, and that she will marry the artist, today of all days.

Edith Schiele. Adele swallows bile at the very thought.

They'll all be at the church by now. Adele heard the preparations this morning: Edith bathing, Hanna helping her into her dress. Mutti had walked past Adele's bedroom, muttering about Edith's complexion. As the grandfather clock struck midday, Papa had knocked on Adele's door to say the carriage would soon be leaving, and he implored her to join them. Only now does she feel that perhaps she should have accepted the invitation. She steps from the bed with shaky movements, the room spinning around her.

Adele gathers herself and slowly puts on a fine dress, applies a pearl pin to her lapel, laces her boots, and looks at her reflection. Her eyes are ringed with red, her cheeks puffy and pale. Her dress hangs off her shoulders. She turns her head to the left, then the right. She's acceptable, she supposes. Those lips, oh yes, at least they're still diabolical. She smiles, despite herself.

Adele moves through the silent apartment. Everyone has left for the church, even Hanna – Edith broke protocol to extend an invitation to the maid. Outside, the thick summer warmth wraps itself around Adele as she hurries along the streets of Hietzing.

The church is up ahead, shimmering in the heat.

Adele stops for a second, a little breathless. The thought comes to her: this should be her wedding day. She should be the one walking down the aisle. She shakes the thought roughly from her mind.

Outside the church a woman, holding a baby on her hip, is smoking a long, elegant cigarette. She has copper hair, flashing eyes and pale flesh. The baby grabs at her collar. Adele recognizes her as the young woman she witnessed standing on this same spot almost a year ago, pregnant on her own wedding day. The woman she had feared was marrying the artist. Adele laughs, a croaking sound.

'They're about to make it official,' the woman says to her.

Adele takes a steadying breath. It's not too late. There's just enough time to make things right again, to undo the ricocheting pain she feels. If she can just see Edith, there's a chance she might not hurt any more.

As she enters the sacred space, she feels a rough hand pulling her back.

Adele spins around. It is the maid, a fierce look in her eyes.

'If you're only here to ruin things, you can leave this minute,' Hanna hisses.

'I beg your pardon?'

'Your sister doesn't need you here, making a mess of her life.'

'It's none of your business. But I want to make things up with Edith, if you must know,' Adele says. 'She's my sister.'

'You're here to put a stop to things, more like.'

'Edith will be terrified. I can't imagine she actually *wanted* to marry the artist. She's never shown the slightest interest in him. Papa gave her no choice.'

'If that's what you need to tell yourself, then fine. But if I hear one peep out of you in there, one murmur of discontent, I will thrash you myself.'

'You have no right to speak to me like that,' Adele exclaims.

Hanna smiles and nods, satisfied. 'For the first time in your life, you didn't get what you wanted and your sister did.' There is a pause in the proceedings as the minister gives Edith, at the front with her groom, the chance to speak. 'Edith knew what she was doing, all right. She is delighted to be marrying the artist. She wanted this. She wanted it very much indeed.'

'You're greatly mistaken.'

'No, Fräulein Adele, I'm not. For I was the one who helped her.'

'You're pulling this nonsense out of thin air, just to spite me!'

Adele can feel the horror rising in her again.

'It's up to you who and what you want to believe,' Hanna replies. 'But all I know is that I won't stand by and indulge your delusions a moment longer.'

At the front of the church, Adele catches sight of Edith. She's radiant, glistening with delight as she makes her promises to the artist.

In the next moment, it is complete. Edith's future is sealed.

And something snaps in Adele – a part of her that can never be healed.

12

October 1916

E dith has been gone for more than a year. Egon was served his conscription papers the day after the wedding and left for his military
training in Prague soon after. He could have been posted anywhere in the
Empire by now. The artist is now a soldier. Her sister came to say goodbye, but Adele had not been able to look at her, the betrayal intensifying
every moment she was in her company. It is better that they're away from
Vienna. The city is falling into a state of decrepitude as the war continues
to rage around them, and Adele feels she has lost more than a sister – she
has lost her sense of place in this world. Everything seems to be crumbling. Only yesterday, she was told that Heinrich had been killed on a
battlefield in some far-flung outpost of the Empire. She thinks of Lina,
the woman he married after Adele broke off their engagement four years
ago. Lina has three small children – a girl and twin boys – and is a widow
at the age of twenty-five. It so easily could have been her.

All this news of death makes Adele increasingly reckless. She gravitates towards insalubrious types, people she would never have shared
a conversation with before the outbreak of war. Now she joins the
throngs in dusky cafés, lingering late into the night, talking about history and politics, anarchy and altruism. She has heard opinions voiced
that she'd never even considered.

'These days we're living through, they're the end of life as we know it. The Empire is over. The Habsburgs have lost control. What's on the horizon? A new, democratic society. The dawn of a new civilization, without the rules and repressions of the past. The old ways are gone,' someone declares.

These people, in their twenties and thirties mostly, those who have so far escaped the calls to fight, typically end the night in an apartment on the outskirts of the city. Music plays loudly, the gramophone jumping as people cram into the small spaces, so different from the world Adele has occupied to this point. A dozen bottles of absinthe are empty by dawn.

One night, a woman brings forth a vial of something that they light and smoke. It's not tobacco – it smells sweeter. Adele takes it when it is offered, the flame blazing in the darkness. She inhales and something swirls free in her, a weight lifting that she has carried for so long. She soars, spinning around the room, her eyes wide and glossy. Men and women soften into one another, doze lightly on cushions piled against the walls. Even the music mellows. Long gone are the classical, operatic pieces that Adele once thought were the only music in the world – in their place she discovers jazz. She never wants to lose this feeling.

Her home, the apartment on Hietzinger Hauptstrasse, seems sterile and fusty, a museum to the past where Papa's unsold curiosities dominate each room. Hanna is gone, they can no longer afford her – Adele, for one, is relieved about that – and Mutti and Papa seem to recede day by day. She argues with them frequently, as they try to intervene in her decisions.

One night, on her way to some backstreet bar to meet her new, unsuitable friends, Adele gets talking to a soldier, a man from Moravia, who follows her, then offers to buy her a drink. She accepts and they spend the evening together, sipping drinks in a candlelit tavern. He tells her of his heroics during the war. She listens to his stories, however overblown, and her mind wanders to thoughts of Egon. How is the artist coping in such a horrific environment? Does he ever think of her?

The soldier asks about her family.

'I'm an only child,' Adele lies. 'My parents are dead.'

'Alone in the world,' he smiles.

They go back to his small room. He shares a bunk with a fellow soldier, who has earned a visit with his fiancée this evening and is therefore absent. The soldier, who says his name is Honza, pats the blankets and asks Adele to join him. He pushes his lips to hers and she doesn't pull away. He puts a calloused hand to the curve of her breast, and she lets him, his thumb stroking with increasing insistence. Her eyes are open, and she watches the ripples of desire as they cross this fighter's features. In one moment he is boyish, fidgeting with his crotch; the next he seems a brute, his hands at her neck.

He pushes her, with some force, back on the bed. The rough hew of the horsehair blankets scratches her flesh. He puts a hand beneath her skirts, pushes them to her waist, roots around with incompetence. Adele doesn't have the energy to say no. In fact, she has no words at all. It's as if she were a mannequin, like the ones she has seen in the windows of elegant boutiques. She sighs, and he mistakes it for passion. He unbuckles himself and enters her. She turns her face the other way.

Adele will bleed, but what does blood matter now? He will have seen enough of it.

There is no Edith this time to intervene and slap his hands away.

And for that, Adele can only be pleased.

13

December 1917

M utti knocks on the door. Adele opens an eye and pulls the blanket over her head.

'Go away!' she says, but the words are inaudible. Her muscles ache.

'Adele! Rouse yourself.' The door creaks. 'There's someone here to see you.'

Edith steps into the dark, dank space, a handkerchief over her nose. Mutti draws the curtains back and opens the windows as wide as they will go. Light bursts into the gloom.

'Edith?' Adele says, her voice breaking. 'I thought I'd never see you again!'

'Don't worry,' Mutti says to Edith, 'the doctor was here yesterday and he assures me she's no longer infectious. The worst is over. She just has to regain her strength.'

Adele reaches out a hand to her sister, touches her fair hair, marvelling at it, pulling Edith closer.

'I am so happy to see you,' Adele says, her voice barely a whisper, the tears beginning to fall. She plants a kiss on Edith's skin with cold lips.

'As I am to see you,' Edith says, blinking at this unfettered emotion, looking to Mutti to gauge whether she's being set up for a fall. 'I've been so worried about you.'

'Influenza, the doctor says. He's seen more cases than normal this year,' Mutti adds.

'I've never known such physical torture in all my life. It felt as if I was burning, in here.' Adele rubs a skeletal hand over her chest. 'The pressure . . . I could hardly breathe.'

'But you survived,' Edith says.

'I saw death. Smiling at me.'

'Don't be ridiculous, darling, you were just overcome with fever,' Mutti interjects.

'You'll live a long life, Adele Harms,' Edith says confidently. 'I promise that you'll be an old woman, a grande dame, before death dares to come for you.'

'I wasn't scared,' Adele says. 'I'd have been pleased to go.'

'Ssshh. Stop talking this way.' Edith looks at Mutti again. 'You're scaring me.'

'She's hallucinating, dear,' Mutti says to Edith, as Adele lapses into a light doze. She can still hear them talking, a gentle buzzing in her ears.

'It's the virus. She's been like this for weeks, getting herself into a state, saying strange things. She was convinced you'd died and there was nothing I could say that would persuade her otherwise.'

Edith blinks, pulling her hand from Adele's grasp. 'How very strange.'

'I'm hoping that seeing you here, in the flesh, will finally put an end to it.'

'I hope so, too,' Edith murmurs.

'At one point,' Mutti laughs, 'she insisted that you'd run away with a fox. Then it was that a fox had bitten you, then that the fox had died, and you were crying. She was not making much sense!'

'I can imagine,' Edith smiles, putting her handkerchief to her mouth once again.

'It's the worst wave of influenza we've seen in Vienna for years. Thousands have died,' Mutti continues, looking at her daughter.

'Egon says the war has made it even worse. But how did she catch it?' Edith asks.

'Oh, you know Adele. She'll have been spending time in another dubious corner of Vienna. And that doctor was no help! He hardly knows where these things come from or how to deal with them. Tried to fob me off with all sorts of useless remedies – Epsom salts, arsenic, aspirin.'

'What business would Adele have in the dubious corners of Vienna?' Edith asks.

Mutti laughs. 'You should spend some time with your sister. She might surprise you.'

Edith strokes Adele's wrist, feeling the pulse beneath.

'This time last week, I feared she wouldn't make it,' Mutti admits.

Edith's lip quivers. 'Adele is strong-willed, she'd never go without a fight.'

'I did the best I could, all by myself. I was nursing her, mopping her brow, administering medicine, preparing bowls of something hot whenever I had a moment, trying to coax her to eat – that was fun, let me tell you! There's next to nothing worth eating, anyway. There'll be rats on the menu next. I've had to pawn the family jewels to buy bread!'

'Well, I'm relieved to be home after all this time. I missed you. I'll be on hand, whenever you need me. Egon has rented a place not far from here, so I can be around often.'

'And how is that husband of yours? Finally making a name for himself?'

'I'm sure he'll be happy for some money to come your way,' Edith replies.

'I've always liked that boy,' Mutti says with a smile.

'Can we not talk about him in front of . . .' Edith dips her head at her sister, who shifts in her sleep.

'Oh, hogwash! She's forgotten about all of that now,' Mutti says, frowning.

'Really? It certainly hasn't seemed that way. After that disastrous family meal, when Papa . . .' She fusses with her sleeve. 'It was all so upsetting.'

'Your sister has been under a great deal of pressure these past few years. You've not been around to see it. I don't know the half of it, I'm sure, and I was never certain how much to tell you in my letters. There was a man – a soldier, I believe, although I never met him. She'll be on to some fresh heartbreak now.'

'Perhaps there is a chance to heal the rift between us after all this time,' Edith says.

Adele stirs, her mouth open, as if she's on the brink of joining the conversation.

'All I know,' Mutti says, standing and indicating to Edith that they should step out of the room and let Adele sleep, 'is that the two of you need each other. We've nothing left, nothing except our dignity, and even that is in short supply these days. Hopefully, this war will end before I'm dead and buried. I'd like to see the back of it. But whatever happens, I want to know that my girls, my darling girls' – and here her voice breaks with emotion – 'are on a firm footing. What hope is there for the future, if you two can't count on each other for love and loyalty?'

14

January 1918

Adele spots the elegant neck of the giraffe, poking above the zoo walls. She's on her way to the entrance to the Schönbrunn Palace gardens, where she has agreed to meet Egon. She is still weak on her feet, not entirely recovered from the ravages of the influenza she caught at the end of the year, but she has made an effort to feel composed for this encounter.

When, a few days ago, a letter arrived at the apartment, addressed to Adele, her name displayed on the envelope in a handwriting that was so familiar, it was as if the words had been stamped upon her heart. She had opened the seal immediately, and instinctively held the letter to her chest, inhaling the paper, before she could finally bring herself to read the words written in ink. It was indeed from the artist. Her mind spiralled.

Your sister tells me you've been unwell, and I trust you're much recovered.

Adele was shocked by the force and familiarity of the emotion that had surged through her body. She shook the trace of it from her bones, blaming the regression on her sensitive state. For her own sanity, she had tried to banish all thoughts of Egon, yet still they rose again.

I wondered if you would grant me the indulgence of meeting with me, privately, to discuss a matter that is close to both our hearts – Edith. In short, I'm worried about her and I would appreciate your sisterly advice. Can I suggest we meet at the zoo in the gardens of Schönbrunn Palace? I've missed Vienna's more exotic animals while I've been away.

Adele blinked as she took in his words, determined not to read more into their meaning than was intended by her brother-in-law.

Tuesday at one o'clock? Please, say nothing to Edith.

'Our secret,' she whispered to herself, ashamed at the rush she was feeling.

Adele folded the letter neatly, tracing her name on the envelope.

She had known immediately that she'd be there at the agreed time.

⌒

Egon walks up, his hands in the pockets of his khaki uniform, sleeves rolled up to reveal his forearms, tanned and toned. He's just as handsome – if not more so, Adele thinks with a pinch – as he was when she first saw him on the street in Hietzing, more than five years ago. They will both turn twenty-eight this year, she realizes. A lifetime has passed between then and now.

'Adele, I was told you'd been completely devastated by the influenza, but you look delightfully well.'

'Charming as ever, Herr Schiele,' Adele replies. She has resolved to keep things formal.

He looks at her from under that pronounced brow.

'Thank you for agreeing to meet me today,' he says, as they set off on a circuit of the park, the light falling in patches across their path. 'I couldn't think of anyone, except you, who might return a smile to my wife's face.'

Adele nods, trying to quell the emotion within her. 'What's the matter with her?'

'Edith is lonely,' he says, as a squirrel darts past. 'She's been bored and at times depressed. She's suffered with being so far from her family and has longed for something to call her own. I know she feels lost. She and my sister Gertrude haven't taken to each other. She's lost touch with her old acquaintances, many of whom are busy as mothers – a position that only exacerbates her distress.' He pauses to kick at fallen leaves. 'I know things have been fraught between the two of you and I blame myself. I was young, foolish and should have behaved better. I wondered if you'd accept my apology?' He looks at her intently. 'Could we draw a line under the past, for Edith's sake?'

'I appreciate your candour,' Adele replies. 'Now you're back in Vienna, there's nothing I want more than to be a part of Edith's life.'

Even as she says it, she knows it is true. But what will a future for her and Edith look like, with Egon there in the middle?

'She has missed you. We both have,' he says.

'And I you,' she replies, sincerely.

'I brought this with me, with you in mind.' Egon reaches into his satchel and pulls out a slim volume, bound in navy, embossed with gold.

'Poetry?' Adele says, leafing through the pages.

'I thought it might interest you. Rainer Maria Rilke always offers me a little light in the darkness.'

'Thank you,' Adele says, holding the book to her chest. She will treasure it.

'Edith intends to invite you over to our new apartment. Please, say nothing of our meeting. I don't want her to think I've interfered, or that I've placed you in a compromised position. She believes I'm visiting my uncle this afternoon.'

'Of course,' Adele says. 'It must be our secret.'

Is this the start of an affair? No, that's a preposterous idea. She doesn't know what she is thinking.

They've reached the perimeter of the park, and Adele cannot quite recall the path, taken by her own two feet, that has carried her from there to here. Her mind is once more full of this man, playing tricks with her.

Suddenly there's a child, a boy, his face smeared with soot. He grabs Egon by the elbow.

'Herr Schiele? Are you the artist? There's an emergency, sir! They sent me to scour the streets, looking for you. I'll get a beating, they said, if I don't deliver this message.'

'Well, now you've found me.'

Egon turns his eyes on Adele, and there's fear in them.

'Spit it out, boy. My nerves are shot.'

'It's Herr Klimt, sir. He's sick. He's sent for you, sir. Urgently. He wants to see you at his studio. Before it's too late.'

⌒

Adele steps into the dimly lit atelier as a svelte black cat runs out of the door, its tail quivering. She has never set foot in an artist's studio before and it is everything she imagined: canvases propped against the walls, the paint splattered in frenzies across the floor, figures sculpted from clay crumbling in the corner. The artist, Herr Klimt, is propped up on the bed, blankets piled high across his legs and around his shoulders. A candle flickers at his bedside. A woman kneels next to him, her face stretched in grief, but he flicks her away with a slight gesture of his fingers.

Egon takes a step closer to this man who is his master. Gustav Klimt is grey, his beard clinging on in wisps. The cage of bones supporting his chest seems to have caved in and he is wheezing gently.

Adele waits in the corner, near the figure of a bare-breasted woman cleaved from stone. She watches as Egon places his hands in Klimt's, presses his lips to the man's thumbs, then takes a cloth and dabs it across his forehead, which is sleek with sweat. She can hear that the younger artist is crying gently, the unnatural rhythm of his breathing an indicator that he's holding back the force of his grief.

'It's over for me; I sense I only have weeks left, maybe days,' Klimt whispers. 'I've known greatness. It tastes not as sweet as you'd expect. But not as bitter, either.'

'Don't speak that way. It's not over; there's life in you yet, old man,' Egon says affectionately. 'I can feel it. You're as strong as a bull.'

'And yet I feel death dancing in the wings.'

The old man glances at Adele.

'Who's that?' he asks.

'My sister-in-law,' she hears the artist reply.

'She has a face that demands to be painted.'

Egon dips his head close to the man's ear. 'May I draw you?' he asks, and Klimt nods. Egon takes out a piece of paper from his satchel, pulls a pencil from a case.

Then, in the silence, he sketches.

Adele watches as the lines emerge, fluid and fearsome. The old master closes his eyes and his jaw slackens. Egon works quickly, tearing his way through several sheets, varying the angle and perspective, but always capturing the same thing: the thin veil of life before him.

Adele sits on the floorboards. She watches and listens. For almost two hours, she's transfixed by the transformation that is taking place around her. Life, lines, power and permanence, the threat of obliteration, transience, all so closely connected. And death, that nimble thief, lingering on its heels, threatening to steal it all. Adele doesn't know if this great artist, Gustav Klimt, will live or die, how long he'll survive. But she does know that he will leave a legacy in this world. His name will be remembered. His art will adorn the walls of galleries. And his face is caught upon the page by Egon's hand.

Adele, too, wants to be preserved, held for eternity, by paint or pencil.

In those moments, an old desire awakens: to pose for Egon Schiele.

15

April 1918

'Thank you for agreeing to do this,' Edith says, as Adele enters their apartment. Edith closes the door behind her. 'It means so much to me. My nerves have been frayed and modelling is the last thing I have patience for. I know you'll be wonderful.'

'I'm only doing this for you,' Adele says, 'so we might spend some time together.' She does want to be close to her sister, to observe her.

'Egon's waiting for you through there. Everything's set up.'

Adele removes her coat and passes it to Edith. Who is this woman she has become?

'I'm behind on Egon's accounts, so if you don't mind I'll just sit here quietly and do some work. You won't even notice I'm around,' Edith continues. Her sister is wary of her, that much is clear. She has invited Adele into her home, but her guarded eyes betray her. She'll not leave her sister alone with her husband; she will not give Adele the opportunity to strike.

Adele walks into the studio space. Egon is there, just as she'd always imagined.

'I'll make sure you're comfortable today. There's nothing to be nervous about,' he tries to reassure her.

'I'm not nervous,' Adele replies. She has never felt more confident.

'Edith always gets the shakes before a session. I assumed you'd be the same.'

'We're very different, your wife and I.'

Egon hands her a sleeveless silk chemise. 'Are you wearing stockings?' he asks, as Edith walks in, fresh lemonade on a tray.

'Why ever would you ask Adele that, Egon?' Edith bristles.

'Your sister will be helping with a portrait I started a while ago. It was never finished, so I need her to adopt the same pose. My last model was wearing green stockings.'

'I am wearing stockings, as it happens,' Adele interrupts. 'But white ones, I'm afraid.'

'No need to borrow a pair from you, then, Edith,' Egon says to his wife.

Adele steps towards the bedroom to undress.

'Keep your bloomers on, and your shoes,' Egon instructs. 'But do remove your dress, please.'

Edith looks nervously in Adele's direction, her fingers fussing with the edge of the glass.

'And keep your hair piled up on your head. There are some pins if you need them.'

Adele closes the bedroom door behind her. She hears Edith whispering to Egon as she leaves. Moments later, before Adele has slipped out of her dress, Edith appears, under the pretext of searching for something she has misplaced. She waits with her sister.

Egon is ready. He takes Adele in with a curious smile, then guides her to a position on the floor. 'Here, please. Sit. Do you need a cushion?' he asks.

'I'm quite happy, for now.' She cannot wait to begin. He, too, seems eager.

'Wonderful. Now, bring your knees together. This is how we replicate the pose. That's it. Keep your left knee in place and let the other fall away.' He breathes, his eyes taking in the composition. 'Can you hold that?' he asks.

'It's not difficult at all,' Adele replies. This is how it begins, she tells herself.

'Now, dip your head to your left knee. Perfect. Don't move!'

Adele does as she's instructed. She feels a pull along the muscles in her spine.

'Bring your hands to that same ankle,' he suggests. 'Hold it there, fingers together.'

He scoots closer to her, across the floorboards, and places his hands on her right calf. His touch is electric. He pulls, gently, widening the arc of her legs.

'Is that awkward for you?' he asks.

Adele senses herself reddening. She feels exposed, the centre of her ruptured for intimate observation. The skin tingles along her inner thighs, the air cool in the bare area between her stockings and the frills of her undergarments.

'Not at all,' Adele lies.

'You're perfect,' Egon says. 'All I need now is for you to look at me.'

Adele raises her eyes to his.

And that is it. Her transformation is complete. There, in that moment, Adele becomes an artist's model. There are no trumpets or fanfare: the only noise is the rhythmic push of the artist's pencil as he works. He can't take his eyes off her.

'I need to acclimatize myself to the shape of you,' he says, more to himself than to Adele. 'The lines of your face and figure, before I begin again with colour.'

This isn't so hard. Adele hardly knows what it is that Edith has been moaning about. She really would have been better suited as a wife to Egon. Perhaps he finally realizes it?

'Adele, concentrate,' Egon commands in a deep voice, bringing her out of her reverie. He examines her with his painter's frown, squinting as he focuses, working and reworking until he's happy with the composition. 'Push your shoulders forward,' he continues. 'Further. Look to the right. A little less . . . yes.'

Egon keeps capturing her on the page for what feels to be an eternity. To hold her pose for so long is difficult, but she has to be bold, she cannot complain, for that is why she is valuable to the artist – she can give him what his wife cannot.

She breathes slowly and marvels at how the hours evaporate.

Finally the work is finished. Egon calls her over.

She notices the way he is looking at her, the way his hand brushes her skin. This contact between them. She observes the mass of her hair in the portrait, her long fingers laced together, that bent knee. Adele hardly recognizes herself in the work Egon has created. Is her nose as angular? Her hands as large? Does she have to look so willing? And what is that in her eyes? Regret?

'You don't like it, do you?' Edith asks, standing close to her husband.

'It's not about whether I like it or not,' Adele says. 'It's art.'

'Very astute, Adele,' Egon says. 'You've been the perfect model today. I'm sure Edith wouldn't mind me revealing that she'd have felt most uncomfortable in this position. I'd appreciate it if you'd pose for me again, soon, if possible? There's so much more we could achieve together.'

16

October 1918

Egon stops abruptly. Adele is standing there, almost nude, before him. She has been modelling for him for almost six months now. In that time, he has produced dozens of drawings and watercolours, lingering over her body. Edith is still vigilant, but she cannot be around all the time. Today, Egon bites the end of his pencil, then turns on her.

'I give up! I can't continue if every time I see you, you've grown fatter.'

'Egon! How dare you!' Adele exclaims.

'It changes everything,' he insists. 'The lines don't work if I use a plump model.'

'Plump?' She runs a hand across her hips, and turns to review her rear.

He looks at her, then relents a little. 'I'm sorry. I'm under a lot of pressure.'

Adele pauses, considers his words. The time has come.

'There's something I need to tell you,' she says. She takes this opportunity to thread together the changes she has noticed recently: her full breasts, a tightening swell across her stomach, an aversion to all things sweet. She cannot remember when her menses last occurred. 'I'm pregnant,' she announces.

Yes, this is how life works out, she thinks, feeling triumphant.

Egon rolls up his sleeves. 'My God,' he responds. 'Well, I hope you're satisfied – that's a considerable mess you've got yourself into.' He returns to the sketchbook and flicks through the pages. Is he looking for the signs he has missed? Perhaps he isn't as attuned to female flesh as he believes. She watches him. He fetches a fresh pencil and sharpens it with ferocious flicks of his wrist. The shavings fall to the floor. His eyes rest on her body again. Silence. Their position isn't straightforward, Adele reminds herself.

When the light fades, Egon goes to his desk and forces the drawer open, rummaging between papers and notebooks, a pot of ink, searching for something at the back. He pulls out an old address book, then scribbles down a number and a street name on a piece of paper and tries to pass it to Adele.

'Go tomorrow. Tell them I sent you, if you must.' Adele is already at the door. He pushes the scrap into her hand. 'Don't worry about the cost. I'll take care of it. It's the least I can do.' Adele reads it, lets the piece of paper fall, then pulls at the door handle. With one hand against the wood, Egon pushes it closed before she can take a step over the threshold. 'Don't be a fool, Adele.'

'This baby will be born in the spring,' she says.

After their session the previous week, he had embraced her as she was leaving, and she had brushed her lips against his. For a second, he'd let the warmth spread between them, but then he'd pulled away. 'I won't mention this to Edith,' he said.

He needed time, was all.

'Think of your sister,' Egon says now, giving Adele a serious look.

'And what about me? Me and you?'

'This has nothing to do with me, and you know it.'

Adele's mind jumps, various scenes colliding. Is he denying their interactions?

'I'm your muse, don't forget.'

'I'm afraid you are greatly mistaken.' He takes a cigarette from an indented silver case in his pocket and rubs it between his fingers.

'You said I was your muse.'

'You're hysterical. I said no such thing. You've always had an overactive imagination, Edith warned me. I'm only helping you as a friend. What kind of life would you have, an unmarried woman with a child to look after?'

'What will Edith say, do you think, if I tell her? About the kiss. This baby.'

He laughs bitterly. 'Don't make things worse for yourself, Adele,' he exhales, pulling a hand through his hair. 'You've already gone too far. I'd advise you to think about your future.'

'My future and yours,' she states. Adele won't be pushed aside for a second time.

He opens the door and places the unlit cigarette between his lips.

'Don't breathe a word of this to your sister, for your own sake,' he warns.

Adele feels a powerful knowledge surging through her: she is the fire that has barrelled out of control. She has never been closer to destroying everything. And she's ready for it.

The streets of Vienna are almost abandoned. A fresh and more virulent wave of influenza is sweeping the city and strict measures have been put in place to prevent the spread of germs. Trams have been cancelled, theatres have pulled their performances, restaurants – already deserted because of the war – stand empty. But still, the virus spreads. Certain back-door services can still be accessed, however, for the right price.

She finds the address that Egon wrote down. The door is unmarked. Adele shakes out her umbrella, then knocks. A man peers through the steamed-up glass before opening the door. The way he takes her in as she removes her hat with its obscuring veil and steps into the low-ceilinged reception hall leaves Adele in no doubt that she's in the intended place. Prickling heat creeps up her neck.

This sort of thing must happen all the time in cities such as Vienna, she thinks.

'Schiele sent me,' she says by way of introduction, the name catching in her throat.

'Follow me,' is all he says.

They walk along the hallway, its walls blossoming with mildew, then descend a winding set of stone stairs, sinking deeper. Adele finds herself in a dim maze of corridors and closed doors, one of which the man suddenly opens and ushers her through. There's another panel, almost hidden, that opens inside the first one.

Adele stumbles and the man takes her arm to steady her, but she shakes him off.

'Get your hands off—' she begins, but she feels she has lost the right to complain.

The final room is exceedingly bright. Adele shields her eyes. The gas lamp fizzes sporadically with a maddening noise that calls to mind a bluebottle trapped in an upturned cup. The room is spartan, with little by way of furniture or decoration. There's a heavy table, similar to the one the Harms family once ate around every day at home. Adele recoils at the sight of an open drawer, loaded with soap, a grater and long-pronged instruments, including a common knitting needle.

In the corner is an older lady with grey hair, who is writing in a ledger. She doesn't smile as her eyes lift to meet Adele's. Before he closes the door, the pockmarked man speaks in an unknown language. Adele can only frown as she takes a seat on a hard chair. The singular word she understands is 'Schiele', spoken with a grimace. The woman raises her eyebrows and looks Adele up and down, taking in her elegant navy dress and the lace-trimmed hat she carries.

'You're a higher class than the usual sort he sends here. Can other measures not be taken for a woman such as yourself?' she asks. 'A prolonged break away from the city? Return with your hands clean? Your family could make such arrangements, surely?'

'They must never know,' Adele says solemnly.

The woman accepts this statement with a small shrug.

'Age?' she asks.

'Twenty-eight.' Adele swallows as the woman records it.

'Older than his usual type, as well. Do you have other children?'

'I'm not married. Is that much not clear?'

'When did you last have your monthly bleed?'

These are things Adele would barely bring up with her own sister. 'I, I . . . can't remember.'

'And when did you last have intercourse?'

'Intercourse?'

'Sexual contact with a man?'

'Contact? I don't know . . .' Everything is so confused all of a sudden. Adele thinks back to how she removed some of her clothes in front of Egon when he was drawing her, the way he brushed against her. There was certainly *contact*. 'I . . . There has been . . .'

She thinks of the soldier pushing her back against the bed, her mind reeling.

The woman looks at her for a long moment.

'And this is your first abortion?'

'I'm not one of those women,' Adele says, jarred by that word and the images it evokes. 'What will happen to my baby?' she continues.

'We'll do our best to terminate the pregnancy. I can't pretend there's no risk associated. It's a dangerous procedure. There'll be pain and a lot of blood.'

Adele feels queasy.

'It'll take a long time for you to recover. Do you have anyone who can look after you?'

Adele thinks of Edith. 'Unfortunately, there's nobody at all.'

'If things go wrong, you must never reveal that you came here.'

Adele takes a long breath and lowers her head, her fingertips to her eyelids.

Egon was right, she must think of the future. Of the mess she has made for herself. An unmarried mother could be sent to the work-house, prison or an asylum.

The woman indicates that Adele should place her coat on a hook behind the door.

'Lift up your skirts. High above your waist,' she instructs. Adele pulls up her undergarments to reveal lacy drawers, the kind Egon likes to draw. They seem ridiculous in this context.

'Remove them too and lie there,' the woman says.

Adele lies down on the divan, its material greasy beneath her head. The woman's hand hovers for a moment over the sharpened end of the knitting needle, but then reaches for a dull metal object that is smooth and long.

'What do you intend to do with *that*?'

The woman ignores her and places her other hand on Adele's belly, pushing into the flesh with her fingers, looking at the ceiling as if she'll find answers there. She prods in several locations, moving her fingers to new positions on her stomach every few seconds. Then, without warning, the woman roughly pushes Adele's thighs apart.

Adele winces at the pressure and focuses on a cobweb on the ceiling as the instrument she'd seen in the woman's hands is pushed into her flesh, further and harder than she ever thought possible. The pain shoots up under her ribs. Adele realizes she may never escape this place, or this feeling.

After a few seconds, the woman mutters something and Adele hears her sigh in exasperation.

'Is something wrong?' She shifts on to her elbows and sees a trace of blood on the rag the woman has used to clean the rough instrument.

'You're not pregnant,' she replies, abruptly. 'There's no baby.' She offers a bright, tight flutter of the lips, as if Adele's problems have disappeared. 'But do tell Schiele I'll have to charge the standard fee. He'll hardly be pleased about that.'

Adele sits up and rearranges her skirts. How on earth can this thing between them already be undone?

'You're mistaken!' she says firmly.

'No. There is no baby,' the woman repeats. 'It does happen from time to time. Women take it upon themselves, for a variety of reasons, to imagine the signs of pregnancy. It's very difficult to tell in the first month or two, one way or another, so I'm surprised it doesn't occur more regularly. It could simply be over-indulgence or something more serious. You should see a physician.'

Adele stares blankly.

'And you should count yourself lucky, you know,' the woman continues. 'You've been spared a horrendous ordeal.'

'You're telling me this baby is a phantom in my belly, that our child is already a ghost. Liar!' Adele shouts.

She needs to get out of here. She needs the light. Adele barges through the first door without pause and hurries through the second. But the third one is locked. She spins. The doors all look the same. She rattles each handle, but cannot escape. She's damned to exist in a place of no life. Screams echo inside her head, inside her womb, from behind the doors she is desperately trying to open. Adele backs away, her head in her hands.

Suddenly the man who escorted her down to the darkness is beside her.

'Stop! Stop all that screaming,' he instructs. 'You're not the first woman Schiele has sent here,' he says. 'Many of his models find their way to this place. He's a greedy, careless man and you should be glad to be rid of him.'

'No! You're lying,' she cries, pushing him away.

Adele is not quite able to recall if she's at fault, or if someone else is to blame . . .

The last thing she registers is the man's pity, before she collapses into a faint.

17

25 October 1918

Adele comes to, hours later. She doesn't know what day it is. She barely knows her own name. She's sitting on a bench, in the gardens of Schönbrunn Palace, the spot next to the zoo where she had waited, what seems a lifetime ago, for a handsome man. It was their secret rendezvous, she remembers that clearly enough. She recalls some lines from the book he gave her.

> *Flare up like a flame*
> *and make big shadows I can move in.*
> *Let everything happen to you: beauty and terror.*
> *Just keep going. No feeling is final.*
> *Don't let yourself lose me.*

She looks up, startled. A giraffe is beside her, outside its enclosure, its long legs bending in unnatural ways, its graceful neck reaching down, its big velvet lips brushing her cheek. She raises a hand and holds it there, relishing the warmth of its skin. When she peers up, the giraffe is gone. Adele looks all around her, but there's no trace of the elegant, exotic animal. She runs through the park, her mind flashing, pain pulsing in her abdomen, a thickening ache moving up from the base of her spine to her skull. She has lost her lace-trimmed hat, is without a coat, and doesn't trust herself to open her mouth, for she fears she might start screaming again and never stop. There are images in her mind that she wants to banish. A soldier and horsehair blankets, his rifle propped in the corner of the room; the letter she received – was it just this morning, or last week? – calling her for an initial assessment with doctors, invoked by her mother. The maze of under- world corridors she passed through earlier, the bright lights and the sterile smell that had swept away her baby. It is gone, it is all gone. She cannot bear any of it. She falls to her knees, clutching at the grass with her fingers.

The word 'sister' floats into her mind.

Edith. Yes, she's the one person Adele needs right now.

But in the next flash, she hears an echo of Hanna's words. Edith chose this. She betrayed her. These thoughts have been trapped in her mind for a long time – more than three years – like a butterfly in a jar, batting against the edges, finding no release.

Edith orchestrated all of this. *She* stole Adele's life. It is Edith's fault this is happening. It's her sister's fault Adele carries nothing but bruises on the outside and a ghost on the inside. She retraces the steps that she knows will lead to the apartment Edith shares with the artist. She must tell what she knows, this knowledge of her betrayal that has scorched Adele, left the wound infested. And she will tell Edith about the betray- als *she* has orchestrated. That her husband is in love with her, Adele, that he invited her to outings without Edith's knowledge, that he gave her gifts, all those cherished afternoons slipping by easily between them as he painted, as easily as the material fell from her shoulders to the floor. She will tell her sister about this baby. It exists, she knows it does. It will be hers alone, something she can love.

She bangs at the door of Edith's home. Egon answers, but as soon as he sees Adele, he pulls the door closed behind him and joins her on the street.

'Adele! What happened? You're covered in . . . what is that . . . blood?'

'I'm going to tell Edith everything,' she announces.

'But there's nothing to tell her.'

'The baby. Our baby.'

'You're not any making sense. Adele, please.' He holds her face, looks into her wild eyes. 'You're scaring me. I'm sorry, it's a lot to bear, everything you've been through. But you need help. Professional help. Let me walk with you to the doctor. Let's not disturb Edith, she's trying to get some rest.'

But Adele won't be moved.

'I'm here to see my sister.'

'She's sleeping,' Egon insists. 'She doesn't want to see you.'

'I won't leave before I've seen Edith. She needs to hear this.'

'Adele, you need to leave. Please, it's for your own good.'

The final piece of her snaps. Adele barges past Egon into the hallway. Edith, wrapped in warm clothes, six months pregnant, is walking down the corridor, disturbed by the commotion.

'Adele?' Edith says, surprised. 'What are you doing here?'

There's wariness in her face and, yes, fear.

Don't do this, you'll regret it for the rest of your days, a voice Adele doesn't recognize whispers in her head. But she cannot hold back any longer. Everything that once made sense has fallen away. And she intends to release, finally, all that she has bottled up over the years. She takes a step closer to her sister, and all her rage rushes out.

The next thing Adele knows, she's on the banks of the Danube. She has no idea what has happened, or what she has done.

What *has* she done?

Her skirts are ripped, and covered with mud and dried blood. There's something firm and round beneath the material. She pulls it out: an orange. She doesn't know where it came from. She hasn't seen one for many months during this war. It glistens like the gems she once admired. It is so vibrant, she weeps. She sits by the river and scratches its bright skin again and again with her thumbnail, the citrus oils bursting into the air around her. Hours later, she throws the shredded remains into the dark waters, and wishes she had the energy to follow.

She returns to Edith's apartment, dazed and exhausted after hours of walking, when it is dark, the dazzling moon lost behind clouds. It's late, so she knows her sister should be sleeping but, even so, she knocks. Adele doesn't want any more trouble. She knocks again. She just wants to apologize. She bangs her fist against the door. She knows she needs help. She is sorry, truly sorry. But no matter how hard she tries, there is no answer.

Interlude

'Comfortable now ...?' the doctor asks, not looking up as he inspects Adele's charts. Adele refuses to look in his direction. She does not want to be here. She'd rather be scrubbing toilets on her hands and knees than be trapped against her will in this stale ward. No medication in the world, certainly nothing administered by this pipsqueak of a man, can dull the ache in her bones or ease the guilt she has carried for half a century. Adele should be out there, searching for the precious ring she has lost. What annihilating pain, to put her hand to her neck and realize the ring was no longer there, nestled close to her heart. She knows she had it only seconds before she was man-handled into the ambulance. Then, yesterday, after a battery of tests, a nurse had proffered a bag containing everything Adele had been wearing or had with her on the day of the accident – not much, and nothing that couldn't be sent straight to the incinerator, but no ring. Adele hasn't been without it for a moment, not a single heartbeat, in fifty years.

She stares at the needle that has been inserted into her hand. The nurse had had to navigate between the crags of her arthritic knuckles and swollen thumb, but had eventually found a vein. Adele scorns her current cleanliness – white arcs are visible under each nail. Her new

clothes are modern, synthetic and scratch against her skin. A comb
has been pulled through her hair. She is practically presentable. She
strokes a thumb across the back of her hand and notes with a certain
swell of pride that a constellation of liver spots and badly healed burn
marks remain. Yes, some things can never be glossed over.

It's a small mercy that Adele has been placed in a bed by the window, furthest from the entrance to the geriatric ward. She looks at her
fellow inmates, and takes in vases of flowers next to each bed, with
gaudy petals destined to fall. Adele's table holds nothing but a jug of
water and she prefers it that way.

'I can call the sister if there's anything you need. Are you thirsty?'
the doctor says, following her eyes. He pours a glass of water without
being asked. Adele nestles her chin into her shoulder to show her defiance. He sighs at her stubbornness and places it on the table. Well!
She'll not touch, let alone drink, this water now that he has told her to,
even if it means she must dry out entirely.

'You won't keep me here another night,' she warns.

The doctor offers Adele a wry smile. 'We need to run through a few
more details, I'm afraid, Frau Harms, and complete more tests. Your
cooperation is essential. It's important that we get the facts straight, so
we understand you better.' He looks once more at his notes. 'It says
here you were born in Vienna in 1890. That makes you – what, seventy-
eight now? Is that correct?'

Adele prickles. She's from a different century, another world. This
man, existing as he does at the forefront of the present, cannot fathom
how life was in Austria's capital all those years ago. The opulence, the
splendour, the spectacle. All gone. He can't imagine who she once was,
that ravishing young woman, those high cheekbones, the heart-
stoppingly plump lips. Staring back at her, reflected in the window, is
a wild-haired witch with a black eye and stitches holding her ripped
skin together. Adele shudders at the sight.

'Our records are incomplete,' the doctor continues. 'We have your
year of birth and the names of your parents, Johann and Josefa

Harms. There's also a record of your treatment at the Steinhof Psychiatric Hospital. Can you tell me why you were sent there?'

Is that pity Adele sees in the doctor's disappointingly dull eyes?

'Please, enough of that!' she interjects. She'll put her fingers in her ears and scream this place down if she has to – anything to stop this man telling her the story of herself.

'I'm sorry if this is difficult. I'm only trying to help. There's so little by way of history in your file. Is there anybody we can contact to let them know you're safe? Family? Friends? Anybody who might be worried about you?'

Adele fusses with the bandage and pulls the needle from the back of her hand. Blood pools from the open vein. She flinches, then moves her legs from the bed, her tough old soles touching the linoleum floor.

'Can I ask what you're doing? Leaving is simply *not* an option,' the doctor insists. 'Not in your condition. Not if you'll only return to the streets. Earlier, you couldn't say when you last ate a proper meal. We've an obligation to keep you safe.'

'There's somewhere I need to be,' Adele states flatly.

That face the other day, before the accident. It's her last chance. Adele needs to know, before it's too late, that everything she remembers, everything she once felt, isn't a figment of her disintegrating mind.

But the doctor has other plans. He gives her a stern look, then, with a flick of his wrist, indicates that a nurse should reinsert the needle and clear up the mess. Adele harnesses her anger, swearing under her breath, but then the fear kicks in, and she almost chokes on it.

Once again, she is trapped. The same awful itching runs up and down her arms.

Suddenly she is a young woman, back in that bare-bulbed room at Steinhof, clawing at the sheets. 'You're mad! You'll never leave here. It's for your own good.' She hears their taunts as the key turns with a clank in its lock and the bolt is drawn across the door. Her thighs are wet and the smell of urine is bitter. A headache spreads to her teeth and she can feel saliva on her chin. 'I can't remember my name,' she repeats. Her finger, with its torn nails, traces indistinct letters in the air. And even in those void moments, certain images surface through the blackness of her mind: his crooked smile, his thick-lashed eyes, his elegant, pale hands.

'Egon,' she hears that young woman whispering to the wall, having wedged herself beneath the bed frame. 'I was beautiful and he painted me. I was rich, and we danced.'

'Somebody needs to be cured of her overactive imagination!' she hears those old psychiatric nurses trill as they attach electrodes and watch her thrash. 'You know that your mind can't be trusted. This is where you belong.'

But, of course, there was never any cure for matters of the heart. Month after month, jolt after jolt, Egon remained. From the depths of her deadening insignificance, Adele recalled the feeling of being captured and held by him, the glory of the artist turning her, Adele, into something eternal.

Then she is back in the present, in this sterile, modern hospital ward, with its bright lights, a jolly nurse in her starched uniform, short cap and white oxford lace-ups, whistling as she wheels a trolley lined with cups of pills around the ward.

Was any of it real? The artist, her sister, Edith, the life she once knew? And if those things are real, then perhaps other memories – horrible, incomplete recollections that have filled Adele with shame and anguish – are they real as well?

Adele whimpers. Suddenly, it is utterly unbearable. 'Please. I'll do anything. Rid me of this pain,' she begs. The nurse smiles with something like understanding, and the intravenous drip flows with beautiful, numbing morphine, offering oblivion. Adele is ready to lose herself in a wave of it. But when she closes her eyes, a trace of her sister's haunted face remains.

~

When she awakes, a young woman is standing at the front of her bed.

'Your granddaughter is here to see you, Frau Harms,' a nurse says, helping Adele sit up on the bed, plumping a pillow.

'Did you say my . . . ?' Adele asks, knocking a beaker to the floor. 'But that's impossible.' The nurse bends to mop the spill and indicates, with a raised eyebrow, the girl who is waiting. 'But that can't be . . .' The old woman squints. 'There's not a soul left on earth who'd want to see me.' The nurse offers a sympathetic smile and moves on to the next patient.

The woman approaches, with hesitant steps, flowers behind her back.

'Good Lord! It's you!' Adele says. 'The bicycle bandit! But what have you done? Your hair! It's as if someone has hacked it off with a blunt knife.'

The woman touches the stubby ends. 'I don't know what I was thinking.'

'You look terrible! Worse than the last time I saw you.'

'You don't look too peachy yourself.'

Adele raises a lip. 'And whose fault is that?'

'That's why I'm here. To apologize,' says the young woman. 'I felt bad for everything that happened. I tried all the hospitals in Vienna. You weren't easy to find. Nobody admitted that day matched your description. And I didn't know your name. I'm Eva, by the way.'

'You really shouldn't have gone to all that bother, you know. I presume your bicycle fared little better than I did.'

'I doubt it'll ever be the same. But you're on the mend, I hope?'

'I'll live, though not for long, I expect, if these doctors have anything to do with it,' Adele says with a jut of her chin, a flash of mischief in her eyes.

'Anyway, I'm sorry that you're in this place because of me.' Eva pushes her hair behind her ear. 'And I believe this is yours.' She reaches into her pocket. 'I found it that day on the street. It clearly means something to you and I thought you'd want it back.'

Adele's heart lurches.

'I'm so pleased to return it to its rightful owner,' Eva adds. 'I also wanted to ask: the woman on the poster. Why was she so important to you?'

'You saw her?' Adele mutters. 'I thought it was my mind playing tricks again.'

'She was right there, in front of us. I can't forget the look in her eyes. I went back the next day to see her once more and look for a name,' Eva continues. 'But all I could find was the name of the artist. Egon Schiele. Have you heard of him?'

Adele's face flushes suddenly, and her nostrils flare.

'Please, I'm tired now. Take your flowers and leave.'

Eva stands, confused by this sudden turn of mood. 'I'm sorry. I only mentioned it because I thought you'd want to know there's an exhibition of Schiele's work at the Albertina. If I'm not mistaken, today's the final day.'

Adele sits bolt upright. 'But I *must* go,' she says, grabbing the young woman's hands. 'Only, I can't make it there on my own.' Adele looks panic-stricken, trapped as she is in this bed, this hospital. Her eyes search Eva's with hope and desperation.

'What about your medication?' Eva asks, looking at the bruising, the charts above the bed, the machines surrounding Adele. 'Aren't you in a lot of pain?'

'Don't let me die here, alone. I need answers.'

'But what am I supposed to do? Sneak you out of here, past the nurses who are looking after you, and the doctors who say you shouldn't be going anywhere?'

Adele brightens. 'Exactly. They'll hardly notice I'm gone. Please, you owe me this, wouldn't you say?'

Eva looks at the older woman's knuckles, still scuffed from the collision, remembers the pain in her eyes as she stood transfixed in front of the haunting image on the poster.

It is a daring thought. She asks herself what she has to lose.

⌣

The taxi pulls away, having brought Eva and Adele to the Albertina gallery. Their escape from the hospital was hurried and unauthorized, and was probably the most fun Eva has had in a long while.

Tourists mill around the entrance to the imposing museum, consulting guidebooks and maps. The air is thick with the sugar scent of caramelized almonds and there's the jolly, wheezing sound of an accordion. A little girl performs a cartwheel across their path, the shadow of her feet falling across Adele's body as they join the queue of people waiting to enter the grand foyer that leads to the exhibition of Schiele's artworks.

Eva takes a thin cigarette from a packet in her bag.

'They calm my nerves,' she says, offering the pack in Adele's direction.

'They're no good for you,' the old woman retorts, but readily accepts. She smells the length of the rolled tobacco, then leans to the proffered flame.

Adele let go of this habit years ago. But now, the familiar lull of the nicotine stirs her. She recalls the stifling days when she worked for the Strasser family in Vienna, between the wars, after she'd been released from the psychiatric hospital. She'd steal cigarettes from a silver case in her mistress's handbag, linger over them on errands.

'Come here, you insolent girl,' the master would say, his belt held high.

After that first war ended, the privileged upbringing Adele had enjoyed became a curse. The Harms family's savings were gone, all their investments wiped out. Adele was unmarried, and past her prime. She had to find work. And, of course, she had no skills – no aptitude for cooking, no experience of cleaning, and no tolerance for children. But she'd been forced to learn.

The hardest lesson had been to forget her pride.

The words *Who do you think you are?* would ring in Adele's ears each time she refused to scrub the flagstones or wipe a child's bottom. She was beaten into submission until she was able to lower her eyes and bite her tongue, until she forgot how to say her name with dignity – until she was nobody at all. There was nothing to live for. The people she had loved most were gone from her life. She doesn't know how she survived, but the cruel days added up to months, years, decades, a lifetime.

Adele extinguishes the glowing embers underfoot.

'Thank you for getting me here. I won't forget that doctor's face in a hurry, as we made a dash for the exit!' Adele laughs. 'I'm grateful. But please, leave me to my own devices. There's no need for you to waste any more of your time.'

'I'm not going anywhere until I see for myself what all the fuss is about,' Eva retorts. 'You *are* going to tell me who that woman on the poster is, and why this artist means so much to you, aren't you?'

As Adele takes a breath, ready to begin, the queue surges forward into the foyer. A man behind the counter beckons to Eva with an impatient flick of his wrist.

Moments later, she is back. Adele is waiting, her nervousness written across her face.

'We have them,' Eva says, wielding two tickets. 'You're ready?'

'I guess it's now or never. But wait! I can't be seen in this state.' The old woman smooths the white hair around her face, brushes her sparse eyebrows with the tip of her finger, then adjusts her shirt beneath her cardigan. She draws herself up as straight as she's able, and attempts a coquettish skitter across the grand marbled opening room of the museum.

It takes everything she has left.

Eva follows in her wake.

GERTRUDE

1

January 1899

'Egon, my heart is wild,' Gertrude whispers into the darkness. 'It's racing so fast.'

The shapes of her words emerge in the cold air, then sink into the night. The candle was extinguished hours ago, and the little girl stares into the flat, faceless dark. She pulls her woollen blanket over her nose. It's rough and smells of horses. She'd woken to a sound – a bark, a thud, followed by scraping. Fear hammers in her heart and pulses in her ears. Something is coming to get her. It's outside the door.

Only Egon can make her safe. But her big brother is snoring, in and out, in and out. She sneaks her hand across the gap between their beds and finds his elbow under the layers. She doesn't want to be caught by Melanie. Her sister sleeps on her back, her arms above the coverlet, in the bed by the door. She's the oldest. Gertrude will be five in April, Egon is eight, and Melanie will turn thirteen next month. She's the grumpiest, firing up whenever Gertrude or her brother makes a noise. It's because of her they're so frequently punished.

Gertrude digs her fingers into her brother's warm armpit and bumpy ribs.

Egon stirs. 'Hush, Gerti,' he murmurs, his eyes tightening. 'Go back to sleep.'

'There was barking, and the door rattled and—' Gertrude takes in the smallest breath.

'Mother will stop telling us her folk tales if all they do is scare you,' Egon whispers. 'You're not a baby. There's no such thing as dragons or witches or water sprites.'

'I know that!' Gertrude sticks out her lower lip. It's not evil sprites with green hair and bulging eyes that she's worried about. It's monsters that are real, such as the farmer's dog with its sharp teeth: Gertrude trembles as, in her mind, she sees it crossing the top fields of Tulln, the neat country town in which they live. The dog rustles through dry crops to reach the train tracks, ambling along the metal lines, past rows of tidy houses and the dozen dotted cottages that belong to their closest neighbours, towards her station home. She imagines it prowling past the ticket office, then up the cold stone stairs, coming closer and closer to their first-floor apartment. Her father is the stationmaster – a man respected for stopping the trains at precisely the right time, and signalling them on their way with a firm blast of his whistle.

Gertrude pictures the dog's fleshy gums dripping as it approaches her door, its nose hooked on her scent. 'Something is coming to bite me,' she whimpers, giving up any attempt at being brave. Tremors reverberate through the floorboards, but it can't be the long, thundering night train as that passed by hours ago, and there won't be any passenger trains breaking the silence until daylight. Dozens of trains pass through this farming town each day, ferrying huge wagons of cargo from mountain villages and countryside settlements further along the route. After Tulln, the trains head off in the direction of Vienna, the Empire's glittering capital, then travel on to a port on the Danube.

The Danube, Gerti has learnt, is the mighty river that snakes from the Black Forest to the Black Sea, all across Austria. Tulln, the town where she was born, is famous, or so Mother's fable goes, as the place where, once upon a time, the feared warrior Attila the Hun met Kriemhild, the princess who would become his wife.

Gertrude's blankets are suddenly too tight. She wriggles out.

'I won't let anything hurt you, I promise,' Egon mumbles, pushing her hand off his arm as he turns his nose to the wall. 'Count backwards to help you sleep, as I taught you.'

'*Zehn, neun, acht, sieben . . .*' Gertrude counts, her mouth forming the words but no sound coming out. Sleep is as distant as Vienna, at the far end of the tracks.

Instead, Gertrude draws her brother's face in her mind: his eyes – dark and large, then the strong nose that's emerging from his squashed-up boy-face. His ears, they're too big, and his lips resemble the plump slugs in the garden. But the hair is easy – a mess of dark curls and sticky-out bits that refuse to be combed. Egon teases her that her hair is the colour of a fox's bottom – brown spiked with bits of orange.

They're inseparable. Egon has told her that when they're older, it will seem as if they're the same age. They'll both be grown-ups and will be allowed to do anything they want.

She wriggles in the firm bed, her toes tingling with the night chill. Gertrude cannot remember a single day when he wasn't in her life, in front of her eyes, being Egon. All the memories that dance in her head include her brother. Like the time they escaped from the house when Father was busy, Egon carrying Gertrude on his back, through the yard at the back of the station, where chickens scratched in the dirt for grain, past the paddock where a horse with a sandy mane thumped its hoof on the ground, until they found a hollow in a hedge in the far field. They'd burrowed inside, arms grazed by brambles, wet leaves stuck to scabs on their knees.

It was worth it, because in their hiding place they could not be seen. Melanie wouldn't pinch her. Mother couldn't shout, and Father wouldn't be able to sit Gertrude on his lap and stroke her hair, even when she didn't want that.

Egon had brought a handkerchief of stolen sugar with him that day. He'd untied the string, licked his finger, then dipped it inside. He'd held it up for her to admire, then popped it in her mouth. The sweetness melted on her tongue.

'More!' Gertrude had said, addicted.

'You're already as sweet as sugar,' Egon teased.

Gertrude had bitten his finger.

❧

Another memory. This time when Egon had done something silly: he'd dangled his sister by her ankles out of the window in Mother and Father's room, the one overlooking the station platform.

'I'll hold you,' he'd said. 'You mustn't squirm.' Gertrude, hands placed on the windowsill, had leaned out. She could see the tops of the passengers' hats as they read their newspapers and checked pocket watches; she saw the signalmen with their flags, and the pedlars and traders, lumpy, heavy sacks at their feet. The hand of the large platform clock pointed to the sky.

Gertrude had looked at her brother. 'It'll be fun,' he'd said. 'You'll see the world upside down.' Egon always wanted her to see the world in new ways. 'First, put your head out, then put your weight on the ledge,' he instructed.

Her brother pushed the curtains aside and she sat on the windowsill, facing him. She'd pushed off her shoes and peeled off her long socks. Egon took her left foot in his hand and blew noisily into the curve of her sole. She giggled and kicked.

'Are you ready? Remember, no wriggling!' He gripped her long skirts and ankles.

'I'm ready,' she'd said, bouncing on her bottom.

'Now, lean back, Gerti. Just let go.'

Gertrude had closed her eyes and taken a deep breath, holding it to show how brave she was. Then she had leaned back and out. Her brother's hands were tight around her ankles. Gertrude could feel the knobbles of the brickwork against her spine, the roughness of the wooden window frame through the material on her thighs. She'd opened her eyes.

'Oh! The sky is green! The fields are blue.' The sound of passengers below reached her ears, some speaking languages she didn't understand. The blood had rushed to her head and she felt heavy. 'Make it go away!' she shouted, but the hissing, huffing chug of an approaching train drowned her out. The force of it passing whipped her skirts from Egon's grasp and they had fallen around her head, obscuring her, revealing her legs and torso, her frilly knickers and the pip of her belly button. Egon's grip had slipped.

He grabbed at Gertrude, catching her around the waist, clawing and dragging her back into the room, her cries muffled by the layers of material. They'd fallen against each other, panicked, before giving way to shrieking, shuddering laughter.

~

The bedroom expands again, and from the dark, Gertrude listens out for her fear. It is gone. There are only the ugly noises of the family – Melanie grinding her teeth until they squeak, Egon rustling his dirty feet against his ankles. Gertrude must close her eyes, for soon the trains will come rattling past, like the sound of galloping horses. That's when the three children must get out of bed, and a new day will begin.

As the youngest, Gertrude must help Mother prepare breakfast: usually it is toasted *hausbrot*, or oats thickened in milk, or bacon dumplings. Gertrude brings salt, butter, curds and cold meats to the table. She lays five places: Father at the head; Mother closest to the stove; she and Egon always sit next to each other, with a view of the trains; and finally, one for Melanie, furthest from the heat. Father comes in from signalling. He's very important and everyone has to do as he wishes, even if they don't want to. He wears a long coat. It has twelve shiny buttons. His hat is embroidered with gold and he wears white gloves that rarely get dirty.

Father makes the rules. He makes them outside the walls of their home and he makes them inside, too. Gertrude doesn't understand them all. She and Egon are never able to keep track of new ones. Father says those two make up their own. He says it as if it were a bad thing, but it doesn't sound so bad to Gertrude. If she made the rules, Egon would be allowed to draw all day and she'd eat sweets for breakfast. Father brings them home from his trips to Vienna. He buys her brother pieces for his toy train set from a shop near Franz Joseph Station, and her Swiss truffles and marzipan, but she's only ever allowed one sweet at a time and always after dinner.

Egon is very good at drawing. He uses pencils, thick crayons or ink, and draws on newspapers and in the backs of books, which makes Father angry. But it's as if her brother has magic in his fingers. He began by drawing the trains with his finger on the windows, but now he spends all his spare time on the platform, sketching the machines with their enormous wheels and wagons. But Father doesn't like it. He thinks Egon should be studying, so his drawing is becoming their secret.

Gertrude enjoys playing with pencils, too. Her drawings are careful, but she doesn't practise, so she can't make them sing the way Egon can. If she were in charge, Egon could have all the paper he wanted; he wouldn't have to steal it or draw on newspaper, and Father wouldn't thrash the backs of his legs. Father would say that Egon's drawings were very good indeed and hang them outside for all the passengers to admire.

Egon draws Gertrude when he comes home from school, throwing his cap into the corner – quick pencil sketches that take minutes and are nothing more than playing. She's his favourite thing to draw, and, because of that, Gertrude has learnt to get what she wants.

'I promise you my share of the marzipan after Father's next trip to Vienna,' Egon says.

Gertrude's eyes light up, but she shakes her head.

'I promise you one item from my collection of blue things.' Egon has a precious box of objects he has collected – wild flowers, which he showed Gertrude how to press between the pages of a heavy book; a gemstone from Krumau, where Mother was born; the cracked shell of a bird's egg. Gertrude envies his collection – she particularly wants the eggshell – but she shakes her head.

'I promise . . .' Egon looks for inspiration. 'Gerti, I promise . . . that one day, when we're older, we'll move to Vienna and live in a beautiful apartment together, just the two of us.'

She considers his words, feels the weight of them. It's the biggest prize.

Gertrude takes up a pose against the wall that she knows her brother will appreciate.

And at dinner, she holds Egon's hand under the table, tighter than ever. This is a promise she'll never let him break.

2

December 1899

'Hurry, children, or we'll miss the fireworks,' Mother says.
'Tonight's a very special occasion. You'll stay awake later than
usual, for a start, so no tears, Gertrude! And you'll be spending time
with the other children in the village. There'll be singing, dancing, the
Danube waltz. I hope you've practised, Adolf – I want to have you spin
me like you used to when we were first married. Aren't you excited?'

'I'm certainly glad to have the evening off. No trains until the
morning.'

'No trains until next year,' Egon says.

'No trains until the next century!' Melanie corrects.

'That's right. It's not a normal New Year's Eve,' Mother explains,
crouching to straighten Gertrude's ribbon. 'It's not just the end of one
year and the start of the next. We're tipping over into a whole new century. The twentieth century. Imagine that . . .'

'It'll be as blighted and blemished as the nineteenth century, no
doubt,' Father says.

'Oh, Adolf, you promised you'd be in a good mood tonight.' Mother
stops to look at him. 'I want us to embrace the future.'

'We must have faith that the years to come will be better than the past.'

'Who knows what the twentieth century might bring? All I pray for is the health of my children. There's nothing I want more than long lives for the three of you, successful marriages and legions of babies for Melanie and Gertrude. And a solid career for Egon, of course. That's my wish.' Mother wipes away a tear and tries to smile.

'I'm never getting married,' moans Gertrude.

'And I won't have children,' says Melanie. 'I've seen how they come out.'

'Well, we can count on Egon, at least,' Mother says. 'A gypsy woman in my hometown once told me I'd have a son, that he'd be the joy of my old age.'

'Enough of your superstitions, Marie. You'll follow in my footsteps, my boy,' Father says, turning to Egon. 'A career in the railways. You'll do me proud.'

In a rare moment of affection, Father swings his son around, then lifts him up and carries him on his back. Gertrude prickles with jealousy. Egon wraps his arms around his father's neck, clinging on, puffing out his cheeks at her, and grinning with smug satisfaction.

Melanie and Gertrude hold their mother's hands.

Father has promised many times that he'll see to it that his son takes over the running of Tulln station one day. But Egon has told Gertrude a secret: he's never going to be a stationmaster. He hates the local primary, he can't concentrate, and he forgets most of what he's taught. He's lonely and shy and the other boys throw things at him. Egon has tried to imagine himself in his father's shoes – the trousers with pressed lines down the front, the spotless shirt with double cuffs, the blazer with gold embroidery along the shoulders – but even with the lure of the accompanying sword and feathered hat, her brother cannot picture himself in his father's place.

Her brother will have to become a very important person in the Imperial-Royal Austrian State Railways – a chief inspector like Uncle Leopold, a man they've heard about but never met; or someone who designs railroads, like their grandfather Karl Ludwig Wilhelm Schiele, although he died a long time ago.

In the distance, music can be heard, as families from all around the town gather for the biggest party in shared memory. Mother hurries them along, her heels tapping.

Gertrude looks up, imagining the burning light and crashing colours of the fireworks that she has been told are coming. But all she sees are clouds, moving across the moon.

3

April 1904

'I'm not a doll, you know,' Gertrude says, covering her eyes with her hands as her brother moves her elbows into position above her head. She sticks out her lower lip. Gertrude is the shape of a smooth seed. She's full of potential – ready to burst into energy that can't be contained. Egon is drawing her on the occasion of her tenth birthday. He arrived home that afternoon on the train from Klosterneuburg. The journey takes less than an hour. He has been sent there to study at the grammar school, where he lodges with the local master blacksmith during term time. It's an improvement on his last school, in Krems, Gertrude remembers, where her brother used to live with a widow whose skin, he said, looked like uncooked cake.

Gertrude misses her brother terribly when he's not around.

Now she watches Egon study the shape of her, all of her, except her face, which she always turns away from him. Gertrude's skin is cream and mottled pink. Her knees are ruby. Egon searches out her shadows: navy in the crevices between her fingers, blades of indigo behind her ears, the sapphire of her tummy button. She knows how to hold herself perfectly still for his eyes. He gets frustrated; he says that he's unable to capture things like 'the movement of her flesh', 'the spark of liquid in her eyes' or the 'flaming orange hair that blooms all around her head like a halo'. He stabs at the paper with his pencil, then crumples it and tries again.

They are in the attic room – with its dusty windows, sealed boxes and old furniture draped with sheets – where Egon often retreats to draw. From the small window, Gertrude can see the train tracks below. She's feeling bored and hungry, is ready to stop, when the door bucks against its frame.

Someone on the other side is trying to open the door and, surprised to find it locked, is trying again, only harder. There's another thud. Gertrude freezes. Egon grabs his materials and leaps towards the cupboard under the eaves, where he stuffs his drawings under a loose floorboard.

'Boy? Open up. Get out here at once,' Father says.

Egon throws Gertrude her dress. 'Hurry,' he instructs.

'Come out!' Father says again. 'What in heaven's name are you doing in there?'

Egon gestures to his sister to hurry. Gertrude fumbles with the fabric, trying to arrange it so she can get her arms and head through. If Father sees her like this, he'll beat Egon.

'Egon Schiele!' their father barks. 'I will break down this door.'

The floorboards creak on the other side.

Would Father be taking off his jacket, rolling up his sleeves?

Gertrude still hasn't managed to wriggle into her dress.

'Must I warn you again?'

The fabric rips slightly as Gertrude struggles with it, but it is insignificant compared to the sound of wood buckling and splitting under a grown man's weight. Their father bursts into the room, the door hanging defeated on its hinges.

Gertrude realizes she has the dress on back to front; its high neckline is choking her.

Egon's hands are balled into fists at his side.

'You scared us,' Gertrude says, breathless.

'It's Gerti's birthday, we were just playing a silly game,' Egon explains.

Splinters of wood are caught on Father's shirt collar and in his hair. He dusts himself down, breathing hard from his efforts. He glares at Egon and his youngest daughter, then looks around for evidence of their corruption.

'Your hands,' he demands. Gertrude holds her long fingers out for inspection while Egon wipes his as firmly as he can against the back of his trousers. When he presents them to his father, they are shaking. Lead is smudged into his fingertips. 'My only son,' Father continues. 'You disobey me. You keep secrets. You make a mockery of my rules. And you're encouraging your sister to be as wild as you are.'

'I'm sorry, Father.'

'Where are they?' he demands. 'Hand them over, or I'll pull up every floorboard.'

Gertrude shuffles further into the corner, her hand on the peeling wallpaper. Egon sways.

'Bring me your damned drawings. Or there will be consequences.' The skin around Father's nostrils is stretched wide.

'No,' Egon says.

Her brother sticks out his chin and Father's closed hand smashes against it, striking him to the ground. Gertrude cries out.

'You're a wilful, disobedient young man,' he says to his son. 'You've hardly impressed with your grades; your report card is abysmal. We sent you to the grammar school in Klosterneuburg – after that embarrassing fiasco, being expelled from Krems – hoping for the best, and now you must repeat the year. We can't keep paying for private tutors to prop you up. At your age, I'd given up playing with a pencil. I didn't have all the opportunities you have; I had to apply myself. I had to show respect towards my father. Your mother has indulged you for too long. She has encouraged this excessive drawing. You're a Schiele! We've much to be proud of in our lineage. People expect a great deal from us, here in Tulln and beyond.'

Gertrude knows how much Egon wants to please their father, how he has tried to follow the path he has chosen for him. Her brother adores the man, despite his bouts of anger. She knows he craves his approval, but he can never be the person Father wants him to be.

Egon glances at her. Gertrude sees herself through his eyes: her body hugging the wall, in the back-to-front dress, her head twisted round, as if the pieces of a puzzle have been badly put together. There is a redness creeping from her brother's mouth, edging along his jaw. In his anger, Father lifts a heavy boot.

'No!' Gertrude says. 'I'll get them. Don't hurt him, please, especially not on my birthday.'

Father kicks the broken wood of the door instead, glaring at his daughter.

'You'll find me in the kitchen,' he announces.

Egon curls up into a tight ball, his arms wrapped around himself, his fingers on his temples. Gertrude runs to the moth-ridden cupboard before her brother can protest. She removes the piece of wood that covers the space where Egon hides his precious things. She pulls out a wad of papers – some huge, covered in detailed drawings of the trains that stop for an extended break in front of their home; others small and controlled – a black feather with white spots, a pebble with intricate markings. Egon has filled page after page. Gertrude removes the most recent ones that her brother hurriedly hid, stuffing them back into the gap before replacing the wood.

Egon's eyes watch her as she leaves the room.

In the kitchen, Gertrude pushes the drawings into Father's hands. Then she sits at the top of the stairs, out of view, to see what he'll do next.

Father settles at the table and looks through his son's work.

'It's a calamity, Marie, this blasted obsession.'

'You mean Egon's drawing?' Her mother tries to smile.

Father cradles his head. 'How is it possible that our son is such a disappointment?' Mother takes a seat. 'We were so happy when he was born – finally, a living boy! But he keeps letting us down. You're failing him, Marie. You and your peasant ways.'

'My father, need I remind you' – Mother sets her shoulders straight – 'was a respectable, wealthy man, with much by way of property.'

'The way things are done in Krumau are not to be tolerated in a modern Austrian household. Your Bohemian superstitions and bad habits should be forgotten by now – all that singing to the children, telling them your ridiculous folk tales . . . why, they only succeed in making Gertrude cry in the night. You shouldn't be encouraging this artistic streak.'

'But what harm does it do?'

'Moments ago, I had to break into the attic.' Mother's eyes widen. Father takes a glass and fills it with amber-coloured liquor, then knocks it back. 'Our children were bolted inside, doing God knows what.'

Gertrude strains closer so as not to miss a word.

'It's her birthday, her tenth birthday, Adolf. You know how significant that is, how painful it is for me. I almost can't bear to celebrate it. Anyway, I'm sure they were only playing.'

'I won't allow it. They're being corrupted. Heading for ruin. All that boy thinks about is drawing! His grades are appalling. Every day, he's threatened with expulsion. How else will he progress, if he doesn't knuckle down and study? I'm at my wits' end.'

Mother's face is heavily lined. There are black shadows under her eyes.

'I'll talk to him again,' she sighs.

'You have to go further than that. There can be no half measures. It's time we drew our own line – no more drawing! Not under this roof. He'll get ten strokes of the cane for every picture he produces. He must resolve never to pick up a pencil again.'

Mother makes a slight movement and leans over the table to look at some of Egon's sketches.

'He does have talent . . .' she ventures.

Father leaps up, towers over her and leans in, his mouth close to her face. 'If he continues, I'll cast him out on to the streets for bringing shame to the Schiele name. And I'll dismiss you, for being a weak mother, incapable of raising the son I deserve. Is that what you want?'

Mother shakes her head fearfully.

'Then get rid of these.'

She tucks Egon's drawings into the pocket of her apron.

Gertrude feels a lurch as Father shakes his head and gestures to the stove.

'No,' Gertrude whispers.

But Father's thin mouth is set. A vein throbs in his neck. Mother seems smaller than before as she pulls the papers from her apron. She closes her eyes.

'Egon would draw with his own blood if he had to,' she whispers. 'He'd etch lines with a knife on his body if he hadn't pencil and paper.'

'Are you disobeying me?'

'This is your dreaded sickness talking, Adolf, flaring up again, making you cruel.'

'Keep your voice down!' he hisses, his face twisted with disgust. 'My only insanity, right now, is that boy.'

Mother turns her back on him, and steps towards the *kachelofen*, with its licking fire.

'What will become of us if you have another episode?' she insists.

'All you need to concern yourself with is that our son be set on a respectable path. Or I'll see to it that you rue the day you married me.'

Mother laughs bitterly, and opens the grate. She pushes Egon's artworks into the flames. The papers immediately begin to split and curl.

'Now, there's a good wife.' He steps towards her, puts a hand on her lower back, and brings his face close to her cheek.

'You've got what you wanted,' she says, rubbing her wrist and pulling away.

Father checks the time, returns his watch to his pocket, then downs another glass of the amber liquid.

Gertrude, tears on her lashes, tries to back away without making a sound, hoping the wood won't creak under her weight. She returns to

Egon, who is still lying in a tight knot on the floor. She kisses his shoulder and fits her body around the curve of his spine.

'Mother burned your drawings,' Gertrude whispers.

'No . . .' he whimpers. 'How could she?'

'You don't deserve any of this.'

'I will never, ever forgive her,' Egon says, his voice splintering like the door.

4

May 1904

'If I find you, I win. Make sure you find a good hiding spot. That's the game, Gerti.'

'But why can't we play here?' Gertrude stares at her hands.

Egon says it'll be fun, but what will she do by herself while her brother is searching for her? It's such a waste, not being together, on one of the rare days when he's home from school. Gertrude misses him.

'Why don't you do the seeking, then, if you're going to pull such an ugly face?' he says, spinning her by the shoulders so that she is facing the wall. 'Cover your eyes and count to one hundred. Then you open them and try to find me.'

'But where will you be?'

'I could be anywhere.'

'I won't have to look outside, will I?'

'The fun is in not knowing.'

Gertrude frowns, thinking of all the places Egon might hide. There's one place he certainly won't choose: Father's study – with its bottles of waxy-smelling cognac, his prized collection of fossils and precious minerals, and a huge map showing the reach of the Imperial-Royal Austrian State Railways – is strictly forbidden to his children.

'Don't look so miserable. This is what normal children do.'

The Schiele children have rarely been allowed to play with their neighbours in Tulln. Father thinks the local children are a bad influence.

She pouts. 'If I can't find you quickly, will you come out? Then you can draw me.'

'Try playing the game, for once. You might enjoy it.'

Gertrude squints, then starts counting. Egon waves a hand in front of her face to check she cannot see, and she pushes him away.

'Keep them closed!' he shouts as he leaves the room.

Gertrude counts to twenty, then walks over to the window. She pushes a dried, lifeless fly to the floor with her finger. She goes to the door and turns the handle. The empty apartment, as she walks around it, feels different, as if her brother could be anywhere, watching her. She steps into each room to see if Egon has made it easy, yet she knows he won't have hidden anywhere obvious. He'd rather hitchhike to Vienna and be gone for three days than be found in the wardrobe in the first three minutes.

She tries the door to Father's study, but it's locked.

In the pantry, Gertrude pulls off a chunk of bread, which she dips in honey. She walks out on to the platform, and looks at the faces of the people waiting for the next train.

She checks their childhood hiding place under the hedge, then starts walking towards the main streets of Tulln, unsure if she should stray this far from home. Suddenly she glimpses Egon's tufty hair as he peeks from behind a wall. She races to catch him, but before she can put her hands on him, he's gone. She spots the flap of his long black coat and launches after him. He's twenty steps ahead by now and moving fast. He'll be taking the path to the Danube. She can catch up with him there and put a stop to this silliness.

But where he should be going left, the dark figure turns right. He's halfway up the hill now, heading away from the busy Hauptplatz, away from the bridge that crosses the river, and towards the abandoned stone fortress that is Tulln's Roman tower. She should have guessed!

From there, once upon a time, a thousand Roman soldiers kept watch on the barbarian tribes across the river.

Gertrude speeds up and feels the heat and tightness in her calves as she climbs the incline. Is he heading towards the vineyards where they have, in the past, crept under the dusty vines and stuffed handfuls of grapes into their every pocket? At the top of the hill, Gertrude spots his face in profile, before he dashes away again, down a narrow alley. She's hot on his heels, but the distance between them is increasing.

The sound of her footsteps echoes off the arched brickwork as she runs through the alleyway. When Gertrude emerges into the light once more, she stops. Sad, angelic faces; ivy covering weather-whitened tombs. She treads carefully, her breath catching in her throat.

What if there comes a day when she can no longer find him, when he is lost to her?

A hand reaches out and touches the back of her neck.

'Found you!' her brother smirks. She punches him in the chest.

'You scared me! Anyway, I found *you*!'

'It took you long enough.'

'I don't like it here,' Gertrude says, looking around.

'I know, but I've got something to show you,' he says, suddenly serious.

He leads her to a white headstone, with two words on it: FAMILIE SCHIELE.

'Grandfather isn't buried in Tulln,' Gertrude says, looking carefully at the grave.

'It's time you met our sister,' Egon says.

Gertrude touches the headstone and looks at her brother.

'You're teasing me!' she insists, her eyes watering.

'Elvira,' he says. 'She was the oldest. She died, aged ten, when I was little.'

'But that's how old I am!'

'That's why you need to meet her now.'

'Elvira?' Gertrude says, the syllables sharp. 'Why haven't I heard her name before?'

'Mother was sad, so Father forbade us from mentioning her. There were three years between her and Melanie . . .'

'But *you* could have told me.'

'I hardly remember her. I wasn't even four when she got sick.'

'I wasn't born then?'

'Mother was pregnant with you. Elvira died in September 1893, and you didn't arrive until April the following year.'

Gertrude considers this information, her breath shallow. 'So I took her place? There'd have been four of us? Melanie wasn't always the oldest? Was Elvira bossy, too?'

'She was kind and quiet. You'd have liked her,' her brother replies.

'Did you like her more than you like me? Would you have preferred it if she'd stayed?'

'That's a silly question. I was too young to remember Elvira ever playing with me. Even before she got ill, she spent a lot of time in bed. Then one day, she just wasn't there any more.'

Fat tears run down Gertrude's cheeks. 'So we can just disappear? Her name's not even on the gravestone. Will that happen to me, now I'm ten? No one will ever speak of me again?'

'I'll make sure that you're remembered, don't worry about that, Gerti.'

'You're meant to say I won't die. Not aged ten. Not ever!'

'This is where we'll all end up, sooner or later. In the same patch of earth as Elvira. Melanie once told me that there were three other babies – all boys, born between her and me – who never cried and were taken away in a bucket.'

'Other brothers?' Gertrude wipes her nose with her knuckles.

'Melanie thought I'd be another blue baby. Maybe that's why she's never liked me.'

'I wish it was Melanie who'd died!'

'You don't mean that.' Egon brushes away an insect that has landed in his sister's hair. 'If I die first,' he says after a pause, 'I promise to come back and haunt you. So you'll never have a quiet moment.'

'I'd like that,' she sniffs. 'But you can't die until you're old – and not before me.'

Egon pulls his sister into a hug, then pinches her ear. 'We'll die together, how about that?' He offers his hand so they can shake on it. 'On the same day. We'll be very old and it will be after a long and happy life.'

Gertrude rubs her eyes, then shakes her brother's hand.

She touches the headstone again, a look of confusion crossing her face, then stoops down and puts her index finger in the mud. 'Elvira,' she writes with her finger across the white stone, beneath the engraving – knowing full well the letters will be washed away with the rain.

5

June 1904

G ertrude wants to send a letter to Egon, to his address in Kloster-neuburg. She doesn't want to write to tell him of the things that occupy her day, of her life in Tulln, how it goes on without him, as there's nothing to report. Instead, she intends to place her hand on a piece of blank paper, spread her fingers wide, and draw a line around it. She knows he'll like that. Gertrude tries the door to Father's study. For once, it's unlocked.

Father is busier than usual, and often stressed. He has become forgetful. She enters, hoping not to be caught in her bid to steal what she needs. He'll hardly miss one sheet of the precious company-headed writing paper. Receiving her drawing on that will make her brother laugh.

Inside, the study is dim, with one low lamp burning in the corner, illuminating a wall of leather-bound volumes. To Gertrude, the room smells fruity, as if Father has doused it in the amber liquid kept in his bottom drawer. Gertrude sits in Father's chair and spins around. She sneaks some of the amber spirit and takes a sip. It burns! Then she takes a cigar from the box and inhales – it smells of wet leaves and bonfires.

She puts her feet on his desk, feeling as if she has nothing to lose.

To her right, a drawer, with a little key in the lock, is open a crack. She pulls, but the drawer sticks. Gertrude pushes her finger into the gap and pulls harder until it gives. There's nothing inside except a thick stack of embossed papers, each one stamped with crimson wax and signed in gold. She spreads them across the desk.

There must be something more in there . . .

Gertrude's fingers feel their way into the dusty corners of the drawer. Jammed right at the back, there's paper of a different texture. Out comes a photograph: Mother in her best dress, her fingers clenched in her lap; Father in his uniform, looking younger, his moustache thicker and wiry, his hand on Mother's shoulder. In the photo there are three children – two girls in pretty dresses and a little boy with sticky-out ears, perched on a rocking horse and frowning. Gertrude recognizes him as her brother. The tall girl behind him is Melanie, with long hair pulled back and tied in a ribbon. So the pale girl on the right, smiling beside Father, her ankles crossed neatly, must be . . . Elvira. She has an upturned nose and a superior look on her face. No, Gertrude wouldn't like her at all. She looks too real, too alive. On the back is the name of the photographer's studio, and a date – 1893. The year Elvira died.

'What are you doing in here?' Mother demands from the doorway. Gertrude pushes the photograph back in the drawer and tries to neaten the pile of boring certificates. 'Young lady?' she continues in the same tone, but her eyes are not on her daughter, but the papers.

Mother dries her hands on her apron and walks over. She picks up the top one with the tips of her fingers and reads it slowly, savouring the words, the hint of a smile softening her face. Gertrude tries to edge away. Then Mother, in one swoop, collects the rest of the pile and runs her thumb down the thick wad. It makes a fluttering noise. Her eyes are shining.

'These,' Mother says, sharing a secret with Gertrude, 'are this family's most valuable possession. We inherited them from your grandfather, and they're the only thing between us and poverty if your father loses his job. They'll be worth a great deal when the time comes to cash them in. They're our investment, our security,' she says. 'Never touch them again.' Mother returns them to the drawer. 'They must stay safe, always under lock and key.'

Gertrude smiles sweetly. She's pleased she hasn't been reprimanded. While her mother's back is turned, she slips a piece of official paper from the tray before running from the room. The last thing she sees is her mother turning the little key in the lock, then slipping it into the safety of her apron.

6

July 1904

G ertrude and her brother escape early, at that boundless time of day when it feels as if everything lies ahead, ready to unfurl.

Egon eases the door of their apartment closed behind them.

'This day is ours,' Egon smiles, as if they've already got away with their plan.

'Ssshh.' She pushes him, anxious to hurry her brother away from the station. It would only take Mother or Melanie peering out of the window to put a stop to everything.

The two of them need light and fresh air today. They intend to follow the railway tracks for a mile or two – stepping along the cracked sleepers, wild plums squashed underfoot, fallen from overhanging trees – then pick up the meander of the Danube and swim in its shallows, before heading along to a quiet spot in the fields. They carry little – Egon has his secret small sketchbook and a sharpened pencil, positioned in the open pocket of his shirt. In a clean napkin, Gertrude has placed slabs of thickly buttered bread that she has sprinkled with sugar, and some slices of dried sausage. Egon has plucked two apples from the tree behind their home.

Now they walk on the firm, flattened ground alongside the tracks, heading away from home, away from Mother and Father, away from

Vienna, where, if you look in the direction of the capital, the skies seem hazy and dark. They are surrounded by fields of sugar beet and sweet-corn. Birds swoop in a drunken dance, skimming the dried husks. They are lulled by the sound of the breeze gently rustling the stalks.

Gertrude is counting her steps. She gets past three hundred before Egon speaks.

'Would you run away with me?' he asks.

'I'm with you now, aren't I?'

'No, I mean properly. Not just for a few hours, or a day, but longer . . .'

'Where would we go?' Gertrude asks.

'I don't know yet. But I'm growing up and I won't have to do things *their* way for much longer,' he says, twisting his face at the mention of their parents. 'I want to leave them behind, but I don't want to leave you.'

'What about money? Mother is always saying how important that is.'

'My art tutor says I could sell my drawings, that rich people would pay for them. Then I could live in Vienna and study at the art school there. There are lots of famous artists in Austria. My tutor says I could be as good as Gustav Klimt one day. His work is like nothing you've ever seen. So, you'd come with me?'

'Would I be able to live with you?'

'I don't see why not.'

'Why can't we go now?' Gertrude asks.

Egon stops walking. 'You're still young. And I'm scared about Father. He's unwell.'

Her heart beats faster. The other day she noticed horrible red sores on his skin.

'He shouts at me a lot,' she pouts.

'That's his illness, it makes him angry. It's not his fault.'

'So you still love him? Even though he hits you?'

'Of course I do. He wants the best for us.'

'But you don't do anything he says!'

'I want to make him proud, I just don't know how yet,' her brother replies.

Gertrude considers this information.

'Melanie won't have to come with us?' she asks, warming to the theme.

'Our sister only toes Mother's line,' he says, taking a bite of his apple. 'They'll be happy together.'

Egon leads her away from the tracks, drops the pips from his apple core on the ground, then pushes them into the soil with the toe of his boot. 'Let's sit for a while,' he says. 'Why don't you pick some flowers? You always find the prettiest ones.'

Gertrude's thoughts are too tangled for her to argue. She kicks off her shoes and removes her socks. The long grasses brush the backs of her knees. Ants hurry over her toes and small spiders scurry up the fine hairs on her legs. She searches, discovers the tiny hearts of wild strawberries and red-shelled scurrying bugs. She inspects the delicate white taproot of an unknown weed, which had been threaded into the soil only moments before.

Gertrude returns to Egon bearing lilac mallows, dandelions and a sunflower as large as her head. Before passing them over, she traces the sunflower's vibrant petals, runs her finger along its thick stem to feel the bristling hairs, then presses the pad of her index finger to the centre. It comes away with a fingerprint of pollen. Some of the dandelions have begun to turn into cottony globes – she blows them with one mighty puff into Egon's face. He laughs, the sunlight in his eyes.

Gertrude puzzles at the transformation that turns one beautiful thing into another.

She passes the specimens to Egon, then wipes her hands on her dress. He arranges them and takes out his pencil, lying on his stomach, his feet kicking the air. He starts with the confident line of the sunflower stalk and its leaf, moves on to replicate the precise curve of the many petals.

Gertrude's eyes wander to an old stone cottage near by – it's missing its roof. The warm breeze plays at the loose hair around her neck. She feels something slipping away from her today, a feeling she cannot name; everything is changing and she can't keep hold of it, like the dandelion seeds being blown away on the wind.

Egon draws for an hour, changing perspectives and rotating his sketchbook. Gertrude is on her knees, searching for a clover with four leaves, when her eyes stray to the distance.

She leaps up. 'He followed us!'

The figure of a man comes into view, on the horizon. Egon jumps up too, and hides his pencil in the undergrowth, followed by his sketchbook. Each step confirms their fear: a head of receding grey hair, shoulders sloped, the uneven gait. He is wearing the burnt red of a stationmaster's uniform.

Egon and Gertrude will get a beating for being this far from home, for not helping Mother with the chores, for making Father come all this way. He'll make them pay.

Their father is stepping from sleeper to sleeper – which is against the rules of the Imperial-Royal Austrian State Railways – and normally he wouldn't hesitate to issue a harsh penalty to anyone found trespassing in this way. Egon pulls Gertrude further into the undergrowth as he approaches. But the hand they expect to feel never leaves his side. The man doesn't alter his pace and continues straight ahead. He stops for a moment, shakes his arms out of his stationmaster's blazer and discards it on the tracks, then sets off again.

'Should we try to stop him?' Gertrude asks.

'We have to let him go,' Egon says.

They shade their eyes and watch him shrinking into the distance.

When the coast is clear, Gertrude runs to pick up the blazer. She returns wearing it, the hem reaching almost to her knees. There's a piece of embossed paper folded into one of the pockets, the same as the certificates she saw in his office, but the crimson wax mark has crumbled off.

Gertrude and Egon then take refuge in the cottage. He pulls the ribbon out of her hair and braids flowers into the plaits he makes.

For many hours, they lie there, staring up at the sky, commenting on the passing clouds, pale butterflies.

From time to time, the rattle of an afternoon train cuts through the calm.

～

It's dusk by the time they return home. Gertrude has left Father's jacket at the dilapidated cottage, but has pulled a shiny button from it to carry as a memento.

They find Mother at the stove, a huge pan of water on the boil beside her. She pushes damp hair from her forehead and wipes her hands on her apron, but the storm they have been expecting doesn't come. Their mother has other things on her mind.

'Tell your sister there's more water ready,' she says, barely looking at them.

Melanie is in their parents' bedroom, a washtub by her side. She's on her knees, sponging Father's back. He's seated on a low stool, naked. The flesh on his chest seems to be hanging off his bones and there are cuts all over the thin skin of his arms. He is staring at the knots in the floorboards, his jaw loose. Gertrude comes closer. His nose is bloody, possibly broken, and the skin is torn around his neck. The water is the colour of charcoal.

'Your turn.' Melanie hands her sister the sponge and leaves with the heavy basin. Gertrude holds the sponge in front of her, but doesn't dare place it on Father's feather-thin frame. Melanie has washed off most of the mud, but there's more in his hair and bristles. Water drips down Gertrude's arm and off her elbow on to the floor, puddling beneath her feet.

Gertrude looks at Father's naked body. Angry welts have flared up around his genitals and spread to his torso and wrists. They're the colour of the red poppies she likes to gather in the fields. Melanie returns, directing Egon, who is carrying the steaming basin of clean water. She gives Gertrude an impatient glance, grabs the sponge, dips it in the water and squeezes, then begins to rub it over Father's forehead, pushing his hair back, making sure the water doesn't drip into his eyes. It's as if she is washing a statue.

'Mother has been out of her mind all day,' Melanie says. 'She's no less worried now that he's home. Look at him,' she continues, as she rubs the back of his neck. 'He's been having another one of his episodes, when he doesn't know who he is or where he's going. He just goes completely blank. Four men had to carry him home. Workers seven miles down the line found him. He was in the swill under the bridge, almost dead! Lord knows what would have happened if they hadn't . . .'

She wipes her forearm across her nose and mouth.

'And where were you, anyway?' Melanie's eyes burn from one sibling to the other.

'We were running an errand for Frau Hogl,' Egon replies. 'She's sick and can't leave the house. It took us longer than expected, and . . .'

Melanie interrupts him with a disappointed shake of her head. 'Frau Hogl recovered days ago. She's in fine health; I saw her this afternoon. Come on, there's work to be done, if you can spare the time away from your games. Father needs to be dried and his clean clothes aren't going to put themselves on.' She stands again to remove the bucket. 'And Gerti, you come with me. You've seen quite enough already.'

7

The train pulls out of the station, on its way to 'Bahnhof Krumau an der Moldau', as the sign would say. At the suggestion of the doctor who's treating Father's illness, the Schieles – including Egon, who is home from school – have taken a ten-day leave of absence, their first family holiday, away from Tulln, its trains and the physical demands of station life. They're visiting Mother's hometown in Bohemia, the place where she was born.

'I prescribe respite, relaxation and fresh air', the doctor had advised. 'Get him away from all the stresses and pollution of the station. Herr Schiele must rest.'

Before they left, Gertrude had seen Mother on the office telephone inside the station. She'd stopped by the door, her ears alert to her mother's hushed tones.

'It started a few weeks ago. He signalled for a train to stop at entirely the wrong time,' Mother explained. Gertrude could hear the familiar sound of her mother lighting one of the thin cigarettes she keeps in a silver case in her apron. She only smokes them when Father isn't around. 'When challenged, he insulted the driver. He dismissed it afterwards, and I, stupidly, chose to think no more of it. But then, last week, he wrestled a passenger to the ground, completely unprovoked.'

There was a pause as the person on the other end of the line reacted to this news.

'Quite! Well, that passenger then made a formal complaint,' she continued, 'and, just our luck, he was a magistrate from Vienna. We were terrified he'd press charges. It didn't amount to that, but it was reported in the local paper.' Gertrude could hear her mother taking a long drag on her cigarette. 'I feel completely humiliated, as you can imagine. Adolf has been reprimanded. We were forced to contact Leopold . . . That's right, the one married to Adolf's sister, and you know there's no love lost between Adolf and Louisa . . . I still think she was resentful when Elvira was born. They've never been able to have any of their own, you know. She never sent her condolences when Elvira . . .' She swallowed her words. 'Anyway, Leopold stepped in on Adolf's behalf. He's very high up in the company. Whatever he said, they listened. They've instructed Adolf to take a break from the station until things blow over, and come back when he's his old dependable self, as they put it. I've my doubts, Kateřina . . . You'll be shocked when you see him. This disease has ravaged him.'

There was a pause as Gertrude's aunt spoke on the other end of the line.

'You know I'll be glad to get away from Tulln,' her mother's voice dropped to a whisper. 'But truth be told, there are times when I can hardly bear to be around him. I just don't know what will happen to us.' She coughed. 'I've missed you dearly, Katzi, you must understand that. I know there won't be room at your house, but I'd be grateful if you could find us a basic, clean pension near by. Somewhere close to the river.'

Gertrude had heard Mother replacing the telephone in its cradle. She had tiptoed away, then rushed to find Egon so she could tell him everything.

⇜

The train is rolling further and further away from what Father calls 'civilization', deeper north and west. A map between his hands, he announces the precise moment when they cross the unseen border into the Kingdom of Bohemia. It's a place Gertrude has only visited once, but cannot remember. In the distance, she sees low, snow-capped mountains and acres of dense trees.

'That's Šumava, the ancient forest,' Mother comments.

'You mean Böhmerwald, as we say in German,' Father says.

'You're going to have to allow me to speak my native tongue in Krumau, Adolf, not chastise me every time I do so. It's only reasonable while we're there,' she says, turning her attention back to the view.

'Legend has it that giants once lived among the trees,' she tells Gertrude.

'Giants?' Gertrude exclaims, imagining their mean eyes.

'There's no such thing as giants,' Melanie says.

'Enough of your myths and legends,' Father interjects. 'You're filling their heads with nonsense.'

But Mother continues her story, emboldened by Gertrude's interest. 'One day, a poor grief-stricken tailor came to the giants with a plea for help. He was not able to support his dozen children. But the giants hurled him down a steep slope and threw a rock at him. The tailor lived, although he was shaken and bruised. But why had he been treated so cruelly, he wanted to know? Would a little kindness have gone amiss? Then he looked at the rock that had caused so much damage. For it was not a rock, but a giant piece of gold.' She smiles, wistfully. 'He lived happily for the rest of his life, could feed his children, and never had to work again.'

'So the giants made him suffer, but he was rewarded in the end?' Egon considers such a fate. 'Wouldn't it have been fairer if they'd just given him the gold? What if the rock had killed him?'

Gertrude looks at her mother.

'Nothing comes easy in this world,' Mother replies. 'We must bear the weight of injustice, to get our just rewards.'

'I don't see the fun in that,' Egon snorts.

'Fun?' Mother laughs. 'Whatever gave you the idea that life should be fun?'

'And when are you due your just rewards, Frau Schiele, for all this suffering you are forced to endure?' Father asks, a little smirk on his face, as he shuffles closer to Mother.

'One day, I will get my pot of gold. And I'll live out the rest of my life in comfort and grace.'

'Until that day comes, you'll simply have to tolerate us,' he says, patting her.

'Indeed, I will.' Mother forces a smile. 'Now, let's enjoy our little trip, shall we?'

⌐⌐

Egon jumps down first and reaches back to take the brass-studded valises stencilled with the Schiele name from Father. Mother, Melanie and Gertrude follow.

'Home,' Mother says, taking in the elevated view of the ancient city – the jumble of red roofs, the jutting spire of the Gothic castle with its pink, grey and green turret; the double horseshoe bends of the river Vltava curving round winding, narrow streets covered in cobblestones.

Mother glances at Father to check if the word has offended him, but he's consumed by the oozing sores on his wrists. The mercury that is rubbed into them and the morphine the doctor has prescribed seem to be making no difference.

'I've not been back since Mother's funeral,' she continues, 'when we spent the summer here eight years ago. You must remember how much you enjoyed that, children?'

They take a carriage from the station to the walls of the medieval old town, where they will have to continue on foot. The driver cracks his reins as they step down. They enter, wandering through corkscrew lanes, the sound of the river dulling the shouts of Egon and Gertrude as they run along the cobbles. They come to the wooden Lazebnický Bridge, which leads to the historic core of the town, and follow the central Radniční street. The buildings are more vibrant than those in

Tulln – painted in ochre, pinks and reds, some with piercing-blue window frames. Washing hangs from lines between windows, white shirts and dresses swaying in the breeze.

'Look, children,' Mother says, stopping at a green door. 'A witch once lived at this address. Oh, the stories that passed among us when I was young, of how mysterious and dreadful she was.'

Then they're in a busy square, náměstí Svornosti, filled with violin players, chestnut vendors and old women, hair plaited in pigtails as if they were still girls, milk pitchers hung across their shoulders. There's a fountain with a towering column in its centre surrounded by stone saints. Egon runs up to it to take a closer look.

'There's Saint Sebastian, shot with arrows,' he shouts back. 'He's my favourite saint.'

'Don't let the water get you, Egon,' Mother warns. 'That column in the middle was built in memory of the town's plague victims. It's bad luck to get wet.'

But it's too late. Egon steps back from the fountain, a seeping splash visible on his shirt.

Vulgar chants erupt from the inns, where men drink frothy beer at tables set out on the street, smashing the tankards together and laughing.

⌒

In front of the town hall, Mother hugs a woman, Kateřina, for a long while. Gertrude does not remember her aunt, but Egon whispers to her that she's a lot fatter than she was the last time he saw her. She has the same dark, thick hair, but shorter than Mother's – and her eyes are the same shape, too.

Gertrude stays close to Egon.

The two women speak in Czech for a minute, their words churning like the river, then Kateřina turns to the rest of the family.

'Adolf, you haven't changed one bit,' she says to Father. 'Still the same strapping young man who showed up here all those years ago.' Gertrude wonders if her aunt is also blind. 'I remember how quickly you wanted to steal my little sister away,' she smiles. 'Mother, rest her soul, turned you away. You had to wait five years, until our little Marie turned seventeen, to marry. Still, a fine match.'

Mother and Kateřina exchange a glance.

'Your sister has no regrets,' Father says gruffly.

Kateřina hoots.

'Hello, young man,' she says to Egon. 'Handsome, indeed. I hear you're possessed by a passion for art? That's your grandmother, that is. Our mother used to paint; she had talent. That's your inheritance. Don't turn your back on it, boy.'

Egon smiles uncertainly. Gertrude looks at Father, who is glaring at her aunt.

'Melanie,' she continues. 'A vision of perfection! Your mother speaks so highly of you. You're steadfast and straight, solid traits in a young woman. Just don't forget to have some fun! It must get boring being so reliable.'

'Don't discourage her, Katzi. I need all the help I can get,' Mother comments.

'And this must be Gerti.' The woman rubs Gertrude's cheek with rough fingers. 'You were knee-high the last time I saw you and an ungrateful little thing, wouldn't drink your milk and screamed the house down. Although still prone to getting your own way, I hear? Nothing wrong with a girl knowing her mind, I say.'

'It's very nice to meet you, Aunt,' Gertrude says politely.

'A fine family, Marie. You've made us Soukupovás proud. Now, you look famished. Drop off your cases. I've secured two spare rooms in the house next door to ours. By the river, as requested. The roof leaks, but you'll be comfortable. I've sent my clan ahead to the tavern, if you can manage it.' She winks. 'Oh, you're a long way from home now!'

The tavern is smoky, the ceiling low and arched and the walls rough to the touch. A boar, rabbits and several chickens are sizzling on a spit over an open flame. The space is packed with men, women, and children of all ages, squeezed on to the benches: gap-toothed children, farmhands, a pair of butchers with blood still on their aprons, plump women in low-cut dresses. It's unlike anything Gertrude has ever seen. Kateřina's husband, Plamen, a bulky man with a protruding belly, and their five children, all boys, are already seated. They're wearing loose trousers that stop at their calves and striped shirts without collars – markedly different from the young men in Tulln.

They all cram on to the benches together, and soon a huge plate piled high with steaming meats, dusted with fragrant herbs, arrives at the table. It's followed by a hot tray of thickly sliced potatoes, cooked until they are crisp and glistening with oil. Kateřina shouts for three large jugs of beer, and barley water for the children. Mother tries to protest, but is silenced by her sister. Gertrude watches her mother sipping at the pale liquid, a puzzled lightness in her eyes.

'Dig in, children,' their aunt orders. 'Before my brutish boys finish the lot. Use your fingers, there are no airs and graces around here.'

Egon jumps at the suggestion, tearing at the meat. Melanie takes a small piece, wiping her fingers under the bench after she puts it on her plate. Gertrude looks at Mother, who looks at Father, who shrugs and takes another gulp of beer. So Gertrude follows her brother's lead, picking up the warm flesh, feeling the moistness of it, the greasy juices on her fingertips. She pulls with her teeth, sucking her fingers. She is ravenous.

Father's aloofness develops into a rapturous mood. He begins telling ribald jokes to Plamen, ones that have been passed on from the workers on the railways, men with muscles, and mischief in their eyes. His illness seems to have been forgotten, even if his sores and sunken eyes are attracting glances from the revellers around them. Soon, even Mother is covering her mouth with her hand, amusement creasing her eyes. Melanie reluctantly joins in, a prim smile on her face. She leans towards her cousin, the oldest of Kateřina's children, saying something to him that Gertrude cannot hear. Gertrude looks around the table, first at her aunt and her brood, then at Mother, Father, her sister and Egon, who is gnawing on a bone like a dog. Her family. A melting feeling starts in her, like a ripple of water, somewhere under her ribs. It rises up her throat, to her lips. And she surprises herself by laughing along with them.

⌒

The noise rips through the night, passing through the thin wall of the narrow, two-bedroom house that has been rented for their stay: a torrent of words in a language they don't understand. Gertrude tries to gather her senses in a space she's not familiar with. Melanie lights a small lamp. The siblings stare at each other, faces swollen with sleep.

'Who's that shouting?' Gertrude asks, her voice trembling.

Then they hear it again – words they don't know the meaning of in their mother's native tongue, but in which the anguish and desperation are clear.

Melanie throws off her blankets and runs to the door that leads to the hallway. Her fingers rest on the handle.

'Wait,' Egon says. 'It's just another one of their arguments.'

There's a rolling clatter from the next room.

'Get away from the window,' Mother says, reverting to German. 'You're drunk!'

'I'm scared,' Gertrude whimpers.

'I should be in there, with Mother,' Melanie says.

Egon shakes his head. 'Don't go.'

They open their door a crack, and peer through. They can't take their eyes from the one that leads to their parents' room.

'Do it, then – jump!' Mother shouts. 'See if I care!'

Melanie grabs the door handle once more, but Egon holds her back.

'He won't do it,' he says.

'How do you know?'

There's a heavy bang from the door to the street and a burst of footsteps. Plamen runs down the hallway in his nightshirt, his thick hairy legs paler than his arms. They hear a scuffle in their parents' room.

Mother raises her voice in her native tongue and Plamen responds with short words, repeated over and over. Egon's fingers dig deeply into Gertrude's shoulder.

'Did Father jump into the river?' Gertrude asks, shaking.

'He'd go to hell if he did that,' Melanie answers.

Finally, their parents' bedroom door is pushed open. The three of them stare harder through the wedge of light and hold their breath. Plamen emerges, steadying his step before he puts each foot down, thrown off balance by the unwieldy cargo he's carrying: Father. He's slung over their uncle's shoulder, rump in the air, his emaciated torso bent, his arms loose down the man's back. Frothy spit dangles from his lips and his eyes are swollen. Mother, in her frilly nightgown, feet bare and hair flowing, follows.

Gertrude almost stops breathing at the horror.

'Let me go with her, she needs me,' Melanie says.

'Mother would rather kill herself than allow us to admit we've seen this,' Egon reasons.

Melanie nods and releases the door. The children huddle on the floor, their arms around each other, aware that what they've heard, and what they've seen, must never be mentioned again.

8

September 1904

As the train crosses the border from Bohemia back into Austria, the dark skies that have been gathering since they left Krumau shed their weight and rain lashes at the windows all the way back to Tulln. Gertrude tries to sleep. Egon reads Father's newspaper and Melanie, her novel. Mother and Father stare out of the window from opposite sides of the carriage. Father was the one to insist that the Schieles leave Krumau three days earlier than planned.

Over breakfast, he'd announced that he wanted to get back to the station, to get himself organized before he resumes his role, with a view of starting afresh and proving he's up to the job. Mother didn't object. She'd merely packed the cases while Father checked the timetables.

'I like it here, I want to stay,' Egon had complained.

'You can return one day, Egon. I'm sure you'll be welcome,' Mother said.

At the station, Mother hugged Kateřina and promised she'd speak to her soon.

Kateřina wouldn't look at Father as he said goodbye.

'Don't let the bastard break you,' Gertrude heard her aunt whisper, her mouth close to Mother's ear as they hugged.

When the train pulls into Tulln, Father is first at the train-carriage door. He straightens his suit, runs a hand over his neatly trimmed beard, checks that nothing is out of place. He's keen to see his colleagues, to flex his authority, to show that he's restored and ready to resume his work.

The doors are unlatched and Father steps off the train, ready to greet his staff.

'Jörg?' Father says, addressing a formally attired man who's waiting to board.

'Adolf?' the man replies, smiling widely and placing his briefcase on the ground.

'What a surprise!' Father pumps his hand. 'It's been years since we last saw each other.'

'Well, it must have been five years ago, at the regional meet-up.'

'You should have let me know you'd be here,' Father says.

'I was told you wouldn't be back from your break until next week,' Jörg replies.

'We returned early. The station would come to a standstill without me,' Father laughs. 'It's the first trip I've taken in my career. Turns out I couldn't sleep without the sound of the trains.'

Jörg laughs along with him. 'This place won't be the same without you.'

'What brings you to our humble outcrop?'

'I saw the advert. I dismissed it at first, but then thinking about it, I felt that picking up your mantle in this region would suit me perfectly. We ran through everything today and signed the necessary documentation. They showed me the ropes and gave me a tour of the living quarters. You've done a tasteful job with it, Frau Schiele,' he says, addressing Mother. 'My wife won't have to change a thing.' He looks around the family. 'We were surprised by the news that you're retiring, of course, but it sounds as if you've had your work cut out here, and you deserve the rest. You'll finally have time to invest in your fossil collecting, as you always wanted. Just don't turn into one yourself!'

Jörg slaps Father on the back.

The train guard sounds the whistle for final boarding. It's a long, sharp sound.

'I, I . . .' Father begins. His eyebrows jump up and down.

'Where are you moving to?' Jörg asks as he steps on to the train. 'I must visit.'

'We, we . . .' Father tries. He's pale, pinched, his elbows crunched against his body. He spins on the spot, looking from the train, to the guard, to their home, and back to Jörg.

'We'll be in Klosterneuburg,' Mother interjects. 'Egon' – she pushes him forward – 'is already living there for his studies; we'll make the move to be closer to him. We're all terribly, terribly . . .' She fishes around for the word.

'Surprised?' Gertrude whispers. Melanie leans into her as a warning.

She can't help but feel a thrill at the thought of living with her brother again.

The train doors are closed between them.

'I'm delighted to hear it,' Jörg says through the open window. 'This is a great opportunity for you and your family, Adolf. I've no doubt about it. And I dare say, for me and mine, too. Now, Godspeed and take good care of yourselves.'

The train rolls into motion. Jörg salutes Father from the window, and Father raises a limp hand. The train's speed increases, the wheels rotating, screeching, until the sound becomes deafening. The family watches the locomotive disappear into the distance.

Father turns to find the regional superior at his side. The man's face is stern.

'We didn't want you to find out this way,' he says, and gestures that the two men walk over to the ticket office. Gertrude huddles beside Melanie, Egon and Mother, who looks on wordlessly. 'I understand this may come as a surprise,' they hear the superior say. 'But I believe you know why we've been forced to take this step. The safety of our passengers is paramount.'

'I'm perfectly capable—' Father interrupts.

'We can't afford any miscalculations on the job. In light of recent circumstances, we're suspending you from duty as stationmaster, effective immediately.' A small moan catches in Mother's throat. 'And I'm sorry, but we're also hereby serving you an official notice to vacate the property by the second week of December.' Gertrude feels her mother's frame shaking as the man hands a document to Father.

His eyes are wild.

'I've given more than thirty years of my life to this company, I deserve—'

'We're very sorry. The decision has been made by commission, your replacement has been appointed. We do value the dedication you've shown over the years, and the sacrifices you've made to uphold the standards of the Imperial-Royal Austrian State Railways. We wish you and your family the very best for the future.'

9

'Leave this goddamn table, if you won't eat your dinner!' Father announces suddenly. His eyes twist violently in Gertrude's direction. Melanie jolts in her seat.

Father licks thick soup off the back of his spoon.

'Adolf!' Mother says. 'The children are eating in a perfectly appropriate way.'

Gertrude sets her cutlery down carefully. Father puts his red-brown fists on the table, the spoon clutched in his right hand. The sores on his wrists are black. Melanie looks up to meet her sister's eyes. Their brother is safely at school in Klosterneuburg, his visits home increasingly rare.

Mother breaks off more bread and butters it, taking a deliberate bite and chewing for more time than is necessary. In just a few days, they will leave their station home. Mother spends all her time picking through their belongings and packing. She wraps items in newspaper, placing them in wooden crates, marking any of value so they can settle their bills in Tulln.

Father slams his palms down on the table and the spoon clatters to the floor.

'Go to your room!' he shouts at Gertrude. 'You hear me! Get out of here!'

Father snorts, then spits over his shoulder. Melanie makes a noise as if to protest, for she was on her knees scrubbing those flagstones only hours before, but Mother shuts her down with a small but violent jerk of her neck.

Gertrude straightens the cutlery to show that she's ready to leave the table. But Father starts bellowing again before she can move.

'Jörg, man. Welcome. Sit. You're here to discuss the station hand-over.' He gestures from the door behind Gertrude to the empty place where Egon would normally sit. Gertrude had not heard anyone climb the stairs. She turns, but the doorway is empty.

Surprise sweeps Mother's face as she also takes in the vacant frame.

'Adolf,' she begins, edging her words out. 'Is Jörg expected to visit this evening?' She dabs her mouth with a napkin. 'I can set another place.'

'He's right there, woman! Are you blind?'

'Don't you speak to Mother that way!' Melanie says sharply.

'You're eighteen, Melanie, time you were married.'

'She'll marry when she's ready, Adolf,' Mother says.

'Well, pull your weight, if you're not the marrying type. I can't be the only one making ends meet while you all slacken off like old rope. Isn't that right, Jörg?'

'You won't be working from now on, Adolf,' Mother reminds him.

'If I have to work, then Egon should as well!' Melanie adds.

'That boy's days of playing around are numbered, mark my words. Now. Eat!'

Mother puts her hands in her lap. Melanie inspects her soup, which has gone cold.

Father picks up the chair and positions it so his guest can take a seat at the table.

'Excuse the mess,' he says to thin air. 'The children are worse than wild animals, and my wife is little more than a peasant.' Father returns to his seat. Mother and Melanie exchange frowns. Father pauses, an ear cocked. 'Yes, yes,' he responds. His tone changes.

'Food, woman!' He snaps his fingers in Mother's face.

'If you insist, husband dearest.' Mother stands, moves to the stove, places the pan on the heat. She warms the rest of the soup, adding water, then ladles it out into a clean bowl, wiping her apron around the rim. She places it on the table next to Egon's seat. Father whips it away.

'Where are your manners?' He turns to the empty seat. 'Do excuse my wife.' Father returns with a jug of cream, which Mother rations, and pours it over the soup in a lavish ribbon. 'Now, let's eat, man!'

'Do pass the salt, Gerti,' Mother says, squeezing her daughter's leg under the table.

Father looks at them, a warning in his eyes. 'Finish up!'

They take mouthfuls of cold soup, each one harder to swallow than the last. Father eventually folds his napkin, stretches his fingers, then laughs, as if responding to a joke.

Mother and Melanie sit in silence. Gertrude fidgets.

'May I leave the table?' she asks, collecting the empty bowls for Melanie to wash.

'Give your father a kiss before you go to your room,' he says, gesturing to her with a wide-open sweep of his arms. 'Come, Elvira, dear. You always were my favourite.'

'Elvira . . .' she stutters. 'But Elvira is dead.'

Mother gasps, then jumps up to take the bowls from her daughter. 'Leave those,' she says.

But the stack slips. The bowls fall from Gertrude's hands, bounce off the edge of the table and smash into a hundred pieces. Gertrude holds her breath, waiting for punishment. But Father only laughs, his deep voice breaking into overblown hooting.

Mother drops to her knees. 'My bowls! My precious bowls,' she wails. She holds the shards, cradling them as if they were pieces of her own flesh. 'Adolf, these were a wedding present from my parents. I've had them for twenty-five years. Now look!' Mother takes a shuddering breath and positions random pieces against each other. She looks forlornly at each of them. 'There are things in this life that can never be replaced,' she cries.

10

December 1904

From a deep sleep, Gertrude senses the heat and light of a glorious summer morning. Her brother is home for the end of the year and to help with the move. She's dreaming that she and Egon have escaped, peeling away from their home in secret as early as they can. They scramble along the tracks, skirt the Danube, dipping in and out of the low sun's glare. They find a hidden spot, take off their clothes and swim in the shallows of the cold river, splashing and dunking each other beneath the surface. They skim stone after stone and count the passing clouds. Egon lies in the long grass and observes her.

The warmth of this promising day draws Gertrude fully from her sleep. Then she hears the crackling.

There's an angry burst, splintering wood. She sits up and feels the heat rising, the swell of it through the cold, dark air. She smells the tarry tang of burning rubber, smouldering earth. The wall by Egon's bed is illuminated, a ricocheting pattern of light and shadow playing across the smooth surface.

Gertrude follows the commotion, walking out of the bedroom – full of packed cases and dismantled furniture – crossing the dark apartment to the living room, drawn relentlessly, horribly, towards the window. The windowpane is hot to the touch. Outside, an intense

160

blaze tunnels into the sky, flecks of burning debris blast upwards before falling to earth with the blackened beauty of snow. Gertrude's lungs are filled with it. She swallows, tasting soot. The flaming mass below fights the space around it, greedy for size and strength. It consumes the tracks, turning sleepers to ash and, as Gertrude watches, it is creeping closer and closer to the platform, and their home.

Gertrude runs to the bedroom and tries to drag Egon from his bed. He pushes back, his eyes shuttered with sleep, and kicks against the urgency of her. She perseveres, fighting him to consciousness.

'Egon! Quick! Fire!'

Melanie stirs, pulling a pillow over her head, uncharacteristically groggy.

Gertrude pulls Egon to his feet and pushes him to the window overlooking the train tracks.

'But someone's down there!' Egon shouts, looking out at the inferno.

'Are they trying to put it out?' Gertrude leans forward to get a better look.

Beside the fire there's the outline of a figure, stooped as if in pain, recoiling from the blast. The intense light masks the person's features. But that's not a pail of water they are holding. Instead, every second or two, they stretch forward to feed the flames.

'My drawings!' Egon's words rise above the noise of the conflagration.

The sound of his cry triggers a reaction in their parents' bedroom. Something clatters to the floor and, after a moment, Gertrude hears quick steps crossing the room. Urgent knocks on the window startle the silhouette. The person raises their head and lifts their right hand, the one that has been feeding the papers to the flames, as if in greeting. Then they bend to pick up something by the side of the tracks. With surprising speed, the arm pulls back and thrusts forward in an arc. An object smashes against the outside wall, between the windows, and bounces gracelessly on to the platform. The figure repeats the motion and a second, heavier, missile reaches its target, crashing through the window of their parents' bedroom. Mother lets out a howl.

Melanie, Egon and Gertrude all rush to the door of their parents' bedroom, jostling each other forward. Gertrude is terrified about what they'll find on the other side. Melanie is the one to push it open, revealing their mother's crumpled frame on the floor, her forehead bleeding. Melanie runs over and pulls her into an embrace, ignoring the shards of glass that dust her mother's shoulders and hair.

At the contact, Mother pulls a long ribbon of air into her lungs, then projects a wail that stretches right across the house and into the darkness.

'Why must he punish me, why must he punish me so?' she moans.

Egon has rushed downstairs and is pounding on the door, the one that leads to the platform. Gertrude leaves Melanie and Mother and joins him. 'We must get out there,' her brother shouts. He fumbles, drops the key and has to pick it up from the cold floor before he can get it into the lock. He twists it twice, then opens the door. A wall of heat hits them; to Gertrude it feels as if they are right inside one of the roaring steam engines.

The man before them is glowing. His sleeve is on fire, his facial hair already singed.

'Father!' Egon shouts. He jumps over the platform edge on to the tracks.

Father turns. 'It's beautiful, isn't it?' he says.

There's not a shred of recognition in his eyes. The heat is intolerable, even from where Gertrude is standing, barefoot, close to the house. Egon grabs the fabric at Father's chest, trying to pull him away, but he fights his son off, taking him by the scruff of the neck.

Sparks rain down on Egon. They blaze in his hair, singe holes into his nightshirt. Father rams her brother to the ground. The pair are dangerously close to the fire.

'Leave him!' Gertrude screams, running to the platform edge and reaching out an arm.

In that moment, she wishes her father were dead.

Egon continues to punch and pull. Father exerts all his strength to hold her brother down. His eyes are bursting from their sockets. Egon grabs a smouldering handful of coal and hurls it against his father's cheek, leaving a bloody, blackened streak from his eye to his chin. Father releases his grip and puts the fingers of both hands to his face. Egon manages to roll away. His hand is already blistering.

'Water,' Gertrude says, running to fetch a bucket for Egon to immerse his hands in.

Neighbours from the closest cottages have now arrived at the platform, alerted by the noise and intense blaze. They are carrying buckets of sand and earth to dampen the flames. One man takes Father by the shoulders and mutely he allows himself to be pulled away. The man sits him down, away from the fire. Father is charred, a cutlet of meat, the hairs scorched off, his skin weeping. A wet rag is pressed to his cheek.

Stuffed into the pocket of his nightshirt, beneath his bedjacket, are three sheets of paper that have managed to escape the inferno. They're covered in soot, but are clearly embossed, stamped with official markings in crimson wax.

'Take these to Melanie,' Egon says, grabbing them. 'Maybe she'll know what they are and why Father has burned them.' She detects his relief that it wasn't his drawings that have been destroyed.

Upstairs, Melanie is still comforting Mother, soothing her, rocking her. Gertrude takes a step into the room and holds out the certificates.

Mother opens her eyes, then crumples again.

'The shares!' she sobs. 'I knew it!'

Egon enters, his hands wrapped in wet rags, and Mother looks up with new doggedness and clenches her free hand into a fist. 'That bastard! Your father! I will kill him with my own bare hands. Our life savings, burned to ashes.'

'What's going to happen to us, Mother?' Gertrude whimpers.

Mother continues, but it's as if she is talking only to herself. 'We're practically homeless as it is, thanks to his recklessness. And he's been hell-bent on punishing me. For what, I'll never know. But to do this? To annihilate his family? I never believed he'd be so cruel. He has taken away the single thing that could have protected us.' She turns to her children. 'We have nothing left. Your future was safeguarded by those shares. Your father has destroyed us all.'

11

December 1904

The grandfather clock ticks heavily in the hallway. It's less than an hour until midnight. Gertrude peers into her parents' bedroom – no longer the one in their station home in Tulln, but in a new, smaller apartment in Klosterneuburg. She can hear her father's juddering breath as he sleeps. Mother has been knitting in the same room, set up in her rocking chair by the window, a glass of amber-coloured liquid on the table at her side. Melanie is seated next to Father's bed, holding his hand, sponging water on to his lips.

'Come on, children, time for bed,' Mother says when she spots Egon and Gertrude in the doorway.

'But it's New Year's Eve,' Egon says. 'We usually stay up.'

'Your father's very ill. A doctor is on his way.'

They've been in their new home for less than two weeks and it hasn't yet taken on familiar dimensions. Their belongings seem untethered in this space. Gertrude notices anew the wilting fern in the hallway by the front door; the colours in the framed landscapes seem less muted in their new position on the wall; and Mother's black-edged mirror, which had been in their bedroom in Tulln, is propped in the front room, too large to fit anywhere else.

They hear a loud knock on the front door and their mother rises to greet the local doctor, an elderly man with a moustache that looks as if it could cut bread. Gertrude and Egon slip out of sight, but remain close enough to listen in.

'I'd hoped not to disturb you on the final day of the year,' Mother says.

'It's my pleasure to be able to offer assistance,' he replies formally.

'What's happening?' Gertrude whispers, taking her brother's hand. He flinches at her touch. The blisters on his palm still haven't healed from the night of the bonfire on the tracks.

'Father's taken a turn for the worse. He's not been the same since the fire.'

The doctor follows their mother into the bedroom, leaving the door slightly ajar. From the obscurity of the hallway, Gertrude and her brother watch.

Mother offers the doctor a drink of the amber liquid and he accepts, making a gesture that it should be a small one. After he removes his hat and coat, he places his fingers on Father's neck, then takes a brown bottle from his satchel. He pours some liquid on to a spoon, then feeds it to Father, whose lips part at the touch of the metal, but whose eyes don't open. The doctor then produces a flame and burns something he has placed in the well of another spoon. He holds it under Father's nose and Father, in response, coughs weakly and spits into a waiting handkerchief. When it is taken away, it is speckled with blood. Father's lips are grey. The sores and burns on his body have worsened, and the smell that has lingered around him for the past ten days is rotten. His frame is thinner than ever, and the burn mark Egon inflicted on his cheek is still a gaping wound.

'He's been this way all day,' Mother warns. 'Struggling to breathe, blood when he coughs, unresponsive. In Tulln, his blank periods were limited to an hour or so, a day at most, but this has been much more prolonged. Isn't that right, Melanie?'

Melanie looks up. 'There's nothing we can do to rouse him, doctor,' she agrees.

'If I may observe him for a while? Carry on as you were.'

Mother settles back in the rocking chair. She pulls a shawl around her shoulders, then works her way back into her knitting.

⌒

The grandfather clock chimes a quarter to midnight. Egon and Gertrude are playing cards in the hallway, Melanie is reading her novel, and Mother is still knitting. The doctor completes another round of tests and observations, then takes a seat for a moment to sip his drink. A few minutes later, he stands abruptly, takes Father's wrist and presses two fingers against the skin there. He picks up a metal instrument, the ends of which he inserts into his ears, then, unbuttoning the top of his patient's nightshirt, he places the other end against Father's chest. He listens, wriggles his nose and runs a thumb across his lower lip.

'Frau Schiele?'

Mother looks up, as if surprised to find the doctor still there.

'It is with regret,' he says, 'that I must inform you that Herr Schiele has, only a few moments ago, passed away.'

A vivid sound of alarm escapes Melanie's mouth. Egon stiffens at Gertrude's side.

Mother glances at the clock. The hand is close to midnight.

The doctor licks the nib of his pencil, poised to write something in an official-looking notebook that he takes from his briefcase. Gertrude's eyes shoot to Father's body. His fingers are curled into his palms. His nails seem ink-dipped.

Mother blinks. 'Now? But I don't believe it.' She peers closer. 'Isn't that his chest rising?' Gertrude, too, thinks she can hear the sound of his breathing now that Mother's long needles have stopped. 'You are sure, doctor?' She places the ball of dark wool on the floor.

'Quite certain,' the doctor says, checking his watch. 'I pronounce death as having occurred at twenty-three hours and fifty-six minutes on Saturday, the thirty-first of December, 1904,' he says solemnly.

'Oh, but it's not yet midnight,' Mother says, checking her own timepiece.

'I don't see what that has to do with it.' He gathers his things from the table.

Mother walks over to her husband's body and leans over, as if searching for something on his skin. 'But he's still breathing, doctor, I can see it.'

'Frau Schiele,' the doctor says. 'Herr Schiele is no longer of this world.' He lowers his chin and raises an eyebrow. 'It appears he has passed away. Quite peacefully, as you'll have gathered.'

Mother slaps her husband, gently, on the cheek. 'There! He opened his eyes.'

'I must say! Please refrain from disrespecting the body at this sacred hour. It is not befitting of you to . . .' Mother places her palms upon Father's chest. His body is limp, the arms flailing. 'Frau Schiele!' The doctor grabs Mother. 'I must ask that you desist. Immediately!'

There has been such a strained silence in the house since they arrived, since the fire, that all this shouting scares Gertrude. She can't hold her tears back. Her brother, his eyes also red and watering, holds a finger to his lips.

Mother looks the doctor in the eye. 'I insist that you appraise him again, *mein Herr*,' she says, rubbing her arms where he grabbed them.

'There really is no—'

'Please, doctor, I beg of you.'

A look of understanding passes between them.

He opens his briefcase with two clicks, then rolls up his sleeves, shaking his head as he does so.

Gertrude watches the doctor conduct his examination with the utmost precision, listening to Father's chest with that same peculiar instrument, feeling once again for a pulse at his neck, determination etched on his features as he looks up at the ceiling, then putting his cheek very close to Father's mouth. They wait.

Gertrude hears the clock toll midnight, the sound of celebration exploding from the adjoining houses. People laugh and clap, voices are raised in traditional song. There's a distant burst of fireworks and Gertrude remembers the New Year with her parents, five years ago, that marked the fresh century.

'I'm afraid it's as I suspected, Frau Schiele,' the doctor says, deliberately. 'Your husband has taken his final breath. I understand that it's upsetting.'

Egon makes a choking noise beside her; the book slips from Melanie's hand.

Gertrude reflects on Father's final breath. Where did it go? Could his air have somehow entered her lungs? She takes a breath, holds it.

'Very well,' Mother replies. She looks at her timepiece. 'But I make it three minutes past midnight.' She shows it to the doctor. 'And I insist you record it as such. Quite the start to the new year,' she sniffs.

The doctor records the new details in his notebook – three minutes past midnight on Sunday, the first of January, 1905.

The doctor nods at her, then slides the notebook into his jacket pocket, tapping it with finality. He offers a restrained bow, places his hat atop his head, and moves towards the door.

'Good evening, Frau Schiele. My condolences once more.'

'And a happy new year to you, doctor,' she calls after him.

12

January 1905

U nder a bright January sky, Father is buried. Gertrude and her family wear mourning clothes, Egon in long trousers, the hems let down, his boots buffed to a shine. Melanie has woven black ribbons through Gertrude's hair. Mother was able to borrow a pillbox hat with a veil.

The gravestones back in the old cemetery in Tulln are tightly packed together. Father's coffin will be lowered into the ground in front of the large gravestone engraved with the words FAMILIE SCHIELE. Pale lichen has grown into the letters since they were last here. Egon vows he will return to scrub the stone clean. Elvira's name has been lost.

Father lay for several days at home, flowers in his coffin to mask the smell. His former colleagues took the train to Klosterneuburg and entered the front room, removing their caps and lowering their eyes, clasping Mother's hands and making promises for the future. Father had been dressed in the gala uniform of a senior railway official, minus the stiff red jacket, which had never been recovered after the day he was found under the bridge.

Gertrude secretly carries with her the shiny button she took from it, is rubbing it now.

There was a short ceremony in the church near by, where Father was spoken of highly, praised for his dedication to his career, his role as head of the family. Prayers were recited over the body, psalms read. Together, they sang a hymn, the words pulsing through Gertrude.

And now, the coffin is being lowered into this gaping hole in the earth. Egon shudders as mud lands in shovel-loads, thudding against the wood. Gertrude holds her brother's arm, while Melanie leans on Mother for support.

'Show compassion to your people in their sorrow . . . Lift us from the darkness of this grief to the peace and light of your presence,' the minister intones.

When the earth has been returned, those gathered bow gently then move on to pay their respects to the family. Mother listens to each and every platitude from Adolf's former colleagues and the many local well-wishers, some of whom she has never spoken to before.

Gertrude notices a short man standing on the periphery of the funeral party. He sports lavish grey hair, with a neat beard and a moustache twisted into elaborate points. She guesses that he can be no more than a year or two older than her father, but it's clear that life has been kinder to him. He steps closer, and places flowers on the ground by the grave. Then he moves towards them, one hand thrust deep into the pocket of his pressed trousers, the other clutching an elaborately carved, silver-tipped walking stick.

'The young Fräulein Schiele, I presume,' he says, removing his hat.

'Gertrude,' she replies.

'The pleasure is all mine.' He smiles, and she accepts the stranger's soft hand.

'And you?' he says, nodding at her brother. 'You must be Egon? The man of the family now.'

Egon shakes his hand. 'And you are . . . ?'

The man folds a silk handkerchief into a tidy square and inserts it into his suit pocket. 'You won't remember me. I'm your Uncle Leopold. Leopold Czihaczek.' He raises an eyebrow and receives no hint of acknowledgement. 'I'm married to your aunt Louisa. She sends her condolences that she can't be here today; she's rather unwell, you see.' He scans their faces. Egon and Gertrude exchange a glance that is laden with suspicion. 'Now. I must offer my condolences to your dear mother,' he continues, his deep voice cutting the sombre conversations. Mother, hearing it, turns to its source, her eyes searching his features. It takes a moment for a look of recognition to cross her face.

'Marie,' he booms, stepping over with a flourish. 'How good it is to see you after all this time.'

'My goodness. I almost didn't recognize you, Herr Czihaczek.'

'Leopold, I insist,' he says, squeezing her fingers. She pulls her hand away before he can plant a kiss upon it. 'No need for formalities between family.'

Mother cocks her head to take in the sight of this well-fed, well-dressed, well-mannered man. 'We didn't expect to see you.'

'I wanted to pay my respects to my brother-in-law. I was always fond of Adolf, you know that. I admired how hard he worked, and his dedication to his family. His demise is a tragedy,' he says, nodding towards the plot. 'Fifty-four is hardly any age at all, these days.'

She purses her lips. 'It was generous of you to take the time to come from Vienna.'

'It's hardly an inconvenience,' he says. He hesitates a moment before continuing. 'Marie . . . I know we haven't always seen eye to eye and for that, I apologize. Perhaps we might agree to put the past behind us now? My wife, your husband . . . their relationship was fraught, but we must let bygones be bygones.' Mother doesn't soften, so Uncle Leopold steps closer. 'I apologize that Louisa and I didn't make the trip when Elvira . . .'

Mother stiffens. 'I really must join the others,' she says.

He nods. 'Before you go . . . if I may be so bold? I'm well aware of all the difficulties Adolf suffered at the end of his career. We spoke at length about his concerns. In light of that, I have an offer, so to speak, that may interest you and . . . be of some benefit, financially?'

'That won't be necessary, Herr Czihaczek,' Mother says. 'We're adequately provided for. There's Adolf's pension – we were grateful he held on until the first day of the new year – minutes after the clock struck midnight, in fact – as it increased the final value. And he saw to it that we were left with a share or two.'

Uncle Leopold looks at her with gentle, knowing eyes. 'If ever you do find that you need assistance, please don't hesitate to call upon me. I have a very comfortable life in Vienna, with little to occupy me. In fact, it's for that reason that I'd like to talk to you about the boy,' he says, gesturing to Egon, who looks up with surprise. 'I'd like to stake a claim in his future, if possible? Before it's too late.'

Mother straightens her spine. 'I assure you, that won't be necessary. I intend to see to it that Egon finishes his education. He has another year at the school here in Klosterneuburg, and we have every intention that he will pass his exams and then train to work for the Imperial-Royal Austrian State Railways, just as his father envisioned.'

'So be it,' Gertrude's uncle says, dipping his hat at her mother. 'But you know where I am if you need me.'

13

June 1906

Gertrude is unpacking Egon's satchel when a folded note falls from his dog-eared workbook, which is covered in doodles – evidence of his endless distraction in the classroom. She picks it up, turns it over in her hands. The note is addressed to 'the loveliest girl'. Gertrude opens it, her heart skipping.

She scans the letter quickly. The words jump out, as if they're trying to bite her.

You rosy, enchanting creature. Seeing you makes my heart ache . . . Gertrude drops the letter on the floor. There's no way he'd confess such feelings for any of the local girls in Klosterneuburg. They're all piggish and dull, he's said so himself.

Her skin prickles, making her itch. Gertrude is furious. She shuffles the piece of paper back into her brother's belongings. She never wants to think about that note ever again.

But the next day, Gertrude returns and searches her brother's satchel once more, her fingers reaching into the tightest pockets. The note is gone. She cannot find evidence of any other indiscretions among his things. Who could it have been for? She repeats a list of names, guessing at connections, trying to prise any hint of sentiment from them.

Her brother, in love? It's impossible. There are no secrets between them.

Now Gertrude is more alert to Egon's behaviour than ever before. She searches his belongings for any clue, looks through his sketches for any hint she can pursue. If she catches him daydreaming, she imagines another girl's face inside his mind. It makes her want to hurt him.

Gertrude is twelve now, too old for the dolls on to which she used to transfer her love, wiping their cheeks and looking into their painted blue eyes. She clears her bedroom of them. One morning soon after, she finds dark streaks of blood on her nightdress and the bedsheets. In the days to come, she bleeds, a rushing, vibrant red. Is she dying like Elvira did? Or being punished? She tries to plug herself with wads of tissue, to no avail. The bleeding stops abruptly, and she prays it will not start again. She looks at her body in the mirror. Her eyes seem bigger, her ribs sharpened. Her hair has grown and she no longer plaits it.

Their home in Klosterneuburg has taken on a quieter, calmer rhythm in the eighteen months since Father died. There are no trains, for a start, and rarely any shouting. Egon and Gertrude attend the local schools, and Melanie has taken on a job as a ticket vendor at the local station. After school, Gertrude helps with the chores – she cleans the windows and tends to the plants, which grow and grow. She reads Mother's recipe books, the ones filled with the traditional dishes of Bohemia, and which are no longer hidden in the pantry. Reading them makes Gertrude hungry, but she doesn't eat – she has come to enjoy the hollow feeling inside.

When the bleeding starts again Melanie notices it, and shows Gertrude how to wash her undergarments. That same week, Gertrude is given a thimble, needle and thread and taught to darn. She pushes the needle into a rip in her skirts, stitching two elements into one.

Melanie shares her geranium-scented cold cream and offers her sister tips on how to rub it into her face. She also shows her how to buff her nails, but Gertrude hasn't any interest in making them look pretty.

There are other changes, ones that are hers alone – coarser hairs on her body, sore lumps beneath her flat nipples. Gertrude is surprised at the stabbing desire she feels for Egon to make drawings of her, to record how her body transforms itself across time. She will suggest it.

~

A week later, Gertrude is rewarded once more for her snooping: she discovers a new drawing in Egon's sketchbook. It's of a girl with hazel hair, pink cheeks, and a sickeningly sweet little smile. Could it be Margarete Partonek? It's a name that had crossed Gertrude's mind in the list of possibilities, but she'd dismissed her outright, for she possesses a traditional prettiness that Gertrude had assumed Egon would scoff at. Margarete's such a plain girl, her face full of symmetry, her lips the shape of a pink bow. She practically lives next door, in the house across the street – she can occasionally be seen going about her business from the window of the main room. Gertrude is disappointed her brother couldn't lose his heart further away than his own front door.

At fourteen years old, Margarete is two years younger than Egon and two years older than Gertrude. She and Margarete have, on occasion, spent time together. They walk home together sometimes, and Gertrude has been to her house, watched her play the piano, looked at her collection of figurine ponies. Gertrude feels a tightness in her chest – she'd assumed that her neighbour considered her brother to be an ass.

Gertrude extends an invitation to Margarete to walk home with her. She wants to observe her up close. They meet at the school gates and, as the older girl approaches, Gertrude watches her every movement. Margarete's hair is so unlike her own copper-red locks, Gertrude notices as they walk along the river path – light seems to bounce off it. Her hands look as soft as a peach, her nails smooth and clean; it makes Gertrude want to stroke them. Gertrude's own are nibbled to stubs. Melanie is quite right about telling her off for the state of them.

When they arrive, Gertrude invites her friend inside.

'Is there anything I can help you with, Frau Schiele?' Margarete asks.

Mother's apron is thick with grease, its pattern faded from repeated washing.

'What a polite young woman you are, Margarete,' Mother says, drying her hands. 'If only a little of your charm could rub off on Gertrude . . .'

Then the front door slams and Egon enters. He stops as he reaches the kitchen.

He frowns, tucking his loose shirt tails into his trousers. The muscles of his throat contract as he swallows. Egon's hair is in tufts, his shirt unbuttoned. Ink leaks through his blazer pocket. Margarete's eyes flit towards Egon and away.

'You've made such a mess of yourself,' Gertrude says to him. He glares at her as he drops his satchel and tames his hair.

'Good afternoon, Fräulein Partonek,' he says.

They talk amicably for a few minutes, before Margarete turns the conversation to his art. 'Your mother says you have aspirations to apply to the Academy of Fine Arts in Vienna?'

'I'd have to take an entrance interview over the summer,' Gertrude's brother replies, trying to look nonchalant as he inspects the bubbling stock on the stove. 'I must present a portfolio of my work, but I'd be the youngest student ever to attend if they accept me.'

'And you prefer art over a more conventional career?'

'My tutors are keen that I put myself forward. Herr Strauch is impressed by my abilities. Besides,' he adds, 'it's unlikely I'll get the grades to do anything else.'

'Enough of that kind of talk!' Mother interrupts. 'You should be leaving, Margarete.' Mother flashes her eyes at Egon as she dices some onions. 'Your mother will be waiting.'

Gertrude is relieved to say goodbye. Egon offers to walk Margarete across the street. Through the window, Gertrude watches them, hidden from view by the thick folds of the curtain. At her door, Margarete hands Egon a piece of paper that he slips into his pocket. Then he returns home with a self-satisfied smirk on his face.

⤳

Gertrude searches for more letters between Margarete and Egon. She's occasionally rewarded. *I do believe art to be a foolish pursuit*, her neighbour has written to Egon. *Perhaps you could channel your passions into design or architecture. My father would be able to get you an apprenticeship, and not one on the railways, as that's clearly not a life you desire.*

We could be happy, Egon, she writes in another. *I promise to love you like you say you love me, but we must have a secure future. When you've completed your studies, and secured a solid career, you can talk to my father about marriage,* Gertrude reads with dismay. Egon would never give up his dreams of becoming an artist. It's the only thing he has ever wanted. It has made his life impossible, earned him beatings from Father, disappointment from Mother, ridicule from most of his teachers. It's all Egon has ever cared about.

Margarete doesn't understand her brother, Gertrude decides. She's asking him to be something he's not. Egon will eventually return his affections to Gertrude, and, when they're old enough, they'll live together in Vienna. Egon will paint and she'll model for him. They won't have to live by the rules, certainly not those once imposed by Father, or society.

Father has made it clear that I can never marry an artist. I must refuse your offer of being your right hand for art. I would not be an able or willing accomplice. Yours, Margarete.

After that, there are no more letters, at least none Gertrude can find.

Does her brother still write to Margarete, making promises he cannot keep? Egon's eyes are sad. Gertrude can see that he believes it might be better if he were able to bury his passion for art. He'd be a better man to Margarete, who'd marry him. He'd be a better son to Mother, who'd be able to live comfortably. He'd be less selfish, less self-obsessed. He'd do the memory of Father proud.

Egon begins to slick his hair into a neat sweep over his ears. He tucks his shirts into his trousers and tries to make sure that the material stays there. He polishes his shoes. Mother is delighted. She believes her words have finally sunk in. But cleanliness and order cannot restore Egon's energy. He speaks less at mealtimes, leaves his breakfast untouched. Egon is lovesick, Gertrude realizes. No, it's more than that. He's trying to starve the artist out of himself, kill the urge that draws him to that world.

For the first time, Gertrude doubts Egon. She feels a sludge of misgiving as the doubt spreads to her heart. He's going to give up on his potential, to be just another man. The thought makes her weak. If love can make you lose yourself so fully, make you kill the best things in yourself, then Gertrude promises herself she'll never, ever succumb.

14

'What's he doing here?' Egon whispers to Gertrude, alarmed, when he enters the kitchen and finds Mother at the table with Uncle Leopold.

Mother stands, her hands on the tabletop, her face weary.

'Good, you're home. We've much to discuss. I've invited your uncle to be part of this important conversation about your future.' Uncle Leopold sits with his legs crossed, smoking a cigarette. Egon slinks into a chair and Mother continues. 'I received your report card this morning. As predicted, you won't pass your final year.'

'All that doodling and daydreaming has finally come home to roost,' Melanie teases.

'You've learnt nothing at all,' Mother says. But Egon does not seem chastised – there are glints of boyish arrogance in his eyes. 'You'll be pleased to know, I went to the school to ask them to let you repeat the year.'

Her brother loses his supercilious expression.

'You can't make me go back there!'

'Hear your mother out,' Uncle Leopold instructs.

'I had no choice but to go to your school, cap in hand,' Mother continues, turning to the stove as the old coffee pot hisses. She fills her cup

180

and one for Uncle Leopold. 'Your uncle came with me and put forward a very pragmatic case. Well, this is where your headmaster has suggested a compelling compromise.' She pauses, looks hard at Egon as she speaks. 'He will let you pass in all subjects, in order *not* to have you back in September.' Melanie's mouth twitches. 'It seems they're as keen to be rid of you as you are to be rid of them.'

Egon leaps to his feet, pulling at Gertrude and spinning her on the spot.

'Delay your celebrations for just a moment, Egon,' Uncle Leopold says.

'Yes, there's more, I'm afraid. Uncle Leopold has gone to great trouble, and has put his own reputation on the line, in order to arrange an apprenticeship for you. If you can't get into the railways through the academic route, we must find another way. So you'll be repairing tracks. You start tomorrow, first thing, at half past six in the morning.'

It seems to Gertrude that Egon has stopped breathing, his face a mask of disbelief.

'What? Did you think we could live on air?' Mother says. 'Poor Melanie's taken it all upon her shoulders since your father died.'

'So I'm being put to work, am I? Manual labour that any talentless mule could perform? May I leave? I've had enough surprises for one day.'

'We're not finished,' Mother says, gesturing that he take a seat once more.

Egon looks from his mother to his uncle. 'Must I sleep in the coal shed, as well?'

'I've been appointed as your legal guardian,' Uncle Leopold announces. 'Yours and Gertrude's, as you're both still classed as children. That means you're my responsibility. I've no heirs of my own, so it's my great pleasure to take on this role. Your mother has agreed to it.'

'Mother!'

'It's what your father would have wanted – a firm hand to guide you both along the path to respectability. Your uncle will make decisions with your best interests at heart.'

'But it's not fair!'

'You realize you must be the man of the family now?' Uncle Leopold says to Egon. Gertrude stares at her uncle, trying to guess what this will mean for her own future, which is never discussed with this kind of fervour. 'These past years have been difficult for you, I understand that,' Uncle Leopold says. 'But your wayward nature . . . It's not too late for it to be rectified. The time has come for you to knuckle down. I've pulled many strings to secure this opportunity. They've accepted you on your father's merit – and on my promise, let it be noted – so do not let me down.'

Egon looks as if he's drowning. 'I don't know what to say,' he mumbles.

Uncle Leopold laughs. 'Thank me when you get your first payment.'

'But I'm going to be an artist,' Egon states firmly. 'My tutors say anyone who can't see my talent must be blind. I've applied to the art school in Vienna. Mother said I could attend the interview.'

'That was months ago! I hardly knew what I was agreeing to,' Mother interjects.

'It's the only profession I intend to pursue.'

'There's no money in art.' Uncle Leopold's stern tone dissolves into bemusement. 'No future. Drawing is for children.'

'I'd rather die than do anything else.'

'So you're prepared to be a pauper, are you? Where's the money going to come from, to fund this expensive habit of yours? All those materials and canvases, oils and whatnot.'

'You're going to pay for it.'

'Am I now?' he guffaws. 'You're having me on!' Uncle Leopold slaps Egon on the back. 'Come now, to bed. You've an early start in the morning and first impressions count.'

'Mother posed for my examination portraits, as did Melanie,' her brother continues. 'The interview is the week after next.'

Mother and Melanie flinch. 'We had no idea that was your intention,' Mother begins.

'What gives you the right,' Uncle Leopold demands, quietly but with power, a finger pointed in Egon's direction, 'to tread such a path? Where does your belief in yourself come from? I have never, in all my years, witnessed confidence such as this.'

'I have talent,' Egon says calmly.

'Talent isn't enough, my boy. Talent doesn't pay the bills. Or provide for a family.'

'It's all I have. And I'm prepared to sacrifice everything for it,' her brother says. 'I know many who'd kill for a shred of the stuff.'

Uncle Leopold almost looks amused. 'Marie, does your son always behave in such a manner?'

Mother and Melanie exchange a look. 'You see what I've had to endure.' She sighs.

Egon takes out his sketchbook, the one he reserves for landscapes and flowers. 'Only take a look,' he says. 'My tutor says that to follow any path other than art would be a waste.'

So Uncle Leopold does look, mystified, flipping page after page – drawings of the blacksmith's courtyard and the local brook and bridge. He puts his hand to his chest.

'It's highly impressive, I'll admit. But . . .' He holds a hand to his brow. 'I'm old-fashioned . . . What do I know? As your legal guardian, my only recommendation can be a failsafe career in the railways.' Egon turns the page for him, to reveal a train, the sense of perspective fault-less. 'But you'll not listen to me, will you?'

Egon shakes his head. 'Don't deny me this, please.'

Uncle Leopold stands up and paces around the room for a moment. Mother dips her head and puts her hand on Egon's shoulder. Finally, Uncle Leopold sighs. 'I have no doubt I'll come to rue these words, but so be it. You have one chance. Take your best shot at this great career you envision for yourself. See if they'll accept you. But if they don't, then perhaps you'll appreciate my offer of a secure and stable future.'

Her brother jumps to his feet and hugs the man tightly. The gesture takes Uncle Leopold by surprise.

'Thank you, Uncle, you won't regret this.'

'My support will continue until you put a foot out of line,' Uncle Leopold warns. 'The day that happens, you're on your own. I mustn't be associated with a scandal of any sort, however minor.'

'I won't let you down,' Egon says. 'And I'll paint you, regularly, to show my appreciation. Your face will be seen on gallery walls in years to come.'

'It won't be my features anyone wants to see. Find yourself some pretty young ladies from good families to paint – that will prove far more profitable. In the meantime,' he continues as Egon skitters from the room, 'I'll postpone the placement until you've done the interview. If you don't get in, I'm afraid there'll be no more argument about it.'

Uncle Leopold collapses into a chair. 'Heaven, arse and twine!' he sighs, downing his coffee. 'Don't you have anything stronger?' he asks Mother. 'I don't know how you've endured this for so long, Marie. That boy is utterly exhausting!'

15

August 1906

'Aren't you going to tell us how it went?' Mother raises her voice so she can be heard from the kitchen where she's sitting by the stove. Egon crashes along the hallway, not acknowledging her question. He's back later than expected – the train from Vienna to Klosterneuburg must have been delayed – and Gertrude and Mother have been waiting for news, barely able to concentrate on the tasks in hand. Mother rises from her knitting and follows him to his room. She watches from the doorway, her arms folded, as he sits on the bed and unties his laces. Gertrude joins her and examines Egon's face for signs of disappointment. There are none, but there's no suppressed joy, either.

'What?' Egon asks. His leather portfolio is flung across the floor.

'If you're reacting like this, it can only mean one thing,' Mother replies.

'I dare say they were impressed.' Egon shrugs. 'They'll interview dozens of young men. Spaces are limited. They told me to expect their decision next week. By letter.'

'But what did they say?'

'That I'm exceptionally talented.'

'Then why so glum?'

'I'm awaiting a decision, that's all.'

'Your uncle was under the impression you'd get a decision immediately.'

'Well, he's mistaken,' Egon retorts.

'He has his hopes pinned on you *not* getting into art school,' Mother says.

'You all do, it seems.' Egon's eyes rest on Gertrude.

That's not fair. She runs to the kitchen and adds another log to the stove. Her nose and eyes tingle with tears. Of course she wants her brother to be accepted, just perhaps not this year. If he delays until she has finished school, they can move to Vienna at the same time and live together, as he always said they would. It won't hurt him to work on the railways for a short while, she thinks. It wouldn't be fair if he was in Vienna, having fun without her.

~

The following day, Gertrude rises before her brother. She hurries, barefoot, to gather the post from the Schieles' designated slot in the shared hallway. She shuffles the envelopes through her hands. There are formal notes, family letters addressed to Mother, but nothing from Vienna. She replaces the letters where she found them and goes back inside the apartment.

The next morning, again, she's alert for the sound of the post arriving. She creeps out to check, but nothing has arrived bearing the stamp of the Academy of Fine Arts.

Each day is the same. Egon behaves as if he hasn't noticed there has been no communication, but after ten days, her brother's temper is short. He writes to Uncle Leopold to say there has been no news.

After two weeks, Gertrude finds a single letter tucked into their box. She turns it over: it bears the blue stamp of the Academy of Fine Arts in Vienna. The letter is addressed 'for the Attention of HERR CZI-HACZEK', their guardian. Gertrude's heart hammers. Her future is sealed inside this envelope. She swallows and feels as if a thousand spiders have spun webs inside her throat. She returns to the apartment, closes the door and stops next to the leafy fern in a pot by the door. She has an urge to dig her fingers deep into the soil. It's moist and they come out covered in muddy grit. She smears the dirt over the envelope, rubbing out the name and address, covering the postage, pushing her thumb over the art school's official stamp.

Floorboards creak. Impulsively, Gertrude digs a deeper hole in the soil and stuffs the crumpled letter into it, then covers it up. She wipes her fingers on the back of her skirt.

'Any post?' her brother asks, his eyes searching her face.

'Nothing today,' she replies, smiling to hide her guilt.

Gertrude is only doing this because she loves Egon so much, but still, it hurts her.

⌣

'I didn't get in,' Egon tells Gertrude. Three weeks have passed since his interview.

'Why do you say that?' she demands.

'I'd have received news by now.'

'They'll have lots of letters to write,' she says.

'Registration starts tomorrow.'

'It's better this way. You can apply again next year.'

'I need to be there now. If not, it's the railways for me . . .'

Gertrude feels a sickening sadness as she looks at her brother. But it hadn't crossed her mind, until now, to wonder what decision the letter contained. When she's sure she won't be disturbed, Gertrude digs into the soil once more. She makes holes until she finds the soggy envelope. She pulls it out and flattens it. The stamp has peeled away. She rips through the seal and pulls out the letter. She reads quickly. Much of the ink has dissolved, and she can only make out patches of the words:

Egon Schiele, she spots.

Delighted to meet such a

Immense potential
Pleased to offer you

Gertrude balls up the letter and buries it back in the soil. Egon will stay in Klosterneuburg. Her brother can still paint and draw, but it will be by her side.

He won't be miserable for ever.

Later that day, Gertrude is completing her homework, eating lemon bonbons sent by Uncle Leopold, when Egon dashes into the room and pulls the pencil she's using from her hand. He kisses her on the cheek, full of joy.

'I'm going to Vienna,' he announces. 'I've been accepted!'

Gertrude looks at the mud under her fingernails.

'I leave this evening!' he adds. 'They sent word to Uncle Leopold asking why I hadn't responded to their letter. He telegrammed Mother, she's just told me the news.' Egon jiggles his eyebrows. 'Uncle Leopold promised to find me accommodation, but for the first couple of weeks, I'll stay at his apartment in Leopoldstadt – it's one of the finest addresses in Vienna – and he'll pay for my tuition up front *and* he's promised to buy all my art materials!' Egon looks into Gertrude's unyielding face. 'Aren't you happy for me?'

She considers his question. 'I suppose I must be,' she says.

Egon has attained everything he ever wanted, his entire future spread out ahead of him, while for Gertrude, there seems to be nothing but an empty frame.

⌒

Hours later, Gertrude, Mother and Melanie accompany Egon to the station. He carries a small case and his portfolio; the telegram is tucked into the front pocket of his jacket.

'Be good for Uncle Leopold and your aunt,' Mother instructs. 'I'll miss you.' She kisses his cheek.

'Don't forget how to draw once you get there,' Melanie says.

Gertrude swallows.

'Goodbye!' Egon calls, his head sticking out of the window in the train door. Mother and Melanie wave as it departs. Egon shouts to Gertrude as the locomotive gains speed, but whatever he says is lost. She counts to one hundred, silently, as the train dissolves into the distance.

16

November 1906

Egon is having the most wonderful time as a young artist in Vienna. He writes to Gertrude to tell her so, weekly, and fills her in on all the exciting things that are happening in his life: the afternoon visits he makes to galleries – the Albertina, the Moderne Galerie, the Belvedere – where he admires works by Gustav Klimt, an older Austrian artist, and a Dutch man called Vincent van Gogh. He includes paragraphs about drinking schnapps in bars with fellow students, banging on the tables, until they are kicked out at midnight. He tells Gertrude about the views he saw of Vienna from the top of a giant Ferris wheel at the city's bustling Wurstelprater amusement park. He went there with two boys, Anton and Erwin, who are becoming firm friends. Uncle Leopold and Aunt Louisa have a stupendous view from their box at the Burgtheater, he tells her. Further news is that Uncle Leopold has secured him an attic room to rent in Kurzbauergasse, which is just a fifteen-minute walk from his apartment. Egon is excited about the move – his first taste of independence – which will happen very soon.

Gertrude scans his letters, then commits them to the stove. She won't give her brother the satisfaction of reading them twice. Some of them appear with elaborate frames around the edges, drawn in red and black crayon, his signature carefully rehearsed. 'These won't be displayed on the walls of a gallery,' she wants to reprimand him.

She considers writing back, but there's nothing to report.

Mother announces that she plans to visit Egon at the start of December.

The same day, an unexpected letter arrives: they are being served notice and must vacate the apartment. Now, once more, they must find somewhere new to live. Mother curses. She writes to her sister, who is unwell, with a view to returning to Krumau, but Gerti still has school, and Mother would like to be closer to Egon than her home-town would allow.

'We'll have to find another place here. I barely know how we'll afford it.'

Gertrude has an idea. 'We could move to Vienna? You'd be near Egon there.'

'We can't just up and leave,' Mother says.

'It is dirty and dangerous there,' Melanie says, taking sides with their mother.

'We've lived here for two years,' Gertrude persists, 'and you're always saying how bored you are, Mother.'

'That's not a reason to move to the capital.'

'But why not?' Gertrude asks.

Mother blinks, searching for the right words. 'Because . . . it's expensive. We can hardly afford our outgoings as things are. The rent alone would cripple us.'

'Uncle Leopold and Aunt Louisa have spare rooms in their apartment. We could stay with them.'

'We'll do no such thing! Get that idea out of your head right away, young lady.'

'What would people think?' Melanie demands, her eyes wide.

'But there's nothing keeping us here,' Gertrude says. 'Not really.'

'What about my job?' Melanie asks. 'I can't just give in my notice and get a new one.'

Gertrude sees something in her mother weaken.

'We could have a better life there,' Gertrude persists. 'You can get a new job, Melanie, maybe even better pay. And you can keep a close eye on Egon, Mother. I can finish school, and when I'm old enough I'll get a job too.'

'This conversation is over. Don't mention it again.' Mother gets up and leaves the room.

Eight days later, Mother announces that Uncle Leopold will be arriving at the weekend, to oversee the move. 'That trip I mentioned, to visit Egon – well, it looks as if it's going to be permanent. We've no choice,' she adds.

It's happening. They're moving to Vienna. Gertrude can't believe her luck.

17

June 1907

'We're running away, just as we said we would,' Egon says, hugging Gertrude when she arrives at the station, carrying a small valise and wearing her fanciest hat.

When the family first moved to Vienna, Gertrude thought she would see a lot more of her brother, now that they were living in the same city. But he never seemed to be free. He kept telling her he had a great deal of work at the art school, yet he always had plenty of time to go drinking with his friends.

'I need to make friends,' he'd said by way of justification.

'I could join you.'

'You don't want to hang around with them,' Egon said. 'They're a bad influence.'

'It's because you're embarrassed by me.'

'No, it's because they'd try to take advantage of you.'

'I wouldn't let them.'

'It's for your own good, Gerti.'

'But what about the promise you made, about us living together?' she insisted. 'You never want to spend time with me any more.'

'That's not true. I'm busy. And I do miss you.' He took her hand. 'I miss drawing you.'

'But you have other models now.'

'If you mean hairy old men in the life-drawing classes, then yes,' Egon replied.

'And pretty girls from good families?'

'Don't be jealous. You'll always be my favourite model. And I'll make it up to you, I promise. How about we take a trip together?' he'd suggested.

Egon has arranged to meet Gertrude here at the station very early. He wouldn't say beforehand where they'd be going, only that she should pack her best clothes, that they'd be gone for five nights in total, two of which would be spent on overnight trains – and not to worry, that he'd leave a note explaining their absence to Mother and Uncle Leopold.

'I paid Anton, my good friend, in cigarettes and croissants, to post my note to the address on Zirkusgasse after midday,' he tells her, smiling. 'I didn't say where we're going, so there's no chance of them dragging us home.'

'But what if he forgets? Mother will send out a search party!'

'He won't forget. Anton Peschka is an upstanding man. He won't let me down.'

'Still, Mother will be very worried.'

'She knows I won't let anything happen to you.'

'It'll be me looking after you,' Gertrude retorts.

'Better to be punished later than denied our adventure now.' He grins.

'Are you going to tell me where we're going, or do I have to guess?'

'We're taking a little trip . . .' He pauses. 'To where Mother and Father spent their honeymoon.'

'Trieste!' she shouts happily.

'Guess what? I sold two drawings, so we've just enough money to enjoy ourselves.'

The train approaches, screeching and clanking, the oily smell reminding Gertrude of her childhood. A flutter rises in her. They've never done anything as thrilling as this. Luckily Egon had kept a ticket book he'd found in Father's desk before he died, with unused coupons with no expiry date and a railway workers' travel card, giving the Schieles the right to free journeys anywhere within the quarter of a million square miles of the Austro-Hungarian Empire. There were enough coupons left for the two of them to travel a great distance, he'd realized. Egon had studied Father's old, faded framed map, which he'd taken with him to Vienna, running his finger along routes across Austria, Bohemia and Hungary, calculating the number of hours it would take to reach the different destinations. He'd quickly settled on Trieste, the jewel of Emperor Franz Joseph's territories, and the place where their parents had spent their honeymoon twenty-eight years earlier.

'Imagine, Mother and Father in Trieste,' Egon continues. 'We can retrace their steps, view the world through their eyes, before it all went wrong. We can see if we can do it better, learn from their mistakes.'

Egon and Gertrude board the train, find their seats in a first-class carriage, place their luggage on the overhead racks and settle in for the journey.

The doors slam and after a long whistle, they are in motion.

~

There's a rattle at the compartment door and a grey-haired inspector enters, dressed in the familiar imperial uniform.

'May I see your tickets, please, young man?' Egon hands over the two coupons, which have been carefully filled in. 'Going all the way to Trieste, are we?' he asks. 'You know you'll have to change in Graz, and take the connecting train. You'll have a few hours to wait, I'm afraid.'

He punches holes in the stubs and hands them back.

'Yes, sir. I've studied the route. I have my father's travel map with me. We plan to have dinner in Graz and catch the overnight train from there.'

'It's a long journey for just the two of you.'

Egon presents the inspector with the railway workers' travel card, emblazoned with their names and stamped photographs.

'Schieles?' the inspector asks, looking at the pass. 'Your father was the stationmaster at Tulln, isn't that right? An honourable servant of the railways. They run a tight ship there, but still, it hasn't been the same since your father retired – what is it, two years ago?'

'Two and a half, sir.'

'And what age are you, young man? Fourteen, fifteen years old?'

'I'm nearly seventeen, sir.' Egon swallows. With his delicate shoulders and slender frame, Gertrude knows he appears younger.

'Ah, a splendid age. Enjoy it. One day, you'll be as ancient as me and you'll pine for these carefree days of youth.' He winks at Egon. 'Now, don't get into any mischief.'

Egon offers the inspector a salute, the kind Father used to execute at departing trains. The inspector returns the gesture with a broad smile. 'You'll make a fine stationmaster one day, my boy,' he says as he leaves. 'I've no doubt you'll make your father proud.'

⤸

The train pulls into Trieste and they jump down into a wall of heat. Men and women bustle in and out of the station, dressed in well-cut clothes that look looser and lighter than those seen in the capital. Egon and Gertrude are surrounded by languages they have never heard before – and those who speak German, she notices, do so with a more complex accent. There's colour, everywhere, revealed with greater intensity; even the people seem less insipid than passers-by in Vienna – their complexions radiant in the heat of the sun.

As Gertrude and Egon exit the station, the vibrant sky spreads wide above them.

'Look at those blues,' Egon says, taking Gertrude's case. 'I told you we'd make it, one day.' She squeezes his arm, nervous, delighted. 'Don't you feel free?'

They head straight for the sea, which is only a few minutes away. Drawn into the flow of people, they walk along the promenade, hand in hand, Gertrude skipping ahead a little and Egon pulling her back. They continue this dance as they admire the view, and listen to the water's pleasing lull. Seagulls balance in the breeze, and wooden boats bob above the waves, the engine oil around them reflecting purples and greens.

Egon pulls them to a halt and takes out his sketchbook.

'Let's sit here for a while,' he says, taking off his shoes and socks and kicking his feet over the harbour wall.

Gertrude does the same, sitting on the whitewashed stone, running her finger along a thick snake of greasy rope. Around her, men carry heavy fishing nets, still dripping, or crates bearing that day's catch; some sit on squat stools, scaling the fish straight off the boat. But Egon is blind to all their activity; he has eyes only for the water, his pencil moving across the paper as he captures the rolling rhythm of it. Gertrude closes her eyes, allows the sun to warm her eyelids. Her brother's style has changed greatly over the past year; his lines are looser, less accurate, better at capturing the spirit of the scene before him.

After an hour, they continue, heading towards the hotel – Egon keeps assuring her that he knows where they're going. They pass women selling trinkets, fresh juices, and boats carved from wood and painted in glossy colours. Egon buys a small one for Gertrude and, further along, he purchases an orange for them to share. Gertrude sucks the sweet liquid from her fingers, and the flavour mingles with the saltiness of her skin.

'That was the most delicious thing I've ever tasted,' she says, smacking her lips.

'It's like eating sunshine,' he says, noticing drips of juice on her dress.

'The hotel's not far.' Egon has a map of the town that Mother kept as a memento of her time here, all the locations she visited with Father neatly marked with a cross. Egon consults it at each new road they pass, turning it in his hands to better direct them. 'This is the one,' her brother says eventually. Gertrude looks up at the sign above the double doors. They approach the reception desk and wait for a serious man to look up from his ledger.

'We've a reservation. The Schieles,' Egon says. 'I booked a room with a sea view.'

The wizened reception clerk makes eye contact with her brother over the counter, peering down his nose. He puts down his pen. 'Just the one?' he asks, adjusting his glasses.

Egon counts out the money, placing it before the man. 'It's all we can afford.'

~

Gertrude wakes first. Her foot is trapped between the scissor of Egon's legs, and she has to pull herself out of his sleeping embrace, trying with each twist of her body not to waken her brother. She sees the familiar birthmark on his left hip, a dark crescent, like the residue of a muddy fingerprint. The parts of Gertrude – her thigh, the top of her arm – that have been in contact with Egon during the night, for the few hours they slept, feel rosy. The rest of her aches, though, for Egon forced her into positions in the room, and on the bed, that she didn't even know she could hold – her spine bent backwards off the mattress, her belly button stretched into a thin line, her arms held, for a long time, crossed high above her head, fingers splayed. Egon's paper and pencils have fallen to the floor. Her own eyes, so distinctive, stare back at her. She feels the challenge that shines out of them, can see mischief in the smile that animates her lips.

The drawings he made in the night are more daring than ever. Gertrude feels a strange power rising in her. She's becoming that most mysterious of all creatures: a woman. They both marvelled at it – the softening skin, the buds under the surface, the darkened hairs. Egon pushed her by candlelight, harder and harder, a circus ringmaster whipping his charge, to get the results he desired. And, for the first time, Gertrude didn't feel the need to hide her face or turn herself away. By the end, though, she was spent.

There's no doubt that he made the most of their privacy, in this cocoon of a room, to enjoy her body to the fullest.

Egon, abruptly, turns over, releasing her. He repositions himself on the other side of the bed, still wrapped in the bedsheets, his mouth slack against the plump pillow. He looks so innocent. But even the act of being together, in this way, is the most outrageous thing they've ever done. Gertrude already anticipates their punishment and it sends a thrill through her.

With a tight feeling in her chest, she looks around the room. The curtains suck in and out against the open window, keeping time with the breeze. Their clothes lie crumpled on the floor. All rules have been abandoned.

Gertrude is hungry. Egon spent all their money on their final night's dinner, so they have nothing to last them until the train home. Egon will be hungry, too. She slips her feet to the floor, dresses quietly, then eases the door shut behind her.

She stops at a small shop a few streets away from the hotel. Crates of fruit surround the door, bright colours and unusual shapes she has never seen before. She examines something small and delicate with purple skin. It smells of sunny days. The sign says 'Figs'. She wants to bite into one but she returns it, reluctantly, to the box before entering the shop.

There's a counter of cheese – some soft and wrinkly, others firm. Her mouth waters. Great lengths of sausage hang from the ceiling. Gertrude eyes up the fresh loaves, warm to the touch; pastries glazed in honey and dotted with raisins, almonds and hazelnuts; moist cakes dripping with icing and topped with candied fruit. She smells the cinnamon. Her stomach rumbles. She walks around the aisles, and stops by a carton of dried yellow chanterelle mushrooms, looking closely at their twisted stems. She digs her fingers into an open sack of pulses – the shiny beans part at her touch and she pushes her fingers in deeper. Gertrude holds a jar with honeycomb inside up to the light. The pattern, through the amber liquid, is mesmerizing. She pulls a leaf off a bunch of herbs and rubs it between her fingers, then holds them to her nose. She thinks of Egon, awakening, reaching out his hand, touching only the cotton of the sheets. She thinks of their shared hunger.

The shopkeeper, an elderly man wearing an apron over his bulging stomach, is busy serving another customer. While he's distracted, Gertrude slips the jar of honey into the ruffles of her skirts, tucking it in at her waistband. She walks around, keeping her eyes on the man.

When he's not looking, she helps herself to cheese wrapped in paper, then retraces her steps to take some chanterelles. She wants to show Egon how beautiful they are.

She feels a slight juddering of nerves as she continues her circuit, but knows that if she smiles sweetly at the man, he will smile back.

Outside, she stops, not wanting to draw attention to herself with a sudden departure. She looks at the crates of fruit again, and picks up two of the figs and holds them to her nose. They smell spicy, syrupy. She badly wants to press one to her lips. She knows all of this is wrong, but cannot resist; in this world where there are no rules, anything is possible. The skin is so soft it tears, revealing moist seeds beneath. She looks over her shoulder. Nobody is watching. Gertrude closes her palm around the fruit, tucks it under her arms, as if she were chilly, and keeps walking. She speeds up now, breathing out as she turns the corner. Egon will be pleased. At the top of the road, she sees the sign for the hotel. Her stomach tightens. After breakfast, they'll return to the port and Egon will draw the boats again before they begin the long journey home.

⁀

Egon swings open the door. He's bare-chested, his braces hanging off his trousers, his hair unbrushed.

'Never, ever disappear without telling me where you're going,' he says, the words sticking in his throat when he notices the man standing beside her, a hand on her shoulder.

'And what's your name, young man?'

He swallows. 'Egon,' he replies, his wide eyes darting between Gertrude and the man in uniform.

'Family name?'

'Schiele.'

'I already told you!' Gertrude says.

'Do you have any proof of that?'

'I . . .'

'This young woman is under your charge, apparently.' The officer's eyes take in the mess of the room, the unmade bed. 'She says her mother resides in Vienna. And the only person here with her, such a long way from home, is you? Her *brother*.'

'That's right. I am her brother.'

'You must think I was born yesterday.'

Egon rummages in the pocket of his jacket on the floor and pulls out the railway workers' travel card. He passes it to the man, who inspects it carefully, examining the photographs, the signature and the official stamp of the Imperial-Royal Austrian State Railways. He holds it up and compares the images of Egon, then Gertrude, his eyes squinting.

'If you're her *brother*, you should be doing more to protect her. Your sister, here, has landed herself in a rather unfortunate mess. She was caught stealing. Luckily for her, the shop owner doesn't want to press charges.'

Egon realizes the gravity of the situation. 'I have no idea what she was thinking, sir.'

'Your parents will need to be informed.'

'Our father's dead,' Egon says firmly.

'Your mother, then.'

Gertrude can't raise her eyes to meet Egon's.

'I'll do just that, sir. I'll explain everything as soon as we get home. Our train is in less than an hour and we'll be back in Vienna tomorrow. I'll see to it that she's reprimanded.'

'We need to go further than that. I think you'll agree, it's a very serious matter.'

'If you say so.' Egon pulls Gertrude away from the man's grip.

'Not so fast. We'll need your mother's address in Vienna. We'll send a local guard there directly to explain what has happened. I'm sure she'll be very interested to hear what you two have been up to.' Gertrude feels Egon flinch beside her.

18

September 1907

Gertrude and her brother are prohibited from spending time together, so they have to snatch it when they can, in secret, Gertrude inventing excuses to get away. Today, Mother believes she's with a friend but in fact she's with Egon, who at the last minute has abandoned their plans to attend a matinee cabaret and is dragging her instead to an artist's studio on Josefstädter Strasse. Egon made a trip there yesterday, alone, but the artist in question, an important man he's determined to speak to, was not available. Her brother was sent on his way, the implication being – he says – that he should not return. But Egon plans to go back every day until Gustav Klimt will converse with him. He has brought his portfolio of drawings, and he intends to show the man his work. Gertrude can choose either to tag along or return home.

They walk through the streets of Vienna's eighth district, then enter an overgrown garden, thick with foliage and flowers, a curved path leading to the front door of the studio. The windows of the one-storey building are wide open, and a woman can be heard singing. A black cat emerges from the undergrowth as they pass; it yawns and stretches its spine before nudging its head against Gertrude's calf. She stops to pet it, running her hand along its body and tickling it under its chin. It purrs, circling.

'We shouldn't be here,' she says. 'He won't want to see you.'

'Just give me a couple of minutes. I only want him to look at my work.'

'I don't see why he's special. What makes him better than all the other boring old men who paint all day?'

'There's no other artist in the whole of Austria that I admire more,' her brother replies seriously. 'He founded the Vienna Secession a decade ago.'

Gertrude looks doubtfully at her brother. 'That means nothing to me.'

'They want to break away from tradition. Klimt hates the conservatism of the past and wants to bring art into the modern world.'

'New perspectives,' Gertrude says, recalling Egon's childhood fixation on the word.

'You can see why I'm so drawn to him,' he says.

'I have noticed that you don't like to follow the normal ways of doing things.'

'Klimt proves it's possible to do things differently.'

'What if he says you're wasting your time?' Gertrude considers the possibility.

'If he says I'm without merit, so be it.'

Gertrude looks at her brother. Is it possible that this man's words could deter him?

She hangs back as Egon approaches the door and knocks. The singing continues, an operatic warble that doesn't falter. He waits, running a finger beneath his collar to loosen it, before trying again. Eventually, the door opens a crack and Gertrude sees a flash of red hair – a darker, more burnt shade of her own. A pale face appears, the eyes wary. Egon speaks, and Gertrude watches as the girl, who can't be much older than she is, shakes her head. She's wearing a red kimono, her arms wrapped around her torso, her legs and feet bare. Gertrude experiences a jolt of envy.

The door closes between them and Egon returns, running his free hand through his hair. 'He's not in, the girl said. He won't be back for a week.'

'You don't believe her?'

'I think he's in there, working.'

'Let's go, then. You can come back tomorrow. But for now, there's still time for you to buy me that hot chocolate you promised me.'

The cat sidles up to her, and Gertrude pauses to stroke its fur once more. When she looks up, her brother is at the gate to the studio gardens, introducing himself to a man. He's large, much older than Egon, with patches of pale-grey hair, and he's wearing a strange blue smock. To Gertrude, it looks like a nightgown – she has certainly never seen a man wear such a thing in the daytime. The older artist waits patiently, his shopping basket placed on the ground, full of scrolls of paper, long brushes and paints. Her brother is fumbling with the clasp of his portfolio.

Egon presents the man with several drawings on pale-brown paper, then wipes his hands, which are slick with sweat, discreetly on his trousers. The man looks through the sketches, adjusting the angle of the works, his eyes probing the lines. Gertrude can see that her brother is holding his breath.

The seconds mount up, a minute passes. Egon seems to be shrinking on the spot. Then he takes a deep breath, and asks the question that Gertrude knows has plagued him, shaped him, ever since he was a child sitting on the platform, drawing the trains in Tulln.

'Sir, may I ask, do I have talent?'

Everything, for her brother, Gertrude knows intimately, hinges on this moment.

'How old are you?' the man replies, frowning.

Gertrude spots the model with red hair watching them from the window.

'I'm seventeen, sir.'

'And what training are you undertaking?'

'I'm at the Academy of Fine Arts, the same one you attended. My

tutors are bores who insist I draw more conservatively. They reprimand me at every turn.'

'They do, do they?'

'I want to form my own art group, as you did.'

'You're ambitious, that's for certain. And you want my opinion on
your talent?'

'I want to know if I'm right to sacrifice everything for art, sir.'

The man laughs, a deep guttural sound that rises from his generous
belly.

'Talent?' he repeats, looking closely at Egon's work. He shakes his
head and Egon goes pale. 'It's as clear to me as my own name that, if
anything, you've much too much. And I know well the sacrifices you
speak of – they never get any easier,' the older man adds.

Her brother loosens, a smile breaking across his face.

Something releases in Gertrude, too, and she approaches. The man
notices her, and she can feel the weight of his appraisal as it searches
her face and scans her body. She experiences a frisson, caught between
fascination and fear of him and his authority. His presence is
formidable.

'Perhaps we could make an exchange of drawings – you can keep
those,' her brother says, gesturing to the works in his hand. 'And I
could have just one of your sketches?'

The man laughs again. 'Your confidence is refreshing. You remind
me of myself, thirty years ago. But why swap with an old man? You
already draw better than I do.'

Her brother becomes bolder. 'They told me I was delusional – my
teachers, my family, my tutors.' Egon fizzes with jubilation. 'Thank you.'

'Now, I must be going,' Klimt says. 'I have lunch with someone special. But I hope to see you again soon, young man. What did you say
your name was?'

19

September 1910

Gertrude arrives at her brother's latest apartment studio on Alserbachstrasse, in Vienna's ninth district, at five o'clock in the afternoon, as arranged. They plan to go to the Park-Kino picture house, but Egon isn't ready. He rages from across the room that a model failed to arrive as planned, and it has cost him a day's progress. He has a commission and has waited all day for the wastrel to show her face, feeling more and more wretched with every passing minute.

'Every model I've ever worked with has been late at some time or another,' he says, 'I hoped this one would be different. I'd even mixed my paints. Now they're ruined.'

Gertrude rubs her finger across her brother's palette of pigments, a hard crust on their surface. She reads the names on the tubes: orpiment yellow, vermilion and verdigris.

Egon clears his throat, complains he has another headache. 'They've been coming more and more frequently,' he says. 'I've eaten nothing all day.' He runs a knife unevenly through a loaf of bread and spreads the slice with butter.

'What about all your other models?' Gertrude asks. 'You're usually boasting that you see more women than the Emperor, that you can't keep up with them all.'

Egon closes his eyes. 'They've all let me down, in one way or another.'

'It can't be that bad. You've still got time, haven't you?'

'I've got people breathing down my neck, debtors knocking at the door at all hours . . . I've lost track of what I owe and where. I've used up all of my chances with Uncle. He's still barely forgiven me for our jaunt to Trieste.' Gertrude reddens. Although that was three years ago now, Egon still blames her for all the trouble they got into – even though the trip had been his idea in the first place.

'I'll pose for you,' she says, 'if that would help. We can see the motion picture another time.'

'No,' he says.

'I used to do it when we were children,' she says. 'And many times here in Vienna. Remember that silly hat?'

'No,' he repeats.

Gertrude jabs a dry paintbrush at him.

'I'm not as pretty as the other girl you hoped would show up today, is that it?'

'Don't be stupid,' he snaps.

'Then why?'

'Because I need a nude. You'd have to take off your clothes. All of them.'

Gertrude stops. 'I've done that before, too.'

'We were children then, we hardly knew better. This work is for an upcoming show. It's far more likely that people will see it. It would do untold damage to your reputation.'

'What reputation?' she snorts.

'Flaunting yourself in a piece of art that will be seen by Vienna's high society isn't likely to impress potential suitors.'

'You sound like Mother!' Gertrude scoffs. 'I hardly think I'd be interested in the kind of man who'd be offended.'

'You wouldn't like it. You're too impatient, easily distracted,' Egon argues.

'That's not true. I'm like a statue.' She strikes a pose, foot raised, then wobbles.

Egon musters a laugh.

'I'm serious, though. The commission is for a nude.'

'I want to do it,' she says. 'For you. I'll turn my face, nobody will know it's me.'

'And you're not allowed to say you don't like it afterwards.'

'Do you need a model, or not?' Gertrude asks her brother.

He shakes his head. 'I can't say I'm happy about this.'

'You don't need to be happy, you just need to pick up a brush and paint.'

〜

Gertrude is dozing on the day cot. Her brother is in the armchair. She returned early that morning to allow Egon to complete the painting.

Egon leaps at the sound of three raps on the door to his apartment.

'It'll be the bailiffs again,' he hisses. He looks through the peephole, then steps back. He holds a finger to his lips.

The knock comes again, a gentle rap. He opens the door and peers out.

Through the opening, Gertrude can see a blonde girl with pale skin.

'Egon Schiele?' she asks. 'We met at Schönbrunn. I'm here for your painting.'

Egon reaches into his pockets and rummages around, then places the coins he finds in the woman's hands. 'The position is now filled,' he says.

'But you asked me to come.' Her eyes are wary.

'Yesterday. I needed you urgently yesterday.'

He closes the door on her. Gertrude can hear her protesting all the way back down the stairs. While he goes to brew some coffee, she wanders over to Egon's desk. There's a photograph in the open drawer: Egon, clowning around, his face and body contorted in a silly pose, sitting on a bench alongside a dashing, slightly older man. The inscription reveals the man's name to be Anton Peschka, one of Egon's friends. She shuffles through Egon's sketches, his calling cards. His diary from the start of the year shows the name 'Liliana', circled, three or four times a week. After July, it does not appear again. Gertrude removes a note from a rough envelope, tucked in the back: *I thought you'd want to know. It finally arrived on 9 August. A baby girl. LA.*

'Just my luck,' Egon says, returning with the coffee pot. Gertrude takes the only cup – chipped – and places it on the table.

The finished artwork looks back at them from the other side of the room. It is otherworldly in its beauty and strangeness. Gertrude has certainly never seen anything like it. In it, she's alone on the page, suspended like a rabbit pulled from a magician's hat. She appears to be sitting on an invisible chair, her knees tucked tightly together, the curve of her buttocks drawing the eye to the sharp dip of her waist, to her belly button, her breasts. Her right arm seems unnaturally long, bent in a triangle, touching the back of her head. It was excruciating to hold that pose for so long and, after a while, her fingers had begun to tingle and go numb.

Egon and Gertrude share the single cup of black coffee, sipping it in silence.

Suddenly, there's a louder, firmer bang at the door.

'I've already told you,' Egon says as he opens it. 'You're too late!'

But it's not the pale-faced girl on the other side, it's a large man, his face red.

'Schiele? You owe my daughter money. You invited her here and didn't pay up.'

'I needed her yesterday. I had to find someone else.'

The man barges into the apartment and sees Gertrude, who is standing by the window.

'So you're taking advantage of another young girl, are you?'

'Please leave,' Egon says. 'You're upsetting my sister.'

The man looks from Gertrude to her brother and back. Then he spots the artwork, which still isn't dry.

'Your sister lets you paint her, breasts, buttocks and all, does she?'

'If your daughter had shown up as agreed, it wouldn't have been necessary.'

'My daughter, pose for you like that? Over my dead body! You should be locked up.'

Egon is silent. The man takes a step closer. 'You listen to me,' he sneers into her brother's face. 'Don't you go approaching young girls on the street. Don't invite them to your apartment, pretending it's all about art, or whatever you call it. You're a menace to society. You'll land in serious trouble one of these days.'

'I've not done a thing wrong,' Egon says.

'You're a pervert, a pornographer, from the looks of *that*.' He points.

'You don't know what you're talking about.'

'I could use some of these' – he holds a drawing aloft – 'to wipe my arse.' He turns to Gertrude. 'And you! You should be ashamed of yourself, flaunting all that flesh like a common whore. You'd get more on the street than you'll get from him in payment.'

'Get out!' Gertrude shouts into his face. 'You're the one with the sick mind, not my brother, you hypocrite.'

20

26 May 1911

*M*y *dearest Gerti. It would be my pleasure if you'd accept this invi-tation to visit me in Krumau. I've missed you terribly. The days are too long without you. I've secured a cottage for the summer. Do hurry! I cannot wait to see you.*

Gertrude reads the letter a second time. She's about to leave for work. She has secured a job at a department store, where she models fancy dresses to encourage rich women, with far thicker waists than she has, that they will look just as elegant in the outfits she displays. With the additional income, she, Mother and Melanie have now been able to rent a small apartment of their own. Gertrude tucks the letter into her handbag. Her colleagues will not tolerate tardiness – if she's late again, she will be fired.

These days she barely thinks about Egon, much less expects him to write. In fact, he does it so infrequently that the very shape of his hand-writing changes from one missive to the next.

But she will ask her boss for time off, she decides. A few days away to visit her brother, the exalted artist, who she has not seen in a long time.

Gertrude arrives in Krumau by train and, having written ahead to Egon to tell him the time of her arrival, is bemused to discover that he's not there to meet her at the station. She waits – no doubt her brother remains the kind of man who often runs late. After fifteen minutes, she can no longer bear the glances she is eliciting from strangers and resolves to set off by herself. She will find her way. Egon will be known in this town, having made a reputation for himself already, no doubt.

Gertrude begins to descend the steps to the historic centre as the sun begins to set. It has been a few years since the Schiele family visited Krumau, the red-roofed town where her mother was born. Going down is easier on the calves. Perhaps that's why Egon has not met her – climbing up is too much effort. Behind her, Gertrude hears rushing footsteps. A hand lands on her shoulder. She turns with a scowl.

'Excuse me, I don't suppose you're Fräulein Schiele, are you?' A man with a little moustache and apple-cheeks is addressing her. 'Do excuse my familiarity. I was back there, at the station.' He points. 'I noticed you waiting on the platform. I suspect we were both waiting for the same person. Your brother?' Gertrude screws up her eyes. 'He was supposed to meet me here. He mentioned you were arriving on the same train and said we could all walk to the cottage together.' He holds his hand out. 'I should introduce myself. Anton Peschka. Egon must have mentioned me? We studied at the *Akademie* together. Rivals in art, but firm friends in life!'

'Gertrude,' she says, presenting him with her hand. Egon hadn't mentioned that anyone else would be there during her stay. Not only that, but he has orchestrated it so they must escort each other to the cottage. 'And no,' she adds, slightly riled, 'I can't recall him mentioning you.'

The man shuffles his valise from one hand to the other. 'Well, he's mentioned you. I've seen his drawings.'

Gertrude feels a blush rushing to her cheeks. Most husbands don't see as much of their wives.

'Follow me,' she says, flinching, then stops and passes him her case. 'Would it be inconvenient for you to carry mine, too?'

⤶

Egon greets them at the door, and immediately thrusts a glass into Anton's hand.

'Gerti, you look sensational,' he says. 'What a delicate wisp you are!'

She lets him embrace her and offers him her cheek. She has to admit, it's good to have his arms around her. He has filled out since she last saw him. She takes in his broader shoulders, a slight protrusion of stomach above his trousers. He's looking after himself very well indeed.

'And I am so pleased you and Anton have met. This old dog could learn a thing or two from me in the studio, but he's not a bad man.' Egon jostles his friend.

Gertrude hears music and looks through the door into the cottage. There seem to be a lot of people inside the small space. In the front room, the furniture has been pushed to the sides and the table is covered in bottles.

'What are we ...' she begins, but Egon has grabbed the wrist of a young girl who arrived a minute after them and is pulling her over. She's expressionless, almost plain in her appearance – but when she makes eye contact, Gertrude experiences a shock of energy that utterly disturbs her. For there is something, impossible to name, that makes this red-haired girl almost beautiful. She also looks strangely familiar.

'This, my dear sister, is someone I'm very keen for you to meet. Vally.' He presents her. 'I first met her at Gustav Klimt's studio. She's been modelling for me for – what, five or six months now?' The girl smiles at him. 'We've become close friends. Vally looked after me very well in Vienna, and I'm rather pleased she's turned up here, too. She's a great help, in my work and my life. I dare say I've made some of the best art of my career thanks to you,' he says, turning to her.

'I'm his sister,' Gertrude interrupts, putting her hand on her brother's arm.

'I don't think you mentioned a sister?' The young woman speaks only to Egon, a cold menace to her tone. She's clearly put out by Gertrude's presence. She too is carrying a valise.

'This is Gerti, of course I've told you about her.'

The girl shakes her head, gently, quizzically, as if she has no recollection.

'She was my first model. Everything I know about beauty, I learnt from her.'

Egon's model turns her cold eyes on Gertrude. But Gertrude won't be intimidated by someone who'll hardly manage to hold Egon's attention for more than a few months, a year if this girl is lucky. There is blood between Gertrude and Egon, an intimacy that can never be written over, not by a mere distraction like her. She frowns at her brother, then reaches over and takes the glass of wine out of Anton's hands. She brushes his fingers and he reddens.

Then she raises Anton's glass to her lips, and swallows every drop.

21

15 August 1914

'I cannot believe you're even contemplating marrying that man. Have you lost your mind? You're doing this to spite me.' Egon turns on Gertrude, his face swollen with anger.

Gertrude has come to visit her brother in his latest studio in Hietzing.

'Egon . . .' she tries.

'He's my friend. You know how much this will hurt me. Marriage is for other people,' he shouts. 'You said so yourself. It's for boring people who have no imagination. Idiots who have nothing better to do!' She exhales and crosses the room. Summer's yellow leaves have gathered between the cobblestones on the street below. 'You said all this to me in Trieste.'

'We were children then, Egon. We've had to grow up. What chance have we ever had of making a life together?' Gertrude is hoping to soften Egon's anger before they say things they'll never be able to take back. But Egon has no control over his own unhappiness. Ever since his experiences in Neulengbach, he has not been the same – Gertrude blames that model of his, Vally, for the situation he got himself into there. His anger has been quicker to rise and he's more easily rattled. But Gertrude isn't the enemy.

She knew he would be maddened by the fact that she'd found love with his friend, that they are building a life together. What she can't say is that being with Anton is the only way she can remain close to Egon, be part of the life he has taught her to admire. This is her way of remaining in his circle, of keeping his attention.

'I thought you were different,' he says. 'I thought *we* were different. But you're the same as everyone else.'

'Anton is your friend, Egon. He's a good man.'

'A good man!' Egon chokes on his disbelief. 'Anton Peschka is an artist!'

'You're an artist.'

'Anton has nothing on my talent. Nothing! How can you settle for that?'

A vein in his right eyelid pulses.

'You're not the only one who I can give myself to,' she replies.

'I don't *want* to paint you any more!'

Gertrude examines her hands and sees the black mark on her smallest nail, evidence of a finger she trapped in a drawer. She doubts it'll grow out before the wedding.

'I haven't painted you for years,' Egon adds. 'You're more like our mother with each passing day.'

Gertrude is amused at his attempt at an insult. 'You should know something,' she says calmly. 'There's a baby. It'll be born before the year is over. Anton and I need to be married before it arrives.' She gives him a firm look. 'It's happening with or without your approval.'

Egon chokes. 'How could you be so stupid? Mother has been on at me, writing me long letters, concerned at the nature of your relationship with that man. *They've been spending too much time together, they're too close,*' he says, an echo of what their parents had said about the two of them all those years ago. 'And I told her, over and over again, that there was nothing to worry about.'

'Am I the only one who has been stupid? What about you? What about that model of yours, Liliana? Don't think those rumours didn't reach my ears, too. Mother turned a blind eye to all that. At least Anton wants to marry me. He'll be a father to our baby. That's more than can be said of you.' She draws a deep breath. 'I'm not a saint. But we women are expected to be perfect and pure, while you men do whatever you please with no thought for the consequences.'

Egon tries to fire back, but Gertrude has not finished.

'So here's something else you need to hear. This "getting married and having a family", Egon, it's what we have to do. You're twenty-four. We have to grow up. Have you ever considered that? Isn't it about time you did the unthinkable and settled down, found a woman – and no, I don't mean Vally, I mean a *respectable* woman, not some low-class girl who takes her clothes off for money. You've proved your point to Mother. Stop punishing her. Stop punishing yourself. You've been an outcast long enough.'

Gertrude pauses, glancing out of the bay window. She sees two women leaving the building opposite.

'Make yourself known to them, why don't you?' Gertrude suggests.

Egon peers down. 'The Harms sisters,' he says. 'The darker-haired one is a little intense. The blonde is easier to be around.'

'It wouldn't be the worst idea for you to get to know them better.'

Gertrude feels the baby quickening. She will become a wife and a mother – for what other choices have ever, realistically, been within her grasp? Egon will no longer be the most important person in her world. That is what's bothering him. That he has to let her go.

'Besides,' she adds. 'You were the one who left me. You made a promise and you broke it. This obsession was always more important ...' Her voice quivers with emotion, but she does her best to swallow it. 'There's nothing you won't sacrifice for your art – me, yourself, your sanity. I only hope it's worth it.'

Interlude

The Albertina Gallery, 9 May 1968

T he first room of the gallery is dedicated to Egon Schiele. A dozen gilded frames are lit by bright lights, the portraits inside frozen. Adele steps into the centre, the rubber of her plimsolls sharp against the polished floor. She stands, caught in the brightest beam of light, and turns a full circle, taking in each and every one of the drawings and watercolours. She breathes deeply. The old woman peers at the female bodies, all rendered by the artist's unmistakable eye – angular lines and amputated limbs, oversized, long-fingered hands and haunting, unflinching eyes. The strangest contortions of shape and perspective. Standing there, Adele takes in a ruby-haired girl reclining, comfortable in her nakedness; a dark-haired beauty thrusting out one hip, her hands raised to her face with its gratifyingly expressive eyes.

Adele feels as if she is twenty-five years old again, the younger woman bristling beneath her skin. Her mind shifts, time dissolves, and the dozen figures emerge from the frames, their eyes glinting with mischief, their pale skin palpably warm, their muscles twitching as they step down and come to stand with her, surrounding her, curling so close that she can feel their breath on her neck.

Adele moves lightly from one foot to another, swaying to a beat that only she can hear.

This is where she belongs. She has made it.

The women look at her expectantly, waiting.

'It's me, Adele. Adele Harms,' she says.

Their eyes narrow. They whisper, their words echoing.

Your fault, your fault.

Lies, lies, lies.

The words spin in Adele's head. Adele had hoped that being in this space would power her memory, provide answers. But the spell is broken, and the women are drawn back once more to their frames – caught there, their essence preserved as if Egon could halt time in its tracks. All she hears is their silence.

'You were going to tell me about this artist . . . ?' Eva interrupts her reverie.

'I knew him a very long time ago,' the older woman admits.

'Why didn't you say so earlier?'

'It's not easy to find the right words when it comes to speaking about those days.'

'What was he like?' Eva replies.

'The artist? Oh, he was charming. Charismatic. The kind of man who breaks your heart. Egon made quite an impression on me.'

'How did you meet?'

'Egon lived in the building opposite the one I lived in with my family. Of course, there were the rumours. Scandal followed him around, but he turned it to his advantage. Some men have a knack for that. I was young and he was the most exciting presence. I knew he was going to change my life for ever.'

'And the two of you fell in love?' Eva guesses.

'He produced this feeling in me ...' Adele grasps Eva's hand and places it against her own chest, above her heart. 'Every time I saw him.' Then she pauses, lowers her eyes and lets go of Eva's hand. 'But it was more complicated than that.'

The old woman's shoulders sag. What does it mean to believe in love, to hope for it, to have it within your grasp, to let it demolish you?

Could she have controlled herself, lived without the obsession she cultivated? Forgiven more easily?

'The truth is, I did something unforgivable. It was a moment of madness, of wild cruelty, and I've regretted my actions ever since. The worst thing is, I've never known what I said or did that day. And I never had the chance to be forgiven.'

'So, is that why you want to be here? To make amends?' Eva asks.

Adele feels a chill creep up her calves. Why is she here? What is it she's looking for, that she can find within these walls?

Eva steps towards her, touching Adele's arm. 'Are you unwell?'

For a moment, she feels dizzy and her breath grows short. Adele has been experiencing more of these episodes over the last six months, moments when it feels as if her heart has stopped or fluttered, when the room shifts around her and she finds herself having to anchor herself back in the world.

'I thought I'd find myself here, find answers . . .' Adele says, unable to conjure more.

'Should we take you back to the hospital?' Eva persists.

'Heavens, no,' she manages to say. 'Just give me a moment.'

They stop to rest on a bench, then continue on into the next room in the gallery. The artworks display women offering up a nipple, a bared bottom, or exposing their genitals, their stockinged thighs open, a suggestive ruffle of material between their legs like petals.

'I've never seen so much nudity displayed so openly before,' Eva comments.

'Society back then didn't know what to make of it either,' Adele says. 'There was glamour, but beneath the surface . . .' She frowns.

'This art caused quite a stir, then?'

'They said Egon was a pornographer, and what his models did was considered tantamount to prostitution. They risked everything – their reputation, their relationships . . .'

Adele stops suddenly. She is face to face with a woman wearing an emerald chemise, her knee raised, her cheek almost resting on it, arms locked around her leg. The look coming off her is volcanic in intensity. She stares out of the elaborately framed painting – powerful, annihilating.

'But let me introduce you,' she says to Eva. 'This is who I used to be.'

'That's you?' Eva exclaims.

'Can you not see the similarity?' Adele leans in closer to the painting.

'I can hardly believe my eyes,' Eva replies.

'Why? Because I was once so beautiful? Beguiling?' Her voice crackles with bitter laughter. 'I suppose it's hard to believe that a woman like that turned into this old crow?'

'I can't really believe that she' – Eva gestures – 'is standing in front of me. I never stopped to imagine that these models had lives of their own. Living, breathing . . .'

'Oh, we had hopes and dreams and failures, let me tell you.'

'But your eyes, they're so full of regret.'

'You're right.' Adele looks closely at her own reflection. 'He saw that in me, too. There was something powerful in letting your guard down. He captured what was left. But we all have regrets. Tell me, Eva, don't you have any?'

Eva frowns. 'You don't want to hear about all my failures and heartbreak.'

'What else do I have to distract me from my own?'

Eva glances at Adele, weighing her words carefully. 'Did you ever get the feeling . . . that all the people you've ever loved would be better off without you?'

Adele looks at Eva shrewdly. 'Perhaps we're more similar than I first thought . . . Take a little advice from an old woman with nothing to her name. Try not to make an almighty mess of your life.'

The next painting shows a woman, naked, arms raised, a triangle across the paper, her face obscured. There's a blue ribbon in her hair.

'That's Gertrude, Egon's little sister,' Adele comments, skimming over the sensual watercolour, admiring the fluid lines and composition.

'That's his *sister*?' Eva asks, leaning in to read the name of the painting: *Seated Female Nude with Raised Right Arm (Gertrude Schiele), 1910.*

Adele nods her head. 'Nothing at all has been left to the imagination.'

'What became of her?'

'She could still be alive for all I know. Living in a world that no longer recognizes her.'

'And what do you think all these women would say,' Eva ponders, 'if they could speak to us today?'

'The same as me. This is who we were – for better or worse. Could we have done it differently? One day you will ask yourself the same thing.'

'This one's striking?' Eva says.

They're faced with a woman with burnt-red hair, her eyes wide and imploring, on her back with one arm beneath her head, her knees raised to reveal her stockings, and her ankles crossed. She wears an orange chemise and a knowing smile.

'That's Vally Neuzil,' Adele says. 'It's fair to say we didn't see eye to eye.'

'You knew her, too?'

'She was Egon's main model, when I first saw him,' Adele replies.

'She was his muse?'

Adele exhales. 'We all hoped we inspired greatness in him. But she, certainly, had a dynamic that shone in his work. She was a better woman than I gave her credit for.'

'What happened to her?' Eva asks.

'I've no idea. I only hope she had more luck than me,' Adele replies, observing the woman in the painting closely, all the jealousy she once harboured diminished.

'Perhaps Vally found happiness in the end?'

'It's possible. But none of us truly escaped our encounters with Egon unscathed.'

VALLY

1

January 1911

'Let me introduce you, Herr Schiele. This is none other than Fräulein Neuzil. She promises to dazzle you, much like the sun. Only don't stare into her centre for long.' Gustav Klimt pushes a pale-faced young woman from the shadows. 'What a gem she is, don't you agree?'

As Vally passes through the drapes that lead from Klimt's living quarters to the studio set aside for life modelling, she feels the full warmth of the fire fall on her as well as the young man's interested gaze. In this space, which she knows well, there are several easels set up at all times. Colourful constellations of paint layer the floor and canvases line the bare-plaster walls. Without looking up, she raises her fingers to the buttons at her neck, brushing a strand of copper hair out of the way. She has been given little opportunity to prepare herself for this viewing.

'Do say hello to our guest, Vally, dearest sweet pea, before you take off your clothes.' The older artist tugs at his greying beard, his habitual gesture of disapproval. The young woman straightens up, her eyes level with those of the young man to whom she is being presented.

'Hello, *sir*,' Vally says, her words heavy with disdain. She raises her chin, but does not let the greeting reach her eyes; instead, she looks the pallid, dark-haired young man up and down, taking in shoulders that don't properly fill his jacket, cuffs frayed around the edges and unpolished shoes. Vally in no way cares for perfection, but she does take the measure of those she meets to better grasp what she's dealing with. This *would-be* does not differ from the other impoverished artists who beg at Gustav's door, keen to feed on the crumbs of his genius.

At sixteen, Vally has seen their desperation in the months she has modelled for Klimt. They come knocking at the door of the studio three or four times a week, and she has to make excuses for the famous artist, or Gus would never get any work done. He's at the very height of his influence and, of course, his success, and it makes inferior men take leave of their senses. Time and again, they fail to produce a work of art as sensual or sought-after as *The Kiss*.

Gustav puts his arm around her shoulders. It looks like a gesture of protection, but Vally knows better than that. He's offering her up to his thirsty guest, like a pitcher of wine to be shared between them, having relished the first sip.

'She's your type entirely, I believe?' Gustav persists. She leans in to the older artist, whose greying hair and thickened girth reveal him to be advancing into his fifties. There must be decades between them, for this younger man, who has yet to sprout proper facial hair, seems barely to have surpassed his second decade of life. Vally feels Gustav plant a kiss on the crown of her head before releasing her.

'Call me Egon.' The young man steps forward, full of the confidence she usually sees fall away within days. The artist offers her his hand. Vally makes it clear that she's not prepared to notice it. He rams it into his pocket and his cheeks darken. Is that embarrassment or anger? She's attuned to measuring men's moods. To get it wrong could be the difference between his tears or hers, his black mood or her black eye.

But in Schiele, Vally cannot draw a firm conclusion. Still, she knows she has got to him. If this man is going to disturb her plans for the afternoon, then she can take a moment's pleasure from ruffling his pretensions. She had hoped to enjoy a nap after a long morning session holding a tight pose. The muscles along her torso still ache from the effort. But now she must be fuel for another artist's divine inspiration. She yawns.

'Now, now, Vally, play nice with this one,' Gustav warns, sensing her mood. 'He has exceptional talent. Much too much, in fact. I told you that before, Egon, when I first met you a few years ago, remember?' So he's a man who must be petted, Vally thinks. He does seem vaguely familiar.

'And *you* must take care of my precious Vally,' Gustav continues. 'She's dear to me.' He squeezes the young man's shoulder. There are hints of gold leaf creased into the lines around Gustav's eyes and as he moves, the smell of turpentine lingers as if it were some kind of *eau de cologne*. 'I have no doubt you'll benefit from one another.'

The older artist returns to his living quarters and Egon draws the curtains. They are alone. The wind rattles the windowpane and the fire crackles. Vally places a log on it, watches it flare. The artist, still bristling, refuses to make eye contact.

He unbuttons his collar.

'You know this isn't a brothel, don't you?' Vally says.

The young man begins to protest, but she cuts him short.

'Don't mistake my role here today,' she continues. 'Gustav said you want to draw me. But I'm not here to pleasure or please you.'

'I've neither the desire nor the means to pay you for such a thing,' Egon replies. 'Besides, you're not my type.' He makes a vague gesture of dissatisfaction, and Vally flares at the insinuation that she is not to his liking. 'I don't want to offend Herr Klimt, so perhaps you could make an excuse . . . pretend you're tired or you've succumbed to a headache. I'm sure another girl can take your place.'

He looks at her now, and his eyes, she sees, have a peculiar depth.

Vally turns on her heel. She walks towards a daybed against one wall of the space they must share. It is covered in patterned blankets and tasselled cushions. She picks one up and plumps it. Then she removes a wide belt that rests upon her hips. The leather groans as she pulls at the buckle and its metal pin is released.

'I told you that won't be necessary,' he says firmly.

The young woman eases her burnt-orange shawl from her shoulders. She takes out the tortoiseshell comb that holds her thick copper hair in its high chignon. Without hurrying, Vally unbuttons her dress – which pinches a little, but only because she is still growing. She lets it fall.

'I said stop!'

She folds it and places it on the seat of a nearby chair. Vally puts a foot on the edge and leans forward to unlace her heeled black boots, which reach up her calves, almost to the knees. She knows, as she does so, that her bottom will stretch the material of her undergarments appealingly. Vally turns back to the artist. He's watching her closely, fury glazed with a hint of desire.

Egon holds up his hand. 'You're wasting your own time,' he says.

She loosens her petticoat.

'I'll discuss it with Klimt,' he continues, 'if you're not prepared to stand aside gracefully.'

She lifts her petticoat over her head. Underneath, all is revealed: the soft flesh of her stomach, the indents of her ribs and a lace-trimmed brassiere; she watches as the artist averts his eyes while she reaches around to unfasten the ribbons that hold it in place. She tugs, then lets the garment drop to the floor. The sound draws his eyes back to her.

Vally watches him squirm and swallow. She is enjoying this. This is her last moment of control, before *he* – as artist, as voyeur – claims her body as his own.

'I don't know why you're looking so very pleased with yourself,' he says. 'This isn't the first time I've seen a naked woman, you know. I've had the pleasure of drawing more than two hundred in the past year alone, all of them far more pleasing to the eye than you.'

'Don't let me stop you, then, if you've seen it all before.' Vally sighs, falling on to the daybed with relish. She pushes the blankets aside and positions herself, her face to the wall. She turns to look over her shoulder, to let him know that she's ready. Vally isn't trying to seduce him;

it's just that she knows her body and how to hold herself. She also knows, if this man has any sense at all, that he'll take the chance to appreciate it.

The artist looks around the room and frowns. He opens his satchel, removes a sketchbook and rolls his shoulders. He produces a carton of pencils and licks the nib of one. 'If you insist,' Egon says finally. How sure of himself he is. 'I, for one, don't have time to waste. I can't keep asking my sister to pose every time another feckless girl lets me down by not showing up at my studio as agreed. That's what I get for approaching them on the street,' he mutters as he lays down the first line, rupturing the blank sheet. 'I thought they'd be grateful for the money, the attention, the warmth. It's not like they have anything better to do, the wastrels who wander this city.'

Vally laughs, her head thrown back.

Egon releases his pencil. 'You should leave.' He says it calmly. 'Put your clothes on and get out. Neither of us has to see the other ever again. This really won't work.'

Vally can't help but laugh again. Something about this serious man tickles her.

'Get out!' he snaps.

He expects her to grab her clothes and flee the room in floods of tears. Vally simply cracks her knuckles, sets her mouth and offers him a serene look.

'You really don't understand women, do you?' she says. 'You don't understand what motivates them, the source of their wants or desires. You clearly don't know how to charm one,' she adds. He opens his mouth to interrupt. 'Have you ever got close to one who didn't give you what you want?'

'Go!' he shouts again. 'You're not what I need! Now, or ever.'

Vally moves as if she were a thief. She grabs her clothes from the chair and is almost past him, but Egon reaches out and grabs her by the wrist. She turns on him, gums bared.

Now it's his turn to laugh.

She could murder him.

Egon stops, bemused delight sparkling in his dark, long-lashed eyes. 'I am sorry,' he says, after a moment.

Vally scrutinizes his features. He looks as if he means it.

'You rattled me,' he adds. 'There's something about you that reminds me of my sister. She knows how to push my buttons, too.' He offers her his hand, and she takes it. It's warm and soft. 'Truce,' he says. Vally smiles, but moves away. 'No, stay, please. I want to draw you. Once, at least.'

'I have one request. You must treat me as an equal if I'm to remain.'

Egon picks up another pencil and nods his head.

Vally relents and returns to the bed. She places her feet together and lets her knees fall wide to either side. There's no need to speak. She allows Egon to work for an hour, and it rolls into two. She changes positions without being asked each time he takes up a new sheet of paper. He selects a tray of pigments – gouache powder that he mixes with water – and lightly works unusual colour choices between his lines: greens and yellows and violet. This surprises her. Vally stays alert and does not loosen her gaze or fall into a light sleep, the way she knows other models do.

Her eyes are on him, the way his are on her. She won't let him beat her.

As they approach the third hour, Egon requests a break.

Vally stands and stretches; her joints pop. She wraps herself in a kimono. 'Gus has an open barrel,' she says. 'I won't tell him if you don't. Wait here.'

She returns with a mug of beer. Egon drinks it down in one go.

'I'd say you read my mind,' he smiles.

'Ready for the final pose?'

Vally removes the robe and positions herself on the floor, which is marked with chalk where models before her have traced outlines of their feet, enabling them to resume their pose. Vally has never needed to chalk a line in her life.

'You'd be better over there.' The artist points across the room. 'This will make for a more interesting composition.'

'Do you even know the meaning of the word?' Egon laughs. 'Or is it just something you've heard other artists say?' Vally looks at him and shakes her head.

~

Egon works for another hour. She gazes through the windows at the overgrown garden and watches the wind blow through the deadened shrubs.

It has been a few years since Vally first showed up at Gustav Klimt's studio. By a young age, she'd already worked her way across Vienna – as a child, tailing her mother as she collected laundry to be scrubbed and steamed, before securing her own pay behind the scenes at the opera house on the Ringstrasse, sometimes washing the feet of the singers. Later, Vally had battled long shifts, roughing her fingers in one of the city's new factories. Positions such as these, occupied by girls such as herself, were always open to abuse. A well-meaning older friend suggested that Vally should visit an artist's studio on Josef-städter Strasse to enquire about modelling, which is how she'd met Gustav. It wasn't work many were willing to take on.

Modelling wasn't much, but it was still better than becoming one of the fragile girls who serviced grunting men in alleyways. Still, Vally remembers the shame she'd felt when she'd first removed her garments, the way the feeling had dug beneath her ribs as she'd hugged her arms around her chest. A more experienced model had taken Vally under her wing, taught her how to encourage her limbs to loosen, how to allow her energy to blossom outwards. She'd stood her in front of a mirror, forced her to look herself in the eye.

These days, Klimt has other models – wealthy women and wives. Vally still sits, when she can, for him and others, but more often she finds herself fulfilling errands: riding the tram to deliver his paintings or an important message; carrying invoices or receipts back and forth between his patrons; buying paper, paint and pencils when the materials cupboard runs low, always securing a discount so she can spend the difference on her favourite sweets; arranging Gustav's desk to his satisfaction; dusting his studio and cleaning the windows with vinegar and paper; setting up his oils according to the colour wheel she has memorized; and arranging the paintings around the room with the care of a curator. She also prepares his morning coffee and slips scraps from her plate to Katze, the atelier's beautiful black cat.

⌣

Eventually, they finish. Vally raises her arms, reaches for a cloth and dabs her forehead, neck and chest. While she dresses, Egon takes his brushes – Vally knows them to be expensive ones made with sable-hair – to a bucket. He rubs soap over his hands, then pushes paint from each brush with his thumb.

While Egon's back is turned, Vally slips behind the heavy curtains.

'Ah, Egon, my boy, how was your session?' Vally hears the deep voice ask as the older artist enters the studio. She pauses.

'I didn't get a chance to thank her. Remind me of her name?'

'Walburga Neuzil. Vally. It's careless of you to forget. We owe our long-suffering models the courtesy, do we not, of remembering their names?'

'She proved as stubborn as a donkey.'

'But quite the beauty! Those wide eyes and that generous mouth . . . We can forgive women for their strong wills.'

'I see why you consider her your muse,' Egon says, relenting.

'My muse?' Gustav sounds amused. 'Vally is many things . . .'

Vally holds her breath. She is nobody's muse but her own.

'She seems to understand art, I mean,' Egon says. 'She has an intuition for it.'

'Vally is intelligent and insightful, despite her provincial background,'

Gustav replies. 'She injects a certain energy on to the page. She has been a comfort to me . . .' There's a pause. 'I don't have as much use for her these days, with all that's going on. I'll be sad to see her go.'

'You're letting her go?'

'You know how things are. I must find a new studio in the coming months. I've worked here for twenty years, but it's time to make a fresh start. Vally senses trouble and is clever enough to flee from it.'

'Then what?' Egon asks.

'I've told her I'll look out for her, whatever happens. But she refuses all generosity. She's an independent young thing, determined to make her own way in the world.'

'Where will she go?'

'Don't you worry about her. Vally is always one step ahead. She lives with her mother and siblings. She says she'll return often, but we can't count on that,' Gustav says.

'And you can't persuade her to stay?'

'I'm surprised at you,' Gustav says with warmth. 'Vally's not the type of young woman to be convinced of anything. She's not dissimilar to you, my boy – an old soul who knows her own mind. And good luck to any man who tries to persuade her otherwise.'

2

'How did you get those scars?' the artist asks, watching her from across the room. His charcoal stick is moving across the paper in front of him, as if with a mind of its own.

Vally touches the pink rivulets on her hips, traces them around her back.

'I've no idea.' She'd almost forgotten they were there.

'They're not painful?' he asks.

'They healed, like all my wounds, a long time ago.'

Vally is tired, has barely slept. She'd lain awake until the weak grey light of morning, nestled in between her tender-limbed little sisters, in the wide bed they share in an attic room in the workers' district of Favoriten. She's haunted by the fear that she has made herself an outcast by rejecting Gustav's hospitality and taking a waitressing job closer to home. Why turn down one job, where coins are handed over regularly for work she mostly enjoys, for another where the hours will be inconvenient, her feet will throb, and she will once again be at the mercy of an unscrupulous boss?

Gustav, at least, is fair, and he's admired by Viennese society, held in high regard. He paints the wives of rich men, bankers and sugar magnates; garnishes them in gold and glory. His work can be seen across

236

the city – there's his famous Beethoven Frieze, depicting three women, painted on the interior walls of the Secession building near the Nasch-markt, the one with an intricate dome like a golden cabbage; as well as his painting of the city's old opera house, the Burgtheater, as seen from the stage. In the audience, Gustav has included miniature por-traits of the capital's elite – a gentleman standing next to Vally had identified the Prime Minister and Johannes Brahms, a composer, then pointed his finger to a woman wearing pearls: Emperor Franz Joseph's mistress, the actress Katharina Schratt. Vally had admired her brazen beauty.

Vally's abrupt decision makes little sense in some ways, but she always trusts her instinct. She senses that things are changing and it is time to move on. Gustav may have been kind to her, but she refuses to be grateful. She has been lucky under his roof. He allows her to main-tain her dignity, most of the time, and she is mercifully not one of the models who has contributed to his growing brood. But she must not become complacent, or she'll find traces of gold at the base of her spine and on the soft skin between her thighs.

Besides, her mother's warnings have been ringing in her ears lately: 'Never rely on a man's generosity,' she'd counselled, having learnt the hard way. 'However tempting, however much you want to believe it'll last. Once they've had their fill, you're out. Hold back and move before you're pushed.'

'You couldn't have been born with them,' Egon persists, still fixated on her scars.

'You can be born with worse scars than these,' Vally replies, a puls-ing at her temples.

'Your parents never mentioned them?'

'As a child, I learnt not to ask too many questions, as I rarely got the answers I desired,' she says. 'My mother told me I'd entered the world with them, marked out by the Devil or an angel, depending on her mood. My sisters – Anna, Antonia, Marie and Berta – don't have them. Another time she told me I'd been branded by convicts, and would be again, if I didn't learn to behave. I've always quite liked that story. I suspect the truth is far more mundane – they were probably self-inflicted, perhaps after I pulled a pan of boiling water off the stove. If so, I'm glad my mind and my mother have kept the memory from me.'

'And your father, what does he say?' Egon asks.

'He always said very little. He was a schoolteacher, serious and steady. He seemed to be a respectable member of society, yet with me . . .' She trails off. 'He died unexpectedly when I was very young. His death had a devastating impact on my family. If I'd not left school and helped, the lot of us would've starved. I was eleven when we arrived in Vienna.'

Egon might act the impoverished artist, Vally thinks, but it's clear that he comes from a decent family and has enjoyed a respectable upbringing, with an education and food on the table. Vally was born in Tattendorf, just fifteen miles south of Vienna, but far from the capital in terms of its ideas, general intellect and wealth. Her mother, Thekla, and father, Josef, could never make money stick around. They only ever had a scrap above nothing. When he died, their situation deteriorated. You'd have thought five daughters would eat little more than birds, but their bellies were harder to fill than a purse on rent day, their mother often complained. She'd clean and take in washing by day, then repair clothes late into the night. Vally learnt to placate her. She adapted, became attentive, appeasing others before they knew they needed anything at all.

Her mother's dissatisfactions were the curse of being born female, the curse of being born poor, and the curse of being born at all. 'My mother once told me in a moment of clarity,' Vally says, thinking of her rough red hands, ' "Do not become a wife to a mediocre man, a mother to thankless children, or spend your days suffering as you perform the duties of the home. There's no dignity to my life. Take your chances wherever you see them, have courage, and don't ever be chastened for doing what you need to do in order to survive." ' Vally takes a breath. 'I intend to follow her advice. Marriage and motherhood isn't for me.'

'My father also died six years ago,' Egon says. 'When I was fourteen.

He tried hard to be a decent man, he was a stationmaster who wanted the best for his family – but we lived in fear. He was the one who taught me that appearances could be deceptive. He was very strict, and had rules for everything, before he lost his mind to the pox.'

'Syphilis?'

'Yes,' he says, reddening.

'I pity your mother, having to endure that,' she replies, her sympathy showing.

'He had the disease for years. It tormented me to see him like that. Now, I have this fear . . .' Egon begins, then tries again. 'I pray every day that it will never catch me.'

'All our fears, especially those we try to fight, catch up with us in the end,' Vally says. Egon's face falls. 'But I'm sure with you it'll be different,' she adds. 'Luck is on your side.'

' "Life is the farce we are all forced to endure," ' he musters. 'That's a line from Rimbaud's poetry.' He puts down his charcoal. 'Alas, the light is going. As for us, we've got tomorrow together and the day after that.'

He's satisfied with how the work is progressing, she can tell. But there's something Vally needs to say to him. 'Gus never makes his models wait, you know, before giving us some payment.'

She has sat for several sessions, and there has been no mention of reimbursement.

Egon stops. 'Forgive me, what was I thinking? My Uncle Leopold arrives tonight. He's the man with the money, and I must charm him into handing over another wad of it. Come to my apartment the day after tomorrow. It's basic, but you'll be comfortable enough. I'll pay you in full. It's an hour's walk from here.' Egon scribbles his address down and passes it over. 'Come early. We can work there from now on.'

Vally looks at the abstract lines of the artist's writing, nothing more than strange black marks to her. Art she can understand. Letters, she cannot. 'I . . .' she begins.

'Don't be late,' he says, with a smile. 'We have much to achieve together.'

3

March 1911

Vally is carrying a heavy stack of plates, silver cutlery balanced precariously on top, when she sees Egon Schiele again. He pushes open the double doors of the bistro where she has been working for the last few weeks and scans the room. He's unmissable – a tall, thin young man with wild hair and those piercing eyes. Blood crashes in Vally's ears, her chest loosens and the plates become dangerously slippery in her hands. She hadn't spared a thought for the artist, didn't care that she'd let him down. He wouldn't concern himself with her vanishing, she'd told herself. She had never expected to hear from him again.

Now Vally tries to return hurriedly to the kitchen before he sees her. A knife, slick with grease from a recent meal, slips over the top plate's ceramic rim and clatters to the floor. Customers raise their eyes. Egon follows the noise. Suddenly, he's beside her. He bends down to retrieve the knife, then straightens up to look at her. She can see the tiny, dashing movements of his eyes as they search hers, appealing for something she can't quite comprehend.

'Watch yourself!' her patron, a stocky man with a brick-coloured neck, implores. 'No more broken plates today, *Fräulein*, if you please.' He gestures to the swinging doors that lead into the kitchen.

Egon and Vally stare at each other expectantly. Egon places the knife back on Vally's pile of plates.

'Thank you,' the owner says. 'Now, we haven't got all day.'

'I've been looking everywhere for you,' Egon says.

'May I help you?' the owner asks, his tone needling. His eyes fix on Vally. 'What trouble have you got yourself into now?'

No words come to her lips. Customers continue to stare, exchange glances and shuffle their chairs. Vally's throat is flushed with heat.

'Is there a problem?' her boss asks, louder. The owner is not a large man, but he usually gets what he wants. He tries to pull Vally away, but his touch throws her arm out of balance and the stack she is carrying tips, then goes crashing down.

The broken plates, the cutlery and half-eaten food explode across the floor. Vally freezes, but the customers erupt with a ripple of cries, gawking, talking hurriedly to the person next to them. Egon steps over the jagged splinters and reaches out a hand.

The heat of his touch is the energy Vally needs. She's jolted into action and propels herself, by his side, to the door, the floor crunching underfoot.

'Mark my words, this is coming from your wages!' her boss shouts after them.

But Egon and Vally are already outside. Vally's thin-soled boots, the holes in the bottom lined with newspaper, hammer the cobbles as they pick up speed.

'Reprobates! The pair of you! Don't show your face here again,' the owner bellows from the doorway.

They run as far and as fast as their energy allows, down the street until they are out of sight, then through a set of imposing wrought-iron gates into a leafy park. Egon steers Vally towards a patch of oak trees on the far side, where they collapse beside a wide trunk. Vally is out of breath, light-headed.

'My wages,' she says, pained. 'That's the second time you've deprived me of money. I cannot afford you in my life, Egon Schiele.'

Egon steadies his breathing, smiling at her. 'And I can't afford for you *not* to be in mine,' he says, taking Vally's hands in his. 'But where the hell did you get to? You disappeared! I looked for you every day. Gustav was as surprised as I was when you didn't show up as planned. At first, I was angry, then I was worried. Now I can only say I'm over-joyed to see you.'

Vally doesn't reject his touch.

'You cost me my job!'

There's something about this strange man.

'Earn your wages as my model,' Egon says, pulling a fistful of notes from his pocket and offering them to her with a wide, unselfconscious smile. 'I promise to be a more charming boss than your previous one.' Vally screws up her face. 'This is for the work you've already done. More than twice the standard fee.'

Vally takes the notes. She counts them, removes two of the smaller bills, hesitates, peels off a third, then gives the rest back to him. 'I suppose I owe you for letting you down.'

'Another girl did end up taking your place. She was remarkable. Striking, dark, with better posture,' he teases. 'A little on the skinny side, though.'

Vally stands, brushing grass off her skirts. 'There's somewhere else I need to be.'

'Don't go.' Egon stands with her. 'I'm not trying to upset you.'

'Please don't assume you have the power to do that.'

'My art wasn't the same without you. I need you,' he pleads.

It's uncomfortable to hear him talk this way. Most men her age, and even those much older, are better at keeping their emotions under control.

'What do you say?' he continues.

'We're all the same to you, aren't we?' She raises an eyebrow.

Men such as Egon Schiele can never truly respect women in her situation – girls without education, who have to shut up to survive.

They mistake silence for consent, for willingness, for a transfer of power. And they take what they can until they eventually fulfil the expectations of their class.

He shakes his head. 'You, my dear Vally, are radically different.'

4

March 1911

Vally arrives at an elegant building with a grey and white facade. She hopes this is the place. Egon had described the location of his studio, Vally subtly pressing him for details along the route that she'd be able to recognize. She has arrived early and approaches the door, presses the buzzer third from the bottom, as instructed, unable to decipher the surname listed there. She waits, her fingers numb. She doesn't have gloves – leather, cotton or otherwise – to protect them.

If this isn't the right address, and she fails once more to show up for their appointment, she's certain he won't bother looking for her again. It would be the end of whatever is developing between them. She feels nervous, as if she is giving too much away. She's about to pull the ruby ribbon out of her hair when Egon flings open the door. She smiles in relief, before a young woman with copper-red hair, a shade fairer than her own, steps past him, kissing Egon roughly on the cheek as she goes, squeezing his arm with something approaching anger. Vally steps back.

'You ask too much of me, really you do,' the young woman says to him, before she flounces away. 'Get the likes of *her* to do your dirty work from now on.'

'Ignore Gertrude,' he says to Vally with a shrug. 'She's always like that.'

They climb the stairs. Once inside his modest, sparsely furnished apartment, there's little relief from the cold. Vally had been hoping to get close to a roaring fire, to warm herself through. But the artist admits that he only adds fuel to the *kachelofen* when his models arrive. He busies himself arranging twists of newspaper, a piece or two of coal and thin strips of wood in the grate. 'It'll take a while to warm up,' he says.

'So that girl was here for pleasure rather than the business of modelling?'

'Gerti? Oh, no. She rarely models for me any more,' he says with a frown, lifting a stack of drawings from his desk and passing them over. 'However much I beg.'

Vally's eyes wander over the pieces. She's assaulted by the fierce energy she saw emanating off the young woman as she blazed from the building.

'She does it to punish me. She's unhappy that she doesn't see me as often as she used to,' Egon continues. 'We used to be very close, but things have changed – you know how it can be.'

Vally is spellbound by the confidence, coquettishness and confrontation that leap off the page. 'These are exquisite,' she says at the sight of the woman's nude body, staged in dramatic poses that show off the taut line between her belly button and pubic hair.

'And she knows it! Gerti doesn't like it that I use other models, despite her words at the door earlier. She thinks everyone else is inferior,' he says, laughing.

'Perhaps she expects marriage?'

Egon stops laughing. 'I thought I'd mentioned it already – Gerti is my sister. And much as she'd like things to remain as they were when we were children, they've changed. I have a new life, new friends, new models . . .' He takes a step closer to Vally.

She is even more disconcerted than before. There is something so brooding between Egon and this Gertrude – witnessed at the door, evidenced in his art – that Vally had felt sure of a love affair. This jealousy and intensity between brother and sister is more troubling.

'Has she always been willing to pose for you in this way?'

'It's perfectly normal for artists to use family members as models, you know,' Egon says. 'Besides, nobody knows it's her. See how she turns her face away?'

'But she's entirely nude.'

'She's my sister. We grew up together. There's nothing untoward.'

'The intimacy on the page is . . .'

'It was her idea. She wanted to do whatever it took to make me a great artist.'

'You are certainly the most talked-about man in Vienna,' Vally concedes.

'I know what they say about me. But I'm not depraved, a pervert or a pornographer. This is what's expected.' He holds up the drawings. 'I was sixteen the first time I used a model who wasn't one of my sisters or my mother. There have been hundreds since – beautiful, ugly, ones so close to giving birth I could see the baby moving beneath their stomach. Don't think I haven't appreciated every one, that I don't value what they entrust me with. And yes, I do want to shock the world – that's why I paint myself in such challenging poses – but it's the pursuit of art, not sex, that drives me. I didn't make the rules. I give the men of Vienna what they desire, what they'll pay for. It's not my fault there's so much hypocrisy.'

'I always defend your work, if that counts for anything,' Vally says.

'If I radicalize society, push its sensitivities a step too far, if I make mistakes, all I am saying is that they are not mine alone.' Egon's defences are up.

'Be careful, that's all,' Vally says. 'They want to see you fall.'

'I know,' Egon sighs. 'I'll watch my step. I don't expect anyone to understand. Now, if you want to leave to protect your reputation, I won't take it personally.'

They look at each other for a moment, and Vally considers her choices.

'I'll stay, but I hope you don't expect me to take my coat off in this temperature.'

'Then let me warm you up, as best I can.'

Egon takes her hands and cups them in his own. He blows on them.

'Where do you want me?' she asks, looking for the best spot in the dimly lit room. There's but a weak flicker of heat and Vally can still see her breath. She blows a tunnel of it towards him, watching it swirl and sink.

'Wherever you'll be comfortable,' Egon says.

'Don't worry about my comfort. Do you want me on my back? Or my knees?'

Vally sticks out her bottom. This charade is how she keeps her distance.

'Let's start with sketches,' he says. He takes a pencil from a carton on the shelf.

'Until it's time for me to take my clothes off?'

The lead snaps against the paper. Egon brushes it to one side, then takes another pencil. 'There's something about you, Vally. You make me nervous. The other models I've found who come here ... they're not as confident, not as bold.'

Vally considers his words. Her eyes roam the sketches pinned to the walls, showing girls in different poses – limbs truncated, torsos headless, eyes blank. 'You should make all of them bold. For what good is any woman if she doesn't have the power to surprise you?'

⌣

Later, Egon places a small lamp close to Vally's body, which is positioned across a mattress on the floor. It casts smooth shadows on the wall and she traces her outline with her finger while Egon sharpens yet another pencil. The space has warmed over the past few hours, and Vally has gingerly removed layer after layer. For the last sketch, Egon has climbed a ladder to get the most interesting perspective on her body.

'I don't suppose you want to stay longer?' Egon asks as Vally returns to her clothes and gathers her things to leave. 'I have cheeses and wine.'

'I'm meeting a friend. I don't want to be late for him,' she says.

The truth is, she's planning to go home to cook for her sisters.

'Let me walk you downstairs, at least. I'll leave with you and see if my friends Anton and Erwin are in their usual haunts. They're always keen on beer and billiards.'

They reach the bottom of several flights of stairs but Egon does not open the door. He just stands there, looking at her. 'Vally . . .' he begins.

She can't bear this feeling that is brewing in her – this growing pull towards him.

She puts a finger to his lips to quiet the words she knows are coming.

5

March 1911

At one of their sessions later that month, Egon entices Vally to stay later than normal by producing cutlets and a carafe of wine he has saved. She's hungry, so accepts, but insists that she prepare the meal. She tenderizes the flesh, seasons it, chops root vegetables, sets a pan to boil, and moves around his basic kitchen, wiping grease from the counter and laying the table for two. The cause for this excess is that Egon has received his allowance from his Uncle Leopold once more. She had noticed a shift in him – he had been in a peculiar mood, generous and brazen one moment, then prone to melancholy the next – and now she knows why.

'It's complicated with my uncle,' he tells her. 'But tonight, with you,' Egon says, taking Vally by the shoulders, 'I want to celebrate.'

She attends to the sizzling meat. Egon leans in, sniffing. 'It's already dead, you know. You've almost blackened them.'

'I wouldn't know how to do it any other way,' Vally defends herself, sliding the meat from pan to plate.

He finishes the food without further complaint. Afterwards Egon and Vally remain at the table, talking, laughing, making their way to the bottom of the carafe. He tells her about his escapades at art school, clashes with his tutor, being expelled from the *Akademie*, forming the

Neukunstgruppe with a band of similarly minded artists, just days after his nineteenth birthday. They now shun him because they're jealous of his talent.

She asks him about his heart. Has it ever been broken?

'No,' he says. 'But the doctors say I have a weak one.'

'There must have been at least one woman who got beneath your skin?'

'Nobody ever came close.'

Vally doesn't believe him. She observes this strange, animated man and his habits. She has never known anyone like him.

At midnight, just as she's about to leave for her shared bed on the other side of the city, Egon asks for one last sketch. Vally wants to go home. She's at the door, but he pushes it closed playfully. She raises an eyebrow, then settles on to some cushions. She hears his pencil, the lull of the lead. She rests her eyes. Just for a moment.

⤜

Hours later, as light transforms the dimensions of the room and the birds begin to sing, Vally sits up. She is cold and cannot place where she is. Then she sees Egon, still sketching.

'I've been waiting for you to open your eyes. I've done some of my best work.' Egon rises and stretches, twisting his back until it pops. 'I drew all night. Look.' He shows her pages and pages of line drawings.

'Why didn't you wake me?' Vally asks, pulling away.

'I didn't want to disturb you.'

'My sisters will be worried,' she says, then looks at the drawings more closely. The sleeping woman in them seems exposed, vacant, and it sickens her that she has been seen and captured in this way. She pushes them back at him. 'These are hideous, Egon,' she says.

Egon searches the drawings, failing to comprehend. Vally is heading towards the door as he approaches the green-tiled *kachelofen*. She turns at the sound of its hinges.

'What are you doing?'

'My art has been burned before,' he says, 'for much less justification than this.'

Vally rushes over and pulls what she can from the flames. 'Why would you care what I think? You could have sold them to some collector, regardless.'

His lowered eyes and pink cheeks make him appear vulnerable. Vally strokes his face, transferring the soot from her fingers. It mixes with tears falling from his eyes. She has never seen a man cry. It is baffling. Egon confuses and infuriates her. But Vally sees an openness in him that's disarming. She lets instinct overtake her and kisses him. Egon succumbs to her, his head in her hands. She grabs a handful of his hair and pulls it back, places her lips on his exposed throat. His eyes are wide and unblinking. Vally unbuttons his trousers with her free hand and reaches inside. She's not a virgin. She lost her so-called purity at fourteen, days after she became legally of age.

Egon flinches. 'Slowly, slow,' he pleads. Men aren't used to women asserting their desire. Vally isn't meek, conjuring up deliberate coyness the way other girls do in order to seduce. She guides Egon into pleasuring her in ways he would never have considered, never expected. Her body is powerful, muscular. In these moments, Vally feels lost, but wonderfully so, in a world that echoes with pleasure. It's her confidence, his vulnerability. Vally is conqueror.

6

April 1911

'Pack your bags, Vally. I can't take it any more,' Egon says, storming into the studio. He has returned from a mysterious meeting in a foul mood. The door slams and the volume of his voice is uncharacteristically loud. Vally has her back to him, her hands in greasy water, washing the morning's dishes. She spins around to get the measure of his anger and flinches as he kicks a chair across the room. For the last month, she has modelled for him and he has paid her promptly. She has enough to survive on, having given what she can spare to her mother and her sisters. She's running low on *papier poudré*, but refuses to spend a thing on herself. She has been staying at Egon's apartment more often, a few nights a week – much to the relief of her sisters, who have more space to themselves in the bed– but is baffled by the suggestion that what she has could fill a travel bag.

Egon grabs her by the shoulders. 'In Vienna there are shadows,' he says. 'The city is black and everything is done by rote. Don't you feel it? The walls closing in? The skies sinking upon us?' He gives her a strangled look. 'Aren't you exhausted by this unrelenting city and its grotesque falsities?'

He examines her puckered fingers. Rain drips from his overcoat.

'The painting's sale didn't go through, then?' she asks.

'This has nothing to do with Arthur Roessler failing to sell my work. It has everything to do with what we're up against. Prejudice. Narrow-mindedness. Those bastards who call themselves my fellow artists. Frauds, all of them! They pray I'll fail, that I'll sink into obscurity.' Vally moves the glassware draining on the counter out of his reach. She knew a bitter mood was gnawing at him, but hadn't guessed the root of his agitation. It sounds as if something, or someone, has finally caught up with him. 'This god-forsaken city suffocates me,' he continues. 'I must see new things.'

Egon runs a hand back and forth across his head. Vally passes him a dry kitchen cloth and he wipes it over his forehead and neck, loosening his tie.

'Where would we go?' she asks.

'Why not Krumau? It's only a few hours from here. It's where my mother was born, where she lived until she married my father. I spent summers there as a young man and I went back last year with Erwin and Anton. My aunt and her husband used to live there, too – the pair of them passed away suddenly within a few months of each other just last year. But the people still know me. There's a magical river and a castle. You'll understand when you see it.'

Vally has never had the privilege of questioning whether she'd be better off somewhere else. She didn't come to Vienna because she fancied a change of scenery, or to indulge any fantasies of escape, but because she and her mother had to find work.

She returns the upended chair to its legs, pushes it under the table. She brushes crumbs off the surface with one hand and catches them with the other. 'I've spent my life trying to escape from such places,' Vally says finally. 'They're full of small-minded people with tedious, conformist ways. I hate to say it, Egon, but I don't think they will appreciate the likes of us.'

'You don't understand. This is our chance,' he continues, 'to live without interruption.'

'Nobody disturbs us here. You've hardly introduced me to your friends or patrons. Let alone your family.'

'My friends are children. My patrons only care about money.'

'It helps that they have money,' she replies. Vally rubs her shoulder. Her class rarely bothered her until she met Egon. His ignorance of his own advantages astounds her. She wonders just how much trouble this man has got himself into.

'Look,' he says. 'I want to live a simple life. Making my art, in nature. Vienna is dirty, Krumau is surrounded by forests. We can be ourselves there. Just you and me.'

She doesn't want to accept his invitation so easily; she has conceded so much of herself to him already. She isn't sure what's developing between them – perhaps it is nothing more than a short-lived affair, the kind young men have every day.

Not for the first time, Egon mistakes Vally's silence, her unhurried thoughtfulness, for some form of blessing. He looks at her, a smile of anticipation on his face. 'Come with me,' he insists. 'My art has never been better. Imagine everything we can do, *together*.'

She rolls the word around in her mind. Egon has many models at his disposal. She'll be entering his apartment as a black-haired one leaves, or there'll be golden strands on the cushions, or other evidence left lying around – items of intimate clothing, smears of rouge, two glasses by the sink.

Vally doesn't care. He seems to need her. Besides, she'd never allow herself to be jealous. But still, the thought of a meaningful bond between her and Egon, a shared agreement, some mutual adventure, excites her. And yet . . .

'You go,' she says, finally. She sees disappointment cross his face. 'Let me know when you're back in Vienna.'

7

May 1911

Vally's family has moved again, to a smaller, sparser apartment, and Vally has to jostle her sisters for space in the bed each night.

'Find a new boyfriend,' Berta complains. 'We sleep better when you're not here.'

Vally's mother is feeling the weight of her thirty-eight years, and is almost cross-eyed with exhaustion. Do other daughters feel as Vally does, the younger woman wonders? That they want to be a shoulder for their mothers to lean on, to offer respite and hold the worry at bay; yet she also wants to flee, to live her own life, to embrace her future and never look back. To do one is to deny the other, and Vally feels crushed with the weight of it all. For now, she resolves to tend to her siblings and bring money into the home.

Vally denies – daily – that she has made a mistake in refusing Egon's invitation to Krumau. He would only have treated her like an unpaid maid; a woman to wash for him, prepare his meals, model whenever the mood took him, and relinquish herself to him when he needed it. No, it wouldn't do. She imagines him there, in Bohemia, then shakes off the thought. Vally has things to do in Vienna. She has people to meet, and it's about time she found fresh work.

She wouldn't know how to reach Egon, anyway. It's better this way.

～

A couple of weeks later, Vally knocks on Gustav's door and he embraces her warmly. She was only passing through the neighbourhood and thought she'd say hello.

'Vally, sweet pea, how tantalizing to see you again. You've been well, I trust?'

'I've been meaning to visit, I just . . .'

'You're here now, that's what matters. Come in. Look at the changes we've made.'

Vally looks around the new studio. It is modern – dark-wood walls, with Japanese furniture, flowers and other evidence of a woman's touch. Vally wonders which one.

'See all this work I've been occupying myself with.' He looks to her for approval.

Vally approaches the canvases that line the walls.

'I like this one,' she says, pointing to an unfinished painting showing an elegant woman sketched in the centre of the frame, detailed wallpaper in the background.

'I suspect it will be one of my favourites, too,' Gustav says. 'This one I intend to paint in muted tones, dusty pinks and reds, none of that gold.'

'How is Frau Bloch-Bauer?'

'She complains, but she's well enough. But we mustn't waste our breath on her. Now tell me, how's our companion, Herr Schiele?'

'He's taken a trip to Krumau, to escape Vienna,' Vally says.

'And you chose not to flee the city with him?'

'He'll find some other girl to model for him there.'

'He told me he'd tried to persuade you,' Gustav says. 'Fools, the pair of you.'

Vally tries to swallow the rising feeling. 'There was nothing to be gained by me going with him,' she says.

'And there's nothing wrong with letting go a little, either, living your life. Lower your defences, Vally, or you might miss out on gentle pleasures. What is there to keep you in Vienna anyhow?'

'Plenty of things,' she says. 'My family.'

'I see,' Gustav says. 'That reminds me, Egon asked me to pass a message on.' He rifles through papers, pulls out a letter. 'Here it is.' He clears his throat. ' "Please relay a message to Fräulein Neuzil, if you see her, which I pray that you will. I'm planning a party in Krumau, the final weekend of the month. It's imperative that she take leave of Vienna and join me. She's welcome to stay with me for as long as she wants. She'll have no problems with directions once she arrives. I'm well known to the locals. It is my greatest wish that she accept this invitation. See what you can do to persuade her." '

Gustav looks up at her. 'It might do you good to have a change of scenery.'

'But that's tomorrow! I can't possibly drop everything for Herr Schiele.'

'Egon possesses a phenomenal talent,' Gustav says gently. 'I've never seen anything like it in more than thirty years as an artist. He's a true visionary. And you, Vally, you complement him.' She tries to protest. 'I'm not saying you should let your guard down entirely. That would be unwise. But allow him to entertain you, however briefly. It could be good for both of you.'

'My mother needs me.'

'A young woman should spread her wings, experience the world. Your mother will still be here when you return. She'll be no better off if you make yourself miserable.'

8

26 May 1911

I t's an unseasonably hot day for late spring. Vally had taken the train out of Vienna in the cool of early morning. During the journey, sweat pools between her breasts, threatening to leave a mark on her freshly laundered dress. Now it's early evening, and she has tried to present herself in the most appealing way, her hair tended to, but the heat has ruined everything. She has never travelled alone, never packed a bag nor bought a ticket to an unknown destination. It has taken every penny she has. She steps off the train and looks down the platform. Klimt wrote ahead to let Egon know the time of her arrival, but she worries he'll have lost track of things, busy as he'll be, collecting barrels and bottles for the evening ahead.

She waits, the minutes passing. Passengers disperse. There's another woman standing at the end of the platform. Vally recognizes her as Egon's sister – that fiery spark of a woman she encountered at Egon's apartment. She has a case and a parasol and keeps turning around with impatience. After several more minutes, she sets off alone. Vally decides to follow her, for they must surely be heading to the same party.

They begin the descent into the town when suddenly a man rushes past Vally and stops the woman with a hand on her shoulder. They talk for a few moments, Egon's sister scowling at him. Vally now recognizes the man as Anton, one of Egon's closest friends, who has stopped by the apartment on a few rare occasions.

She follows the pair as they continue to descend the steps leading away from the station, towards the high walls of the old town, which nestles around the snaking form of an ancient, rolling river. Vally hears the Vltava before she sees it. When it comes into view, the sinking sun glints off its bold curves. Egon's friend doesn't falter as he leads the way through the enclosed town. Even at dusk, it is a striking place: tight stacks of dense stone and brick, interlocking ochre and carmine, pinks and pale green. Men drink in the many taverns, their energy spilling out into the streets along with their beer. Smoke carries the scent of mouth-watering food, with pungent spices Vally cannot identify. Bow meets string, and the noise lifts. Vally understands the sounds of Vienna – its screeches and hisses, clangs and shouts – but these new rhythms unsettle her.

As they pass a fountain, Vally spots an old woman begging on her knees, her eyes cast down. Vally delivers her the only coin she has left in her pocket.

Women with the lace collars she'd once worn in the countryside hurry their children home, wanting to get behind closed doors before night falls fully. Egon's sister and her companion move on and finally they arrive at the house, on the edge of the Vltava. The gathered crowd is in a rambunctious mood, barrels have already been opened and laughter erupts.

Egon embraces his sister and hands his friend Anton a glass of wine. Then he spots her, following close behind them. 'Vally!' he says, his eyes glinting with pleasure. Egon looks improved in Krumau. His clothes are looser, his form more relaxed, with the rugged lick of colour that comes with spending more time outdoors. 'You made it! I'm delighted – and a little surprised. I thought you'd stand me up again. Now, come and meet my sister.'

Vally listens as Egon introduces her, braced against the piercing gaze of this entitled young woman. She won't give her the satisfaction of recognition. So Egon's sister takes a glass from Anton's hand, and drinks it down.

❧

Inside the cottage there is music and dancing. Egon pulls her into the centre of the space and passes her a drink. There are five chiselled farmhands there, young men her age and older, who Egon introduces as his cousins. They are strapping and self-conscious; they watch the party with wary eyes, whispering to each other. Vally decides to dance with the youngest, a bashful boy whose hands seem as if greased with butter, he is so out of place. He rejoins his brothers, smiling, proud to have taken to the floor. An ash-haired young man pulls Vally towards him and whispers in her ear. She bursts out laughing. This man, Willy, is whippet-thin and his eyes dazzle. Over the course of the evening, he's never far from Egon's orbit, Vally notices, always on hand to top up his glass, roll a cigarette or change the gramophone record. Vally likes him. He dances with a liquidity to his spine that she has not seen before in a man. He's quick to laugh at her jokes, even quicker to tell a crude one of his own. Then Vally is taken by the hand and spun by the magnetic Moa Mandu, a cabaret dancer with masses of untameable hair and the daring modern style of dress that comes straight from Paris. Her eyes crinkle with warmth and laughter as she twirls Vally across the room, into the hands of Erwin, her partner, Egon's dear friend. Moa curtsies with a playful pout and then pirouettes for him. He responds with a set of jagged mimes, for which he is famous across Vienna. Two of Egon's friends, fellow artists from the *Akademie*, try to mimic his moves – unsuccessfully – and he repeats the performance, to show them how it's done. One of their girlfriends passes Vally another drink, and she manages to take a large mouthful before she's pushed back into the throng.

Egon appears by her side, grinning, but she can't hear what he's saying. He pulls her closer, and she nuzzles into his neck. He grips her around the waist and sways with her, in time to the music. She softens against him, feels his muscles beneath his shirt, then plucks the cigarette from his fingers and lets the peaty taste filter to her lungs.

'I'm so glad I came,' she says. His sister is watching them from the corner.

'I can't hear you?' he replies, his lips brushing her ear.

'I said, there's nowhere else I'd rather be.'

Vally sees herself reflected in his eyes. He takes her face in his hands. 'So you'll stay?'

She squeezes his wrists in agreement, and he kisses her, there, in front of everyone.

9

June 1911

Vally tries to imagine this space filled with the two of them – his sketchbook, her small pots and powders on the ledge, the table set for two, her dress hanging behind the door. She imagines sipping coffee, her feet tucked up, in the wicker chair each morning, Egon's easel positioned to harness the light, the comforting silence between them.

It would have been hard to imagine such solitude in the immediate aftermath of the party. Egon's sister, for one, thought she'd been invited for an extended stay, so had been quite put out – Vally later learnt – to arrive in the midst of such a gathering. There had been some awkward conversations between the siblings, with the result that Gertrude had decided to return to Vienna the following day, in the company of Egon's friend Anton.

Vally steps outside, into the shadows of the overgrown garden that runs the length of a stone wall.

'We'll clear these weeds,' Egon says, coming out to join her. 'Cut the nettles and thistles, fight back the scrub. We can grow our own vegetables, if you want?'

Vally won't admit how unsettling this is, this ominous calm that's creeping in.

'Look, wild sunflowers!' she says, crouching to pull back weeds. 'The soil is thin, but they're pushing through. It's better that we give them a chance to grow.'

Clearly Egon has already made quite an impression on the local population over the weeks that he has been living here. Older men take a detour from their usual routes to stop at the red cottage. They stand by the gate. 'And this must be little Gertrude Schiele, grown into such a strapping young woman.' They open their arms wide to Vally. 'You were such a terror, too, as we remember. God bless your long-suffering mother.'

Vally holds herself apart, and does not contradict them.

Egon laughs, kindly. 'Your eyes must be failing you . . .'

'Ah, your wife!' they say, chuckling with friendly understanding.

'This is my friend, Fräulein Neuzil. She helps with the administration of my art.'

Vally notices their apprehension.

'Your male friends won't be accompanying you this year?'

'Herr Osen and Herr Peschka have just left. They may return in a week or two.'

'And your mother?' they ask. 'It's been several years since she last came. Perhaps it's that she doesn't feel the same draw to the place, now that Kateřina is no longer with us.'

'Mother lives in Vienna with my sisters.'

'And how are they?' the locals ask, looking at Vally with suspicious eyes.

'Melanie works as a clerk on the railways, so one of us, at least, has followed Father's wishes. Gertrude is modelling clothes for a department store.'

'Are your sisters married?'

'Melanie will remain a spinster for ever. Gertrude's too young to be thinking of marriage. As for me, I feel no need to think of such things yet.'

'It's never too soon to settle down, set up a steady life and start a family. Your mother was seventeen, was she not, when she married your father?'

'An artist's life requires some of those old rules to be broken,' Egon smiles.

Egon relays such updates several times a day, then bids the locals farewell. Vally observes the subtle dance on their faces. Are they wondering how can it be that a once respectable family has fallen so far? A woman widowed, with an artist for a son and unmarried daughters . . .

During these conversations, Vally feels suspicious eyes on her, weighing her up, wondering. Egon shrugs her worries away. 'People aren't concerned about such things. The locals are not so old-fashioned and they'll never know we share a bed. They'll imagine you're the maid.' Vally regards him. 'Besides, we're doing no harm.'

⤺

Weeks pass, and the locals still walk by as they used to, but they rarely raise a hand or start a conversation. Instead, they watch the artist at work in the garden, his easel set up on the grass and Egon before it, as if he were the captain at the wheel of a grand ship. Vally models, covering herself when they appear. She is attuned to the locals' intolerance. They seldom address her, but when they do, there's ice laced into their words. Egon they can forgive, just about. They have done so in the past – when he has come to visit with his friends, students from the *Akademie*, they have indulged his boyish larks. They know him and his ways, saw how his poor mother despaired, and have high hopes that he'll grow out of it.

But with her, it's different. Look how she walks, as if she thinks she belongs here, they seem to gossip. Look at her buying alcohol. Has she no shame? *We see them laughing together*, Vally imagines them whispering. *She only washes one set of bedsheets in the river.*

Egon refuses to acknowledge that they're making themselves susceptible to criticism. He continues to work – planning another party to which he sends intricate invitations to all his friends. Of course, he will sleep off the aftermath without a care in the world. He won't go to church on a Sunday and he's unconcerned when the town's schoolchildren start showing up at the garden, kindled by gossip they have heard from their parents.

Groups of girls hide at a respectable distance, sharp eyes peeping over the bushes, watching Egon. Vally often glimpses a swaying plait or the pleats of a skirt. Soon, in the same way foxes gain ground, they become brazen. They throw small stones. She hears giggling. By the end of the month, two girls have garnered the courage to stand, then sit, behind Egon, their eyes on him as he works.

'They're harmless,' he repeats to Vally when they're alone.

She passes a darning needle through a hole in his sock.

'They're young, that's all I'm saying,' she says.

'They're but a few years younger than you,' he replies. 'Were you not intrigued by the forbidden at that age?'

'Young girls have unpredictable minds,' she warns.

'You're forgetting that I grew up with Gerti.'

'Oh, yes,' she says. Vally pricks her finger. It draws blood.

Summer swoons in and the two girls return day after day after day as the heat intensifies. One is tall and willowy, with glossy dark hair; the other, shorter, is still chubby with a sullen face. Vally watches them from the cottage as she secures her hair. Their flat eyes make her uneasy. They don't see Vally standing by the window, for they're not searching her out. They're watching Egon work.

These girls are trouble, she can feel it. Vally resolves to make her feelings clearer to Egon. She thinks of the sunflowers she unearthed – the small, unfurled buds. She waters them daily now. Finally she has something that she can care for, that she's invested in.

'The little birds have been coming into our garden again, in search of breadcrumbs,' Egon says that evening over dinner.

'You must send them away, Egon,' Vally replies. 'And whatever you do, don't draw them. If word gets out, you'll get us both into trouble.'

'They're just schoolchildren, Vally, don't be so ferocious. Remember how it was when we were thirteen or fourteen and bored to death? Don't you recall the terrible passions that tortured us at that age? How else are they to entertain themselves?'

'So we must provide the scandal? Think what they might be saying to their parents.'

'They came, uninvited,' he insists. 'The locals know such things. They wouldn't be as idiotic as to think we actively sought this.'

Vally envies Egon his certainty. People are, she has discovered, more often than not, ignorant, threatened by what they don't understand or cannot appreciate.

'It's the children, if anyone, who'll be punished,' Egon persists.

How can he be so stupid?

She could leave Krumau, and start afresh. But the truth is, she wants to remain by Egon's side. She wants to nurture what's growing within her. She just needs him to be more cautious. But still the girls come, day after day after day, as the petals of her sunflowers unfurl.

10

August 1911

'Wake up, Vally,' Egon urges, shaking her shoulder. 'I need you to run an errand.'

'Really, must I be disturbed?' she complains from the small bed they share, turning her back on him. It's late afternoon, and she has been trying, unsuccessfully, to nap. Her head had been pounding all morning while she was doing laundry, and now this, just as she's finally managed to rest . . .

'I have work that must be sent urgently to Vienna.'

'Go yourself.' The clouds are low and dark, and she can't face the walk.

'There's more work to be done. I'm in the middle of it.'

She sits up, the blood pulsing in her head in a fresh, ugly rhythm.

'Can't it wait until tomorrow?'

'Roessler's expecting my latest drawings and watercolours, for which he'll pay handsomely. We're low on funds. Dangerously so. We can't exist on thin air,' he says, with impatience. 'In here,' he adds, tapping the thick postal tube secured with string under his arm, 'there are some early sketches for a large oil painting I want to begin and other works I hope he can sell. He'll gauge the appetite from my buyers and send me an advance. I've included a note. Tell them at the district office it's for Vienna,' Egon continues. 'I've scraped together enough to pay for postage. You can be there and back in less than an hour.'

Vally laces her boots and pulls on her shawl. She closes the door behind her without saying goodbye. The sky thickens above her.

'Wait!' Egon waves after her. She stops. He comes running with an umbrella.

She smiles, softening. Perhaps he does care, after all.

'They mustn't get wet, whatever happens,' he says, patting the parcel.

～

At the district postal office, Vally stands in line. Her feet are sore in boots that pinch and all she wants to do is sleep. But she must wait for the cashier to attend to the half-dozen townspeople in front of her, as the queue grows behind. The man behind the counter has no intention of hurrying.

'To Vienna,' Vally says eventually, passing the postal tube over the counter. She searches in her pockets for Egon's *kronen* then looks up, aware that the cashier has not taken her offering. 'Please,' she adds, with a tight smile. The cashier examines the address that Egon has included. His eyes are heavy. He turns them to Vally and looks her up and down.

'This is a delivery request from Herr Schiele, the artist?' he asks. 'The one who throws noisy parties that echo across the Vltava?'

'Yes, that's him,' Vally replies.

'And what's inside?'

'Artworks,' she says, letting a note of irritation enter her voice. 'For his patrons in Vienna.'

'And what is the nature of this so-called art?'

'Drawings, watercolours depicting people, the fields, the hills. This beautiful town.'

'Open it,' he demands.

Vally stares at him. 'I can't do that.'

'Then I'm unable to process this request.'

'But it's urgent,' she says, recalling Egon's words. Their financial situation is precarious. The cashier opens a drawer, takes out a pair of scissors. 'You have no right!' she objects.

But he has already cut the string. He pulls out several works of varying sizes. His eyes rush over the contents, eager to take it all in. He removes sheet after sheet, letting them drop on to the counter in front of him. The customers behind Vally start murmuring and surge forward, their faces animated. Vally can see drawings Egon has made of her, in her petticoats and stockings, and more erotic ones in which she has removed her underclothes.

'Put them away,' she instructs.

But the cashier is enjoying himself too much. 'This is *you*, isn't it?' he says, looking from the page to her bosom. Vally hears little gasps behind her.

'It's art,' she says.

'Pornography!' the cashier replies.

'Only if you have a corrupt mind.'

'It is your artist who's perverted.'

There's a loud ripple of agreement from those in the room.

'I will report you,' Vally snaps back.

'No, I'll report *you*,' he sneers. 'The pair of you should be locked up for this!'

Vally feels her desperation rising.

'And what is this?' The man holds up a drawing of the girls who have been spending time with Egon in the garden, the 'little birds', as he calls them. They are sitting next to one another, arm in arm, the hems of their pale-blue dresses raised. Vally has never seen it before.

'I know these girls. They're children. From respectable families. They are not whores for your artist to paint and sell on to his patrons in Vienna.'

'I, I . . .' Vally is unable to find the words to defend Egon.

The anger of the people around her is suddenly deafening.

Then the cashier drops another sheet as if it has burned him – it is one of Egon's self-portraits. In it, the artist is naked and masturbating. It falls from the counter to the floor and lies there, for everyone to observe. The sudden silence is cavernous. In the portrait, Egon grips his swollen penis, a finger held over its orange tip, a wild look in his eyes.

'Shame! Shame on you!' the man splutters.

Vally lunges at the man. She rams her fingers into the puckered flesh of his throat, and he falls off his stool. She's dragged across the counter, across the drawings, the customers swelling around her, pulling at Vally, shouting and spitting.

'Whore!' the man shouts as he regains his balance. 'You and that Schiele are scoundrels. You're not welcome here. We're a peaceful town, with decent people. You are not only corrupting each other, you are corrupting our children. The magistrate will hear of this. Now get out! Get back to the gutter where you belong.'

Vally gathers the sheets in one swoop, before she's manhandled out on to the street.

She runs back to Egon, their words crashing in her ears like thunder.

11

August 1911

Vally and Egon are sleeping, naked, their bodies close, early morning light streaming into the room. There is a sense of peace, at last. She'd returned home yesterday afternoon, dripping wet, having abandoned the umbrella at the post office. Egon had started as she came through the door, the sodden tube of his art tucked beneath her thin coat, and was clearly about to protest, but she got there first, erupting with the news of what had happened. She screamed at him for his idiotic betrayal, beat her fist against his chest, shouted into his face late into the night, delirious with the pain in her head, and furious with herself for having known this was coming and not having left while she had the chance. Egon apologized, held her, tried to reassure her, railed against the locals and their narrow-minded ways, said it would blow over. He'd talk to the girls' parents in the morning, he said, say sorry for any offence. He'd explain. No harm had been done. Then he'd pay a visit to the postal office and try to make amends. The incident would soon be forgotten, he promised.

'It would have been different if I'd been there,' he said. 'I'd have reasoned with them.'

'Run your own damn errands next time, then,' she'd replied.

Finally, when all their anger and disbelief had been spent, Egon had managed to make Vally smile – despite herself – as he tried to conjure the idea of the thin-lipped postal worker holding a drawing of Egon's enlarged member.

Afterwards Egon took Vally in his arms, and they'd made love, tenderly, exhausted, before falling asleep.

Now, in the balanced calm of dawn, their even breathing is all that can be heard in the room. Until the window explodes with a crack of broken glass.

Egon throws an arm over Vally as a missile flies across the room. It lands near the fireplace. They huddle together, arms over their heads, hearts hammering. Vally is the first to jump out of bed, cursing, and go to the broken window. Three men run from the porch. Vally doesn't see their faces. Egon races to the door.

'Did you see who it was?' he demands. 'That bastard from the district office?'

'It could have been any of them,' she says, shaking.

Vally stares at the missile: a brick, dipped in tar. A dead rat has been tied to it with twine. Its tail trails off the edge; its small mouth, with a neat row of sharp teeth, is open.

Egon collapses, his back against the wall, his eyes fixed on the tarred brick. Vally pulls on the shirt he discarded the previous night. The blood is pounding in her ears, but the urge to fight has left her, too.

'I can't believe it. My mother was born in Krumau. I deserve to be here,' Egon says. He punches his fist into the wall. 'I'm an artist, not a murderer,' he continues. 'They want to hound me out. But you cannot censor art.'

'If we stay, what'll be next?' she asks. 'Bruises? Blood? The next brick might not miss its target.'

'It's ignorance,' he says with resignation.

Vally sits next to him, puts her head on his arm. 'We'll never fit in – here or anywhere. It's time we leave.'

⌒

Vally hadn't realized it, but she's ready to return to Vienna. She misses her sisters, and the way they wriggle in their sleep. She has even missed the city, with its coffee houses brimming with debate, and the women who gather where they can to reflect on the important issues of the day – equality, suffrage, Freud, the existence of the female soul.

Everything in Krumau moves at such a dawdle. Aside from the breadth of colour she has seen – undiluted daylight, fields of corn, the cheerfully painted taverns – Vally has experienced little by way of friendship or kindness in this place.

'Bring me paper and a pen,' Egon says. 'I must write to Roessler. I'll tell him about the disaster yesterday. It's a miracle you salvaged my works,' he adds. 'And get packing. We're leaving for Neulengbach on the next available train.'

'Where?' Vally gets up, follows him, stepping around the broken glass.

'My Uncle Leopold has a summer house in Neulengbach. It's less than an hour from Vienna, but far enough from here. It's even more rural, untamed.'

'I can't fathom why you'd want to swap one provincial outpost for another precisely the same?' she says.

'I can't return to Vienna. Not with a scandal hot on our heels.' Why does Egon insist on making it all so complicated? 'We'll keep our heads down. I'll make the best art of my life, and you'll manage the business side of things. We'll stay out of trouble, make love every day, drink wine each evening. We'll endure.'

Egon begins his letter. He turns serious as he writes. 'These people,' he mutters. 'Lack of education. Primitive. It's a witch-hunt. What threat did I pose?' he continues, not expecting an answer. 'I'm an artist. Is that a crime? To corrupt their young by filling their imaginations with art, a ladder to the moon?'

When Egon finally looks up, all his bravado has gone. 'I used to love this town so much,' he says. 'The people have no idea what they've done.'

'One day, they'll regret this,' she says to soothe him.

Vally goes to the window once more.

It's then she sees that her beautiful, budding sunflowers have been trampled underfoot.

12

April 1912

'Herr Schiele, he is no longer here.' An acne-ridden Neulengbach youth steps from the shadows and stops Vally with a hand on her arm. The cottage that she and Egon have rented for the past eight months is atop a steep hill, overlooking fields. Vally is weary from the exertion of the daily climb. It's clear this man has been waiting.

She hugs her basket of vegetables and bread tightly. The tone he uses seems almost proud. He leers at Vally as he speaks, making it difficult to grasp his meaning. She stares at his mouth as he repeats himself, sees his fat tongue flicking against his rotten teeth.

'Two policemen came,' he continues. Vally whips her head towards the whitewashed cottage with its low-hanging roof, her eyes going straight to the window at the back, where she would normally expect to see Egon, smirking back at her. He's not, but that doesn't mean anything this man says is true. 'He has been taken to the station.'

'What would they want with Egon?' she asks, addressing not the man, but herself.

'Herr Schiele has been arrested,' the youth insists. 'They took him away.'

Vally shifts her heavy basket. A white cabbage tumbles over the top on to the road and begins to roll away.

'Schiele belongs in handcuffs,' the young man sneers. 'Next, they'll be here for you!'

He walks away while Vally hurries towards the house. The door is open.

'Egon? Egon, are you here?' His work has been pulled from the walls and tossed to the floor. Faces stare up at her, some familiar, others unknown. Pencil, gouache, perspectives skewed. Landscapes trodden underfoot, marked by heavy boot prints. Egon's eyes in his self-portraits stare back at her, his mouth open. He didn't even have a chance to tidy away his brushes, their bristles already hardening in the early afternoon sun, and the colours, his expensive pigments, are ruined.

Egon and Vally have lived uneventfully in Neulengbach. It's a small, boring town – precisely what he'd wanted – surrounded by miles of fields and innumerable shades of green, with an old church and a squat castle sitting on a mound. They have kept to themselves, disturbing nobody. Vally has held the flock of schoolchildren, those who are drawn to the artist's studio like moths to a flame, at a safe distance. There is one girl to whom Vally has shown kindness, but Tatjana has no interest in the artist himself.

Vally salvages what she can of Egon's paints and hurriedly cleans his brushes, the water silky beneath her fingers. She gathers his works and smooths them out on the table.

She wants to believe there has been a terrible mistake.

⁓

'You cannot take a man's liberty without explanation,' Vally insists to the official at the entrance to Neulengbach's District Courthouse, off the town's main street. The man's uniform is grey and humourless, matching his face.

'And your name is?'

'Neuzil. I'm an acquaintance of Egon Schiele.'

'Neuzil? No relation to the arrested, then?'

'He's my friend.' Vally notes the way he looks at her. 'I'm the artist's assistant.'

'Unless you're his wife or an immediate relative, I cannot disclose to you the crimes with which Herr Schiele has been charged.'

'Crimes? He paints. He goes nowhere, except for walks in the countryside and occasional trips to Vienna.'

'His charges will be released in due course.'

'But he should be free today.'

'We've received serious complaints against your . . . *partner*.'

'Complaints? For what, exactly?'

'I have said, I cannot share that information with you, Fräulein Neuzil.' His tongue quivers before he says her name. 'Come back tomorrow. And think about how you can be a little more . . . accommodating next time.'

'I'm not paying you a *heller*.'

'No money need exchange hands.'

'Egon will hear of this,' Vally says.

'Not that he can do a thing about it,' he replies.

She feels the guard's eyes roaming over her as she leaves. The door swings shut, and Vally steadies herself against the wall, her fingers clenched.

⌒

Vally wakes early the next morning. She rubs the back of her neck to soothe the threatening migraine. She's not sure she has slept at all, anxious about Egon – isolated, powerless. He hates to be alone.

Vally must do whatever it takes, today, to set him free. But first, she'll have to swallow her pride and approach the locals to discover the crime of which he has been accused. She sets out in her smartest outfit – a neat skirt made of thick material, double-breasted jacket and wide-brimmed hat. White clouds gather beyond the castle as she walks along the dirt road towards the bakery where, yesterday morning, before the arrest, she'd bought bread. She couldn't describe her interaction with the baker that day as warm, but he'd taken her money and relented when she'd requested that she not be given the cob that was overly crusty on top.

Yet today he sees her coming and scoots around the counter to turn the sign in the window to 'Closed' before she can even push open the door. Vally gestures that she wants to talk, but the man makes it clear that he's busy.

Word has clearly spread. Three women cross the street to avoid her, whispering and glancing her way. Vally enters the nearest public inn. Two roughly hewn men, forearms bulging, are drinking there. They put their heads together when she enters. She approaches the thickset woman behind the bar, who has served the couple in the past. She's called away to the back of the alehouse, but not before Vally notices a deeper coldness in her eyes. What has Egon done? Who has he angered? She leaves without answers.

The black church spire comes into view. Vally observes it grimly. She does not appreciate religious places. Her lack of faith makes her defenceless.

'Ah, the artist's mistress,' the priest raises his voice as she enters.

Vally ventures down the aisle between empty pews on either side. Stained sunlight falls across her path.

The priest gestures that she take a seat beside him. The bench is hardly wide enough.

'You're in trouble,' he continues.

Vally inhales the scent of woody incense and dust.

'Why have they arrested Herr Schiele?' she asks.

The priest raises his thick eyebrows and all the moles and liver spots on his face seem to move with them. 'I hear troubling things about Egon Schiele. Perhaps you can tell me if they're true.'

'Should a man be punished for his talent?' she ventures.

'Schiele has a singular talent for ruffling feathers. It has come to us that he – in fact, the both of you – were hounded out of the last town you settled in.'

'We chose to leave after a misunderstanding. Egon has done nothing wrong. He has not stolen, murdered anyone, or started any fires.'

The priest looks at her sceptically. 'He's a pornographer. I've been told so, and on good authority.'

The priest crosses himself.

A murderous rage surges through Vally.

'In the name of art, a man has been arrested, denied his liberty, and languishes in a prison cell? For his pictures of the human body, as God created it? There are striking representations of the human form, right here.' Vally gestures to a painting of Christ on the cross – his taut, near-naked body, the loincloth gathered around his thighs, the folds of the material not dissimilar to the way Egon depicts her petticoats. 'Tell me, what is the difference? I can see *his* nipples, can I not?'

The priest blinks at her outburst. 'It's quite a battle the two of you have chosen to undertake. Against religion. Against society. You've lost the approval of upstanding people. It doesn't bother you to forfeit order and conformity?' The priest does not take his eyes from Vally. 'I'm a simple man,' he continues. 'I care nothing for art, if that's what you insist on calling it. But Herr Schiele has transgressed not only in this matter. He is being held for more than his proclivity for drawing female flesh.' He pauses. 'What say you of morally corrupting young children by showing them erotic drawings? Of the seduction of a minor? Of kidnap? Should an artist, in your view, be outside the law?'

All the shadows in the church fall upon Vally at once.

'You can't mean Tatjana?'

The priest swallows a smile of satisfaction.

'What a coincidence that you should mention the young Von Mossig. Her father, the Captain, has indeed lodged a formal complaint.'

'But I welcomed her into our home! I was the one who accompanied her to Vienna. It's absurd to claim that she was kidnapped. And seduction? Egon never laid a finger on her.'

'That's not so, according to Tatjana's version of events.'

'I must speak to her at once.'

'It's too late for that.'

Vally knocks a prayer book to the floor and kicks it out of her way, scuffing the pages as she scrambles out of the pew.

How has it come to this?

Does Tatjana not realize her games have cost a man his freedom?

13

April 1912

In Neulengbach, Egon had heeded Vally's warnings and been much stricter about keeping the town's young admirers at bay. Their rustic little cottage on the edge of the town did provide some refuge from prying eyes, but still the youngsters gathered in the garden of the atelier, desperate to defy their parents and catch a glimpse of forbidden art. Mostly Egon ignored them or chased them from the garden if they came too close. Vally even had to remind him to play less of the *tatzelwurm*, one of the terrifying creatures from the region's folklore, or he'd give the children nightmares. Egon's sterner stance meant Vally could be the one to offer a glass of sweet lemonade or a hazelnut biscuit from the batches she liked to bake.

One girl, the quietest, caught Vally's attention. She had chestnut hair, almost to her waist, and a blunt fringe. Her features were delicate and she was smaller than the others, despite being, at fourteen, one of the older girls to venture to the cottage. The others often teased her, Vally noticed, so she tried to reassure the girl and told her to pay them no heed. Tatjana said that her parents were strict, that she had no siblings, no friends. Her father was important, apparently – a retired naval officer – and never had time for her. She seemed lonely and bored.

Egon, much to Vally's chagrin, had urged caution. But the girl reminded Vally so much of her little sister Berta that she couldn't resist wanting to spend time with her. She braided her silky hair and offered butterscotch sweets, telling Tatjana stories of Vienna. As they sat on the stool at the cottage's old piano, she'd even promised that one day she would take the young girl there.

'Vienna is where my grandmother lives,' Tatjana commented, playing simple scales that Vally failed to copy. 'Father promises me every year that we'll visit her, but it never happens. I want to show her how I can play this.' The young girl began an elaborate tune.

When Egon arrived home, all the joy on Tatjana's face curdled. The girl only ever came to the house when Egon wasn't there, often waiting outside, unseen, until he left, then flinging the door open without knocking, and throwing her arms around Vally.

'Will you read to me?' Tatjana asked Vally one afternoon. She had brought a book from school and opened it expectantly.

'Not today,' Vally replied. 'There's too much to do. Look at all the mess you've made.'

'Can I read to you, then?'

'Egon will be back any minute.'

'You said he'd be out all evening. Please. I'll read to the end of the page.'

'One page, no more, then you can help me with the chores.'

Tatjana began to read aloud, putting emphasis in all the right places and giving a different voice to each character. An hour later, she turned the last page.

'That's it. The end.'

Vally jumped up. 'Where has the time gone? Tatjana, really!'

'But you enjoyed it.' A line of watery annoyance brimmed in the girl's eyes.

'I did, but it's time for you to leave. Do your parents never wonder where you are?'

'I'd only be in my room, reading to myself.'

'They must worry about you. Offer them this address. I should meet them. I can let them know what a great help you are to me.'

'Fine, I'll do that,' Tatjana said, planting a quick, bird-like kiss on Vally's elbow.

A day later, Tatjana arrived with a new book. She showed Vally the cover and asked her to read once more. When Vally finally admitted she couldn't read or write, Tatjana began to teach her, pointing to words and explaining how the different letter combinations made specific sounds. Over the next few days, the girl helped Vally to learn the alphabet, then write down the letters. Her attempts were wobbly at first but grew more confident with practice, and soon Vally could recognize several words, enough to read a full line, then another. As the weeks progressed, she began to tackle full pages at a time, even venturing to read some verse by Egon's favourite poet, Rimbaud, with his tales of foolish virgins and their infernal bridegroom.

⌒

It was past midnight, one week later, when Egon was interrupted by an urgent knock at the door, in the middle of a story he was telling at the dinner table to his friend Erwin Osen. Vally had heard the same anecdote several times before, so she laughed at the correct point, then excused herself.

She opened the door on to the dark, wild night, expecting to find Anton Peschka, who'd missed the earlier train. Instead, her eyes fell on Tatjana, drenched from the rain, her blouse clinging to her shoulders.

'Tatti, what's happened? It's so late. We have a friend staying,' Vally added, looking over her shoulder. Egon was still caught in his story. Tatjana thrust her wrists at Vally – there were bruises streaked all the way up her arms.

'My father,' she hiccupped. 'He tried to kill me.'

Vally pulled the girl into her, and she stood trembling against her chest.

'Come, let's get you out of these wet clothes. You'll dry off in seconds by the fire.'

She held the girl by the shoulders and a look passed between them.

'No, it's fine. I'll explain. Don't worry about Egon.' Vally led Tatjana down the corridor to their bedroom, then closed the door and pulled the sodden blouse over the girl's head. Egon's art was pinned to the walls, crisp sheets of Japan paper showing contorted self-portraits, jagged limbs, intense watercolours displaying a rosy nipple, pubic hair, protruding ribs.

Vally tried to block them from Tatjana's view.

'I'm sure I've got something that will fit you.' Vally rummaged in a trunk as the girl stood in the shadows cast by the low-burning lamp, her arms folded awkwardly over her chest. 'Here, quickly, put this on before you catch your death. I'll see if I can find something else in a moment.'

Vally handed her the garment without looking at her body and Tatjana pulled it over her head. It hung off her delicate frame.

'Give me that sodden skirt and your socks, too,' Vally said, passing her a towel to dry her hair. 'I'll put them by the stove to dry.' Tatjana shuffled the remaining clothes off her body and handed them over.

'Wait here,' Vally instructed, stepping out of the room. She would explain the situation to Egon, as soon as she had dealt with the wet items – the last thing she needed was to have the warnings she'd given him in Krumau thrown back at her. As she spread out the clothes on a chair by the stove, Vally noticed with a start that the girl's drawers were furled within the layers of skirt. She tucked them hastily away, then left the room.

When she pushed open the living-room door, she found Tatjana in the middle of the room, cast in candlelight, angelic with her tousled chestnut hair and the white scalloped shirt brushing her thighs. She had pulled a dry pair of socks up her calves.

Erwin was instructing her to pirouette while Egon captured her loosely in his sketchbook.

'Our little friend has returned, I see,' Egon said, resting his pencil. 'Imagine my surprise when I found her in our bedroom when I went looking for you.'

Erwin erupted with laughter and knocked over a glass of wine. It trickled down the table leg, pooling on the floor. 'What a mess,' he said, jumping up to fetch a cloth, still smiling.

'Tatjana didn't have anywhere else to go,' Vally replied. 'She just turned up uninvited.' Tatjana shot her a betrayed look. 'She was drenched. I told her she could dry off here before we send her home. When the storm is over.'

Tatjana burst into sobs. 'You can't make me! I'm never going back there.'

Egon looked at Vally with steady eyes, his brows raised in a weary challenge.

'Well, it's not going to be possible for you to stay here,' he said to the girl.

'Vally said I could come any time.'

'Tatjana! That's not what I said. Egon, I never—'

'You can't stay here. We've a full house as it is,' Egon continued.

Erwin dropped Vally's clean dishcloth into the puddle of wine. 'It's hardly likely Anton will make it from Vienna tonight. We can sleep in here, Egon. Vally and this little lady can take the bed. You can't send her back out into the night looking like that, for Christ's sake. You'll be the talk of the town. You're already an ogre, from what I hear.' He knocked Egon's shoulder, playfully.

'Please,' Tatjana pleaded.

Vally could see the desperation in her eyes. 'She'll be on her way first thing, won't you, Tatti?'

'I'll be gone before you even wake up,' the young girl promised.

⏤

The next day, Tatjana was at the table, having prepared four plates for breakfast, by the time Vally emerged. When she'd found the other side of the bed deserted, Vally had hoped that the girl had made good on her promise and left at first light. But there she was, cheerful to the point of obnoxiousness, cutting bread and setting out jars of fruit preserve. Tatjana had also picked daisies and colourful weeds from the garden and had placed them in a jar filled with water.

'I thought you were leaving?' Vally said, taking a seat.

'I am!' Tatjana replied. 'I'm going to Vienna to stay with my grandmama.'

'You can't go all that way by yourself!'

'I'm heading back to Vienna today,' Erwin said, entering the kitchen. 'And Egon's coming with me, aren't you?' the young man shouted into the other room, where the two men had slept on the cot and the floor. Egon came in with his shirt unbuttoned, his teeth stained crimson from the previous night's drinking.

'Am I?' he asked, giving Vally a stern look when he noticed Tatjana. Vally busied herself with the coffee on the stove.

'You said you wanted to visit Roessler, about that commission. You were complaining that he never sells your work.' Erwin helped himself to the lion's share of the bread. 'And we can find Anton and ask him what, or *who*, kept him from turning up last night.'

'Erwin and Egon can accompany me on the train to Vienna,' Tatjana said to Vally.

'You'll be safe with us,' Erwin smirked.

'Tatti should return home. She's fourteen. Her parents will be worried,' Vally said.

'I'm never going home. It's dangerous. My father will hurt me,' Tatjana said, exposing her arms once more. 'I said I was going to Vienna. He told me to go and never come back.'

'Oh, Tatjana,' Vally said. 'People often say hurtful things in anger. He'll apologize.'

'Your father did that to you?' Erwin interrupted, examining her bruises.

'I'm going to Vienna whether you agree or not,' she said.

Vally sighed. There was a softness in Egon's eyes, telling her he wouldn't argue with her on this.

'Fine. But I'm coming with you all,' she said. 'Someone has to make sure Tatjana gets to her grandmother's apartment.'

'On your head be it.' Egon gave a half-smile, and took a sip of coffee.

⌒

Vally and Tatjana made the trip from Vienna's West Railway Station to her grandmother's house in the west of the city. Egon and Erwin had more important business to attend to. Tatjana faithfully recalled the address. She was certain about the street name and number. They arrived at a neatly painted door in a well-to-do neighbourhood.

'This must be it.' Tatjana knocked with vigour. 'Imagine Grand-mama's surprise when she sees me.'

She knocked again.

'Are you sure this is the right place?' Vally asked.

'Of course I am!'

A few moments later, the door opened a crack.

'Shoo! I'm not expecting anyone.' A wrinkled hand gestured them away before closing the door once more.

Vally knocked until the man opened it again. 'Excuse me, we're looking for Frau von Mossig. She's my friend's grandmother. Is she here?'

'Never heard of her,' the old man wheezed.

Tatjana reddened. 'She lives here, she does.'

'I'd know about it if she did. Now, push off, the pair of you.'

They tried three similar addresses, Vally growing increasingly desperate as the day wore on. 'I've no idea what we'll do if we don't find your grandmother,' she said. 'We've missed the last train back to Neulengbach. We'll have to stay the night.'

There was nothing else they could do. So, they found a cheap place to stay near the station, then left at first light. On the train back to Neulengbach, Tatjana was sulking. 'I don't want to go home,' she repeated.

'You have to go,' Vally urged. 'You've already caused enough trouble.'

At the corner of the road to her home, Tatjana had hugged Vally, almost crushing her. 'I wish it could be just the two of us, always,' she said, with longing.

Vally looked into the younger girl's eyes, never imagining what would follow.

'I'll see you soon,' she promised. 'Now, go! Try to make amends with your father.'

14

April 1912

The basement cell in which Egon is being detained is stuffy, claustrophobic, with a high, curved ceiling and an iron-barred slit for a window. On the other side, Vally knows well, is a sheer drop, for she has considered trying to reach him that way, to offer reassuring words and throw any small tokens she could through the gaps.

Now she's at the scuffed wooden door, looking through the grate at him. She reaches out to touch his fingers.

'Vally! You came. Thank you. Everyone else has abandoned me,' he says. 'This is the first human contact I've had in almost a week,' he adds, pressing the tips of her fingers to his lips. He breathes her in, as if she were a fresh bloom. 'Nothing has ever seemed sweeter. But how did you convince that tyrant of a guard to let you in?' Egon asks, pressing his face to the grate.

'Never mind that,' she says sadly, rubbing his cheek. 'You've not shaved,' she adds, after a moment.

'They won't allow me a paintbrush, let alone a razor blade,' he replies.

'Ah, bristles on a stick, the deadliest of weapons,' she says, trying to raise a smile in return.

'They've denied me everything. My muscles ache. My hands act out the motion of drawing, of painting, in thin air. I've begged, but they won't

288

let me have even a pencil. I've been forced to mark lines upon the wall, using my fingers and spittle from my mouth. It dries before I move on to the next stroke, but the image remains, in here.' He touches his temple.

'It's an outrage,' Vally tells Egon. 'To contain you in this way.'

'I'm powerless,' he replies. 'They have the key to this heavy door, with its lock that cannot be broken. I'm in their system. I could be in this dungeon for weeks, months, years, even.' Vally sees fear and anger in his eyes. 'Yesterday, the guard made me scrub the floor. I scrubbed until my fingers were raw. I was almost proud of what I'd done, but he offered no praise. He spat on my efforts! How do people find joy in humiliating others?'

'It's senseless,' she agrees.

'And how is it that mere words – a malicious or careless complaint – can deprive a man of his freedom? I don't even know what it is I'm supposed to have done.'

Vally looks past him, through the bars, into the cell. Against the rough-plaster wall is a narrow cot, covered in grey blankets. There's a washbasin and a wooden chair. A bucket, covered with a rag, is pushed into the corner.

Vally tries to steady her voice. 'Egon, you're going to be put on trial.'

'It will be a circus. My guilt is already decided.'

'They say you seduced a girl, that Tatjana was kidnapped,' she explains. 'You're here so you can't influence her, or influence her father to retract his case against you.' She wipes her eyes with her sleeve. 'It's all my fault. We should never have accompanied her to Vienna.'

Egon closes his eyes, finally comprehending.

'Oh, Vally.' He gives a deep sigh. 'We can't blame Tatjana. Or our-selves. If not this, now, it would have been something else, later. They have always been out to get me. I suspect Uncle Leopold has also played a hand in my humiliation. He knows people in the courthouse in this town. He could have stopped this if he wanted to, yet his silence is deafening. I've heard from no one, not Roessler, Erwin, not even Gerti. You're the single person who has stood by my side.'

'Perhaps the news hasn't reached them yet?'

'Bad news travels faster than light. With every hour that passes, I fear I'll lose my mind, like my father did.'

The guard bangs open the door at the other end of the corridor. Vally flinches. 'Time's up,' he drawls.

'You will endure,' she promises Egon.

He swallows. 'Wait, I made something for you.' He passes it to her; it is the texture and size of an apricot stone. 'It's not much,' he says, as she examines the tiny carving of a face in her palm. 'I squeezed some bread into a ball and sculpted it with my nails.'

'I mean it,' the guard shouts down the hallway, hacking his throat clear.

Vally returns her hands to her pockets. 'Ah,' she says. 'And I have something special for you.' She pulls out an orange, its skin glistening. 'They're in short supply, but I knew you'd appreciate it.'

Its fierce, ripe scent lingers in the air between them.

'It's the most unspoiled thing I've ever seen. Please, see if you can charm the guard once more, and bring my watercolours, for I want to paint it, on the cot in this cell.'

'A splash of colour amid all this grey,' she replies.

'It will be my only light.'

She turns to leave, aching at the thought of being separated from him again.

'I love you,' she thinks she hears him whisper.

15

May 1912

Vally sits in the second row of the dark-panelled courtroom in Sankt Pölten, waiting for the hearing to begin. Egon has spent three weeks under arrest in Neulengbach prison. His fate – and hers – will be played out today. She scratches the skin around her thumbnails.

She has spoken to others little more than Egon has in these past weeks, and has lived as a hermit in their cottage, sipping vodka in the daytime, walking from room to room, forgetting where she's meant to be and why. If she has talked, it has been to the girls in Egon's paintings, which she has pinned on the walls once more. They stare back at her, silent, their eyes challenging, their shoulders set, hips thrusting. Before she met Egon and became familiar with his work, Vally had never seen women presented in this way, with such unabashed confidence, as if they might step off the paper and grab the viewer by the scruff of the neck, ready to deliver a kiss or a kick. Even Gustav wasn't as bold.

Vally's thoughts circle around an image of herself. She envies the woman trapped there.

There's a flutter of activity as the judge enters. Reporters from Vienna strain forward, pencils poised. Locals Vally recognizes from Neuleng-bach, and others from as far away as Krumau, have made the trip to see Schiele get what he deserves. Egon's sisters are in the front row with his mother. They wear black and their expressions are serious, drawn. None of them, when they'd been waiting to enter earlier, had acknowledged Vally, or invited her to join them. Anton Peschka arrives just as the room is quietening to a hush and takes a seat next to Gertrude.

The judge adjusts his heavy black robes as he sits. The elderly man is smaller than Vally expected, with compact features and oversized ears bristling with grey hairs. In any other walk of life, he'd be a laughable figure.

People fidget in their seats. With the sound of a key grating in an old lock, the courtroom inhales collectively. The door opens and, for a few moments, everyone stares into the space it exhibits. Then, with shuffling footsteps, an officer with glistening buttons emerges, his prisoner cuffed by his side. Egon is gaunt, his leg in a heavy brace. Despite the indignity of the excessive restraints, he enters with his head held high, his eyes resting on an undetermined point in the distance, his shoulders straight. He looks around the room, takes one deep, steadying breath, as if admiring the sea's horizon, then takes his seat in the dock.

The judge arranges his papers. He doesn't look in the artist's direction.

'Name?' he demands.

'My name is Egon Schiele.' He stands, bringing both hands up, cuffed as they are, as if to straighten his tie. Vally can hear the smallest wobble in his voice.

'And what is your profession?' The final word rolls off the judge's tongue.

'*Maler*, your Honour. I'm an artist.' He draws a deep breath before he takes the opportunity to continue. 'For twenty-one days I've been under arrest, Your Honour. Five hundred and four hours. Would you concede your liberty for that length of time? What has your investigation into my behaviour revealed? Tell me, what wrongdoing have you unearthed?'

The judge raises his eyes. 'Herr Schiele, you're in this courtroom, today – the fourth day of May, 1912 – under very serious charges.' Egon steadies himself on the dock's rail. The people on the benches lean forward to better devour the indictment. 'You are hereby charged with immorality – that is to say, the careless or wilful display of erotic drawings in your studio, to be viewed by children, which could contribute to their corruption.' Vally thinks of the explicit drawings pinned to the walls of the bedroom that were found by officers the day of his arrest. Tatjana had seen them the night she came to the house. 'Furthermore,' the judge continues, 'you are charged with seduction of a minor, and kidnap.'

The courtroom bursts into animated whispers. Egon closes his eyes. His fingers against the wood look bleached. Vally feels the ground shift beneath her feet. Such charges are absurd. The woman next to her tuts happily.

'The girl in question is Tatjana Georgette Anna von Mossig, aged fourteen, daughter of Captain von Mossig of Neulengbach. The court understands that you did unlawfully detain her at your property, Au 48, in the same town, for one night without her parents' knowledge or consent. You then abducted the minor, taking her to Vienna, whereby you spent one night together at an unknown location. Captain von Mossig, fearing for his daughter's safety, immediately reported her missing and identified you as the culprit, on the basis of ongoing questionable interactions, between you and the child, that have taken place on your property over the course of several months. The girl, upon her rescue, exhibited serious bruising to her forearms, proving she resisted your advances, Herr Schiele.' The judge pauses, cracking his fingers. 'Charges as serious as these incur a maximum of five years in prison.'

Vally sees the swirl of Egon's crown as his head falls forward in disbelief.

'How do you plead?' the judge demands.

The courtroom settles into a deep silence. Egon, ever the performer, makes them wait. Then he raises his eyes and looks at them with insolence. 'I am without guilt, your Honour.'

The judge slams a palm on his bench. 'The artist pleads not guilty.'

The woman next to Vally tuts again, her shoulders shaking from the sheer joy of it.

'I had no interaction with Fräulein von Mossig. My companion, Fräulein Neuzil, will attest to that.' Vally's stomach lurches. 'The girl was never out of her sight. As for abduction, I was trying to protect her. She begged for my help. I would have been a monster to deny help to a child in distress. Distress initiated by her own father.'

A gasp whips round the courtroom.

'Captain von Mossig is an upstanding member of our community.'

'Fräulein von Mossig is the victim in all this,' Egon continues. 'But I believe you'll find the abuse of which you speak has occurred much closer to home. Of course the Captain would want to protect his reputation. The girl has been examined, I believe, and was found to be perfectly intact. That excludes any possibility of seduction.'

'Are you calling Captain von Mossig a liar?' he asks.

Egon does not reply.

The judge continues, referring to his file. 'Let the record show that one hundred and twenty-five incriminating depictions of the human body were confiscated from the property. Such content is not fit for decent society.'

Egon takes a breath. 'I do not deny that I have made drawings and watercolours that are erotic. But they are always works of art – to that I can attest, and people who understand something of this will gladly affirm it. Have other artists made no erotic pictures?'

The old judge narrows his eyes. 'I've had the misfortune of seeing the works in question. They are vile, the product of a degenerate mind.'

'No erotic work of art is filth if it is artistically significant. It is only turned into filth through the eyes of the beholder.' Egon has to raise his voice to be heard.

The judge's eyes bulge. 'So we're the ones at fault.' He points a stubby finger at himself, then directs it around the gallery. He fumbles under the desk, reaching to extract something from a leather case. 'Let's see, shall we? Here is an example of one piece of "art" that an innocent girl of fourteen years old was forced to view in your residence.' The judge pinches one corner of a piece of paper with his fingertips, as if the nude woman rendered in charcoal and gouache might crawl off the page and up his arm with the speed of a spider. It's an artwork that Vally knows Egon values highly. It is of her.

'That has been taken without permission!' Egon shouts.

'I apologize to those gathered here today,' the judge continues as the spectators lean forward to get a closer look, 'that you must witness this.' He dangles the artwork. 'But this, *this*, is the work of the perverted perpetrator who is the subject of this trial. If this is what he freely portrays of his dark nature, imagine how much deeper the layers of depravity run. No right-thinking person should be exposed to this. We fail our children by allowing this to exist.'

The muscles in Egon's neck are strained. The judge fumbles beneath his desk again, then produces a box of matches.

No, Vally thinks. The guard has to restrain Egon. The courtroom shifts, balancing itself as if there's a swell underfoot. With a perverse smile, the judge runs the match against its coarse strike paper. It sparks brightly at its tip.

The judge holds Egon's artwork and edges it towards the flame. But the heat moves up the short match with such speed that, in seconds, it has burned close to his fingers.

Vally sees anxiety cross the judge's face as the paper fails to light.

But then it takes.

Vally, as she is captured on the page, stares out, unflinching. She rests her eyes on every person in the courtroom as the paper twists and spins, is consumed in an instant. The real Vally has lost something of herself, again. The judge flicks his wrist to extinguish the match and releases the burden of the burnt artwork, letting the ashen remains drop to the stone floor. For Egon, it is as if he's witnessed part of himself perishing. Tears hang off his nose and chin.

'Order! Quiet!' the judge shouts.

But the courtroom is already silent.

～

His solicitor presented a firm case in Egon's favour, calling on written statements from his more esteemed patrons in Vienna, including Roessler. The charges against Egon – seduction of a minor and abduction – have been dropped. The Captain admitted he'd been hasty in his accusations. But the count of public immorality, for displaying his artwork in his own home, was upheld. The judge sentenced Egon to twenty-four days in jail, twenty-one of which had already been served while he awaited trial. Egon must spend the three remaining days in Sankt Pölten prison. At the conclusion of the hearing, the judge asked Egon if he repented of his sins. 'I feel not punished, but purified,' he declared.

Tatjana was not called to speak. Vally wonders why she lied, or if the young girl truly believed that Egon had behaved improperly. Did Tatjana say those things to protect her father? Had the Captain feared for his daughter's safety, whipped into a panic by the hateful gossip? Perhaps it was all an attempt by the girl to get closer to Vally?

She'll never know.

Vally has just hours to pack up the cottage and Egon's materials, arrange the delivery of trunks, and settle outstanding bills. This time, no question about it, they'll be returning to Vienna. Vally refuses to discuss going anywhere else. She leaves the key on the table and closes the door behind her. There is nobody to say goodbye to.

The train speeds them back to Vienna. Vally watches Egon as he stares at the shifting landscape. He doesn't speak. He sits close and she feels his fingers digging into her arm.

16

August 1912

'Don't leave me, Vally,' Egon says, as she tightens the laces on her boots.

'I haven't left your side for weeks,' she replies. Vally looks over at the artist, who is still in bed, his torso bare, the sheets twisted beneath his arms. 'I'll only be an hour.'

The air in the studio is heavy with masculine sweat and summer heat.

'I don't want you to go,' he complains, his eyes screwed up.

'Come with me, if you can't bear your own company,' Vally replies.

'I'm not ready.' Egon has been lethargic for some time now, unwilling to move.

'What are you waiting for? The whole world is out there, if you want it.'

'I can't be around people. But I don't want to be alone.'

'Not even for a short while?' She kisses him, a peck on his forehead. She has been looking after him, tending to his needs while he retreats further into this shell of himself. 'I need to buy food and wood.' She picks up her bag and shawl. 'And you're low on tobacco.'

'If you leave, don't come back,' he pouts dramatically.

It has been months since his imprisonment and the trial and Egon has been in a strange, changeable mood ever since. Vally isn't sure how to help him out of this latest episode. When they first returned to Vienna, Egon had been taken in by his mother. She was distraught for him, and he needed the cocoon of her protection in the early weeks – but before long, his mother's attention became suffocating. Vally, during this time, returned to live with her mother and slept top-to-tail with the girls, waking with headaches and a stiff neck. Erwin then offered to put Egon up for a month until he found a place of his own. They drowned their sorrows, argued about art and philosophy, the downfall of empires, and Erwin invited friends around to lift Egon's spirits. Erwin's support broke some barrier within him and encouraged him to return to painting. 'You are, after all, the *enfant terrible* of the art world, now more than ever before,' Erwin told him, raising a glass.

Egon has taken part in group exhibitions in Budapest and Cologne and has been invited to submit work for his first solo show, in Munich. He now rents a cheap space in an elegant but run-down building in Pfeilgasse, where he can paint, when he feels like it, and where Vally can see him freely and tend to his needs.

'Do you want tobacco or not?' she asks, as she sits on the edge of the bed and strokes Egon's chest.

'Stay,' he repeats, as if he were a spoiled child. Vally slips her hand under the sheet. She feels the warmth of his leg, the firm muscle of his thigh, the bristle of the coarser hairs. She squeezes, then moves her fingers up. There's a damp heat between his legs where the mass of hair is softer. She goes further and further. Egon lets his head fall back. Vally knows how to make him feel better.

'I'll always be by your side,' she whispers. Then she pushes the sheets aside and lowers her lips to him.

↬

As the weeks go by, Vally leaves the apartment with increasing regularity, bringing back what cheap joys she can find. She buys fruit and flowers, when she can afford them. She fills empty jars with water and cuts the stems, then places them inside, arranging each one to offer its best angle. Those flowers, with their fleeting beauty, are one of the few things that can brighten up the place and banish a little of the dreariness that seeps in.

'Look at this,' Vally says as she returns home, holding a long stem with peculiar orange petals like delicate lanterns. Egon turns at her voice.

'It's extraordinary,' he says, taking the physalis from her. He holds it up to her face. 'The colour complements your hair,' he adds. Vally fills a tall jar and places it inside.

'I want to include it in a painting of you and me.' Egon smiles.

He prepares two canvases of equal shape: one to capture him, looking defiant, self-confident yet fragile; the other is for her. 'It will be an important work of art,' he adds. Egon has never said that about any of the paintings he's made of Vally before, even though she knows they hold value for him and have sold successfully to his patrons.

Egon sketches her from various angles and finally settles on a composition where she is facing him, her eyes level with his. 'That's it,' he says. 'There. Look at me. Look me straight in the eye.' He squeezes oils from several tubes on to his palette, opening one with a knife to scrape out the last of its colour. Egon picks up his brush and touches it to the canvas. He works for hours.

It's strange, but when Vally poses for Egon, she goes into an otherworldly trance. Her mind unhooks itself from the present and time speeds by, like a pebble launched across a frozen lake. She can see the ghostly eyes of strange people, wearing strange clothes and strange expressions, staring at her. They walk around the room where she is posing, peering at her from every angle. They come close, fingers to their face. They move away. They think they know her, but she does not know them. She does not care for them, nor eternity. She does not want to be remembered. She is here for Egon. Egon alone.

'It's all for him, the artist, my friend, my lover,' she thinks. 'I don't owe you a thing.'

Their intensity, their insistence that they can own something of her, by seeing her, by being before her, only makes her look more penetratingly into Egon's eyes.

He returns her gaze with appreciation, with equality, his brush capturing everything between them. This is their union; this is the connection she craved.

17

31 October 1912

V ally wonders what the likes of Egon and herself are doing in such a wealthy district.

'Your paintings must be selling better than ever if you're going to live in Hietzing,' she says, as they walk down the wide, tree-lined road. Women with frilly parasols walk arm in arm along the main street; men wearing top hats, the tips of their moustaches waxed into points, wait on corners while their shoes are being polished. Maids sweep leaves off the steps to grand apartment buildings, the facades painted in neutral tones embellished with white; some buildings even have coats of arms above the entrance. There are none of the stray cats or beggar children Vally is used to seeing in the parts of town where she has lived.

'It's about time we enjoyed the finer side of life,' he says. 'Don't we deserve it, after the year I've had?'

Vally is alert to any hint of 'together' in the way Egon speaks of his new apartment. She's welcome at her mother's for as long as she needs, but she can't impose for ever.

Egon's artworks have been in wild demand for several months now – and the requests that flow in from across the city and beyond show no signs of abating. Each time he gets an invitation to take part in a new exhibition or somebody important calls about a commission, Egon radiates boyish satisfaction. The scandal, after all, has been good for him.

Only men can navigate disgrace and spin it into success, she thinks. But he deserves his success. If it means he has less time for her, and has to pander to the upper echelons of Viennese society a little more, then so be it. For the first time since Vally has known him, money flows easily. He doesn't owe anyone anything, least of all his uncle Leopold.

They reach the address they have been looking for – Hietzinger Hauptstrasse 101.

'Here we are,' he says. He pushes open the heavy door and steps ahead of her. 'Wait until you see it. It's spacious and light, right at the top of the building – the front room is north-facing, so I'll use it as my studio. I have every intention that this place will be my base for longer than a month. I need roots, Vally.'

They reach a dark-green door at the top of the stairs. Vally feels a tug of vertigo as she leans over the banister, glimpsing the mosaic-tiled hallway below. Egon's belongings will arrive by cart any minute now. They will have to carry everything from the street up all these stairs, Vally realizes. It'll take hours. Her shoulders ache in anticipation of the back-breaking chore. Egon takes a key from his pocket and unlocks the door.

'It's bigger than all the other spaces you've lived in combined!' Vally spins, her arms outstretched, in the middle of the room that has been earmarked to be Egon's studio. 'And the light from this window,' she sighs, drawn to the wide bay which offers a view of the street far below. 'But look at that.' Vally frowns. 'We can see right into those apartments on the other side of the street,' she says, her fingers on the dusty glass.

Egon isn't listening. 'My mother's mirror will hang here,' he's saying, pointing to a wall by the door. Vally can see how well the vast mirror will fill the space. All the better for capturing his own reflection, she thinks. 'And the chair I made will have pride of place right there,' he adds, gesturing to a desk left behind by the previous tenant. 'Father's

Germanic tomes can go at the top,' he says, running a hand along the bookshelves, 'then Nietzsche, Shakespeare, Rimbaud, my art books . . .'

The bell rings. 'That will be the coachman, delivering my belongings,' Egon says.

The couple make several trips up and down the stairs. Vally's thighs burn on the upward climb, her calf muscles snapping on the downward trot. 'Careful with that piece,' Egon instructs as she lifts a canvas. It's a daring large-scale painting he has been working on over the summer, a rebuff to conservative society – showing himself as a cardinal and Vally as a nun, far more erotic and daring than Klimt's *The Kiss*. 'We have to store it carefully until we find a buyer.' Her fingers throb with the weight.

⤿

It's dark outside now, and Vally stands at the bay window, looking at the view. The lights in the building opposite reveal the occupants inside even more clearly.

'We're being watched,' she says to Egon when he returns with another bundle.

'Somebody must be exceedingly bored, if that's true,' he says, joining Vally.

'A pair of eyes,' she says. 'A young woman. There. She's sitting on a chaise longue. I noticed her earlier and thought nothing of it, but she hasn't moved all afternoon.'

'Resist paranoia, Vally. Nobody cares what we do here in Vienna. We're unknown. It's a big city and people have more important things to do than watch us. Nobody will mark us out here for being unmarried.'

Vally flinches. 'Marriage,' she says, 'isn't a possibility, is it? For a woman like me?'

'It's too late for you to decide that your heart's desire is to be a wife.'

'It seems there isn't much I am good for.'

'I didn't mean it in that way. Besides, there's plenty you're good for.' Egon pulls Vally to him and kisses her neck.

Vally keeps her eyes on the window below, where the prying young woman had been sitting. She has gone now.

Egon smiles at her, then dashes back downstairs to retrieve one last thing. A few moments later, Vally sees the same woman leaving the main door of the building opposite, wrapping her furs around her neck, looking serene and satisfied. She takes the arm of another young woman of similar age and build. Vally watches them dip their heads together and cross the street, giggling, the darker-haired one leading the way.

18

15 August 1914

Vally has spent the afternoon with her sisters. Beautiful Berta hugged her tight before she left. The girls are growing, and she sees so little of them. She sends any money she can spare to her mother, and she knows the whole family benefits, but they're making a life away from her. She can't shake the need to be elsewhere these days, but it's not clear where she would go or why, and she can't bring herself to leave Egon, not when he needs her. And now that war has been declared, the world is even more uncertain than before.

She climbs the stairs and reaches into her pocket for the key to the apartment.

But then, Vally hears raised voices inside. There's a woman pleading, and Egon's responses are angry. Vally stops and listens for a moment.

'This obsession,' she overhears Egon's sister say. 'It was always more important.' Vally can imagine Egon's face as he receives these words, his eyes cast down, his mouth set. 'There's nothing you won't sacrifice for your art,' the woman continues, her voice rising. 'Me, yourself, your sanity. I only hope it's worth it.'

Vally shifts, reeling from the monologue, but the floorboards creak beneath her.

The door swings open and Vally is caught on the threshold. Egon's sister darts past. Rarely have they been in the same room, let alone shared a conversation, but Gertrude's presence looms large. It's clear Egon both adores and is infuriated by her.

Vally steps gently into the studio and approaches Egon, who is standing by the window.

'What happened?' she asks.

He refuses to look at her. It's possible he is crying.

'Why did Gertrude leave in such a hurry?' Vally tries again.

'My sister has got herself into a mess,' he says, his voice rough.

'Tell me what's going on, please?'

Egon is usually guarded when it comes to Gertrude, but this time he relents.

'There's a baby, if you must know. It will be born by the end of the year.'

'And you're not happy for her?'

'You haven't asked who the father is.'

'I . . .' Vally looks around. Her eyes rest on Egon for a moment, and she banishes the treacherous thought that flashes through her mind. 'I couldn't possibly imagine.'

'Anton Peschka,' Egon announces. 'A man I considered my friend.'

'But shouldn't you be happy for them?' Vally persists. 'You and Anton have always been close.'

'It's a betrayal, by both of them.'

Vally doesn't know what to say. She feels a mixture of jealousy and relief – that Egon's sister is getting on with her life, that she will have new preoccupations.

'When will they marry?' she asks eventually.

'Soon,' he replies. 'And it will change things for all of us.'

⁓

Vally now stays with Egon most nights. That evening, she takes herself to bed early while he continues to paint in the main room. She takes with her a bag of her favourite sugary treats and a game of dice she found at the back of the desk drawer. She has been playing for an hour when she hears the sound of Egon laughing. What does he have to be so amused about, alone with his art? Vally shakes the dice vigorously and rolls, but can't get the combination she needs.

Later, he joins her. The candle is still burning but Vally has been dozing. 'You should have done this an hour ago. We have money, but not to burn.' Egon blows out the flame. Vally opens her eyes at the sound of his voice, and an image of his face lingers in the darkness.

'You were laughing in there,' she says. Her voice sounds strange to her. Egon removes his clothes in the dark, the buckle of his belt cracking against the floorboards.

'What?'

'Earlier. I heard you laughing.'

'It was nothing,' he says. She hears him cross the room.

'There must have been something to entertain you.'

'Oh, it's those women, Adele and Edith, the sisters from across the street. I could see them from the window. I waved. They waved. They're a distraction.'

'You know their names?'

'I met them at a gallery opening a while ago.'

It's a blessing that Egon can't see her expression.

'Why didn't you say something at the time?'

'If I told you every time I spoke to a woman, you'd hardly appreciate it.'

He hurries into bed, slipping under the blankets, searching out the area her body has already warmed. He reaches out to pull her to him, but Vally turns away. He has a hunger in him, but Vally is not in the mood. She squeezes her eyes shut, but still cannot shake from her mind the faces of those neighbours, the entitled sisters, who've been on the receiving end – without hard work or consideration – of everything they've ever wanted, their entire lives.

19

January 1915

V ally dashes from room to room, searching for her handbag. She'd left it on the bookcase, as she always does when she arrives at the apartment, but it's not there. She rummages through discarded clothes, empties a drawer. She crouches on her knees to look under the bed, but there's nothing there, except crumpled sweet wrappers pushed out of reach by the broom.

'I'll meet you downstairs,' Egon shouts. 'Do hurry, or we'll be late.' The door slams and there's something fitting and final in the sound.

Eventually Vally finds her handbag on the ledge of the bay window in the front room, a space she's increasingly drawn to. She pulls on her boots, rushes out of the apartment and hurries down the stairs, her breathing shallow. Near the bottom, she steps on a trailing lace and is thrown off balance. She's propelled forward. She cannot regain her equilibrium or grip the banister in time. She lands, hard.

Vally is on her knees, panting. She stares at the loosening tiles, then rises up, rubbing her sore, burning palms on her skirts. Her muscles ache. She will bruise for this.

When she walks out on to the street, Egon has a scowl on his face. He doesn't even notice her blotched cheeks, the sweat streaked across her forehead, the dust on her knees.

'At last!' he exclaims. 'Let's go. It's very important I make a good impression tonight.'

'I don't want to do this, Egon, please.'

'You said you wanted to see this film.'

'Not sitting beside those spoiled sisters.'

'You'll enjoy their company. I thought it would be nice for you to spend some time with women your own age, instead of old men and artists.'

Vally shakes her head, her temples throbbing. 'It will be intolerable. Go without me,' she says, turning back.

'Impossible. Herr Harms won't let his daughters out of the door if you're not there.'

Vally bites her lip. This is torture. 'I'd rather face a firing squad,' she says.

'Don't say such idiotic things,' Egon snaps. 'I could be called up to fight any day now, sent into battle, unless I can avoid it. This weak heart of mine has saved me so far. But I'm scared, Vally, and you should be, too.'

Vally slumps further, the air leaving her. What was she thinking, agreeing to this? She said she'd do it so as not to appear jealous, ignoring the feeling in her gut, but now it seems like madness. 'Promise me this will be the only time. We'll never have to see them again.'

'I promise,' Egon says, taking her by the arm and dragging her across the road.

∽

Two nights after the disastrous cinema outing, and Vally still has not regained her pride. Her trust in him has evaporated, and she doesn't know which way to turn.

Egon, full of boyish confidence, has gone out for the evening to meet a friend.

'Who were you with?' Vally asks as soon as he is through the door.

'Erwin,' he replies, taking off his coat and hanging it up. 'We played billiards, we drank. I did tell you I'd be out till late.'

Vally refills her short glass to the brim. She has worked through one bottle already. Or is it two?

'How was your evening,' he asks. 'Did you manage to entertain yourself?'

It's then that Egon notices a second, empty, glass on the table beside Vally. He stops rolling his cigarette and runs a hand over his head.

'Erwin called,' Vally says, looking up at him. 'He came to see you.'

'Vally, I can . . .'

'He's wonderful company.' She smiles and scrunches up one eye. 'I see why you are keen to spend so much time with him. We laughed all night. Who were you really with? One of your models? Or another girl I don't even know the name of?'

Egon sits down beside her. 'Listen, Vally, I owe you an explanation,' he says. She turns her head to listen. 'Circumstances have been challenging. As you know, my uncle hasn't sent any money for a long time. My art is selling, but buyers are slow to pay.'

'What's that got to do with you not being here?' Vally slurs.

'It means that life has been difficult. You've not had the energy to work, or for other things . . . I needed time, on my own, to see to things.'

The rim of the glass knocks against Vally's teeth as she takes a large sip. 'So you lied?'

'To protect you,' he says solemnly. 'I didn't want to hurt you.'

'Hurt me? You couldn't,' Vally says abruptly. 'I've never *loved* you, you know.'

'Vally, I feel a world of tenderness for you. The way you stood by me during that ordeal in Neulengbach. I wouldn't have made it through without your support.'

'But you don't love me either?' she says.

'I appreciate your company, if that's what you mean?'

Vally lurches across the room and grabs a fountain pen. 'Write it down,' she says.

'What?'

'Get your sketchbook. I want you to write something down for me. Say that on this date,' Vally announces, 'the eighth of January . . .' Egon grimaces. 'Write it down!' she insists, her face blotchy. 'Write: "I am not in love with anyone in the world."'

'Vally?' He tries to take her hand. 'How is this necessary?'

'I want it to be recorded. It's the only voice I have. One day, people will need to know.' Egon faithfully registers her words. He passes the sketchbook over.

'Forgive me,' he says. 'You don't deserve this. I promise things will be different.'

'Let me see,' Vally says, tracing the words with her finger. She takes the pen, then signs her name at the bottom – graceless letters that could have been scrawled by a child. 'Walburga Neuzil,' she repeats into the gulf between them.

20

May 1915

'A re you not sick and tired of this stinking city?' Vally accosts Egon the moment he returns to the apartment. He never seems to be around any more and this feeling, as if he always has somewhere else to be, that she's always waiting for him, has been brewing inside her for some time now.

'What are you talking about?' he asks, distracted, checking the pockets of his coat.

'It feels more stifling than ever, doesn't it?' she continues. 'The coffee houses are crammed with bores. Your friends have been drafted to fight. It's impossible to get the most basic supplies. This war is stripping all the joy from our lives. What's the good of Vienna if we can't enjoy it? Let's get away, anywhere the war will allow us. How about that place on the coast your parents visited after they were married?'

'That reminds me,' he says, 'Gertrude has promised to visit tomorrow. My sweet sister, the mother.' Egon hasn't looked at Vally since he came through the door. 'She's bringing the baby with her, little Anton Junior. A fine name, I suppose. But I still don't understand why they couldn't have named him after Father.'

'Egon, please stop talking about your sister and the baby, I'm talking about us.' Vally angles herself into his line of sight. 'Leaving Vienna would restore us. Let's go. Think of the work you could make.'

'You're forgetting the horrors of Krumau, and you hated Neulengbach. It's not the right time. I could be called up to fight at a moment's notice.'

'You said you'll be excused, on account of your heart?'

'But I'm exhibiting, selling work, meeting new people . . .'

'Ghastly people!' Vally says, her mind on Adele Harms and her pathetic sister, who they keep bumping into on the street. 'I need to get away. Please.'

'And *I* need a little peace. You've been uptight and irritating for weeks.'

'You're the one who has pushed me away,' she says.

'You've become needy.' Egon knows she will recoil from this accusation.

'You never listen to me any more,' she insists weakly.

'I'm tired of listening! There's so much to be done. Important things! I'm making a name for myself. For the first time, things are falling in my favour. I don't want to ruin that. I don't want complications. And I don't have the time to stand here arguing. I still haven't replied to Roessler and he's been waiting on my response for days. He's been pestering me about all kinds of things, putting ideas in my head about the future, about the path I have to take. He's expecting my answer.' Egon pulls out the chair and takes up his fountain pen. He composes a few lines, determination and annoyance shifting across his face.

'Must your art always come first?'

'Would you prefer it if we didn't have any money?' he snaps. 'Both of us can't lie on our backs all day doing nothing, filling our faces with sweets without a care in the world.'

Vally emits a choked noise. Anger surges. She grasps Egon's glass inkpot with the silver lid and, before she knows what she's doing, Vally hurls it at the bay window. It flies through the air. For a second, two, it is suspended. Then it explodes against the wall. Black ink splashes across one of Egon's artworks.

'You're hysterical! Are you trying to destroy me?' Egon inspects the piece, bending over it, while Vally flings insults at his back. He grabs his jacket. 'Enough! I've had all I can take. Of you, of this! I expect this mess to be cleaned up before I get back.'

The door slams and Vally collapses on to the floor. She cannot remember the last time she cried. She won't do it now. She wrenches the emotion out of herself as if wringing an old dishcloth. Her ribs ache. She has lost so much to that man. There's nothing left. All her pride, all her confidence. He has taken it all.

~

After an hour, she stands, shakily. The apartment is quiet. It's still bright outside. The ink remains wet to the touch, and her hands are covered in it. Vally walks to the desk. Egon has left the letter he was writing to Arthur Roessler exposed on the table. He believes she can't read, so no need to hide it. She pulls the page towards her. Egon had managed a few sentences before abandoning it. The letters swim before Vally's eyes.

There's a line about Egon's art and the new exhibition.

Vally keeps reading. The final sentence catches her eye.

I intend to get married . . . Egon has scribbled.

The words pulse on the page. Vally is holding her breath.

'Ad-van-tageous-ly,' she reads out loud. But what does it mean?

I intend to get married, advantageously.

Her heart hammers. She spots her own name, written in the hand of the man to whom she has devoted herself. Then the words, underlined, and their meaning, slap her.

Not Vally.

21

June 1915

'Vally, it's wonderful to see you.' Egon stands as soon as she pushes through the doors of Café Eichberger. The sound of his voice stops her, the energy and enthusiasm in it.

'I don't have much time,' she says.

'Take a seat,' he insists, pulling out a chair for her.

Vally sits and puts her hands together above the table, determined to show him they're not shaking. She turns her head to avoid his kiss. Egon's eyes are tight. Empty coffee cups sit on the table and an ashtray is strewn with the remnants of several cigarettes. She has turned up so late, she'd barely expected him still to be waiting for her.

'You look terrible,' Vally says. His clothes are crumpled, his fingers tobacco-stained.

'I've missed you,' he replies. The silence stretches. Vally has no intention of breaking it. 'Have you not missed me?' His fingers tap the side of his cup.

'Don't ask questions to which you won't like the answer.'

He sighs, his eyes pleading, and she wonders if he is enjoying this, the flagellation.

'I've invited you here . . .' He takes her hands in his and runs his fingers over her skin. 'I want to propose something.'

Vally flinches. She can't bear the promise that has seeped into his voice.

'Please. Don't waste my time,' she says. 'I came here for one reason and one reason only. I wanted to look you in the eye as I say this to you, so it doesn't get back to you that Roessler told me and you think I'm crying in some corner, or that you've succeeded in hurting my feelings in any way.' She pauses, tries to steady her breathing. 'Congratulations,' she manages.

The air is heavy with smoke and it stings her eyes. Egon groans and pulls his hands away.

'No, I mean it,' Vally continues. 'I wish you all the best for the future. I hope you have a very long and successful marriage.'

'You know I didn't mean for it to be this way.'

'I've been in your life for four years. I stood by you when you were imprisoned. I followed you around to god-forsaken places. I travelled with you to your exhibitions, slept next to you, listening to your damned snoring. I managed the business side of things, dealt with the buyers, and dare I say it, I inspired your most profound works. I'd have liked to hear it directly from you that you're marrying another woman. I mean, imagine my surprise to find out you had proposed to someone else while we were practically living together, while we were intimate.'

'I asked you here to tell you myself. I never wanted you to hear it from anyone but me. I'm sorry, I know that's not enough, but I didn't mean to hurt you,' he says, confirming everything she hadn't wanted to believe. 'It all happened so fast.' Vally had hoped, in her deepest core, that there had been some misunderstanding, that he'd deny it all.

'I'll never allow you to hurt me,' she says.

'I still want to be with you, if that counts for anything?'

It crosses her mind that he has been drinking.

'And does Fräulein Harms know you're here, saying these things to me?' Vally asks, her chest constricting. Egon shuffles in his seat. She stands to leave.

'Wait! Hear me out. You may view this as a marriage of necessity, of convenience, perhaps, but that doesn't mean *we* can't continue as we were. It's perfectly normal for married men to have certain . . . liaisons. In that spirit, I have something for you.' He reaches into his satchel. Vally sinks back into her seat. She needs a moment to breathe.

Egon places a thick envelope on the table between them, with the satisfaction of a man presenting a bouquet of expensive flowers. 'It's not much, but it's something. A proposal of your very own.'

'There's nothing you could offer that would interest me.'

The unopened envelope sits on the chequered cloth between them. Her name is written, in his hand, across the front. Egon offers Vally a bemused glance.

'It won't kill you to at least consider it.' He nudges it across the table. His fingers form a pyramid in front of his face as he watches her. Vally pushes the corner of the envelope away from her. What is Egon playing at?

He grabs it now and rips open the seal, pulls out a sheet of paper and passes it over. Involuntarily, Vally's eyes scan from left to right.

'It's a kind of contract,' he explains. 'I drew it up myself, so it's not official, but it is a promise of sorts, formalizing our commitment to each other. It entitles us to two weeks away together. Alone,' he says, with emphasis. 'You and I, as we've always been, each and every summer. To all intents and purposes, you'll be my model, but we can continue as before.'

Vally sucks in a long stream of air.

Egon mistakes it for delight. 'Exactly,' he says, encouraged. 'We can go wherever we please. To Trieste, to walk along the coast arm in arm, as you've always said you wanted. We can be together. That time will be ours. All you have to do is sign *here*.' Egon places the sheet on the table and runs a finger along the dotted line.

'How dare you . . .' she whispers. 'How dare you think I'd be your whore.'

'It's not like that, Vally. I know it's not much, but it's something.'

Vally bursts out laughing. 'Your darling Adele won't like this one bit.'

There's a pause and Vally sees his eyelids flicker. The late-afternoon light catches in his dark hair. She will never touch him again, never kiss him. Adele Harms has won.

'Edith,' he says so faintly she can barely hear him.

The world seems to shift.

'Edith?'

Egon juts out his chin in the smallest gesture of confirmation.

'After everything! You want a pretty doll for a wife!'

'There's more to her than meets the eye,' he says, his shoulders sagging.

'Adele, at least, has some spark.' Vally would have understood the attraction. 'But Edith . . .' Vally jumps up. Egon stops her, a hand on her arm. His tone changes.

'Edith will agree to it,' he insists.

'No doubt she has no idea that you're here making these promises to me. More fool her.'

'I'll reason with her.'

'What did you expect from me today?' Vally demands, her voice rising.

'I thought you might be pleased?' His face takes on a boyish hopefulness.

'You take and take,' she says, 'yet you're unwilling to give anything in return. When you've had your fill, you discard us, throw us away like a spent tube of paint. They were right, in Krumau, in Neulengbach. They should have thrown away the key!'

Egon's face crumples. She knows how much that will wound him.

'I know you're hurting, but I am, too,' he says, defeated. 'Come to my studio, I beg of you. I want you to see the painting I've been working on, *Death and the Maiden*. I've painted you and me. In it, we're embracing, clinging to each other, knowing we must go our separate ways – you'll see the agony I'm going through at the thought of losing you. But this' – he picks up the contract once more – 'means we can hold on to what we had. You'll be my model, my muse. I treated you badly, Vally, and you didn't deserve that.' He pauses. 'I've always loved you, you know that, in the only way I could.'

Vally takes the piece of paper.

For a split second, she sees hope, relief, victory cross his face. Then she looks Egon in the eye as she rips the agreement solidly down the middle, then again and again, until it has been shredded into so many small pieces that it can never be put back together.

'As I said, congratulations. The two of you deserve each other.'

22

June 1915

'Do something life-changing!' A plump woman catches Vally's eye, her voice insistent. There's a stall set up on the street, decked with bunting. The woman, older and soft around the edges, is handing out leaflets, stopping passers-by, encouraging young women to sign up to the Red Cross as nurses.

'Support the war effort,' she calls out cheerfully.

Earlier, Vally had dismissed the idea, but now she's intrigued. It would be a relief to do something good for a change. And she needs to get away.

'I've never been asked to serve my country before,' she comments.

'It's not only the men who can make a difference, you know? Women's work is vital to the survival of the Empire.' The older woman is wearing a tabard, her hair tucked into a crisp, white cap.

'It's never women who leave a legacy,' Vally says. 'Never women who are remembered for their efforts.'

The woman has kind eyes. 'What keeps you here in Vienna?' she asks.

'Nothing's keeping me,' Vally says. Not her family, not Egon. She touches the posters lining the stall, trying to imagine herself in the uniform.

'You look like a decent young woman.'

'Appearances can be deceptive.'

'How old are you, my dear?' the woman asks.

'I'll be twenty-one on the nineteenth of August.'

'Can you read and write?' she asks.

'A little,' Vally replies.

'Then I've just the thing for a bright young woman like yourself,' the older woman says, shuffling papers. 'How do you like the sound of Dalmatia?'

'I've never heard of the place.'

'It's five hundred miles south of here, a stone's throw from the Adriatic Sea. You'll be in the mountains, stationed near Sinj. Our men are fighting there and dying.' She passes Vally a photograph of a dozen men, injured soldiers, lying in hospital beds. One of them is smiling. 'They need the care of a good girl' – the older woman takes Vally's hands in her own, and it's mortifying, but Vally can feel tears brimming in her eyes – 'to restore their strength, help them recover. With the right care, at the right time, these men don't have to suffer. You can make the world of difference.' She pauses. 'It's you they're waiting for.'

'I'm not that person,' Vally says. 'I never have been.'

'You can be,' the woman says, with emotion. 'As a military nurse, you'll be fully trained. No experience necessary. You'll learn how to fix broken bones, administer medicines, treat the sick and injured. You'll experience very difficult things, but something tells me you can handle it. You'll be paid. You'll be respected. You'll have a place with us.'

Vally struggles to stop the tears from coming. She bites the inside of her lip.

'It might be just the fresh start you're looking for?' the woman adds.

Something hot runs down Vally's cheek. The sensation is so strange.

'All you have to do to make that happen, is sign here.'

Vally thinks of her mother, her beautiful sisters, and the life they will lead without her in it. She thinks of Egon and Edith, their upcoming marriage, the babies that woman will bear. *Frau Schiele*. She thinks of the hours she spent modelling for Egon, the poses she held, the hunger that rumbled within her as he created his artworks – the playfulness he captured, the pain, hanging on walls where she will never see it, viewed by people who will never know her name.

Tears continue to fall down her cheeks.

But finally, here is the promise of potential, something she can call her own.

Vally takes the pen. Her hands are trembling. She steadies herself and moves the ink across the page in one graceful motion. She has been practising.

Then she spells her name out above the signature, in looping, lavish letters.

Vally Neuzil.

Her future awaits.

Interlude

The Albertina Gallery, 9 May 1968

'Oh my, oh my! It's really him,' Adele whispers, entering the next room of the exhibition.

She walks over to a series of paintings depicting a young man in exaggerated poses, with various expressions on his face. She gravitates to the one that is most similar to the man she carries in her memory, then gets as close as she is able to the surface of the painting.

In this space, with his sweat in the pigment, his intention in every line, Adele feels his presence. She can smell his skin, hear his breathing, see the tightening of his throat as he swallows. She cannot drag her eyes from his. He is so very real.

But this feeling in her – it is as if her heart is tightening. The reality she once knew is so close, yet unreachable. There's no portal for her to slip through, to step back into those golden days and do things differently, behave better, make it right.

'Let me introduce you,' she says proudly in Eva's direction, 'to Egon Schiele.'

She has missed him, so very much.

'He clearly admires his own face,' Eva comments as she takes in the dozen self-portraits around them, showing the artist as a teenager and young man. She peers closely at one in which the artist's eyes are closed, his long limbs filling the space, his hand raised, fingers splayed in greeting. '*Kneeling Nude with Raised Hands*,' Eva adds. 'I like the pinks, purples and greens he's used to portray his own flesh.'

'He's handsome, wouldn't you agree?' Adele asks.

'How old would he be here?' Eva steps closer. 'It says it was painted in 1910.'

'Twenty,' Adele says, turning to look at the portrait. 'He was born in 1890, the same year as me. He was older by a few months.'

'I've never seen self-portraits like this. It's like he's almost mocking himself. Some of his models were very young, though, and the paintings are so raw,' Eva remarks, pointing to a portrait on the opposite wall of a dark-haired woman, seemingly asleep. The figure is undressed from the waist, her ribs and breasts exposed, her body taut as if she were holding her breath.

'The women he painted knew what they were doing,' Adele replies. 'Society had dismissed them but Schiele wanted them. Many would have been grateful – for the attention, for the money. It wouldn't have been much, but it was a victory of sorts.'

'Are you saying he sought out models who couldn't say no?'

'Pah! You don't know what you're talking about. He barely had any money himself. He'd go without food or firewood to be able to pay these girls. Now here they are, in a gallery, elevated above anything they'd ever dreamt possible.'

Eva looks around. 'But don't you feel sorry for them?'

'Don't you dare pity us. You modern girls think the world is made up of choices, but you forget that often there are none. There are worse things in life.'

Eva mutters words that Adele doesn't hear, then a painting of a young girl in the corner catches her eye. 'But look at this one,' she says, stepping over to the image. It shows a girl, her skirts lifted, revealing her bottom. 'Doesn't that make you uncomfortable?'

Adele sniffs, looking into the girl's eyes. 'Egon certainly crossed a line at times in the name of art. But he had his reasons. And besides, he paid the price.'

'I don't mean to upset you,' Eva says. 'But let's not turn a blind eye to such things.'

'With Egon,' Adele says, her chin raised, 'there are always more questions than answers. But, to me, he radiated an energy that I never felt with anyone else.'.

'I knew that feeling once.'

'How old are you now?' Adele asks, her eyes piercing.

'Twenty-eight,' Eva replies.

'Old enough to know better. But not so old that you can't right your wrongs.'

'The same could be said of you,' Eva suggests gently.

'Nonsense. At your age, I had the world in the palms of my hands. Then I managed to lose it all. Take my mother's advice: get married while you can, have children, make a respectable life for yourself.'

'Is that what you did?' Eva asks.

Adele's thin lips stretch into a smile. 'What do you think?'

'But did you want all that?' Eva asks.

'With him, maybe. But that was madness, on my part.' She looks up at Eva, sharply. 'Why are you crying?' Adele demands.

'I'm not.'

'It's as plain as day.'

Eva takes a deep breath and releases it. 'I've not told anyone,' she whispers.

'What exactly?'

Eva puts her fingers to her stomach.

Adele flinches. 'You're pregnant?'

'Sshhh,' Eva pleads, looking around. A passing museum security guard makes eye contact and Adele scowls at him.

'It's not the kind of thing you can keep secret for ever,' Adele warns.

Eva lowers her eyes. 'I can try.'

'Weren't you just implying that there are always choices, that you young women can do anything?'

'You don't know me,' Eva says. 'You don't know the mistakes I've made.'

'The cruelty of this life,' Adele says, 'is that we succumb to our fate and then we have to live with it, day after day after day. We're sculpted by choices we often don't have the liberty to make. Then we find ourselves shaped into something we never intended to be. You end up left with just the tiniest bit of yourself, something you hardly recognize.'

'Well, I've made my decision. It would all be over by now if I hadn't run into you.'

Eva wipes her cheek with the cuff of her lilac top.

'It doesn't have to be this way,' Adele says, softening. She puts a hand on the young woman's shoulder and gives it a gentle squeeze. 'Things can shift,' she insists. 'You have a chance to make the decision that is right for you.'

The final tour group of the day enters the room, pushing up close behind Eva and Adele, manoeuvring their shoulders to get a better view of the art. Their guide speaks with authority, gesticulating at the paintings on the walls.

'Schiele's total oeuvre includes more than three thousand works on paper and three hundred paintings,' he says. The dozen tourists dutifully listen. 'The poses seen here are sexually explicit. The most striking element is the line: jagged, energetic, tension-revealing.'

The guide catches Adele's eyes.

'But the presentation of the figures,' he adds, 'defies conventional beauty and accepted standards of depicting a nude. Schiele's models are naked, not nude; he displays their genitals without shame.' The guide takes a few steps towards the other side of the room. 'Look closely at this one, created in 1918, after the artist returned to Vienna, towards the end of the First World War,' he says. 'It's clear that Schiele saw the female figure as a raw material necessary to the construction of his art.'

'What do *you* know of Schiele?' Adele interrupts. She is struggling to keep her balance and Eva takes her by the arm.

'Excuse me? Are you part of this group?' he says.

'I could tell you a few things.'

'Madame, I'm afraid you'll have to book on to the next tour. That will be tomorrow now.'

'You know nothing about the artist or his intentions,' Adele snorts.

'I'm only an expert in art history.' The man holds up a booklet.

'Come now, let's find somewhere to sit, before you get us thrown out,' Eva says, guiding Adele towards an empty bench facing a striking painting in the next room.

'You can read my essay in the catalogue guide, available in the gift shop,' the man calls after them.

The old woman collapses on to the seat. She's tired and weak.

'Why do I have to listen to all these men telling me how it was?' Adele asks.

'You don't, Adele. Not any more,' Eva reassures her.

They remain that way, Eva comforting the old woman in the middle of the gallery, the tourists milling past.

Finally, Adele lifts her head. Her eyes seem darker, less focused.

'Edith?' she gasps, pulling away from Eva's grasp.

Adele is already hobbling into the next room, clutching her heart.

A portrait of a young woman hangs in the centre. Her large, doleful eyes look out, her cheeks stained with a blush. Her hair is the colour of straw. She's wearing a dress with an oversized ruffle, her hands clasped in front of her, her fingers long and spindly.

'This is the woman from the poster,' Eva says. 'I saw her that day I ran into you.'

'My sister,' Adele reveals. 'I've been waiting my entire life to be close to her again.'

Eva looks from the painting to Adele. 'You must be confused. It says here' – Eva leans in to read the title – 'that this is a portrait of the artist's wife, from 1915.'

'Her name is Edith Harms.'

'The name that was in the letters, the bundle you carried tied in ribbon?' Eva asks.

'She wrote to me every week, during the war. I'm ashamed to say I never replied.'

'I don't understand. Egon Schiele was your brother-in-law?' Eva says. 'I thought you had a relationship with the artist.'

'He chose her,' Adele replies slowly, drawing in air. She wills the woman in the painting to turn those eyes upon her. Standing before her in this way, bowed and broken, with Edith looking exactly the same, so serene, makes Adele's legs begin to buckle.

'I had to see you again,' Adele whispers to the woman in the frame. 'One more time, after that frightful day, to speak the words that I've needed to say for a lifetime.'

EDITH

1

17 June 1915

A veil, carrying the scent of its storage box, obscures Edith's view as she steps down from the horse-drawn carriage alongside her father and approaches the entrance to the local church in Hietzing. Inside, everyone will be waiting for her. Egon, her groom, at the altar.

Today, especially, she doesn't feel like herself. Edith had barely recognized the woman steadily looking back at her from the gilded mirror in her bedroom as she'd prepared herself that morning. She had watched as the stranger rubbed cold cream into her face, blotting away the excess before her cheeks, forehead and neck were dusted with pearly powder. Rouge was patted along her cheekbones, her lashes rubbed with petroleum jelly and coal dust. Finally, a cosmetic was dabbed into the pad of her lower lip. Edith and the reflected soon-to-be wife closed their lips at the same time, rolling the top against the bottom, before releasing them with a dull pop. Then her mother had come between them, as she clipped a string of pearls around her neck, spritzed the atomizer in her direction and secured the borrowed veil.

Now Edith holds on to Papa's arm as he guides her across the uneven flagstones. He's wearing a fine dark suit and sweating gently in the heat. When they stop at the church entrance, Edith turns to him, a small smile on her lips. She wants this, she really does, but she must appear chaste, demure, not let on to those around her that she played a part in orchestrating her own fate. Instead, she allows herself to be carried along, smiling sweetly, acquiescing all the while, not consumed by needs of her own – for where does demonstrable desire lead you, other than to madness and disappointment?

Papa squeezes her arm and gives a small nod of confirmation. She wonders if he can hear the stretched, scissoring sound of her nerves, heightened at the thought of seeing all those people in the church. A high-pitched pulse rings in her ears. But when Edith walks through the arched entrance, the noise inside her head is drowned out as the organist rouses the guests to their feet.

She steadies herself and smooths the creamy fabric of her dress. It had belonged to Edith's cousin and neither fits well nor suits her. It's too heavy for a summer wedding, with a suffocating high neck and an excess of material for her height and frame. But this marriage came about so abruptly, and was organized in such haste, that there has been no time to find a more suitable gown or for alterations to be made. It has been doused in lavender water to hide the scent of camphor. In any case, because of the war, Edith has had to make do. The rush was intensified because Egon was determined that, if they must marry in a hurry, and if the wedding were to fall in June, then they should follow in the footsteps of his parents thirty-six years earlier, and marry on the seventeenth – on that, there could be no negotiation.

In the time she has known him, Egon has barely mentioned his father, other than to say he was a respected stationmaster who died after a long illness, and that he'd admired the man greatly, even if they hadn't always seen eye to eye. Edith had come away with the impression that the two weren't excessively close, and yet here he is now, fervently attached to honouring his father's memory. Edith can't help but wonder why it means so much to him.

The music booms around her, and the friends and family who've been able to make it turn to observe Edith, their eyes taking in every detail. She must get used to this, she supposes – the probing eyes of others – if she is to model for the artist, as she understands she will have to.

Some of the guests she has met only recently. Conscription has taken away many of Egon's former classmates, and travel has been increasingly difficult as the war continues, so it has been impossible for them to return for a visit, however brief. Egon's wealthy patrons and his distinguished friend Gustav Klimt – all older men – have remained in Vienna, however, and have come to show their support. At the very front, Edith can see Frau Schiele smoothing her skirts and Egon's sister Melanie in an extravagant hat. Edith only became acquainted with them a few days ago, but both women had been welcoming, if gently staggered at the news that Egon had proposed marriage. Egon's uncle Leopold, beaming at her from a pew, told her they were delighted that Egon had finally come to his senses and chosen such a charming and respectable young lady.

Edith concentrates on putting one foot in front of the other. Up ahead is the artist, the man she had secretly set her heart on and whose affections she is astounded to have won. But who is he really, this man who she must know for ever? He waits, his back turned, moving from one foot to the other.

Then he turns to face her. His smile, as his eyes lock on hers, is wide and devoid of self-consciousness. His hair is brushed back, the skin below his hairline glistening, his cheeks flushed. He looks so handsome, it's heart-stopping. Happiness sharpens beneath her ribs. She notices a nick of blood on his neck. He'll have shaved this morning, a fresh blade, no doubt.

This, then, is her moment.

Her darling Papa looks at her. He seems reluctant to leave, but after a brief squeeze of Edith's wrist, he moves to take his seat next to Mutti, who's squashed on to the narrow wooden bench between the Brons and elderly aunts and cousins from the Harms side of the family.

Then the minister speaks. His words slide into one another and she cannot distinguish much except her own name and Egon's. There are hymns and Bible readings.

Behind her, from the pews, comes the sound of a child crying. It's distracting. Edith turns. The culprit is a fat little thing, perched on its mother's knee. The woman ignores it, simply jiggles the child up and down. She has a pale, thin face, a straight nose, and a halo of copper hair. She looks so similar to Egon that this must be Gertrude, Egon's younger sister. She did not attend the family meeting; Egon had tried to downplay the suggestion that she had refused the invitation. 'She can't wait to meet you,' he'd said. But now, here she is, her cool eyes on Edith, taking in every thread of her. Edith feels uncomfortable under the scrutiny, as if she has been found lacking. The woman whispers to a man to her right, her husband, who Edith knows to be Egon's friend Anton. Neither one is smiling. When the baby continues to cry, the woman gets up, slips past the other guests, and takes it outside.

Edith quickly scans the faces of the other guests. Adele is at home, supposedly suffering from a migraine. She has remained in bed since the announcement, refusing even to open the curtains. She has not spoken to her sister since the day she found out about the wedding and, in her rage, launched a champagne glass at Edith's chest. In fact, Adele has not spoken to a soul. Edith was forced to move from the bedroom they shared, fearing for her safety, and sleep in the same small room as Hanna, the maid.

Edith is nudged back into the moment. Everyone is waiting. It's so very hot.

The minister repeats his question. In a daze, she has placed a band, which once belonged to his father, on Egon's finger and heard him speak, although she's not sure exactly what he said.

'And will you, Edith Anna Harms, take this man . . .' Egon's eyes are on her. Her name sounds so strange coming from the minister's mouth, as if separated from her actual existence. Edith focuses on the movement of the minister's lips. '. . . Egon Leo Adolf Ludwig Schiele, to be your wedded husband?' he repeats. She has never heard his middle names before. Edith sways. It is suddenly as if she cannot get enough air.

Then, at the back, stepping between the shadows, Edith sees a woman in black, a shawl wrapped around her shoulders, with her face partially obscured, despite the heat. The eyes are so dark and menacing, they take her breath away. Could the woman be Adele? Or a scorned Vally? Whoever it is, Edith is worried she might try to put a stop to the union.

'I take thee to be my lawful husband,' Edith says quickly and decisively, her throat dry.

Egon takes a ring from his pocket. The beautiful gold band glints and shines. He slips it on. It catches for an awkward moment on the knot of her knuckle so he pushes again while she holds her breath. She intends to wear this ring for the rest of her life.

'Now that Egon Schiele and Edith Harms have given themselves to each other by solemn vows, I pronounce that they are husband and wife, in the name of the Father, and of the Son, and of the Holy Spirit. Those whom God hath joined together, let no man put asunder,' the minister says.

'Edith Schiele?' she whispers to herself. Yes. The artist's wife.

Edith looks back at the shadows, wondering if the woman was a hallucination from the heat. Whoever she was, she has gone. Edith spots lovely Hanna standing at the back of the church and smiles.

Egon's face is very close to hers. He takes the edge of her veil between his fingers and lifts it up over her head. As he does so, his fingers brush her hair. Then he takes her by the shoulders. She's electrified by his touch. He leans in, closer, closer. Edith shuts her eyes as his lips meet hers.

2

June 1915

The truth is, Edith had not been as passive in the sequence of events as everyone believed.

She'd seen the artist from the window that first October evening more than two years ago, as he moved his belongings into the apartment opposite theirs. She, too, had experienced a flutter of intrigue and desire as she watched him. But of course, her sister got there first, staking her claim, declaring him her own.

Adele had always passed things down to her little sister. It began with the dolls she no longer cared for, books she'd finished; later it was dresses she'd outgrown – the natural order in a family with two girls. By the time they were older, Adele had grown accustomed to taking things first and without thought. Edith never minded much.

But when they'd left the apartment that night, hurrying to the opera, and the artist brushed past them on the street, Edith had seen a look in his eyes and felt a kind of knowing pass between them. It was a look she had been unable to shake from her mind the entire night. Adele, of course, had been oblivious, and had prattled on, leaving no space for Edith to admit her own feelings.

In the past, Adele's passions had usually burned themselves out, and Edith had assumed this new one would suffer the same fate – that her sister would grow bored and move on. But that did not happen. Instead, Adele's obsession seemed only to intensify, as if magnified under a lens.

Edith may not have been honest with her sister about her attraction to Egon, but she'd have stepped aside gracefully if she'd witnessed a great love blooming between Adele and the artist. Instead, Edith saw the way he looked at *her* on the occasions when they met in the street – his eyes glistening with questions that no man had asked of her before. He seemed to be the first person who saw Edith for who she really was, and she couldn't bear to be unseen again. In every interaction, she felt the threads tightening between them. Adele was ignorant, too caught up in her own chorus, and so triumphant over every perceived conquest, that she never noticed that the artist did not look at her in the same way.

After more than a year of this budding attraction between them, and more than two years since she'd first caught sight of him, along with the disastrous trip to the moving pictures with that woman Vally in tow, Edith knew she had to find a way to talk to the artist, alone. But with Mutti on high alert because of her worries over Adele, there was little opportunity.

That all changed one day in May, when Hanna lumbered up the stairs holding another letter from him, playfully addressed to 'Ad and Ed'. There was very little Hanna did not see or have influence over in the Harms household, despite appearances. Long ago, Adele had made an enemy of Hanna by treating her with disdain, and she paid for it, every day, in trivial ways. Edith recognized the writing as the artist's, for he'd written before, but she'd barely seen those letters. Adele had claimed them, devouring the words, owning them, and sleeping with them under her pillow.

This time, Edith intended to read the letter at her own pace, savouring the message, before sharing it with her sister. Edith took it from Hanna with a kiss and escaped to the privacy of the linen closet. It was the only place where she could be safe from prying eyes. Nestled amid the towels, blankets and bedding, Edith ran a finger over the creamy paper. She took a grip from her hair to prise open the envelope. Then she unfolded the paper and scanned the words: *Are you under house arrest? Why not visit me? I realize this would not be considered appropriate.*

Reading his words, Edith felt something speed up inside her. And with those short lines, she devised her plan. She knew that Mutti had her salon the following day, so she would only have Adele to deal with. Edith wrote her response, saying that indeed, living under such scrutiny was entirely suffocating, and would Egon be kind enough to meet briefly at the corner of the road the next morning at eleven thirty. *Only to have the chance to say hello once more*, she wrote, signing off from both of them.

Adele found the artist handsome, but Edith had caught glimpses of something deeper in him that her sister failed to grasp: a sensitivity in the way he considered things, his gentleness when he was around her, his way of looking at the world, as she'd witnessed at the gallery. All the other suitors her mother kept trying to press upon her paled in comparison. Edith felt guilty about betraying Adele, and she didn't want to hurt her, but why should she allow her sister to claim Egon just because she'd seen him first?

Edith tucked the letter in her blouse and headed towards the kitchen. She needed an ally.

'Hanna . . .' she began. How best to phrase it? Edith had to tread carefully. 'I know this will seem like a strange request, and not one you'll relish, but could you see to it that Adele accompanies you to the market tomorrow morning while Mutti is entertaining her ladies? And please, don't hurry home.'

Edith thought Hanna might ask why, but the maid gave her a warm, knowing look.

'For you, my dear, anything,' Hanna replied, as she busied herself with lunch.

'And please could you pass this note back to the artist this afternoon?'

'I know he'll be pleased to see you,' Hanna replied, squeezing Edith's arm.

Adele must never find out that Edith had taken matters into her own hands in such a reckless manner. Edith took Egon's letter from her blouse, held it to her lips, and opened the grate to the stove. The gold flicker of the fire was mesmerizing. She admired the flames as they consumed the paper and felt relieved. For the first time in her life, she might have something to call her own.

~

Meeting Egon alone that day sealed Edith's fate. The busy main street of Hietzing was dotted with elegant men and women, well-dressed children holding the hands of their nannies, and horse-drawn carriages heading in the direction of the Innere Stadt. Adele, protesting, had left with Hanna some time earlier, chased out of the apartment by Mutti. Edith, waiting in bed for her sister's departure – under the false pretence of a cough – had felt truly queasy at the thought that Adele might not leave, or that she'd dither and delay to the extent that she'd bump into the artist herself and ruin it all.

But at the last moment, things had come to pass just as she'd hoped they would.

Egon was waiting, hands in his pockets, rocking gently on his heels. He'd politely asked about Adele. Edith said she'd been called away.

He raised his eyebrows and smiled conspiratorially.

'Just you and I, then, Fräulein Harms? Shall we take a walk in Park Schönbrunn?'

'I can spare half an hour, at the very most,' Edith replied, feeling nervous.

They headed in the direction of the park, Egon walking close alongside her. As she stepped off the pavement, his hand brushed against hers. He apologized immediately.

'Forgive me,' he said, grinning. 'I know what is said of me but I can assure you my intentions are pure. I have the utmost respect for you, Edith.'

She couldn't help but smile at his manners. This was the same young man who had shocked Vienna.

They talked, circling various subjects, a dance of words that mirrored the emotion brewing between them. She asked about his art, his ambitions for the future. He asked the same question of her. What did she want from her life? Who did she want to become?

An admiral butterfly landed on his lapel and he stopped in the middle of the path, dipping his hat to an elderly couple a few steps behind them. He lifted it off, gently, examined it, its dusty pigments on his finger.

He held the insect up without telling her what to see.

'I should go,' Edith said, reluctantly. 'My sister will be returning any minute now.'

'Of course,' Egon replied. 'Let me walk you back to your door, at least.'

Edith winced. 'Adele might see us together, and that would be . . . problematic.'

'I've noticed that she looks at me rather intensely,' Egon said with a wry smile.

They stopped on the corner of the main street in Hietzing. 'Before you go,' he added. 'I want to say something . . . it's about Vally.' He cleared his throat. 'I intend to talk to her and bring things to a dignified end. I hope you understand what I'm trying to say.'

His eyes searched her face.

Edith shook her head. 'What do you mean?'

'Edith,' he said, 'I can't shake the feeling that there's more to you than meets the eye and every time I'm with you, you prove me right. I want to know you, deeply. Will you allow me that privilege?'

⁓

Edith was playing cards, weeks later, after several more clandestine meetings with the artist, each with its own excitement, when there was a knock at their door.

'Herr Schiele, greetings,' she heard Hanna say from the hallway.

'Hello, Hanna,' he said warmly. 'I'd like to speak with Herr Harms, if I may?'

Edith jumped. What was Egon doing here?

'What may I say it's regarding?' Hanna asked.

'A private matter, I'm afraid,' Egon replied.

Edith crept into the hallway.

'Herr Harms doesn't like to be disturbed, especially at this time in the morning.'

'Tell him we have serious business to discuss.'

What business? Edith wondered. Her mind jumped.

Hanna, grumbling, approached the room where Papa took his breakfast. She knocked.

'What is it now?' Papa demanded. Hanna's reply was lost as she went in and the door closed behind her.

'What are you doing here?' Edith hissed at Egon.

'I saw your mother leave with Adele, so I'm taking my chances with your father.'

'Egon, surely you're not . . . this is too soon!'

'But I am sure of my intentions, Edith. And how much longer do we need? Besides, this war is building. My brother-in-law, Anton, has already received his conscription papers. This might be our only chance.' The door opened and Hanna beckoned him in. 'Trust me,' he said nervously as he went into the room. Hanna approached.

'This is men's business. Come, I'll make camomile to calm your nerves,' she said.

Edith put her ear to the wood. 'I'm not going anywhere, not with my fate being discussed.'

'Herr Harms, I regret that I've disturbed you, but this matter can't wait,' she could hear Egon saying. Hanna joined her by the door. 'I'm here to make a proposal. I want to ask for your daughter's hand in marriage.'

Breath pooled in Edith's lungs and Hanna gripped her arm.

'You've come here, Herr Schiele, at this unsociable hour, hoping to find me in an agreeable mood, so that you might ask to marry my daughter?'

'There's no time like the present, sir.'

'If I were your age, I'd be satisfied to wait a while,' Papa replied.

'With respect, I'm almost twenty-five. And this war has changed everything. I want to step into my future as a better man – and draw a line under the foolish days of my youth.'

'Ah, yes, all of Vienna knows of your misdemeanours. What gives you the idea I'd allow my daughter to marry an artist – and a convict, no less?'

'I was found guilty of nothing more than creating art, sir. I've learnt my lesson. I can assure you, I'll not abuse the trust you place in me with your daughter. I've much to offer.'

'Much to offer?' Edith could hear the derision in Papa's voice. 'Let us be frank, Herr Schiele – what way of life can an artist seriously offer my daughter? What have you by way of financial stability? You offer little in terms of respectability.'

'My name is beginning to hold value, abroad as well as in Austria. I have accepted three commissions this month alone and I expect many more. My situation is improving.'

'Is that so? And what about your family?'

'My uncle, Leopold Czihaczek, was chief inspector for the Imperial-Royal Austrian State Railways. My father, a stationmaster. I was brought up with rules and taught manners.'

'How does a respectable man such as that end up with an artist for a son?' Papa mused out loud. Egon suffered a moment's silence. Papa realized he'd gone too far, for he turned the conversation. 'Your means are not stable, but adequate, so you're asking me to place my faith in your potential. The stakes are very high. This is my daughter we're talking about. Are you a man who's capable of making sacrifices?'

'I've made countless sacrifices for my art.'

'Your art! I want to know if you can make sacrifices for your family.

Can you follow a straight path, stay out of trouble?' He paused. 'Will you put Adele first?'

'Edith,' the young man said simply.

'What could you possibly want with Edith? Adele's the one who should marry first. Edith's too young, you must see that.' Papa sounded as if he was in pain.

'She's twenty-two. My mother was five years younger when she married.'

'She's delicate,' her father warned.

'She'll cope perfectly well,' Egon replied.

'No, it's simply impossible.'

Edith felt dizzy.

'I'm afraid I've fallen in love.'

'Love! You young men, always confounding expectations.' Papa paused. 'You've got some nerve, son. Now, you've said what you came to say. My coffee's cold. I'll think on it. Will that satisfy you for now?'

'I'll return later for your answer.'

'I'll need to discuss this with my wife. Nothing happens around here without her say-so, let me tell you. You've a lot to learn.'

'This morning, a young man was here,' Papa said later, entering the room Edith shared with Adele. 'He arrived at our door with a proposition.' Edith looked at her father, frowning, taking in the bottle of cognac and two glasses he held in his hands. 'The artist,' he said, setting the items down.

Edith straightened the remaining cards in her hands, noticing that the cognac was well below the pencil line that her mother drew on it each night. She moved her head to encourage Papa to continue, unable to trust herself to speak. Her father filled one glass and held it out to her. He'd never offered his daughter alcohol before. The scorched smell of it was terrible.

'The artist is keen to marry,' Papa continued. He positioned himself at the foot of Adele's bed and coughed into a silk handkerchief. 'He wants to marry *you*.'

Edith dropped her playing cards and rose to her feet. 'And what did you say?'

'That you were too young and too sensitive to marry an artist. But he wouldn't be swayed.'

Edith reddened and her heart was pounding. Things had moved far quicker than she'd ever imagined and this made it all too real. This was what she wanted, but it was also the point of no return, when she had to choose between the artist and her sister.

'What about Adele? She will be terribly unhappy about this.'

'He was clear. Edith, he said. So here we are.' Papa examined his hands. 'This war is doing untold damage. Battle brings spectacular upheaval. We're already feeling the repercussions. Belts are tightening, food is harder to come by, fuel is running low and the hostility grows. Many of my former colleagues are feeling the strain financially. For some, it may end in bankruptcy. Even Herr Bron is struggling.' He looked away. 'I must tell you something . . .' She'd never seen Papa like this, so ragged. 'We've been dealt a bad hand. There's no money for second chances. In fact, there's scarcely any money at all.' The family finances had hardly entered Edith's thoughts. She knew the war had made things scarce, but now that her father had confessed the truth about their situation, she recognized the small economies that were being made, the household damage that had gone unrepaired, the smaller cuts of meat, the strain in Hanna's eyes.

'Egon Schiele is far from being my first choice of husband for you,' he said. 'But circumstances have conspired against us. Young men have been sent away to fight. Married, you'll have a place. Unwed, you may be waiting a long time for our soldiers to return.'

'So I'm to marry the artist?' Edith said, her voice faltering.

'Do you want to?' Her father looked up, as if seeing her properly for the first time.

The chambers of Edith's heart constricted, caught between conflicting desires. On one side there was the deep love she held for her sister. She knew how much this course of action would hurt Adele. To agree would be to cut her down, as if Adele were a tree, Edith wielding the sharpened axe. On the other side was Egon, and a future by his side. Edith saw herself coming into bloom, unfurling from the old ideas about who she was and turning into this new version of herself. To say no to her father now would be to nip that woman in the bud, deny her, take away the source of light she gravitated towards. She weighed up her loyalties. Edith would lose part of herself, whichever way she turned. It was impossible to have both – a relationship with her sister and a relationship with Egon. But she had to make a choice.

She looked into her father's eyes and said, 'I do.'

Then she began to cry.

3

June 1915

The carriage pulls to a stop on Hietzinger Hauptstrasse. Egon gets out first and holds the door open for Edith. 'My wife!' he says theatrically, and offers her his hand. She takes it. Her feet still tingle from the wedding waltzes she performed with Egon and their guests late into the night. They had danced together in front of everyone. At one point Egon had taken her by the waist and dipped her back, her pearls skimming the underside of her chin as she hung as gracefully as she could from his arms. Egon even succeeded in dancing with Mutti, much to her chagrin. Without a father of the groom, Edith had partnered with Egon's brother-in-law, Anton. He had taken her energetically around the room, spinning her off her feet with an elegance and strength she'd not expected. Edith had laughed, out of breath, while Gertrude glared at the pair of them.

Of course, the wedding reception had been smaller and more restrained than what might have been expected before the war. But the families and friends had shared a modest meal in the side room of a respectable restaurant and, afterwards, the tables had been pushed to the sides as the music began.

Now Edith stands in the middle of the street that she has lived on her entire life. She looks up at the windows of the tall apartment building she'd left that morning, at the entrance through which she has walked all those times without a second thought. Egon takes her arm and turns her towards another door. He reaches into his jacket for the key. Edith can feel the sting of hidden eyes on her as clearly as if a hand were nipping at her back.

'Hurry, please,' she says. Egon opens the door, then sweeps his arms beneath her to carry her into the building. 'Really!' she laughs. 'Put me down.' Edith feels heavy, cumbersome, in his arms. She shifts her weight and kicks her feet.

'It's not often I say it, but some traditions,' Egon says, 'should be maintained.' Edith's ankles bash against the door frame. Adele's laughter rattles in her head.

Back on her own feet, they climb the stairs to Egon's apartment.

'Your new abode, Frau Schiele,' he announces. 'I intend to make you very comfortable here. You must make yourself at home.'

Edith walks into the large open space. She intends to brighten the place up. Egon's painting and drawing equipment overwhelms the room. She'll buy colourful fabrics to make rugs and cushions and fill the space with leafy plants. Egon's easel is set up in front of the bay window. She notices that to the left of it is a large ink stain across the wall, great splatters dried into the plaster. Edith is surprised that the spill wasn't cleaned up at the time.

There's also a wall of books, a desk, a chair, and a gigantic mirror. Edith stands before it. The heavy cream wedding dress isn't as bad as she thought. But still, she's surprised at how uneasy she always manages to appear, her arms straight before her, the tips of her fingers resting nervously against her thumbs. She almost looks idiotic.

Very soon, she'll be expected to perform the duties of a wife. She has no doubt that Egon will know what to do, even if she has no idea.

Edith watches as her reflection steps out of the frame of the mirror. She walks past the kitchenette towards the bedroom. She passes a small room with a sink, a speckled mirror and a washbasin, with a damp flannel draped across the ledge. Edith brushes her fingers over Egon's cologne, his cracked soap, his razor in its pouch, cataloguing their positions. She notices that there is stubble clinging to the enamel of the washbasin; she runs her little finger around the inner curve, then blows the residue from the tip.

Egon is in the bedroom, sitting on the bed, his feet up, his shoes kicked off, rolling a cigarette. His shirtsleeves are turned up and all the buttons down the front are undone, revealing his chest. This man, her husband, is still little more than a stranger.

Three large trunks of Edith's belongings were delivered to his apartment earlier that day, and she goes to them now, keeping her back to Egon. They are full of brocade skirts, loose tea gowns for the afternoon, lace-trimmed petticoats and frilly bloomers. Edith kneels to open one and removes her nightgown, which she had placed on the very top that morning. It's freshly laundered. She removes what she'll need to prepare for bed: her wash things, a sleeping bonnet, a silver-handled hairbrush.

Edith carries them to the privacy of the bathroom. Egon runs his tongue along the rolling paper of his cigarette, his eyes on her. He looks mildly amused, but it's unfathomable to Edith that she might undress in front of him. No husband would expect that of a wife.

Many minutes later, Edith emerges. She carefully twists the knob of the bedroom door, not wanting to disturb Egon, but he's still awake, fully dressed, sitting on the bed reading. Light music plays quietly from a gramophone in the corner.

'Well, you look ... very neat,' he says, the sides of his mouth twitching.

Edith can hear his tone is teasing. 'This is what I always wear to bed.' The hem of her loose, long-sleeved nightdress sweeps the floor. It is buttoned carefully up her neck. Her hair has been brushed one hundred times, plaited and tucked away under her bonnet.

'Well, for a start, we won't be needing this.' Egon stands, walks over to her, then undoes the white ribbon under her chin, pulling on its length until the bonnet shifts and her plait comes tumbling out. He lets the bonnet drop, then holds her braid in his fingers, bringing the tip to his lips.

'But ...' Edith says, pulling away slightly. Egon undoes the buttons at her throat. One by one, his fingers do the work. He's gentle, but insistent. Edith can't swallow her fear.

Egon pulls her close, breathes into her exposed neck. 'You'll enjoy it,' he says. 'In fact, you'll learn to love it. This is what couples do.' He steps from his trousers, then leads her towards the bed. Egon wants what is owed to a husband. He loosens the last buttons on her nightgown and pulls it up over her head. 'There's so much material!' he says, holding the fabric aloft, daring her to reclaim it.

He throws the gown across the room and it lands in a heap by the door. Then he removes his white shirt. Edith is embarrassed. She has never seen a man exposed in this way before. Egon's chest is pale, his muscles slender beneath his skin. There are a few dark hairs between his nipples. His forearms and torso are sprinkled with freckles. Edith notices a leaf-shaped birthmark on his hip.

Egon eases her back, gently, on to the pillows, then takes her wrists and straightens them above her head. He looks at her with an artist's eye, but there's a hunger there that's not professional. Egon does not rush. He lies next to Edith and strokes her skin, starting at her hips and moving up. She's electrified.

Disgust, desire. She thinks of Adele. Shame.

She can't take it any more. She runs to the bathroom.

Egon gives her a moment, then comes to the door. He speaks from the other side. 'Edith, come on, don't cry. It's not such a terrible thing.'

'I can't,' she says. 'I won't.'

'My mother was the same. On her wedding night, she locked herself in the bathroom and refused to come out. It sounds strange, but in a way it pleases me to see history repeating itself.' Edith doesn't reply. 'Of course, so the story goes, as a result my father went to visit a prostitute, and that's how he contracted the syphilis that sent him mad and eventually killed him. So maybe some parts of history are best left forgotten.'

Edith strokes the back of the door.

'I'm sorry,' he adds. 'I'll be here, waiting. Take your time. I'll entertain myself with Rimbaud.'

Edith hears Egon step away from the door.

She looks around the space, her heart pounding. She wanted this, she made it happen. And now ... Edith cannot shake the sickening sense that she has done something wrong. She looks at her hands. How strange it is, to wear a ring, this gold band that rubs against her skin. It belongs to her. She slips it off, and looks at it. Inside are two elegant initials: E & E.

It moves something so deep inside her it hurts.

Then her eyes fall on the blade of Egon's razor.

⌒

Her husband knocks once more on the door. 'Edith? What's going on in there? Are you unwell? It's been almost an hour.'

She doesn't reply. Egon tries the door and it opens, a little. He exerts more force and is able to squeeze through. Edith is lying on the floor, curled up. She has been crying. His razor glints in her hand. There's blood on the blade.

'Edith, this is no joke!'

He runs his hands over her body, her wrists, looking for the source. He lifts her hands to reveal thin slices on her thigh. Angular lines have been scratched into her skin.

There's an A, a D.

'What have you done to yourself?' he asks, his voice tight and scared. Egon grabs a flannel and tries to soak away the blood, but it only exposes the lines of the cuts.

ADELE.

Edith has cut the word into her skin. She has caused her sister so much pain by marrying the man she loves. And oh, the guilt she feels for the pleasure that is promised by him. She can't escape the pain she has caused.

'It hurts,' Edith whispers, her eyes closed.

Egon pulls her to him. 'Hush.' He rocks her, for a long time, until all the tension in her dissipates. Her fingers tighten around his arms and she can hear his heart beating.

'You chose the wrong sister,' Edith says.

'What? Is that what this is about? You think I should have married Adele?'

'She'd make a better wife for you. She'd know what to do.'

'Adele always scared me, truth be told.'

'She believed you were going to marry her.'

'But I didn't give her any reason to think that. I never felt anything for Adele.'

'You broke her heart. Then I broke it again when I accepted your proposal.'

'Edith, look at me.' He holds her face in his hands. 'Love doesn't work that way. You can't make conscious choices, that would be absurd. You find yourself in love, and it's always unexpected. The joy is that it takes you by surprise.'

'Do you . . . love me?' Edith asks.

'Of course. The first time I saw you,' he adds, 'something leapt inside me. The more I got to know you, the more it grew,' Egon says. 'That's the beginning of a great love, I'm sure of it.'

He pauses, repeats her question back to her.

'I don't know,' Edith whispers. 'I have no idea how love is supposed to feel.'

'It's meant to feel warm, and safe. It's meant to feel as if we have all the time in the world and we only want to spend it with each other.' Egon rubs his hands up her bare arms.

'Adele will never forgive me.'

'She will forgive you. She's your sister. I promise. All this will be forgotten.'

Egon kisses Edith. He holds her. 'Now?' he asks. 'Are you ready? I hope you are.'

Her husband leads her back to the bedroom. He lays her down and pulls the blankets over them both. Edith closes her eyes as he enters then pushes himself in deeper. Blood soaks into the sheets. Pain throbs from the cuts on her thigh and between her legs.

And pleasure? It blooms.

4

June 1915

Edith wakes when the light can't be denied any more. She hears her husband moving around in the kitchen. Before long, the smell of coffee reaches her. He brings her a cup in bed. The rim of it is chipped. 'Cream, please,' Edith says, dressing.

He comes back. 'We've no cream, but I added a little sugar.'

It still tastes bitter.

'I'll be working in the main room,' Egon says, 'where the light is best. I intend to start a painting of you, *The Artist's Wife*. The first step is to prepare the canvas.'

It feels strange to wake up in such a different space, in a bed that's made for two. The sheets are twisted – the bottom one is stained with blood – and the blankets have been pushed to the foot of the bed. The pain between her thighs is pulsing and sharp. The blood has dried, and Edith scrapes a little off with her fingernail, wincing as she does. The lines she has cut into her flesh will take months to heal. The scars might last a lifetime.

Edith takes her embroidery hoop from the trunk and begins working on a piece she'd hoped to have finished by now – she's talented with needle and thread, conjuring scenes, patterns, poems. It's a gift for Egon – his name and hers. She wants to hang it somewhere in their home. Perhaps it can sit alongside Egon's artworks, in the main room? She harbours the hope that his subject matter will change now that he's a married man. No more nudes, surely?

She works for an hour while Egon paints. She hears him moving around and enjoys this feeling of accomplishment. It's official – she is no longer a child, and the physical act was not as brutal as she'd expected. She enjoyed the recklessness of it, and wonders what will happen next.

There's the ringing of a bell. 'I'll go down,' Egon shouts.

A few minutes later he returns. The colour, and all gaiety, has gone from his face. In his hand is an envelope. He comes and sits on the bed, scratching the backs of his wrists.

'Aren't you going to open it?' Edith asks, looking at him.

'I can't,' Egon whispers. 'I already know what it will say.'

'What?' A feeling of dread is spreading under Edith's skin, racing towards her heart.

'It's the worst possible news.' Egon's jaw is set. His eyes are wide and unblinking. Edith takes the envelope from him and rips it open. She reads it quickly, the page fluttering between her fingers. She struggles to take it all in, but one phrase is clear.

'It says you're fit to fight.'

Egon squeezes his eyes closed. He takes the letter from her and reads it himself. He's shaking. 'I leave for Prague in three days.' He runs a hand down his face. 'On Monday, they'll begin training me, an artist, to be a soldier. I knew this day might come. But I'd hoped enough strings had been pulled by the right people.'

'And what will happen to us?' Edith asks.

'You'll come with me, as my wife. But there goes our honeymoon in Trieste.'

Edith knows nothing of Prague. She has hardly left Austria, and certainly never been to such a far-flung corner of the Austro-Hungarian Empire. It does cross her mind that at least she won't have to worry about Adele there. She won't have to see her face every time she looks out of the window or fret about bumping into her on the street.

Egon breathes into cupped hands. 'What does an artist do with a gun?'

'Can you not stay in Vienna?' she tries. 'Get some kind of office job to help the war effort?'

'That was the plan. My heart was meant to save me. The doctor promised that this thing' – he thumps his chest – 'would excuse me from anything too strenuous, from getting too close to danger. They must be running low on men to call on weak ones like me.'

'You're not weak,' Edith tries, pulling him into an awkward embrace.

'I'm not strong enough for this.' Egon's words are thin and strained. 'My talent will be entirely wasted. And for what? So I can die in some god-forsaken country, fighting a war I don't believe in? I've seen them! Injured soldiers, poor young bastards from all kinds of backgrounds – Czechs, Magyars, Bosnians, Slovaks. They've been shipped off in their thousands, only to return bleeding and butchered, missing limbs and most of their minds. Artists should be exempt from that kind of battle!' He pulls at Edith, grasping the nightgown she'd pulled back on when she woke. Egon speaks quietly, his words muffled against Edith's chest. 'What will become of me, Vally? Oh, Vally,' he whispers.

Edith freezes. Did she hear him correctly? Yes. That name was unmistakable. Why did Egon marry her if Vally is the one he's crying out for in his darkest hour?

'I'm not Vally,' Edith says slowly, removing herself from him, and stepping away from the bed.

He looks across at her. 'I know that,' he says. He hasn't realized his error. Egon picks up the patch of embroidery Edith has been working on and turns it over, as if he doesn't know which side is the one to admire. 'You're worlds apart.'

Edith feels the prickle of tears coming. 'Why didn't you marry her, then? Why am I wearing this ring on my finger, when Vally is the one who—?'

'You know why.'

'I haven't a clue!'

'I couldn't marry Vally. And I didn't want to! I wanted to marry you.'

'You couldn't break the rules for her?'

'She had no interest in marrying me. She even signed some stupid bit of paper to prove it. "I'm not in love with anyone in the world,"' Egon mimics.

'But you told me you're expecting your modelling sessions with her to continue.'

Egon laughs bitterly. 'She said no to that proposal.'

'Well, that's for the best,' Edith says. She is relieved at the news.

'She's joined some do-gooder organization as a military nurse, according to Roessler. She left Vienna before the wedding, I suspect.'

Edith would have to rethink what she thought she knew about Vally Neuzil.

'You were in such a hurry to marry me. Why?' Edith asks, eventually.

'You'll be able to enjoy my success. Vally was too proud ever to succumb to that notion. You're a nice girl from a good family,' he adds, looking at his hands. 'And you're beautiful. You don't know it, so that only makes it all the more endearing.'

'A nice girl,' Edith says, perplexed.

'Yes, the kind who wears a bonnet to bed on her wedding night,' Egon says, making his point. Edith reddens from her core. It wasn't her fault that nobody had thought to warn her. She'd hoped – naively, as it was now clear – that Egon wouldn't think her ridiculous. 'That counts for a lot. It wasn't just your beauty and the way you see the world that I was attracted to, but also your innocence. Your purity,' he adds.

Edith is suddenly aware that she could throw something. But much to her annoyance, she's too well brought-up for that. Instead, she picks up the lace-trimmed bonnet from the bedside table. She intends to throw it away.

'You should rest that delicate heart of yours,' she says finally, heading out of the bedroom door. 'Don't you have a war to fight?'

She feels gratified at the dash of anguish she sees on her husband's features.

5

'Goodbye, Adele,' Edith says. She and Egon leave in a matter of hours, but her sister won't even raise her head from the pillow. The curtains are drawn and the room they shared until recently is dank, earthy, a cavern. Adele has reverted to a prehistoric self, devoid of language, manners, basic hygiene.

'I'm leaving for Prague. I don't know how long I'll be gone,' Edith continues. She thinks of the travel document she'd collected that day, bearing her photograph and new signature: Edith Schiele. Adele stares at the wall. Edith considers touching her sister, squeezing her shoulder, or placing her lips to her cheek, but there's something active and dangerous in Adele's silence that holds Edith back. 'Please talk to me,' she goes on, shifting her position on the bed that used to be hers, which is now covered in Adele's discarded clothing, her dress shed as if it were an old skin. 'I'd be so glad if we could go back to the way things used to be between us. I know it won't happen straight away, but I'd like us to find our way as sisters again. You must remember the good times, our secrets, all our escapades. I think of them now more than ever. How much we used to laugh . . .' She waits. 'Do you remember the time I knocked my carton of ice cream off the balcony at the theatre, straight on to that woman's lap? Or the time we hired bicycles to go around the lake in the Salzkammergut and you were talking so much you cycled straight in, and had to be rescued by Father, looking like some monster from the deep?' Edith smiles sadly. 'Then there were all the dances. Men circling you for attention, me off to the side. I'm not sure you realize how much I've always looked up to you, the extent to which I wanted to be like you.'

She twiddles a button on Adele's dress and sighs.

'Before I go . . . I want to say that I know I've hurt you, and I'm sorry.' Edith waits a few moments, to see if anything she has said will stir even the slightest gesture of goodwill. 'Goodbye, then,' Edith repeats. 'I'll keep you in my thoughts.'

Edith leaves the room and closes the door, wondering when she'll see her sister again.

'If she carries on this way, she'll end up in an asylum,' Mutti hisses, loud enough for Adele to hear through the door. 'Almost two weeks and she hasn't uttered a single word. She refuses to eat, won't wash. There's a toilet pan under the bed that poor Hanna has to empty!' Edith pulls a face. 'That girl really must pull herself together,' Mutti adds.

'But how long does it take?' Edith asks. 'To heal a broken heart?'

'Broken heart?' Mutti scoffs. 'She'll get over your artist in no time at all.'

'I mean how long until she forgets the pain I've caused her?'

'She'll have forgotten all about you before you've even stepped off the train.'

⤙

Edith hugs Hanna for the longest time. The maid feels delicate in her arms. Ever since the government declared war on Serbia, with other European countries quickly joining in, the world has been changing at a dangerous rate. The future is no longer as they'd anticipated. Edith is now acutely aware that money in the Harms household is scarce, and she fears Hanna won't be around when she returns, whenever that might be.

'Thank you,' Edith whispers. 'For everything.' She kisses Hanna's cheek warmly. Edith is about to embark on a journey that might never have happened without Hanna's intervention.

'It's grand to see you bloom, Diderlie,' she says, using Edith's childhood nickname. 'I remember what it's like to be young and hopeful. Enjoy it.'

'I'm proud of you,' Papa says, bestowing a hug on her. 'You've retained your composure very well throughout this ordeal. I've always had faith in you, ever since you were a girl. There's very little that life can throw at you, I believe, that would derail you. Take care of yourself. And each other.'

Mutti must be able to see the sadness in Edith's eyes, for she says in a quiet, comforting tone: 'Darling. Adele simply can't hold a grudge for ever.'

Edith plays with the beads of her amber necklace. 'I'll miss you all,' she says, trying to freeze in her mind the image of her parents and Hanna, as they are in that moment.

This space, these people, are her sanctuary, however broken they may be.

6

Summer 1915

I t's late when Egon and Edith arrive at the station in Prague. But even at that hour, soldiers in dull-green uniform patrol the streets, their heavy boots clomping against the cobbles, their rifles pointed at the darkening sky. Egon and Edith hurry past. They don't want to break the bubble of their life together with the realities of war, at least until the morning. Edith feels a long way from home. She has been married for less than a week, and already she has had all her expectations ripped away.

The directions they've been given are vague and they navigate under a blanket of cloud. Egon struggles to read the map, and they circle back on themselves. Finally, they find their way to a squat hotel, where Edith must live for at least two months.

'Is this it?' she asks, looking up at the dreary frontage.

'I expect this may well be a palace compared to where I'll be,' Egon tries to reassure her. In the morning, he'll move to a military flat a few miles away with his fellow conscripts. He has been assigned work as an administrative clerk in a prisoner-of-war camp, thanks to his exemplary handwriting. His connections in Vienna have indeed pulled strings to prevent him from being sent straight into battle, and for that they are both grateful. 'I'll be able to visit one or two nights a week,' he adds, a grim set to his mouth.

The thought floods Edith with joy. Already, she yearns for his body when they're apart.

'I have no idea what I'll do in Prague the rest of the time,' she says. Edith doesn't know a soul. She intends to relax for the first few days, restore herself, for on the journey her menses arrived, the blood coming as a surprise now that she's a wife. After her interactions with her husband, she'd assumed she wouldn't need to think of them for a while. But she supposes it's not unusual for conception not to happen the very first time. Next month, perhaps, a seed will be planted.

'Just make sure the bed's warm when I return. Now, let's go inside. We mustn't catch our death out here, of all places.' He rushes her through the door. 'Good evening,' he says to the receptionist. 'We have a room booked for Herr and Frau Schiele.'

⌒

'Do you have to go already?' Edith asks as Egon dresses in his smart army uniform. She's lying in bed, the sheets pulled across her breasts. They have to make the most of every opportunity to be together, infrequent as they are. 'I'm bored out of my brain without you.' Edith rolls a cigarette, her fingers much more adept these days at navigating the thin paper. She licks the edge, twists it and passes it to him.

'Another truckload of prisoners arrives today. I can't be late,' Egon says, accepting the cigarette and putting it behind his ear to smoke on his return journey to the camp on the outskirts of the city. He has been working with captured Russian soldiers, recording in a ledger, as they arrive, their names, dates and places of birth, and regiment numbers – before they're sent on for labour elsewhere in the Empire. In the weeks he has been there, he has met hundreds of men, almost all of them younger than he is – Mikhails, Nikolais, Dmitris – and has learnt to decipher the sharp inflections of their language, picking up a catalogue of coarse profanities that they mutter at him as they wait in limbo between one kind of hell on a bullet-strewn battlefield and another, rotting in a prison cell.

Her husband has also catalogued, in his own mind, the textures of the wounds the Russians have received in battle and beyond – the coarse pocks of shrapnel damage, the deep splice of a bayonet wound, the dull dent of a rifle butt to the chest. Many men have teeth missing, an eye sewn back into its socket, a hole in the head. Egon was sickened when he first encountered them, imagining, no doubt, his own body riddled with such injuries. But now he finds a strange beauty in the marks and the men who bear them.

'They all have such haunting faces. I intend to draw them, if they'll let me. It will make a change from administrative tasks,' he says.

After his own experiences in Neulengbach, his twenty-four days in a cell, Egon despises that he has become the jailer, and that he has a degree of control over these men's fates. He shows an excess of kindness when he can, and neutrality at all other times. He slams the other guards for their ruthlessness, which puts their noses out of joint, and they come after him. As a result, Egon has already jammed fists with another private – they had to be separated by Oberleutnant Grünwald, their superior – and he returned to her with a bloodied nose. Edith had cleaned it as best she could, working around the swelling with a wet flannel and kissing the tender cartilage. He hadn't expected to be injured by his own comrades, he'd said with a sour laugh.

'I'll be back on Friday,' he says now as he picks up his kitbag and swings his rifle over his arm.

'I'll miss you,' she says. 'The hours seem endless without you. But I suppose I—'

'Why don't you—'

'If you suggest I go to the library one more time, I'll scream.' She smiles.

'So not the library.'

'I've seen every sight in the guidebook. I've traipsed around all the parks and viewed the cathedral. Twice!' Edith is aware she sounds like a spoiled child. She just wishes she could be doing something more useful, that there was something more to her role than waiting around for Egon.

'You could read my books. I brought Goethe and Shakespeare with me. Or play around with my typewriter – you can type up those poems I've been working on.' Egon kisses her along the shoulder. 'Anyway, I expect it won't be too long before you have your hands full . . .' he says, almost shyly.

'Not this month,' she says, embarrassed to have failed once more. She's not even sure she wants a baby just yet, but felt a hollow sadness at the sight of blood in her undergarments once more. Still, best not to worry about these things.

He kisses her. 'We'll have to try harder, then.'

'I'll miss you!' she says again as he leaves, wrapping herself in the sheet.

He does look handsome in that khaki uniform, with its stiff, high collar, Edith thinks. Being a soldier almost suits him. Egon spends at least a few hours outdoors most days, so he's tanned and muscular and brimming with energy. She can't get enough of him. But this way of life doesn't suit her – she feels pointless, wandering about the city with no tasks, no duties, no friends. Here, she is nobody's daughter, nobody's sister. She could do anything she wants, yet the options are limited. She never particularly enjoyed the social whirl of Vienna – or certainly not as much as Adele did – but at least it gave a rhythm to her days. In Prague, she has nothing to fall back on. Edith has abandoned her embroidery projects once and for all, read all her books, and has no intention of borrowing new ones. She's sick to death of playing card games.

She is acutely aware, of course, that her boredom seems petty when compared to the destruction of the battlefields, the lives being lost. Adele is the one person who might understand, but what could she say to her that hasn't been said already? She can hardly mention Egon in her letters, nor her own loneliness as a wife, so she tries to find humour in everyday moments, anything to heal the rift with her sister. She determines to write to her every week. Whether Adele reads her letters or puts them straight on the stove is anyone's guess, for Edith has yet to receive a reply.

⌒

Edith begins a walking loop around the city. She doesn't intend to return to the hotel until evening. Many of the buildings are boarded up, the coffee shops closed, the galleries abandoned. Before the war, this would have been the ideal place to spend a honeymoon, she thinks. Truckloads of munitions clang past her, horns beeping. Edith prefers the quiet backstreets, to avoid the telltale stomps of marching troops. For the first few days, she hadn't known any better, and the young men would leer at her as they passed, the ones at the rear wolf-whistling, earning jeers from their compatriots.

She's almost at the park, where she can lose another hour, when a man steps in front of her.

'Excuse me, miss? I don't suppose you can help me?' He's a soldier, in uniform, alone. Edith is instantly wary. He's larger and broader than Egon, with a square jaw and blond hair. 'Do you recognize this address?' He holds out a piece of paper.

'I do, as it happens.' Edith stands next to him and points in the direction from which he has come. 'Turn right, and right again; it's at the top of that long street, on the corner by the station.' His cologne is very strong. 'You can't miss it. Unless you're determined to.'

'You know your way around.'

'I have plenty of time on my hands.'

'Don't suppose you double as a tour guide?' He starts to walk away, then turns. 'Look,' he begins. 'My meeting is at midday. I know this is unacceptably forward, but if you're free in an hour or so, and want to join me for a drink, or lunch, I'd be delighted. My treat. I'm in the city for two days and I don't get many opportunities to speak to young ladies, or anyone not holding a gun, for that matter.'

Edith looks at him. It's the most attractive offer she's had in weeks.

'It's up to you. I won't be offended if you have somewhere else to go. But you know where I'll be at one o'clock, if you're feeling sociable.'

The man waves and Edith watches him take the route she directed him along.

She's so very tempted. To have a conversation, share lunch, exchange anecdotes, with an interested human being . . . but really, she should decline.

Edith is waiting when the soldier comes out on to the street an hour later.

'Klaus,' he says, extending his hand, his face expanding in surprise when he sees her.

'Edith Schiele. You're the first man I've spoken to in months who isn't my husband.'

'My wife is in Berlin with our children,' he smiles. 'I miss them terribly.'

'What a pair we are. I miss my husband and we're in the same city.'

'I'm honoured that you'll allow me to take up a little of your time. I know how precious it is. Can I buy you a meal?' he asks. 'A hot drink?'

Her mouth waters. 'I know the most pleasing place.'

∽

'Ah, my beautiful wife! I've been waiting for this moment,' Egon says, as he joins Edith at the military bar where they'd arranged to meet. 'A good woman, a fine beer. What more could a hard-working soldier want on a Friday evening?'

He laughs, pulling her into an embrace that is quite intense for such a public space.

Edith wriggles out of his grasp. 'Your comrades are staring.'

'Let them! Their jealousy is nothing new. How was your day?'

'It was fine. You said it would be. I missed you, of course.'

'So it wasn't all doom and gloom. What fun did you get up to?'

'I wouldn't go as far as fun,' she says carefully. 'But I did make a friend.'

'I told you you weren't unapproachable. What did you war wives get up to?'

'We had lunch, we walked along the river. We spoke a lot about you and—'

'Will you see her again?'

'Actually, he leaves the day after tomorrow. He has a stopover of less than forty-eight hours.'

Egon puts his beer down on the table. 'You've been cavorting with another man!'

She laughs at his reaction. 'He's married.'

'You're married, must I remind you of that? So what's your excuse, then, for carrying on with someone else?'

'I wasn't carrying on. Or cavorting! It wasn't like that.' Edith hadn't been naive to the fact that befriending another soldier might provoke jealousy in Egon. Perhaps he wouldn't take her for granted so much from now on. Or stare quite so openly each time a pretty young woman passed by on the street. 'You know how bored I've been . . . Is it against the law for me to speak to any other man who isn't you?'

'Given the circumstances, it should be.'

'What circumstances?' Edith notices his fellow soldiers looking at them.

'You. Alone. Bored. We all know what happens next.'

'What are you suggesting?'

'Don't play the innocent with me. That can only get you so far.'

'It was purely cordial. He showed me photographs of his little boys, his wife.'

'And you believe that means he didn't have other motives?' Egon asks.

'I told him what a talent you are, how even this war can't slow you down. I even told him that you've been working on a portrait of me.'

'Now's not the time to butter me up.' Egon glares, but she can see that her words have touched him. 'I mean it,' he continues, his voice low. 'I don't want you getting caught up in something you can't control. You're too nice for your own good.'

'I wouldn't have told you if I had anything to hide,' she says.

Egon pauses and Edith hopes he can see the logic in what she has said.

'You know how important I believe it is that we're honest with each other,' she continues. 'I asked, when you proposed, that we start this marriage with a clean slate. That meant cutting your ties with Vally, which you did, and I appreciate that. We couldn't have started a relationship with your past hanging over us. Our happiness relies on us being able to tell the truth and not have any secrets between us. That may be uncomfortable at times, but isn't that what we agreed? So why would I lie to you now?'

'I apologize,' Egon says. He finishes the last of his beer. 'You're right. I don't know where that came from. Marriage has changed me.'

'Believe in me, as I believe in you, and we'll be the happiest creatures on earth.'

Three months later, Egon unveils the portrait of Edith that he has been working on, snatching time here and there between his duties as a soldier to complete it. She has posed for him, standing straight and solid. She wore her favourite dress for the sittings, a modern colourful one that she had fashioned at the start of the year from excess curtain material. Up until now, Egon hasn't let her see the artwork itself. For many hours, she has stared at the wooden frame of the easel, the back of the canvas, Egon's face peering round to examine her from time to time. He covers the painting with a sheet whenever he leaves, and she made him a promise that she would not look until it was ready. 'I don't want you to be swayed before the paint is dry,' he said. 'Don't look anxious. You'll love it.'

Now, he pulls the sheet away, and watches her reaction.

'Oh, I . . .' she begins. 'Do I really look like that?'

Edith peers into her wide blue eyes, which shine back at her with childlike innocence from a pale-skinned face. Her hair is a darker shade than her natural colour, her fingers pressed together uncomfortably at her sides, an uncertain smile on her lips. Her striped dress looks foolish in this context; she feels he has gone to lengths to make her look almost idiotic.

'You look beautiful, what are you talking about?'

'Why are my feet turned inward like that? Do I truly stand in such a stupid position, as if I need to be excused for an urgent visit to the washroom?'

'I deliberately avoided all trace of the erotic, and I think the result is powerful. Perhaps it is my first truly mature piece of work.'

'I look like a doll, all stiff, hanging there in a sea of white. No, worse, I look like a puppet!'

'You look very sweet. It's a portrait of the artist's wife – it's meant to be serious.'

'You give the impression I'm not entirely in control of my own limbs.'

'My little marionette,' he says.

'You're not my puppeteer. And I'm not yours to be manipulated, Egon. Why on earth would you suggest such a thing?' she demands, throwing the sheet back over her portrait.

7

Autumn 1917

It has been more than two years since Edith last set foot in Vienna. During the intervening months, she has become better accustomed to life as a war wife. In normal circumstances, if they'd been in Vienna, she'd have learnt how to run a household with Hanna by her side until she'd adjusted, but here she is just making it up as she goes along. Egon veers between laughter and horror at her attempts.

After that first strange summer in Prague, Edith had been consumed by loneliness. She'd never been so untethered, so freed from the roots of her existence. She saw her soldier husband whenever possible, they made love and fought and made up again, getting used to the rhythm of each other and themselves occupying these new identities, people they'd never been before. In the empty days between, Edith found herself wishing that her education had prepared her for more than visits to the theatre and elegant soirees.

She punched the pillows each time her monthly blood stained her underwear, and wondered what was wrong with her. How was a baby made, if not from intercourse in this way? Perhaps she was doing something wrong? Adele would probably know. Edith knew now that she wanted a baby, and felt like an insomniac, bemused at the ease with which others fell into a deep sleep with no effort or delay whatsoever. She thought of Egon's sister, Gertrude, who'd fallen pregnant without even intending to. Edith saw other war wives every day pushing perambulators, babies pawing the air with their small mittened fists, their plump-peach cheeks visible beneath knitted shawls. She wanted the same, badly.

Edith readied herself when she knew Egon would be returning to their rooms, washing her hair in cold water with whatever sliver of soap remained, roughly rubbing her skin with the last of her lotions, setting her blonde hair in curls as best she could without the tools she'd had to hand at home, pinking her cheeks and lips. She had to prove that she was worthy of his choice. Would he, one day, regret it?

She felt so ill prepared for the path her life had taken.

She wrote long letters to Adele, angry, then apologizing, then desperate once more to recover the sister she felt she had lost. She was furious that her sister had lost herself in her obsession, that she'd failed to be happy for Edith, even after the marriage and months of separation; she felt deeply guilty and sad that her own break for happiness had caused so much pain. And could she ever be truly happy if the person she had once been closest to in the world wouldn't even acknowledge her existence?

She rewrote the letters when she was more lucid, deleting all but the apologies. She included a return address on every envelope, but never once received a reply.

☞

In the spring of 1916, after Egon had completed his basic training, they left Prague and Egon was stationed at various locations – some closer to Vienna than others. They are in the countryside now and Edith feels calmer and restored away from the war-steeped city. She worries for Egon's safety a little less and takes better care of herself. From their new home Edith can see the snow-capped Otscher and the Erlauf river flows past their little house, where, thankfully, they are able to live together. But the rigour and oppressive hierarchy of the army is getting too much for Egon. His disregard for the rules can no longer be laughed away by his superiors and he is frequently punished. Egon spends more and more of his time on his art, working in a disused storeroom at the base. His commander, it has been revealed, had assumed Egon was a painter-decorator when they met, before Egon explained that he was, in fact, not a painter of door frames and walls, but a painter of people and landscapes, ideas and visions.

His work is still being exhibited internationally – Berlin, Zurich, Munich and Dresden. He has been invited to organize an exhibition at the Prater in Vienna next year. 'We need this damned war to be over, then I'll take on the world,' he says.

Egon tries to stay up late after dinner, to purge the images that spiral through his brain, but Edith has become skilled at tempting him back to bed. She feels bold and reckless whenever it is just the two of them. These days, when Egon is working, she goes for long walks, up to the castle. Edith collects cowslips and other flowers to press between Egon's heavy art books – it is her new hobby. Cafés are starting to open again where the customers play a curious game, *karambol,* at which Edith has become adept. Egon takes pleasure in bringing her gifts – an apple from a stranger's tree, a single rose, scented soap, a tortoiseshell comb. For the first time in her life, Edith believes she is beautiful. She believes that she will be remembered.

She and Egon often spend many 'nice hours' at home in the afternoon, drawing the curtains against the outside world, finding solace in the soft curves of each other's body. He brushes her hair when they are done. Yet still, each month, she bleeds.

She can't shake the feeling that it's a punishment for her actions, a curse.

⌒

Letters arrive sporadically from Vienna. In this way, Egon hears from Gertrude, who recounts news of her husband. Anton is fighting a much rougher and dirtier battle than Egon, up to his neck in mud in Macedonia. She includes a drawing by Anton Junior, who's starting to talk. *Hasn't he talent?* she asks. 'He takes after his father,' Egon mutters as he holds the drawing of a train in his hands. Egon dashes off a reply and asks Edith to post it.

Dear Gerti. We live in the most daunting times the world has ever seen. We have grown used to every kind of deprivation. Hundreds of thousands of people are perishing miserably. Everyone living or dying must bear his fate. We must become hardened and fearless. Whatever happened before 1914 belongs to a different world. This is why we should always look to the future. Yours, with affection, Egon.

Egon's mother writes and tells him of her many ailments, of the demonstrations and hunger riots that have shaken Vienna, her fear of catching a new strain of influenza that has been gaining ground in Europe, more deadly than the seasonal variety that usually knocks her out each winter. 'It's taken hold in other countries, but shows no signs of reaching Vienna,' Egon mutters, 'yet fret she must.' His mother also writes of Melanie, who has set herself up as a milliner and, despite limited supplies, is receiving a steady stream of orders for her designs. Through her work, his mother writes, Egon's sister has met a man, a tailor, and she has high hopes for a marriage after the war. Uncle Leopold sends a short but affectionate note, and encloses a little money, the first since Neulengbach.

Gustav Klimt writes that he is determined to paint the town red as soon as Schiele returns – he's putting bottles of absinthe aside for the occasion; and Roessler and his other patrons mourn the diminishment of Egon's painting time, while reporting news of invitations for exhibitions across the continent. Everyone is trying, as best they can, to navigate the war. But there are many casualties, much by way of loss.

Edith receives long letters from Mutti, who recounts news of bankruptcies among their acquaintances, and shocking suicides from within their social circle. Friends are fleeing, and with good reason,

Mutti notes ominously. The Brons have left Vienna, along with Emilia and her new family, seeking safety in the countryside. Houses have been boarded up, shops looted; beggars abound on the streets and people have gone missing without a trace. In this way, Edith has also come to learn that Hanna has, indeed, been let go. The war has made things too precarious. Sugar, soap, milk, meat and paraffin have become scarce. There have been riots over potatoes. With rationing, Hanna was another mouth to feed, and then the mayor had hiked taxes drastically, which meant the Harms family, like so many others, was stretched to breaking point. *It's better Hanna go*, Mutti wrote. She had family in the south and had left a forwarding address for Edith's letters. According to her mother, the Viennese were dancing towards destruction and the Habsburg monarchy was on its knees, with all the civil unrest and upheaval.

In one of her letters, Mutti makes a light-hearted comment that Papa has been unwell. *Your father is as depleted as Vienna by the ravages of war.*

Edith worries about what has not been stated plainly.

And Adele? Adele is much revived, apparently. She has undertaken a course of the talking cure, with a sought-after psychoanalyst, and her headaches and hysteria have abated. *She has discovered that she's been imprisoned and repressed by the traditional role of a dutiful daughter in a bourgeois family! She wants to know why we didn't encourage her to broaden her horizons*, Mutti writes and Edith has to smile. *Nevertheless, she has found her old lust for life, makes an effort to pay social visits whenever possible, and spends long evenings with friends, doing who knows what.* All the old rules have been abandoned, Edith notes. Mutti suspects there may be a suitor on the cards, *But who am I to know? I'm only her mother, after all.* Edith finishes the letter and lets go of the great swell of tension she has been holding on to for so long. Perhaps, at last, Adele has moved on.

⌣

Today, Edith picks up the familiar envelope bearing Mutti's writing and looks at it carefully. It's clearly her mother's hand, yet it seems different: neater, more deliberate.

Edith sits to read it with a fresh coffee. She wonders, briefly, what Adele has got up to now and hopes there may be news of an engagement.

Dearest Edith, the letter begins. Her eyes move quickly to take in the words.

It is with the saddest, heaviest heart that I write to tell you . . .

Edith crunches the page into a tight ball and drops it. She positively throws it to the ground as if it has grown teeth. She cannot read any more than that first line. She simply can't. Her mind boils with twisted thoughts of what on earth could have happened. It is the worst possible disaster. She grabs her coat and runs out of the door, intending to lose herself in the hills. There, for a short time at least, she can delay the unthinkable.

That evening, Egon returns late.

'I'm hungry!' he calls, as he comes through the door. Usually, she rushes to greet him, but tonight, a pale Edith sits at an empty table. She's still wearing her coat, frozen in place, as if her elbows are jointed to the wood.

'Are you sick?' Egon rushes to her, placing a hand on her forehead. 'You're very pale, have you eaten anything today? What is it? What's wrong?'

Edith watches as his eyes scan her face. He has always been alert to, and fearful of, any signs of sickness in those closest to him. 'A letter came,' she says simply. 'From Vienna.' She passes the crumpled ball to him. He takes it, perplexed.

'What does it say?'

'It's from Mutti.' Edith's voice is weak. 'It arrived today.'

'And?' He smooths the page in front of him.

'It contains bad news. The worst. Could you read it to me?' Edith says. 'I couldn't bear to look past the first line.'

Egon runs his eyes from left to right. He puts a hand over his mouth.

'Oh, Edith. I am so sorry. You really don't know?' He lowers himself to her.

She buries her head in her arms. This feeling of being on the brink of world-collapsing news, irreversible tragedy, is unbearable. But it can't be worse than anything she has already imagined in the hours alone in the hills.

'You need to hear this,' Egon says gently. 'I'm so, so sorry.'

'Adele?' It has finally happened. She has lost her sister for ever.

Egon waits a moment, unsteady. 'It's your father.'

Edith feels the air leave her lungs, everything slipping around her.

'It says there was nothing that could be done.'

'Papa!' Edith shudders violently, her body racked with sobs as she absorbs the news.

'Your mother says it happened on Friday. He was taken ill, unexpectedly.'

'How? Why?'

'It was his heart.'

Edith feels as if she has plunged into a bottomless hole.

'I know what it's like to lose a father,' Egon tries to soothe her. 'But he'll always be with you. Your mother says the funeral will take place this week. In Vienna.'

Edith is sinking, sinking, sinking. 'My papa . . .'

Her husband wraps his arms around her, rocking her. 'We'll both go. I'll take compassionate leave. There are no two ways about it. We must pay our respects.'

8

November 1917

'W e should order a bottle of something special,' Adele announces to the table.

'I'm not sure that's appropriate, darling,' Mutti says. A waiter stands to one side, ready to take their order. Edith and Egon exchange a look.

'It's what Papa would have wanted,' Adele replies, her voice rising above the noise of the other diners. 'Here we are, together, after all. It's been such a long time, more than two years since we could last say that. The war doesn't have to ruin everything.' She looks at each of them, her eyes resting on Egon for a fraction longer than her mother or sister. 'Besides, it's a celebration of sorts, is it not?'

The low lights flicker. The piano that once would have played slow, soulful notes is dusty and dormant, and the stool's legs don't look as if they could support a grown man's weight any more.

Mutti pats Adele's hand. 'We'll start with water.' The waiter makes a note.

'Champagne!' Adele calls after him. 'Your most expensive bottle! We're at a restaurant, are we not? This was your decision,' she says, addressing her mother. 'We're burying Papa in the morning! Are we not expected to let loose a little? How else can we drown our sorrows?

With this endless war and all these reports about the damned influenza, we're lucky to be out at all.'

'It's impossible to source champagne these days, I'm afraid, *Fräulein*,' the waiter says. 'We can offer you a sparkling Chardonnay?'

Egon shuffles in his chair while Edith rummages in her handbag for a tissue. Her nerves are frayed, but she's determined to put on a brave face. Returning to Vienna has been an ordeal, not in any way helped by the fact that Adele has been acting strangely – breezy one moment then bullying the next. There's nothing about her that Edith recognizes.

The waiter returns with a bottle. He presents it to Adele, who reads the label. With deft movements, he untwists the wiring around the cork. Adele watches his every muscle, intently. He grips the neck of the bottle firmly in his left hand, then twists the body of it, slowly, with his right. There's an almost imperceptible pop, which prompts an audible murmur of pleasure from her sister. The waiter leans forward to pour the fizzing liquid into Adele's outstretched glass.

'Precisely what I need,' she says. Mutti holds her hand over the glass that has been placed in front of her. Egon accepts some and holds Edith's glass out, too, even though she has no intention of drinking it. Adele takes a long sip, her head tipped, the tender white skin of her neck revealed. 'Delicious.' She swallows. Her eyes rest on Egon again. 'So, the artist-turned-soldier returns. How have you been? Fighting the great fight?'

Egon smiles. 'I've been lucky, as it happens, been kept from the horrors of the front. I've been stationed in a small town, in a menial role, which suits me perfectly. In Prague, I oversaw prisoners of war. Russian men, the strong, silent types. We couldn't communicate much, but they let me draw them.'

Adele examines the rising bubbles in her glass. 'Fascinating.'

The waiter returns. He addresses Mutti. 'Madame?'

'I can't say I'm feeling hungry. Good job, as there's hardly a thing on the menu.'

'I want the veal cutlet,' Adele interrupts.

'Wiener schnitzel for me too, please,' Egon adds.

'No veal, I'm afraid,' the waiter says apologetically. 'The meat rations . . . We have a little horse meat, if that's of interest?'

'Fine,' Egon and Adele say in unison.

'Broth, please, however it comes,' Edith says.

'Make that two.' Mutti sighs. The four sit in silence while the waiter rearranges their cutlery.

'And you, Edith?' Adele asks. 'Not pregnant yet?'

'Adele! What a question.' Edith catches her mother's eye.

'You've been a wife for two and a half years now. Why the delay?'

'It's none of your business.'

'There's clearly a problem. And Egon isn't the issue, I hear?'

'Adele! I'll leave if you're planning to continue like this.' The tips of Edith's ears burn with humiliation. 'I've come all this way for Papa's funeral. I am beside myself with grief and I don't appreciate being harassed and insulted by my own sister.'

Adele takes another sip and looks over her glass.

'Or perhaps you're barren?' she mutters.

Egon grasps Edith's hand under the table.

'That's quite enough of that! Show some respect,' Mutti instructs.

'I just feel as if you're hiding something,' Adele says. Her eyes have that snake-like quality Edith remembers from the days after her wedding – cold but all-seeing. Adele puts her glass on the table, but not before Edith experiences the notion that she might throw it at her again. 'You know what it's like to have a secret, don't you, Edith?'

'Enough!' Mutti interjects. 'No more squabbles. As well as my heartbreak, I was about to say that your father's passing makes things difficult for me. Financially.'

'Oh, Mutti, please don't start this again!' Adele interjects, a warning in her eyes.

'Adele will get a job in the new year,' Mutti says decisively.

'You know I've set my heart on being on the stage, once the theatres open again. I'm no Isadora Duncan, but I've been told I have potential,' Adele says defensively.

'Nothing too strenuous,' Mutti continues.

'You expect me to become a chimney sweep or street cleaner?' Adele says, rolling her eyes at her mother. 'Or how about a tram driver or a postwoman? Is that what you want?'

'Don't be ridiculous! A little light endeavour in a department store will do you good.'

'You know how I feel about that!'

'And you know how I feel. You may think such work is beneath you, but needs must. We're one step away from pawning the family heirlooms.'

Adele looks thoroughly chastised.

'We have news too, actually,' Egon says and everyone turns expectantly. 'It seems the army has finally had enough of me. I've annoyed all the right people. Edith and I are all set to return to Vienna fully in the new year.'

'Finally!' Adele mutters as the waiter positions the plates on the table.

'I'll still be enlisted,' Egon continues, 'but I'll be around more, back on the scene. We'll find another apartment in Hietzing. My superior, Oberleutnant Grünwald, has taken a shine to me. Before the war, he was an arts and textiles dealer in Vienna. He recognized my talent and keeps me away from all the danger. Unofficially, I'm a war artist.'

'Wonderful!' Mutti erupts. 'I can't wait to have you around again. There's plenty you can help me with, Edith, there won't be a dull moment.'

Adele raises her eyebrows at Edith a fraction, and her lips twitch. For less than a second, there's some sisterly warmth there, a shared frustration.

'Maybe, just maybe,' Mutti says, 'after all this turmoil with your dear father, God rest his soul, we might still anticipate brighter things in nineteen eighteen.'

9

January 1918

'And this . . .' Egon announces, 'is our new home.' He walks behind Edith into the apartment, a hand over her eyes. She can see enough to put one foot in front of the other without tripping. He pulls his hand away and spins her in the middle of the room so she can take it all in. It's a large open space, the walls painted white, the floors polished cement. The windows let in a huge expanse of light. 'A few of your colourful rugs, and it won't feel so damp,' he admits. 'And at last, we have the money to heat it.'

Edith weighs up the feeling of this new space. She tries to imagine where their possessions will go, and how she'll decorate it. They're on the ground floor, with views on to a small garden.

'You can plant the seeds you've been collecting there.' He points. 'They'll thrive, there's so much sunlight. We can finally put down our roots, too. And look! The last tenant left us some window boxes.'

For the last three summers, since she married, Edith has planted small black and white sunflower seeds wherever they've been. She admires each stage as they grow – the emerging stem, the promising balance of small double leaves, then the tight knot of the head, which unfurls and expands into brightness, the broad faces angled towards the roaming sun.

'And we're not far from Klimt's studio. It has been wonderful to see him again; he's as strong and significant as ever – even if my talent is on the brink of overtaking his. Never repeat that to his face!' Egon adds hastily. 'He put in a good word to help us secure this place.'

Edith strokes the plaster by the door, and some falls away at her touch.

'How strange to think we'll have a place to call our own, after so long away,' she comments warily.

'You don't want to live here?' he asks.

'Of course I do, but so much has changed, it doesn't even feel like the same city we left. Papa and Hanna, the wave of new faces, rationing, strikes . . .'

'It's time for us to celebrate. Even caged birds sing from time to time. We can't let this dreadful war bring us down. Here, we can entertain, invite family and friends. I'll send word to Gerti. I'd like to see little Anton Junior. And Anton Senior, the old devil, can bring whatever wine he can get his hands on now that he's back! It'll be good to raise a glass, remember the dead, see some familiar faces,' Egon says.

'You're right,' Edith says. 'We're back at the centre of things, together.'

'We're here, we're alive and I want people to know it. Let's be happy. Everything has been so out of kilter. We must find our feet again.'

'Sometimes I feel as if I barely know anyone in the city any more. I know it won't be that way for ever.'

'Why not soften the feud with Adele? You're bound to bump into her; it's only a matter of time. You don't want to be looking over your shoulder the whole time, worrying yourself to death . . .'

'Do you hear what you're saying?' she teases. 'And you know I tried, back in December, but this is Adele we're talking about.'

'You're right to be wary. She was unbearable that evening at the restaurant! It was a disaster, but all our nerves were shot that night before your poor father's funeral. And she was better behaved the next day, so there's hope, isn't there?'

'She's had long enough to get over her infatuation with you, I suppose.'

'Ah, but once you've fallen for Egon Schiele, do you ever recover?' he replies, grinning.

Edith pushes him, gently. 'She'll have found other distractions by now, I'm sure. Mutti says there have been plenty of suitors.'

'Call on her,' he suggests. 'It'll be good for you.'

'I'll consider it.'

Egon dances a few steps with her across the wide-open space, waltzing her towards the window. 'This,' he says when they stop, 'is our new beginning. Vienna might be battered by the war, but we're about to launch. I'll have more time for my art and you can model for me again. And perhaps we might even be blessed with the baby you've been longing for?'

Edith laughs but feels a pang at his words. 'That would be a miracle. What kind of world would we be bringing it into, anyway?'

She would like a baby. Something of her own to love. And with a child, there would always be a part of Egon that she'd have access to, something they would always share. She'd never feel alone. She'd have purpose, direction – something of which to be proud.

'There's death, destruction, uncertainty and upheaval,' Egon reels off. 'Not to mention insanity. But there's also love, tenderness, talent and hope. I know the last few years have been painful, but maybe now that we're home, you'll be able to relax more.'

'But what if Adele is right?' she whispers, flinching at the memory. 'What if I'm barren?'

'It will happen. I'm sure of it. These things take time.'

'There's no harm in continuing to try, I suppose,' she says, smiling.

10

January 1918

'I'll take it to my deathbed,' Egon says. 'Now open them wider. The longer you complain, the longer this will take.' Edith is in the most undignified, uncomfortable position, sprawled on the makeshift bed in the front room. At Egon's behest, she has removed all her undergarments and hitched her skirts above her waist. Her boots and stockings remain on.

Edith has been very careful to position herself so she cannot be seen from the window. At first, she'd pulled the curtains, but Egon tore them open again, complaining about the light. She worries about what the neighbours might think at the best of times, let alone if they caught sight of her now.

'I wish you'd warned me that this was what you had in mind.' Edith has a headache from gritting her teeth.

To add insult to injury, Egon says she must touch herself.

'Try to enjoy yourself,' he instructs.

'Enjoy myself? I don't want people to think I'm on the brink of hysteria,' she says.

'Come on, don't be a prude. Bring your hand around. There should be a place that feels very satisfying. Do you need me to show you?'

'I doubt you'd have a clue,' she mocks. The index finger of Edith's hand pushes between her legs. Never in her wildest dreams did Edith imagine Egon could put her in a position as degrading as this. 'Don't you dare show my face!' she says. 'Promise me.'

She doesn't want the world to think she spends her afternoons with her hands down her undergarments, cavorting with the devil, as Mutti would say.

'I've already told you, I'll take it to my grave. Nobody will ever know it's you.'

'At least change the date and let people assume it's Vally. They'd expect this of her.'

'You know I can't do that,' he says. Edith removes her hand and raises her head to stare at him. 'Now please, put it back,' Egon instructs and carries on sketching, a glint in his eyes.

Edith returns her gaze to the ceiling.

'How much longer must I hold this ungodly pose?' she says after a while.

'You're obviously enjoying yourself – I've been finished for ages,' he says, grinning.

Instantly, Edith pulls herself into a sitting position, swinging her skirts into place. She shoots Egon a disgusted look, and goes to warm her hands at the stove.

Egon brings the sketch over to her. He's rather pleased with himself.

'Look,' he says. 'I've captured the very essence of you, my model: a tightness, an unwillingness to yield, but also a childish vulnerability. This woman can experience none of life's pleasures, let alone her own. The brutal wound demands to be seen, above all else.' He stops. 'Don't cry. I'm only teasing!'

'It's pornography. Women have been jailed and maimed for less!'

'This is art. You have to see that. Klimt has drawn women in much the same way.'

'But I could be mistaken for a common whore.'

'This is what pays our bills. Pays for this space that you've made so homely.'

'I don't want to be seen in this way ever again. It doesn't suit me,' Edith says. 'Your buyers don't even value the art you make with me in it.' Edith is very aware that Egon's images of her don't command the highest prices. She remembers that look she caught from Gertrude on her wedding day – the sense that she has been found lacking. The grand oil painting Egon made after they were married, in her striped dress, didn't even sell when it was exhibited recently. Many of her portraits go unsold, while the ones of Vally are in great demand.

'How can I work, create, if you won't pose for me?'

'There are other, far more willing women.'

'You nearly tore down my canvas when you arrived and a model was here without her clothes on.' Egon gives in to his bad temper. 'My buyers, my patrons, they want my radical style, my nudes. If I can't supply those, they'll go elsewhere. Anyone can paint a nice woman in a dress. It doesn't have the same impact.'

'But I'm your wife! I deliver your paintings. I speak to your patrons. I shake their hands. I can't hand over works of myself with my legs splayed apart for them to display on their wall.'

'Nobody makes that association, except you.'

'How would you know? We're recognized. They know our faces, if not always our names. They know that this one's Vally and that one's your sister. Think of how you compromise us.'

'Vally never complained.'

'Vally had years of experience spreading her legs. Why didn't you marry her? Oh, that's right. You couldn't. You had to find a nice girl. And now you want to tar me with the same brush.'

'Damn it, Edith. You can't have it both ways. I'm being inundated with commissions. Ever since it was announced that I'd curate the Secession exhibition and even before then . . . And, as I've said, it's the nudes that people are prepared to pay for. So what will it be? You model for me, and be prepared to take your clothes off, or other people will have to instead. You choose.'

Edith feels trapped. She can take her clothes off and damn the consequences, or let an unknown woman into her home to do the same *and* pay her for the privilege. That means less money for food, fuel and the treats they can still purchase. And who knows what Egon and this model might get up to behind closed doors. There must be another way.

There's one person she can think of. Whether Edith can trust her sister or not is an entirely different question – but she knows Adele would be willing to strike a confident pose. And at least Edith could be around at the same time, to keep an eye on her of course, but also it might help the three of them come to some kind of reconciliation. Edith buckles gently at the memory of her betrayal. For years, she's felt a muddy guilt about Adele's heartbreak, the wretched feeling colouring most of her days. The letters scraped deep into her thigh on her wedding night may have healed, but the scars have not entirely faded.

Why, yes – perhaps this wouldn't be the most outlandish idea? Adele has always appreciated Egon's art, appreciated it in ways Edith has never been able to fathom. Perhaps this would be the chance to make amends, to let Adele enjoy a little of what she thinks she is missing, and perhaps realize that it is not something to pine for, after all.

11

February 1918

Despite her best efforts, Edith is nervous about having her sister around to their apartment. They've been spending some time together – tentatively. Two weeks ago, Edith and Adele met in a coffee shop. It was civil. She'd go as far as to say it was nice to see her sister again. They spoke about common acquaintances, Edith's take on Prague and the war, Vienna and their hopes for the future.

Her sister had kissed her cheek as they parted, and there was a hint of forgiveness in the gesture.

The next week, Edith had gone to the family home and spent an afternoon drinking weak coffee, Adele sitting on the chaise longue, observing the goings-on on the street below, as she used to do in days gone by. But it wasn't the same, not at all. So much of what Edith remembers of her former home has gone. Much of the silver – be it teaspoons or photograph frames – is missing and the atmosphere feels sluggish, stupefied. Adele confided to Edith that she was bored to death so, as she was leaving, Edith had invited Adele to their home the following week, and wrote out the address on Wattmanngasse. However, for the past six days – and she's sure it's her own paranoia – Edith has felt eyes on her, in the morning as she dresses, in the afternoon as she washes the dishes, as she reads books on photography and philosophy, or arranges bulbs in the window boxes and positions them for the light.

Edith cleans the apartment for Adele's arrival. She arranges her perfume bottles and fluffs the cushions. She spends so much of her time up to her elbows in soapsuds these days that she has taken to removing her ring and putting it in a saucer by the sink. Egon will be out for the day, spending time with Roessler or Benesch, or another of his ever-demanding patrons. Edith hasn't yet told him that Adele will be coming to their home. She's still testing the waters, and after this visit, if it goes well, she'll speak to Egon about their reconciliation. She'll—

Several harsh knocks ring out on the front door. Adele isn't due for another fifteen minutes. It's unlike her to be early, unless she has undergone quite the transformation.

Edith dries her hands and removes her apron, slips her wedding ring on, then opens the door. There's a man in uniform, who takes off his cap as he addresses her.

'Schiele?' he asks.

'I'm Frau Schiele.' She searches the man's weather-reddened face.

He presents a letter. 'This has been returned from three of the last-known addresses associated with the deceased. We've been trying to track down Herr Schiele as the subsequent next-of-kin, hence the delay.'

Edith turns the letter over in her hands, searching for telltale information.

'I'm sorry for your loss,' the man adds, before walking away. Edith closes the door, the letter clasped to her chest. The postmark is Dalmatia. She knows no one there.

She should wait. Edith should wait for Egon to get home and open this himself. It's addressed to him, after all, and it's stamped 'Private and Confidential'.

Edith takes it to the kitchen and boils a pan of water, steaming the envelope open carefully, a trick she learnt from Adele. She'll be able to seal it again once she has the information, and Egon will be none the wiser. Gently, Edith removes the stiff paper from the envelope. It bears official stamps and the mark of the Red Cross. She scans the page quickly, looking for a name. And there it is.

Name: Walburga Neuzil

Occupation: Military nurse

Date of death: 25 December 1917

Cause: Scarlet fever

Age: 23

With no response from immediate kin, WALBURGA NEUZIL has been interred in SINJ.

Vally, dead.

She eases the letter back into the envelope with shaking hands and reseals it. She didn't admire the woman, but she takes no joy in the news of her death. But Egon? How might he respond? They were close. She was his model, his muse, even. Egon maintained that their relationship wasn't serious, that she'd professed not to love him, that it was more of a professional union, a fondness, but Edith has always had her doubts. Especially after she witnessed the painting *Death and the Maiden*; the way the figures there, Egon and Vally, clung to each other at their impending separation. That hurt. So this could be a blow to Egon. Edith realizes she is crying.

Another knock disturbs her. She slips the letter under the window box, goes to the door, and is relieved to see Adele rather than another man in uniform.

'Come in, make yourself at home,' Edith says politely. She thinks of Vally, not as she was towards her, cold and indifferent, but as she appeared in Egon's enigmatic portraits.

'And I brought you these.' Adele extracts a brown packet from her overcoat. 'Sunflower seeds. Flowers are impossible to buy, as you know, but these are just as charming.' She hands them over. 'They'll grow to be as tall as Egon by the end of the summer.'

Edith pours the seeds into her palm, then clasps them.

'So you did get my letters?' she says hopefully.

'Coffee?' Adele asks as she does a loop of their apartment. Edith has made the bed and removed any intimate, personal items from view.

'Of course,' Edith says quickly, embarrassed to have forgotten her most basic manners. 'I'll just put some on.'

'Well, it's small, but jolly,' Adele concludes, looking around the room.

'Yes, indeed,' Edith replies. But her mind is still on Egon's possible reaction to the news about Vally. Perhaps it would be better if he didn't find out?

They sit, Adele making herself comfortable, running her thumb around the cup, as if to clean it. They talk for a while, of what happened to Heinrich, and other acquaintances.

'I have something to ask of you,' Edith finally says to her sister. 'It may not be appropriate, so do think it over and feel free to decline if you feel it is necessary.' Adele politely blows across the surface of the drink, her eyebrows raised. 'Egon needs a model.' Edith lets the words sink in. 'You know me – I'm not comfortable with that side of things. I never get it right. I'm asking if you'd be willing to sit for him,' Edith continues. 'He has an important commission and he needs someone who's confident. Someone we can ... trust.' Adele takes another sip, keeping her eyes steadily on Edith.

'I ...' Adele begins.

The door crashes and Egon runs in, clattering along the hallway, tripping over the shoes and satchels that he has left there. It takes him a moment to gather his breath. 'Edith?' he begs, close to tears. A strange, unfathomable look passes between him and Adele. He turns to his wife. 'Edith! I've received the most terrible news. My heart is broken. Everything I ever held dear has gone.' He's shaking. Edith's eyes shoot to the window box as she jumps up. He crumples against her, his knees buckling. Edith is mortified that Adele must witness this. She tries to hold him up. 'Nothing will ever be the same. I am destroyed by grief. I don't know how I'll face the future. The person

I held in the highest esteem, the one I admired more than any other – gone.'

'Egon, I . . .' Edith looks around, at a loss. 'I had no idea she meant this much to you.'

Edith catches Adele's eye. Her sister is frowning and seems to be uncomfortable at this display of emotion.

'What are you talking about?' Egon grabs Edith by the shoulders. 'There is nobody else. He was irreplaceable. A man in a million. My hero, my mentor. Gustav Klimt is dead.'

12

February 1918

G ustav Klimt's funeral is held on a Saturday, the ninth day of February. It is a cool, vibrant-skied day. Egon and Edith woke that morning to frost upon the ground, but the warmth of a bright sun has lifted it everywhere but in the deepest shadows.

The news that Austria's most resplendent artist had died was a walloping blow to the country, sending shockwaves around Vienna and beyond. It was known that Gustav had caught influenza at the start of the year. In itself, such an illness was not unusual, and indeed, 1918 had already seen a high number of cases. Adele herself had been struck down the previous December and had suffered terribly, but had soon recovered. Klimt's case, however, had developed into a suffocating pneumonia, which left him breathless and bed-bound for weeks. Edith knew that Egon had visited him during this time; she had seen some of the sketches he'd made of his master, admired the tender pencil lines. She had not known Klimt with any intimacy – she'd believed they'd have decades to solidify their friendship – but she'd met the revered artist on a few occasions, including her wedding day, when he had gifted the couple a beautiful Japanese vase. But Egon's bond with Klimt was intense. She saw the respect that passed between her husband and this man who was almost thirty years his senior. Edith could admit only now that she'd been wary of Gustav Klimt, of his wild impulses, his gargantuan hungers, his advances. She hoped her husband would not commit too closely to following his path.

Still, it was hardly anticipated that the great artist, the creator of *The Kiss*, would die. But at the start of that week in early February, Gustav's condition had worsened and he had been rushed to the General Hospital in Alsergrund. Within hours, he had suffered a stroke and could not be saved. He was fifty-five years old.

The funeral is a lavish affair. All Vienna's most prominent citizens – those who have survived the war so far – have come to pay their respects: a mass of black moving along the street, following the horse-drawn carriage. People who never met him but knew his name, admired his art, line the streets, throwing long-stemmed flowers. Egon has pride of place among the cortège as Gustav's coffin is transported along the main road in Hietzing to the local cemetery. Gustav had made it clear long before he knew he was ill that he wanted to be buried next to his mother, Anna, who'd been laid to rest three years earlier.

Edith's husband's head is bowed, his eyes ringed with red. This morning, he had confided that he was worried that this affair would bring back memories of his own father's funeral, thirteen years before. The artist's hearse is strewn with winter garlands. Gustav's paintbrushes, bearing crusts of paint – for he left many unfinished canvases – have been placed among the wreaths. Her husband and other artists have added their own, etched with their names, as a mark of respect. Egon had dipped the bristles of his in liquid gold.

He had spent the night of Klimt's passing at the mortuary. Egon bribed the *angestellter* to allow him time with the body in order to draw the face of the corpse and, with the blessing of Gustav's closest relatives, he prepared a death mask – a likeness of the great artist's features, to be preserved in perpetuity. With his own fingers, Egon had spread plaster of Paris over his mentor's cheeks, his forehead, his eyes, working it into the bristles of his moustache. He had waited, in silence, until the plaster hardened and could be pulled loose.

Edith is wearing a mourning dress and black veil. She drops back, holding her sister's hand. Adele had sweetly, almost bashfully, requested to join the funeral parade, having been present when the news of Gustav's death broke. They enter Hietzing cemetery through the main gate, the procession having trebled in length since the outset of the journey. Gustav's family lead the way. There is no wife, but there are many women – models, lovers, friends. Edith has heard that Gustav fathered a dozen children, probably more.

'Who's that?' Adele asks, her eyes caught on a beautiful woman, her hair a voluptuous mass on her head.

'That's Emilie Flöge,' Edith replies. 'A friendship, by all accounts.'

'They say Klimt was unrestrained in his liaisons.'

'Egon says it went deeper than that between Emilie and him.'

'She's weeping,' Adele points out.

They follow a winding path through the graves, past weather-worn headstones and statues of angels. The procession turns left by an imposing crypt. All these old bones beneath the surface, Edith considers. She prays it'll be a long, long time before she ends up encased in wood below the earth.

Space at the graveside is limited, and Edith and Adele weave through the crowd to join Egon, who is closer to the front.

'You're Schiele,' Edith hears a woman comment, pocketing her handkerchief and extending her hand.

'Egon, yes,' her husband replies.

'All this – the future, the hope of our culture – falls upon you now,' she says.

Egon looks at her with desperate eyes. 'It does?' He swallows.

'I do hope you're up to it. For there is nobody Gustav admired more to carry his legacy forward. You bear the torch. Use it wisely.' She touches his shoulder and leaves.

Eulogies are read, hymns sung. The flowers atop the coffin tremble in a gentle breeze. Then, the ropes of the coffin are being slowly released when a wild, choking cry goes up.

Emilie steps forward, her face obscured. She throws her arms on to the coffin, her fingers white against the grain, and places kisses on the polished wood. The mourners hold their breath until another woman steps forward and takes Emilie gently by the shoulders, allowing Gustav to make his final descent.

The low sun catches the wings of a stone angel. A shudder goes through Edith. Egon throws a handful of earth into the deep hole.

As they're leaving, Egon looks around, peering into faces covered by veils.

'I thought I might see Vally here,' he admits. 'It's strange for her to miss this.'

13

March 1918

E dith puts the finishing touches to her outfit. She has curled her
fair hair and tied it with a navy ribbon, and dressed in her finest
silk and organza gown – an ornate embroidered garment that hasn't
been touched since before the war, but has lain wrapped in tissue
paper in her wardrobe at Mutti's apartment. She has repaired it carefully and washed it especially for this occasion. She has also taken
great care with her appearance, touching powder and pink pigment to
her cheeks. Now she hopes Egon will appreciate the efforts she has
made in order to look her best: for tonight is the opening of the Vienna
Secession's forty-ninth exhibition – a show that Egon has curated,
inviting the artists he admires most to contribute. He'll display nineteen large paintings and twenty-four drawings of his own – all for sale
to the highest bidder. Edith and her husband must leave imminently
in order to arrive on time.

Egon is hunched over the kitchen table, his shirtsleeves rolled up,
his dejection framed by the window. 'Are you unwell?' Edith hurries
over to him. 'Egon, look at me.' Edith takes his face in her hands and
directs her husband's gaze towards her. The skin around his eyes is
purple, and they glisten with tears.

'I can't go,' he whispers. 'I can't face them. I can't pretend to believe in it all.' He gestures loosely. 'Not with Gustav gone. I drew him on his deathbed. The look in his eyes still haunts me.'

'You've been working for months to prepare for this evening. People are expecting you.'

'They won't even notice that I'm not in attendance,' he says.

'You designed the poster. Your name is upon it. Everyone has been talking about you and this year's exhibition. You can't stay away and let the show go on without you.'

'All I know is that I can't be in that room with people looking at me, expecting me to shine, without my friend. How can we be expected to celebrate the art that he lived for, in the space that he established, without him?'

'He'll be there in spirit. His art will be on the walls, will it not? People are eager to get together to talk about him and celebrate his passion.'

'He's been dead less than a month. It should have been cancelled, as a mark of respect.'

'Art lives on, you told me that.' She looks at him tenderly. 'Gustav admired you greatly. You told me the story of when you first met at his atelier a decade ago, and you asked him if you had talent. And how did he reply?'

'Edith, no, please. It's too painful to remember.' Egon grips his head in his hands.

'"Much too much!" he said after looking at your drawings. He saw that in you. He'd want you to go, to honour his memory, to continue the movement he so believed in.'

Egon's shoulders are shaking. Edith puts a hand on his back and can feel the juddering vibrations through his shirt and skin.

'He was like a father to me,' he says eventually.

'And it is a tragedy that he died. But you are his successor. It's up to you to carry his mantle, continue as he would have wanted you to.'

'I can't do it.'

'You have to. You have made him proud before and you will do so again. The Vienna Secession was Gustav's pride and joy for more than twenty years. And you've worked so hard for this show. You were so happy to be invited to participate and make it your own, and you said, before this happened, that it would be the making of you. You must overcome your grief,' Edith says, 'if only for an hour. Now is not the time to fade away.'

〜

Egon and Edith leave the Ringstrasse and walk up the steps to the imposing white and gold Secession building. It's a charmingly unconventional structure: squat and windowless, with sharp white lines and a ball-of-gold crown. It was designed to reflect the idea that art could free culture from the grips of the establishment, and is a sharp contrast to the historic buildings that line the grand boulevard.

Inside the exhibition space, well-dressed people have turned out in force for the occasion and to honour Gustav Klimt. Egon and Edith step into the large central room which is dedicated to Egon's works; the effect is instantaneous and dizzying. Instantly, the couple are handed long flutes fizzing with chilled sparkling wine, and Egon is feted as a hero, men coming to shake his hand and women casting glances in his direction, whispering to their friends. Edith catches him smiling. Every patron in the room wants to talk to Egon and she is edged away from his side, but she's sure this worship will revive him.

She admires his artworks, these great paintings and drawings, featuring her and other models, many of whose names she does not know. They look different on the wall of a gallery.

'Is that you?' one woman asks Edith as they stand in front of a painting. Edith turns to look at her. She has always believed she is impermanent, as if her features shift over time, and will be neither remembered nor remarked. Yet here she is now, captured on the canvas.

'Yes,' she says. 'I'm the woman in the painting.'

'You're the artist's wife?'

'Edith Schiele.'

'I admire your husband greatly. And for that reason, I admire you. It's very brave to do what you do, to pose so openly and present yourself to the world. You have my respect.'

'It's not so difficult, really.' Edith blushes, looking into the woman's beautiful pale face, with its halo of dark, wild hair. Is she mocking her?

'I'm Serena. Lederer? My husband and I were close friends of dear Gustav, and he's a keen collector of his work. Your husband may have mentioned that he has painted my son Erich over the years. They enjoy each other's company immensely.'

'Of course, I know of Erich. He's been a wonderful model, so natural and confident.'

'We've missed Egon greatly during this interminable war, which is perhaps why you and I haven't met earlier?' The woman takes Edith's arm, conspiratorially. Her fingers drip with diamonds. 'You must come and stay with us at our castle in Weidlingau.'

'My husband would be delighted, I'm certain of it. As would I,' Edith says.

'Elisabeth, my daughter, is keen to learn from him, too. She takes after me and wants to pursue her own artistic interests. Art isn't just for the boys.' The woman smiles. 'But it sounds as if I may have to wrestle Herr Schiele from the clutches of every patron in the room, if his success tonight is anything to go by.'

'In what way?'

'Do you see how everyone is fawning over him? This is his moment. He has already sold a portrait, and it's the one of you, I believe.' She looks at Edith warmly, appraising her with her dark eyes.

'My goodness,' Edith says, looking around for Egon. 'Can it be true?'

'Tonight,' Serena continues, 'is the start of Egon Schiele's glittering trajectory. Your husband is destined for great things. The scandals of his past – oh, I know all about those – are behind him now. He has talent, *much too much*' – she smiles shrewdly – 'and a remarkable woman by his side. He has what it takes to be Austria's greatest living artist, if he isn't already. In the coming months and years, Egon will become unstoppable.'

⤸

'Is it true?' Edith takes Egon by the elbow. 'That man wants to buy your painting?'

'Herr Haberditzl has made an offer I can't refuse.' The lights twinkle in Egon's eyes.

'The one of me?' She searches his face, hurrying his answer.

'Yes, the director of the Moderne Galerie wants *you* – the artist's wife, sitting, with your hands clasped, wearing that old chemise and the plaid skirt. It's the most significant sale I've ever made. And what a price! You've no idea how much more this will bring our way. And how it will silence my critics.'

She kisses his cheek, blooming with joy. Edith can't believe it. With this sale, something is confirmed: her place, by her husband's side, as a worthy woman and model – one who is appreciated, even with her clothes on. She glows as she turns the thought over in her mind. At last, she is valued.

'Only, he wants me to paint over your skirts.'

'What?'

'He finds it all too indecent.'

'My skirts?' Of all the things Egon has painted over the years – the wide-open legs and darkened interior of a woman's thighs, the breasts and all that *touching* that has characterized his work, it's Edith's skirt that has caused offence?

'What, precisely, is his objection?'

'It wasn't quite clear. Perhaps he thinks the pattern is too lewd, or the way the material falls is overly suggestive. You should ask him.'

'I'm not going to do that.'

'Let me call him over here to speak to you,' he bluffs.

'You'll do no such thing!' Light flashes off the crystal, and Edith squints against it, a sudden defiance rising in her. 'You shouldn't do it. You've always said you won't pander to these men who only have a commercial head for art. What will they demand next – that you paint over my face? That you get a new wife altogether, because the one you have doesn't suit them?'

'This is the biggest sale of my life, Edith. For what they're about to pay, if they require me to marry another woman and paint all day in the nude, I'd happily oblige – and so would you.'

'I won't let you anywhere near my skirts with a paintbrush.' She's serious.

'But you didn't object after our wedding when Roessler instructed me to paint over Vally's bare buttocks in *Death and the Maiden*.'

'That's different.' Edith stiffens at the mention of Vally.

'Herr Schiele?' a man interrupts. He's carrying a heavy camera. It flashes brightly in their faces and the world goes blank for a moment or two. Edith rubs her temple with her thumb.

'Come now, enjoy yourself. It's not every night that your husband is crowned the star of the show.' He smiles. 'Look at these people, this glittering crowd. I'm on the brink of something here, I can feel it. This is the first night of many great nights,' he says, so sure of himself as he downs the rest of his drink. Edith can't shake a growing discomfort. 'And once the news gets out, everyone who approaches us will talk of a portrait or painting of their daughter, or how to get their hands on my latest offering.'

A waiter passes and Egon takes a flute and hands it to Edith, as more people gather round to clap him on the back, shake his hand and discuss the finer details of his style. He's lost to her again. She fades away, finding solace in the familiarity of his work, in the eyes of the women before her, who have been silenced, but for whom others now speak.

Edith must pull herself together. This is wonderful news. It's progress, as they say. The start of a dazzling new era for the artist Egon Schiele.

For the past must fall away, and he is the future.

14

June 1918

'Mutti's waiting for you,' Adele says when Edith opens the door. 'She refuses to come in. She blames that ache in her hip, but the truth is, she doesn't want to be accosted by your rats.'

'They're only mice, you know that,' Edith chides. She hears them in the night. And now that Adele comes here, modelling in silence, she has noticed them, too. Edith tried to buy traps at the market, but as with everything else, as a result of this war, they're in short supply.

'Is Egon ready for me?' Adele asks.

'I'm sure he will be,' Edith says. Mutti and she are taking a day trip to the grounds of a country house. Egon's work on the painting has 'run over', so Adele will not be joining them. Edith has done her best to see to it that Egon and Adele are rarely alone together, but it has happened on a few occasions over the past couple of months. After-wards, Egon always says that nothing was amiss. 'Adele is Adele,' he shrugs – a declaration that doesn't fill Edith with much by way of reassurance.

Adele begins to undo the buttons at her wrists while she walks Edith to the door.

'Could you get this for me?' Adele turns around. 'Egon has rather unwieldy fingers.'

Edith works her way down the spine of buttons at Adele's back. Her sister's skin is pale, entirely unblemished. When was the last time she was even touched? 'Don't keep Mutti waiting, now,' her sister adds, opening the door as if she were hurrying Edith out of her own home. It's only when Edith is halfway down the street, striding along beside her mother, that she realizes she'd not had a chance to bid her husband goodbye or gather her things. She imagines Egon discovering Adele, half-dressed. Would he make himself busy, keep the relationship professional, or would he reveal that rakish smile, and invite Adele into the bedroom?

Edith feels sick. Mutti notices her chalky face and, after a quick embrace, rummages in her handbag, and pushes a pill at her.

'I worry about you,' she says. They board the tram, one of the few that runs a regular route during the war. Edith hurries to take a seat. Everything is moving too quickly; the abrupt jolts of the tracks below are making her dizzy and she has a strange taste in her mouth, as if she has bitten her tongue.

'Oh, Mutti, I feel terrible.' Edith lowers her head towards her knees and breathes deeply. 'I fear I must go home – I can't face a day on my feet, sniffing flowers.'

'Nonsense. We're together – you know how much that means to me. I've been looking forward to this for weeks!' Mutti nudges her back into a sitting position. 'Walk it off, that's what I say.'

Edith thinks of Adele's creamy skin. Another wave of nausea washes over her.

At the next stop, Edith hops from the tram. Her mother shuffles down after her, a look of concern on her face as she searches her daughter's features. 'You're not coming down with anything sinister, are you, darling?'

'Perhaps it's something I ate.'

'A little sickness before lunch could be a good sign, you know? I had that with both you girls,' her mother says, the lightness of hope creeping into her voice. Mutti has been hoping for a grandchild for the last three years, ever since the moment Edith and Egon married.

Edith frowns and finds a bench. 'Mutti,' she says. 'I'm worried about Adele. I fear I've asked too much of her over this business with Egon and the modelling. Does she seem like herself, do you think?'

Mutti strokes her daughter's back. 'Since you returned to Vienna, Adele has been happier than I've seen her for a very long time. You're the light of her life. She gets up in the morning with a spring in her step, and never stops talking about how much she enjoys spending time with you again. As for posing for Egon, she's doing it for you, darling.'

Edith's stomach lurches. She gets up and vomits in the bushes. The pale liquid burns her throat and lingers on her lips. She stares at the mess on the ground, among the fallen petals and leaves.

'Goodness!' Mutti pulls a handkerchief from her skirts and presses it to Edith's head. 'You're hot to the touch. Let's get you home, you'll feel better there.'

~

When Edith arrives at her front door, a thick anticipation still rumbles through her, the taste of bile in her mouth. She cannot stop imagining what's going on inside.

She enters with care. The scene that will present itself is clear: Adele, in her bed, legs wrapped around her husband's torso. But Egon is painting quietly, a spare brush behind his ear. Adele is lounging on Edith's cushions, half-asleep.

'You're back earlier than expected,' Egon says. He puts his palette down and kisses his wife's cheek. 'We thought you'd be out all day.' Is it her imagination, or does Edith sense something between them, a frisson of relief, of giddiness that they have been caught in this moment and not another? 'I've wanted to show you this,' he says. It's an almost-finished painting of Adele, demure, with an innocence she does not possess. The image resembles Edith.

'You've not captured her likeness at all,' she says.

'What about the gaze? You know what's going on behind those eyes, don't you?'

'And what is going on behind her eyes?' Edith asks.

'There's power there,' Egon replies. 'There's passion behind the deadpan sweetness. Innocence belies intense sexuality. It stalks the viewer. Can you see it?'

'Now you're talking as if you were a critic,' Edith comments.

Adele stands up, her eyelids heavy.

'You're wearing my pearls!'

'Are you sick? Is that why you've rushed home?' Adele replies.

'I'm queasy through and through,' Edith admits.

'Something must have gone down the wrong way,' Adele says. She sweeps her hair up off her shoulders. Will Edith find long strands of it on her pillows, again? 'Am I dismissed?' she asks, not entirely to Egon. 'We'll get to it quicker tomorrow, shall we?' Adele squeezes her husband's arm. Then she takes Edith by the elbow as she walks to the door. 'I'm saying this because I care for you,' she whispers. 'But your clothes look tight, your cheeks are . . .' Adele puffs her own out. Edith sucks in her stomach, straightens her back. Adele smiles. 'Men can't stand it when their wives let themselves go.'

Edith cannot shake the ice that settles on her heart whenever Adele is near.

'I'm . . . pregnant,' she announces. It's startling to say it out loud.

Edith watches the muscles on Adele's face twitch.

'Oh, are we now? Well, I see now why you've been acting in such a peculiar fashion.'

Edith raises her chin. If she opens her mouth, she'll start screaming and never stop.

'Adele, if it's a girl?' she whispers into Edith's ear. 'Adele Schiele has such a nice ring to it, I've always thought.' Adele strokes her sister's hair. 'Oh, before I forget. These are yours.' She lifts the pearls from her neck. 'I'd never be able to forgive myself if I walked away with another thing that belongs to you. I'll be back tomorrow. Egon needs me. Now more than ever.'

Edith has always known, deep down, that this was going to happen, that her sister hasn't changed at all, that it was impossible for Adele to wish the best for Edith. She's unwell, that's what Edith tells herself. But the last thing she wants is to give her sister the satisfaction of knowing that she's got to her. So she holds the door for Adele with a small shake of her head, her lips pinched.

'Goodbye, Adele,' she says, and closes the door behind her with a solemn click.

She returns to Egon. If she has anything to do with it, Adele won't ever pose for him again.

'Is the painting finished?' Edith asks.

'We need another day or two, three at most,' he replies.

'Last week Adele said it was nearly done.'

'Adele can barely tell the time, you've said as much yourself,' Egon says.

'I'm sick of having her around. She rattles my nerves.'

'Adele's been a good model, you should give her that much.'

'Too good, one might say.'

Egon sighs. 'This was your choice, not mine, Edith. She's doing us a favour.'

'But she's always here! Being Adele.' Edith steadies herself against the sink.

'We'll not use her again, if that's what you want.'

'What was I thinking? I'm not even sure she's in her right mind. The looks she gives me, the words that come out of her mouth . . .'

'My father succumbed to madness. It was hell. Adele seems a long way from that.'

'But there's something not right about her, the way her eyes cut through me . . .'

'Your sister has a lot of faults, but she loves you. She talks about you all the time.'

Edith wonders if Egon is being deliberately naive, or if she is being particularly sensitive.

'Egon, I . . .' she begins. 'I've not been feeling well. I don't know how to say this. I'm always tired and today I was sick.' Edith stops. 'I wasn't sure at first, but now, I think . . .' She sweeps a hand across her belly and looks into his eyes until something clicks.

He takes her face in his hands. 'This is such happy news! Edith, look at me.' He pulls her into a tight embrace.

'Is it?' She looks up, her eyes brimming.

'I thought you wanted this?'

'I'm scared,' she says. 'It feels too good to be true.'

'I'm terrified,' Egon admits, letting the news sink in. 'Nothing will ever be the same.'

'I suspect I'm a month or two gone; I've lost all track. I'd given up even hoping it might happen. I'll need to see a doctor, but just think, if it all goes well, we'll have a baby in the new year, at long last. I can't wait to meet the little thing.'

'My God, I'll be a father. It's unthinkable. Perhaps I'll finally understand my own.'

'I only wish Papa was alive, so I could tell him the news.'

'Both our fathers would be proud. Grandfathers! Imagine that. We must raise a toast.' Egon takes down a glass and pours schnapps into it. 'A sip for you.' She smells it, then he knocks back the rest. He looks dazed and delighted. 'I'm in awe of you, Edith. I love you. And what's happening in there,' he says, putting a hand on her belly. 'It's unbelievable.'

'Lots of women have babies,' she says. 'All the time.'

'Yes, but this one is ours. Some hope, in the darkness, at last.'

15

25 October 1918

'My mother was here,' Egon says. 'She came asking for money again. I gave her what we could spare, which isn't much, and I showed her the painting I've been working on. It's the one I exhibited in March at the Secession, and I had the idea, after you told me you were pregnant, of adding a child, to make the squatting couple into a family. Well, she took one look at the baby and came right out with it, without any preamble – she asked that if we have a daughter, we might consider naming the child Elvira. I said I'd discuss it with you. You know how much it would mean to her.'

'At least she didn't ask us to call her Marie,' Edith says, moving dishes around in the kitchen.

'She became very emotional, talking about the past, about all the things that have been lost, her babies that died in the womb – hardly appropriate, given your condition.'

'Well, I'm open to the idea of that name,' Edith concedes. 'Now, have you seen my ring?' she adds, getting ready to leave. The buttons of her coat no longer fasten around her extended, firm stomach, so she leaves it open, despite the cold. She's looking around the kitchen, in all kinds of unlikely places. She thinks she left the ring on the soap dish – only she can't remember when.

'As she left,' Egon continues, 'she was keen to tell me that the Spanish influenza is making itself known again in Vienna, this time with a vengeance.'

'I washed dishes yesterday,' Edith says, retracing her steps. 'I'd have taken it off then.' She rubs the place on her finger where the ring had been. The skin there is indented and shiny.

'Listen to me, Edith. It has spread around the globe. We need to be aware of these things. There's a growing sense of panic. She left the newspaper.' Egon passes it over. 'Read it.'

Edith glances at the article. *More than eighteen thousand people dead in Austria as a result of Spanish influenza.* 'It's worrying, certainly. But I'm already late for the check-up you arranged with Von Graff,' she says. 'I don't want to leave without my ring.' Edith rubs a hand over her belly. 'I'll go to the market after to get food and fuel.'

The baby, at six months, moves often. Edith can feel its energy, so intense it crackles.

'The article advises staying indoors and some say you should wear a flu mask when outside.'

'Caution doesn't suit you,' Edith says. 'And neither would a mask.'

'Death wouldn't suit me, either. Or you, for that matter,' Egon replies. He joins her by the sink. 'You always leave it in that saucer,' he adds. 'I've not touched it.'

'This will be the same as the three-day fever in spring,' Edith says. 'People get it, but they recover. It's the old and frail who are dying.'

'That's not true. Some think that Gustav died of it – that it's what caused the pneumonia that put him in hospital.' Egon pauses. 'But reports say that people can die within hours of their first symptoms. Doctors are powerless; they're blaming it on all sorts of things, from jazz music to the bombs disturbing graves and the soil releasing noxious gases.'

'You won't die, Egon. You're only twenty-eight. You're young, you're strong.'

'It's the young who are susceptible. And women in your state have almost no defences against it,' he warns. When there's no response, he continues, 'Edith, you're not listening. The tram system is shut, schools are closing. People are confining themselves to their homes. They say this influenza will claim more lives than all those lost during the war.'

'My state? We'll freeze to death without firewood. We need to stock up. This is already the coldest winter since the turn of the century.'

'Edith, I don't want you to leave the house. I'm serious. I'll send word and ask Dr von Graff to come here.'

'In another few weeks, I'll barely be able to walk. I need the exercise,' she says.

'Please, think of me, the baby,' he begs. 'Stay here, where it's safe.'

Edith looks at the rain lashing against the window. Her shoes have started to pinch and she can't replace them as leather is no longer available.

'Fine. If you're willing to send a request that he visit me here, then I'll stay, wrapped in cotton wool. In the meantime, please, help me find my ring. I can't bear to be without it.'

16

25 October 1918

L ater that day, Edith is lying in bed, swathed in woollen blankets, reading a periodical and eating toasted war bread, which is dry and dusty because flour is so hard to come by. Crumbs tumble on to her rounded belly and, as she's taking the final bite, she hears the bell. Egon goes to answer it. It will be the doctor. In truth, she's quite pleased to have been saved the journey.

Edith waits to hear footsteps in the hallway, but there's nothing. No voices or the sound of the door closing. Only an airborne energy, rippling. She sits up, brushing the crumbs to the floor. The mice will eat well tonight.

'Egon?' she shouts. 'Who's there?' There's no reply. Edith raises herself awkwardly. At six months, she's becoming large and ungainly. She pulls her soft leather shoes on to save her bare feet the indignity of the cold floor, then lumbers out of the bedroom. She can hear Egon, speaking animatedly in a low voice. There's anger in his tone. Urgency. He's trying to calm someone down. A woman.

'Adele?' Edith says in surprise. 'What are you doing here?'

Edith looks from her husband to her sister. Adele is on the threshold of their home, her expression wild. Egon has his hand on the door frame, as if trying to prevent her from coming any further.

'Come in,' Edith says cautiously. 'I'll catch a chill.'

'Adele is leaving,' Egon says.

'Your husband won't let me pass.'

'What do you want?' Edith asks.

'I need to see you,' Adele says.

'She's trying to cause trouble.' Egon looks anguished.

'Adele?'

'I have news I want to share.'

'Go back to bed, Edith,' her husband says. 'I'll see to it that Adele leaves immediately.'

'I'm not leaving!'

'You are,' Egon replies.

Egon tries to close the door but Adele worms her way around it. Edith feels something dark and porous gathering in the air.

'I'm pregnant!' Adele shouts to Edith as she turns away.

'What did you say?'

'Aren't you going to ask me who the father is?' Adele demands.

Edith stops and takes a step back towards the door, closer to Egon and Adele.

'It's as you said, she's not in her right mind,' Egon says, reddening.

'You're not the only one who can be happy!' Adele says defiantly.

'Nothing ever happened between us!'

'You couldn't resist,' Adele retorts, her eyes on Egon.

'You're lying,' he swears.

The ground sways beneath Edith's feet. This is unbearable.

'Ah, but you made me promises,' Adele says, her face up close to his.

'Adele is insane. I've seen it before. She has all the signs.'

'Bored, he was, of such a *nice* girl,' Adele wheezes in Edith's ear.

'That's not true!' Egon musters, wedging himself in between the two of them.

Adele smiles at Edith, satisfied. 'Some truths are too hard to handle.'

'Edith, she's a liar. She has lost her mind.'

'One of us has to satisfy your husband,' she hisses.

With all her strength, Edith slaps her sister across the face.

Adele straightens, a hand to her cheek, looking as if she doesn't know what day it is.

'Adele Harms,' Edith spits, anger in each syllable. 'You are the most poisonous person on the planet. I'd rather die than lay eyes on you again. I'm horrified to call you my sister. To think that I once looked up to you, that I loved you.' Edith is trembling. 'And you!' She turns on Egon. 'I don't know what or who to believe any more. One of you is lying to me! My sister or my husband. It's the greatest betrayal imaginable.'

Anger explodes in waves and she continues to shake. Edith pushes past both of them and runs out into the street. She's not dressed for the weather and has no money, but she can't bear to be around either of them for a second longer.

'Edith, wait, it's not what you think,' Egon begs, coming after her, but Adele holds him back. 'Please, give me a chance to explain,' he calls out.

'It's not my fault your husband chose the wrong sister,' Adele screams as Edith runs into the rain, her face burning, the baby kicking at her ribs.

17

25 October 1918

E dith walks the streets aimlessly, for an hour, two. Her feet are sodden, her hair wet, her hands ache with the cold. But she won't go home. Adele's words still ring in her ears. Over and over, she hears her nauseating voice. And with each exclamation, it's as if the slap Edith so violently administered lands on her own cheek, rather than her sister's.

Edith is beaten, exhausted, emptied of all permanence. It was all a pretence.

She is almost certain that Adele is lying, but the chill remains in Edith as if it were stitched into her bones.

Hand on heart, could Edith say that Egon wasn't capable of doing such a thing, of hurting her in this unforgivable way? She thought he loved her. But can a man change? All the models he has been with over the years, the girl in Neulengbach, the way he'd discarded Vally. She had wanted to believe he could. But now, she can't tell with any certainty, one way or another.

Edith passes theatres and concert halls, restaurants and drinking dens. Most of them are boarded up, a combination of the war and the fear around the influenza, but some smaller establishments offer bright lights, even on this murky day. There's a bowling alley on the corner and a sign for a cabaret. Why did she always think these things were for other people? There's so much *life* all around her. How is it that she has never lost control, always erred on the side of caution and care? And where has that got her?

The middle of a war, a pandemic, a challenging marriage, a poisonous sister, a pregnancy that could kill her if things don't go well? What's the point of living at all?

⤙

It's raining harder by the time Edith arrives at Vienna's Prater amusement park. The mud has splashed up to her knees, but pickpockets remain undeterred. She can be careless, though, as she has nothing left to steal. The space jostles with frenetic noise and energy. Edith roams past its eye-rolling contraptions – flying swing-chairs, wooden-horse carousels, a rickety roller-coaster and a ghost train. She has experienced frights enough for one day.

She is soaked through. She looks for refuge and finds it in the short queue for the giant Ferris wheel. The modern steel construction towers above, and she feels a flutter of trepidation, but it is the only sanctuary on offer. She's at the front before she realizes she has no money. A grubby man with few teeth nods her past conspiratorially – he can see what state she's in, and in that brief moment, she is grateful. She enters the red-painted wooden cabin as it swings to a stop.

Mercifully, she's fully protected from the downpour there, entombed in a space where there are no choices left to be made. He slams the door shut behind her.

It's only then that Edith casts her eyes over the frame and tightened bolts, and she wonders if the structure will hold. Could everything come crashing down, with her and this unborn baby in the middle of it? It cranks into motion and she feels the rattle through her body.

Edith holds her breath as the wheel moves along a fraction. Then the whole thing heaves into motion once more. Beneath her, the distance grows, until she's high above Vienna, the autumnal trees and copper spires and familiar landmarks shrinking. She sees the purple-grey smudge of pigeons, red roofs streaked with rust, a bird's-eye view of chimneys and grassland and cobbles. People moving through the rain become pinpoints on the ground. She sees tramlines, the city's veins, and a weak horizon cut into the distance. This is her orbit. Up she goes, higher and higher. Near the top, the wind whistles through an open window, whipping her hair against her neck. The cabin rocks unsteadily, and she's breathless, light-headed, scared of looking down. Her heart races, the baby twists, and she begins to pant.

Then she experiences the tipping point – a moment of balance before the descent – the sensation manifesting itself first in her belly. She puts her hand to her stomach, desperate, scared that somehow the baby is in danger, that it is all her fault. Why is she being so reckless?

She remembers, then, that she has been pushed to the edge by the people she loves most.

It takes less than half an hour for the wheel to complete its circuit. In that time, she has thought of death and love, of blood and betrayal, and where her loyalties lie.

Who can we trust in this world? Edith still hasn't a clue.

⌒

She begins walking again. Where else can she go? She feels as if she were a homeless rambler, one of these unfortunate types who have frittered everything away and must wander the streets, with no chance of redemption or return. She is sure she's mistaken for such a figure too, grubby as she has become, shivering and shaking. She warms her belly, thinking only of the baby, of its emerging limbs and eyes closed against the darkness inside her.

Edith approaches the market. Stalls are closing up for the evening, men and boys packing away the produce, piling up crates. She runs her hands over wrinkled fruit and meagre vegetables, the prices sky-high.

'One for a pretty girl, down on her luck,' a man says, putting his hand beneath his stall and pulling out an orange. He holds it out and she is transfixed. Edith sits down. He produces a knife to peel it. She's so empty, and the juice is so sweet. It's rare.

As she is leaving, she touches a stack of tall, brittle firewood, the only type that can be sourced during this sad war, and imagines the flames that will consume it, given time. They promise so much: life-giving warmth, and destruction.

A line that is so terribly fine.

18

25 October 1918

E dith knocks on the door. It's almost midnight. Egon is there in less than a heartbeat.

'Oh, my God, where were you? I've been looking all over the city.'

She stands there, shivering. Water drips from her nose.

'Come in, right now,' he says, hurrying her inside. 'Get out of those wet clothes.'

Edith coughs into her blue hands. She's finding it difficult to swallow. He leads her to the bedroom and removes her thin coat, then undoes the buttons of her dress and helps her step out of it. He pulls the shoes off her feet. He fetches a dry towel and runs it over her back, rubbing her for warmth. He follows the line of her arms, then puts it on her head to soak up the rain in her hair, which the downpour has turned a darker shade of blonde. Egon disappears and comes back with her silver-handled brush, then runs it through the length of her hair, brushing out the knots ever so gently.

'Adele is lying,' he says quietly, after a time. 'She tried to kiss me. It was weeks ago. I turned her away. I told her she was insane to even consider it. I thought she'd get over it. That's why I didn't tell you. I wanted to give her a second chance. But my rejection only made her more demanding. I know she loves you, but I'm certain she's jealous about your pregnancy. Perhaps that pushed her over the edge? All I can say is that, if she is pregnant, it isn't by me.'

Edith coughs again, wrapping her arms around herself.

'It doesn't matter now,' she whispers.

In her wanderings, she had eventually concluded that she knows her sister; knows her sensitivities, her weaknesses, her bad side and the good. Edith understands the part she herself has played in cultivating the person Adele has become. She's sorry, too, for everything.

'She did tell me she was pregnant,' Egon admits. 'I sent her to my doctor friend. I wanted to help. All that talk of suitors and her reckless behaviour. But I'd no idea she was going around saying the baby was mine. That's preposterous, Edith, you have to believe me.'

There's nothing Edith can say. She has already made her choice.

'I thought I was helping,' he repeats. 'I never touched her. I wouldn't dream of it.' He stops. 'Edith, look at me.' He takes her face roughly in his hands. 'We're happy. We have a future. I wouldn't do anything to risk that.' He pulls her to him and she yields.

'All is forgiven,' she whispers, her voice hoarse. 'I love you.'

If one of them is lying, then perhaps it stands to reason that at least one is also telling the truth. Edith holds on to that. She doesn't want to draw a line down the middle. She will find a way back to them both, given time, given tenderness, given the strength to forgive the most terrible transgressions.

'And I you,' he whispers. 'Eternally.'

The two of them curl up together on the bed, their bodies entwined. Egon wraps his arms around her and she kisses his wrist. The baby kicks. Edith places Egon's hand to the movement. There's something transcendent about the proximity of their beating hearts, three simultaneous pulses.

The potential, the possibilities, are endless.

Edith coughs. She holds Egon tighter.

'I need you to feel warm and safe,' he says. 'We have all the time in the world.'

There's only one choice Edith can make, that much is clear: to believe in love.

For without it, we are nothing.

Interlude

The Albertina Gallery, 9 May 1968

'I'm sorry.' Standing in front of the painting of her sister, Adele lowers her head and gathers her words, unfurls them from her heart and offers them from her lips with tenderness. 'There isn't a second that goes by, not a moment, when I haven't regretted ... absolutely everything, to my very core. There's no punishment I haven't deserved. The things I did, the things I said to you ...' She tries to smile at her sister. 'You must believe me, I never wanted it to end the way it did. If I'd known, I'd have run after you, begged you to stay. I'd have been brave enough to tell you the truth.'

It's all coming back to Adele now. In this space, after half a century, the contours and colours of her memory are being restored. Scenes return to her in snippets, as if painted by Egon's brush. And now that they are surfacing, she barely wants to see. But she must. She must relive her ugliest actions. It's the only way to forgiveness.

Truth, truth, truth. The word echoes in Adele's head.

With a clenched heart, Adele now sees the look on Edith's face when Adele told her she was pregnant. Did she really say those words? What had possessed her? Her own delusions had got the better of her, she can see that now. Adele moves through the chambers of her rusted memory, sieving through pain and shame, to unearth the shrapnel of truth. The slap – my God, she can still feel it as if it were administered afresh – the stinging shock as her sister's palm thrashed her cheek. There is only betrayal in Edith's eyes, a deep hole of it, as the pain compresses the air from her lungs.

Adele shakes and shakes. Eva holds her, stroking her hair.

'There came a point when I couldn't contain my jealousy any longer,' Adele manages to say eventually, explaining to her younger friend what she remembers from that fateful day so long ago.

'You see why I've never forgiven myself,' Adele concludes. 'My actions were so terrible, the pain cut me off from life.'

She looks up at the portrait once more. Is that clemency she can see in Edith's glistening blue eyes? It is what she has been searching for her entire life.

Adele looks at the woman pulled into being from brushstrokes. Her hand reaches out, as if to brush a tendril of hair from the side of her sister's face.

'*Die gnädige Frau!*' the security guard's deep voice ruptures the quiet. 'Do not touch the artworks!'

Adele snatches her hand away. People turn, their eyes upon her.

Edith's eyes are mere strokes of oil paint – pigment that has hardened and cracked over the years.

Adele takes a seat on a bench and breathes into her hands. She feels weaker than ever, a putrefying soul. Eva sits alongside her, reaching a hand to the old woman's back, not saying a word, looking instead into the soulful, sad eyes of the woman in the painting.

'Oh, Adele. I've no doubt your sister loved you very much. Whatever happened between you, I'm sure you're forgiven after all this time. You couldn't have known where your words that day would lead . . .'

EGON

1

Saturday, 26 October 1918

The pillow by Egon's head is moist. Its heat rises, smoking in the cold, bright room. He focuses on the shape of Edith next to him. Her eyelids are grey, her cheekbones sharp through yellow skin. Her lips are dry. Egon recoils to the furthest corner of the bed, pulling his knees up to get as far away from her as possible.

Jesus Christ, is his beautiful wife even alive?

Movement flutters across her chest, almost imperceptible.

She lives, but she has it. He knew this terrible illness was always going to find its way to him. He'd felt it in his bones, as surely as he'd felt the ferocious pull towards art as a boy.

He knew he'd never escape it.

Egon is aghast. He retches at the strength of his horror and fear and anger. He cannot bear to touch his wife. He's ashamed at the wave of sudden hatred he feels for her. Edith has brought this illness here, into their home, into their bed, and he has to make her better, pray that she will survive, while also protecting himself. Did she not think of him and the baby when she fled?

The world seems smaller suddenly, microscopic; it no longer revolves around the sun, but a minute nucleus of disease. He stares at his wife. How much damage has already been done? He thinks of life peeling off in layers, the weight of her diminishing as she sleeps. His wife, affected by gravity in a new way, sinking out of existence.

Edith already looks as his father did, on his deathbed. Egon remembers watching from an almost closed door that night as the life ebbed out of him. He thinks of all that has happened in that time – his imprisonment, his marriage, this interminable war, one that could end any day now – and everything that failed to happen to his dead father, turning to bone, dust, to nothingness.

He tries to calm himself. Edith is sleeping, he tells himself, only sleeping.

Maybe this isn't the Spanish influenza, but simply a fever, something that will pass through them. He's overreacting. But Egon can't deny that he feels death flexing all around him. He's prepared to fight. For his life, for hers and their baby's. He will win.

Still, he stuffs a corner of the bedsheet into his mouth and cries soundlessly.

◡

Egon slowly recovers his senses and tries to make Edith as comfortable as he can manage. She almost wakes as he drags the bed into the living room and pulls her into a sitting position, tucking pillows in behind her. He sends word with a boy on the street for a doctor, to arrive as soon as possible, then fills a bowl with vinegar and warm water and puts it by her side. He lifts her damp nightdress and places his hand on Edith's belly.

Is their baby still moving?

Yes. It shifts its position, an elbow or foot rippling beneath her skin. He hadn't noticed quite how much her body has changed. Her stretched skin offers a luminescent pattern, like marble or the inside of an eggshell, where it has widened to accommodate their child.

How wonderful the body is, to incubate life.

For now, he'll make some broth, flavour it with spices, encourage

Edith to drink, restore her strength. Egon examines the silence around him. He checks again that she's still breathing. Is there any way to save the baby? He cannot bear to think it, but it is there: his darkest thought. He has heard that they can be cut out, pulled through the layers of a woman's flesh and muscle. Is it possible? Could theirs be rescued if the absolute worst occurs and Edith does not survive?

Egon takes a knife, one that badly needs sharpening – he'll get it done, on his next outing – and attacks the meagre vegetables they have acquired. He slices at an onion, cutting indiscriminately, messy chunks that Edith would tease him for. Egon pushes the pieces into a pan with whatever else he can find, and covers it with water, setting it to boil. He dries his face, then watches the bubbles gather, then roil to the surface. The windows steam, and he loses sight of the world beyond.

Egon approaches the pane and, with his index finger, writes his name on the glass, in capital letters, his first name atop his family name, and draws a box around it, the way he sometimes signed his artworks when he was younger. He looks at it and through it. Then he rubs it out.

What else can he do? Egon picks up a pencil and his sketchbook, and tries to draw the lines of his wife's face. He doesn't want to forget anything about her. Oh God, why is he thinking this way? But the sharpened lead scratches against the page, powerless. Edith opens her eyes. Her hair is wet on her forehead. He should fetch her silver-handled brush. Instead, he returns the sketchpad to the table. He dabs a cloth, soaked in vinegar, across her forehead and down the contours of her neck – the water pools in her delicate hollows.

'Egon,' she whispers, the word faint. She breaks into jagged coughing.

'No, don't speak.' He strokes her head. 'Save your energy. I need you to get better.'

'Egon, I'm freezing.' It's an effort for her to say it and she gently gasps at the exertion. He takes another blanket from the bedroom and wraps it around her shoulders. He holds her, rubbing her to create more warmth. He blows upon her fingers.

Where is the doctor he sent for? He should have been here by now. Egon is fearful of leaving to find him. But what could be taking so long?

'It's fine, you're going to be fine. You're already getting better, I can see it.' He touches her forehead. She's burning up. An image of Elvira, the sister Egon barely knew, comes to mind. She died all those years ago, at the age of ten. She'd been Egon's first experience of death – but not his last. How calmly it comes, how quietly, leaving the living afraid and fully in its shade.

He fetches Edith a bowl of broth. 'Here, have a little of this. I can't claim any great skill in the kitchen, but it's warm, at least.'

He raises the spoon to her mouth, and she lets him feed her, a mouthful, two.

'I do feel better,' Edith says, one side of her mouth sagging. 'So much better.'

Egon pulls the blanket more tightly around his wife. He offers a spoonful of medicine the doctor prescribed to help her sleep during the early stages of her pregnancy, when she'd complained of lying alert for hours, while Egon slept soundly.

Is this her end? It cannot be. He thought they'd have so many more days together.

Egon busies himself as best he can. Later, at nightfall, he picks up the sketchbook once more and tries again to map her face with his pencil, first forming the line of her cheek, her eyelids, the bump on her nose. The candle flickers. It has grown short in the hours he has sat there. Egon fears the dark almost as much as death.

Edith's eyes close. His art comes back to him.

He could draw her for an eternity.

2

Sunday, 27 October 1918

The next day, Edith's breaths are short and shallow, and her cough has worsened. Egon is alert, and has been all night, watching for the rise and fall of her chest, the movements that indicate she's still alive – a flutter of an eyelid, a twitch in her features, fingers that play a burst of tiny notes on an invisible piano – anything to demonstrate that she still has a chance. They are faint, but they're there, and offer reassurance. She will get better.

Life is only ever the next breath, Egon tells himself, and he's thunderstruck that he never understood such a thing before.

Edith coughs violently, abruptly, gasping for oxygen, her lurid eyelids closed. Egon's arms go weak. He can no longer uphold the pretence that everything is fine. He can barely breathe against the injustice of this. He's back before an unforgiving judge, a sadistic jailer. He's suffocating, paranoid, desperate. What hope has he, this time, of escape?

He wipes his forehead with the washcloth. It stinks of vinegar. He takes the last candle from the nightstand and sits down at his table on the other side of the room. He looks back at his wife. Egon can only see everything he's about to lose.

He takes a piece of paper from the shelf. He's irritated by the unblemished whiteness of the page. He's reluctant to mark it, but, before the light fades entirely, he must compose himself and begin. He considers writing to Gertrude: hard, beautiful Gerti. How tight they'd once wound themselves around each other. She'd known the inner chambers of his heart. He misses her, the comfort of loving her, but she has a family of her own. She made it clear to Egon that he could never be a part of that. She doesn't need him interrupting the woman she had to become.

Edith's coughs rattle the silence.

Egon thinks of Vally. He occasionally encounters her in a dream, where he experiences an intense wave of relief and satisfaction at seeing her. There's something in his soul that recognizes her in the deepest of ways, and it feels so essential to be in her presence again, after causing her so much pain. He has had no word from her since their final argument, many summers ago; that hot, sweaty day when he didn't know which way to turn and said all the wrong things. It was then that his delight at being freed from her had turned sour. Where is she now? Somebody had mentioned in passing, almost as if he did not know the woman in question, had not loved her in his own way, that she'd gone to Dalmatia, to be a part of the war effort. Could it be true? The thought raises Egon's upper lip – a sneer that's not entirely unkind. It's simply that he cannot imagine Vally mopping brows and administering medicine. She, who posed for Vienna's most celebrated artists and who will be admired in galleries one hundred years from now, swilling out bedpans. Oh, she'll have found someone to tie herself to – someone older, with influence and wit. Vally, better than any of them, knows how to survive.

Mother, he writes.

Edith is unwell. He puts the pencil down. This is going to be so very hard to write.

You know that she is in her sixth month of pregnancy. Our baby is due in January 1919. Egon is startled once again by the thought of the child Edith is carrying. The potential that's wrapped up inside her. His life. His blood and energy, becoming. He wanted that to materialize, to be real, so strongly it sickened him. He wanted, so badly, to become a father. Now it looks as if that dream wasn't to be. He swallows it like a rock.

Her body has been so strong and she has complained so little. But now, it seems, she has fallen victim to the dreaded Spanish influenza that is raging through Vienna and across Europe. She's always cold and cannot stop coughing. She has turned weak. I fear the worst. It could become pneumonia, and then . . .

Egon wants fate to prove him wrong. There's a chance, isn't there? He prays. He promises the very essence of himself, everything he once valued, to keep his love safe. All my success, all my talent. I offer it to you. Let me offer it graciously, Lord, where once I would have thrown it in your face. For what is talent worth, if I have to suffer alone?

The doctor has still not arrived, and I can't bear to leave her.

Egon doesn't want to start again. He thinks of the eternal joy he'd hold in his muscles, carry in his blood, if Edith lived, the baby was born, if it screamed in their faces, full of the life it had almost been denied. How close he would always know he had come to disaster. He would never forget this brush with death, never not live with it in the depths of his heart, the same way he still carries the memory of the prison cell.

My heart is breaking. I can only hope that fate will be kind to us all.

Egon signs his name – *Your son, Egon* – and folds the note into an envelope. He'll send it tomorrow.

Tomorrow.

Will the world have changed by the time his mother receives this letter?

Edith coughs, once, then again and again and again. He wonders how she has the energy to do it with such force. He feels sorry for the pain she must be in. He's exhausted, too. His eyes ache and he's freezing. But he needs to look after Edith. He takes the candle to the bed where she's sleeping. She looks puffy and grey. He holds it closer to her lips. Are they blue? She's still breathing, he can see her chest rising, but her lips are definitely darker and her ears are tinged purple, too. This is a very bad sign.

Shaking, Egon takes Edith's hands. They're cold. This cannot be happening, please, God almighty, do not let this happen. He kisses her fingertips. Her nails are grey, as if they have been dipped in ink – the wet ink from the wall, from the pot that Vally threw.

No, he's getting confused, losing track of things, but suddenly it seems as if all the women he's ever loved, ever needed, ever painted, are in the room with him, all playing out their singular roles at the same time. Who is he to each of them? He changes, from one light to the next, according not to his own characteristics and drives and urges, but theirs. What *do* they need from him? Did they ever get it? Christ. He rubs his eyes, but the women he has known continue to dance through the space – their faces contorting, bodies bent, through every emotion he's made them feel.

He has let down each of them, assuredly, and he never even noticed.

And who is he? This man – he runs his hands up and down his own limbs and torso – who he thought was so real and sure. He's nothing but a question mark, if not seen through their eyes. He doesn't exist at all without the prism of each of them, combining into one image like a hallucination. It changes everything.

He tries to pull himself out of all this by turning his attention to his wife, to the living, breathing woman in front of him. Could he have done things differently?

Perhaps her strange colour is because she has not moved for two days, since she came back, heartbroken, close to midnight on Friday. He turns her gently.

Edith opens her eyes. They are wild and dilated. Her gaze soon fixes itself on Egon's face and she smiles.

'The baby,' she whimpers, her hand on her stomach. 'I can't feel it moving.' Hot tears stream down her cheeks.

He whispers into her neck, weaving love into her with kisses. A cough tears through her. He holds a handkerchief to her mouth. There's blood on it when he takes it away.

'I carry death, not life,' she whispers.

Egon can barely breathe, but he must say these words to her, keep her talking. 'You are living, right now, and that's all that matters. Live. Live. For me. I love you. We have each other. We have everything.'

They look at each other for a long time. He feels numb, yet terribly alive.

He licks the pencil's nib, rests it on a blank sheet, and tentatively draws a line – the curve of her neck to her collarbone, a singular mark – but it's all wrong. His art has deserted him. It's agony to move the pencil; the connection is severed. But he'll do it; he'll keep trying. It's torment, but she holds his gaze, angles her head back so he can draw her more easily. She tries to smile, but on the page, by his hand, it resembles a grimace. His beautiful wife, Edith, he cannot capture her. For the first time in his life, he cannot capture on paper what he sees before him. He's blind. Something in Edith fades. He waits a minute and puts his ear to her mouth, listening for sounds that mean she's only sleeping. Thank God, he thinks, she's still here. Thank God, thank God, thank God. Spare me. Spare my love. You owe me this.

Egon shivers. The chill stirs from within his bones. He takes a seat in the armchair. He'll watch her until morning. Tomorrow, he'll call again for that god-forsaken doctor. He'll ask him to prescribe the strongest opium to help her through. Egon will wait all night for death to dare arrive here, he thinks. And he'll beat it into retreat.

3

Monday, 28 October 1918

E gon awakes to the church bells ringing. He counts. Seven. Why is he in the living room, in the armchair, his shirtsleeves rolled up?

The stub of the candle in the foreground focuses him into the moment. It has burned out in the night, the wax pooling on to the table. He stares at it for a long time, transfixed. The hairs on the back of his neck are taut. Egon doesn't dare look around the room, which is cold and quiet, bathed in flashes of pale autumn light. It's too silent. It feels overwhelming, as if he were alone.

Egon listens to the void, waiting, praying for a cough, a small sigh or the sound of his wife turning. There's nothing. Only birds outside, oblivious, singing to the sky.

Egon steels himself to look. He sees death. Edith is frozen, her eyes slightly open, her lips apart, her body fallen awkwardly to one side. He moves over to it, slowly, as if she might pounce on him. He takes her dainty wrist, and presses his thumb there.

Her skin is cold and mottled. There's no beat, no sign of life. Her right hand is clutching a pencil. He takes her left hand in his. It's missing her beautiful wedding ring. She couldn't find it, and now she never will. He will look for it, for ever, as soon as he gets the chance. He will never let it go. Egon can't take his eyes off her. He's appalled to see

434

spots of scarlet blood on the pillow beside her mouth. He'd known that the influenza could turn to pneumonia and block her lungs, but he hadn't expected this. She'd drowned in the night. Alone, while he slept.

Egon vomits into the bowl of vinegar water.

Edith must have woken, he realizes with desperation. Why did she not call out to him, wake him? He falls to his knees and howls. His wife. Dying in the darkness.

A piece of paper falls from the bed. It's the sketch Egon made of Edith only hours before. He cannot take his eyes from the life in her. Her open eyes. Her mouth poised, as if she were about to speak, with words she would never whisper. There's so much he should have said to her, when he had the chance. Then he notices the shape of her writing on the back.

My dear love – Egon struggles to follow the loose cursive script, so familiar.

I love you eternally and love you more and more infinitely and immeasurably . . .

Egon curls himself into a tight ball, smashes his forehead against the floorboards. He's in so much pain that he cannot cry tears. He cannot go on.

Everything in him is depleted. But with a sharp impulse, he rises to be near her. He curls up next to her hard body, his hand over her swollen stomach. It's as if he has caught the moon in the palm of his hand. Egon stays that way, muted, listening to the waxing and waning of the church bells as they strike the hours over the course of the day.

He hears the doctor, banging on the door to be let in.

He ignores him. It's too late. Everything is too late.

It's dusk when he hears an echo of his wife whisper, 'Survive.'

Egon traces the word in the air with his finger and feels breathless, feverish and aching. Hasn't everything Egon has ever done been leading to this moment? Marching him to this fate? How many wrong turns has he taken, every single day, without knowing? Could the outcome have been different if he'd done one thing otherwise along the way? Could he be living an alternative life, with a wife who was breathing, his baby kicking at the universe inside her?

Egon finally leaves his wife's body to go to the desk and get down the facts – *Edith Schiele no more* – to send to whom? The only person Egon needs now is his sister. She's the one living soul who can soothe him. He stares at the words as they fade in and out of focus. The death of Edith. The death of everything. It is inconceivable.

Egon is finally, irrevocably, alone.

He cannot see more than a handful of seconds into the future. He can barely see the corners of the room. On the far walls, the figures in his work appear as if they've been rubbed out with turpentine. Did he do that? He steps closer to see wild strokes of paint up and down the walls. He doesn't remember. His eyes sting and he stumbles. His lungs have tightened and he's cold. He coughs a shuddering expulsion into his hand. There's red paint – or is it blood? – in his palm. Egon is too tired to notice. He lies on the floorboards, delirious, beaten by his own emotions. Heat grows in him, gnawing. Let it devour him, the way a dog devours a bone. He has nothing left to give.

Life is only ever this breath, and this breath, and this breath.

Egon needs someone – saviour, doctor, friend – anyone who can push death aside and save him. Now the pounding at the door turns into something physical. Is it his heartbeat? Is it a fist, belonging to a debtor or a dealer? What time is it? Which day? The pounding is urgent. Faster. Harder. Is it Adolf Schiele again, reddened, enraged, ready to kill? He will break down that door, as he'd done years before, when Egon and Gertrude were children, caught in their riptide, drowning in each other's mysteries.

'Gerti,' Egon rasps, his eyes dilating. He sees her face in a weak sunbeam, a memory surfacing from a day in their childhood when they escaped along the train tracks, and she wore their father's blazer. He tries to reach out to her, his long fingers extended in her direction, but she only laughs and blows dandelion seeds into his face.

He jerks his head back as if she has punched him.

'Egon! Let me in!'

Will it be Edith, innocence written across her face, before a halo of light, her hand held out in an unsteady, self-conscious gesture, beckoning to him to follow her and his unborn child? He longs to join her, but he hasn't the energy to reach her right now.

Or will it be Adele, perhaps, pulling her knees up, her stockings tight, such a deep invitation in her eyes, full of the promise to fulfil his desires and rip his heart out?

'Egon, please!'

Or maybe it is Vally – unhurried, tender, quiet Vally, looking so self-possessed and serene? She's waiting for him, on the steps of this prison he has found himself in, the bright globe of an orange in her hand, the smell of it rising to his nose and filling him with the radiance of summer and hope and redemption. Vally is standing there, offering Egon everything she had. Sanctuary and love. He won't ever reject it again.

'Egon! I need you to hear me!' It's a woman's voice. 'Open this door.'

But he can't.

The pounding continues. Whatever it is, it's coming for him. It won't stop until that door has been ripped from its frame, as he has ripped apart so many things that came into his orbit.

He shudders, stalls. He writhes on the floor.

Egon is wild-eyed, purple, a rancid collection of organs, a grimace upon his lips.

He howls. Then he stops.

Life is only – ever – this breath.

The Final Frame

It's late in the day and the remaining visitors are sluggish, like heat-addled flies. Adele wipes her cheek, exhausted after all that she has revealed to this woman, more than she's ever admitted to another soul. She eases the ring from her finger and passes it to Eva.

'Take it, please,' Adele says. She sees surprise in Eva's eyes as she offers her the neat circle of gold. 'The truth is, it was never something I could call my own.'

'Adele, what are you saying? It's yours. It's clear how precious it is to you.'

'It's not mine. It never was. It belonged to Edith. I stole it from her.'

'Oh, Adele.' Eva touches the ring, slips it on to her finger.

'I took it from her own home, and I never had the chance to give it back. If you look inside, it's engraved – E & E. I couldn't bear that. I tried to change an E to an A. By the time I came to my senses, Edith, my beautiful, sweet, silly little sister, was dead. She was only twenty-five years old, and six months pregnant with her first child. How I've lived beyond that, I'll never know. Three days after her death, Egon died, too,' Adele continues. 'I never knew grief could crush you like a boulder. It was all my fault. Edith ran out into that cold, wet night because of me. She never stood a chance.'

'I'm heartbroken for you, Adele.'

'Egon nursed her and caught the influenza from her, too. He was just twenty-eight.'

'I had no idea it ended like that. That they were so young.'

'We buried Edith in Ober-Sankt-Veit. I could barely stand. I wanted to crawl into the mud beside her. Frau Schiele, Egon's mother, had to hold me back, and my own mother was in no fit state to comfort me. Rumours were spreading through Vienna like wildfire, that the end of that first war was only a matter of days away. Egon died on the final day of October. Six years after I first laid eyes on him.'

Eva holds the old woman. 'Adele, listen to me. It's not your fault.'

'Imagine the future they could have had,' Adele murmurs. 'Imagine who they could have become. The art he would have made. He had everything to live for. I think of their child every day. I have seen them everywhere, on every street corner. They have never left me.'

'You can't blame yourself. There was a pandemic. It swept right across Europe, it was deadly.'

'But I lied. I stole from her. I was racked with jealousy. My own sister! There's nothing that has happened to me since that moment that I didn't deserve. I was sent to an asylum, you know. My mother signed the papers. She couldn't cope. She'd lost her husband and her daughter in little more than a year. She'd threatened it before – she'd seen I was on the brink of a breakdown for a long time. I'd got a letter the morning of my argument with Edith saying I was to be assessed, and it tipped me over the edge. After their deaths, I was ready to implode. Mutti thought that place could save me. It was her one hope: that I'd be cured and she'd have something left, something to show for her life. But there's no cure for guilt and grief. By the time I was released, after three years, she was gone, too.'

'Adele, there are no words I can utter to make any of this better.'

'It should have been me who died. They could have been happy together.'

'Are you sorry?' Eva asks.

'Yes.' Adele turns those grey eyes on her. 'I am so very sorry.'

'Edith would forgive you. I saw her back there, the gentleness in her eyes. I feel I know a little of her and I've heard the way you talk about her. It sounds as if she loved you, very much.'

'Do you think so?' Adele clutches at the young woman, warmth flowing between them.

'I do.'

Adele closes her eyes, satisfied.

Then she suddenly gasps. The pain that has been blossoming shoots up her left arm. It vibrates through the muscles and ricochets into her neck before it reaches her core. A clamp squeezes around her vital, pulsating centre. She cries out, then collapses, the lights of the gallery spinning.

Eva drops beside her and cradles Adele's head. 'Help! Somebody, please, help!' she cries.

'Perhaps the parts of us that are broken can be made whole,' the old woman manages.

Tourists gather around, staying a polite distance away, hands to their chests, concern creasing their eyes.

Adele stares back at them all, her mouth agape. From her position on the floor, the people in the room have taken on the strangest perspective. Adele's pupils roll and roam.

There's something unhooking in her.

Electrifying pain forks along her nerves.

But Adele is calmed by one thought: she is exactly where she's meant to be.

She catches the eye of one woman . . . Edith.

'Stop staring and do something!' Eva cries to the crowd.

Someone rushes in, a guard, here to help.

'What's her name?' he demands.

'Her name,' Eva shouts, her panic clear, 'is Adele. Adele Harms.'

The words echo off the walls; the eyes in the paintings flicker, seeing once more.

Adele's knotted fingers cling tightly to Eva's. Then, out of the frames, two figures emerge and walk towards her. They're smiling, holding hands. They've come for her at last.

His brush moves a final time, the paint smudges, the lines turn abstract.

Adele feels Edith's calming touch, a kiss on her cheek. It is everything.

And the light runs through her.

Epilogue

T he young woman walks back through the gallery, retracing the steps she'd taken with Adele. Her new friend is dead. Eva is horrified, heartbroken, but she knows it was worth the huge risk to her health to bring Adele to the gallery. There was nowhere else she wanted to be, in the end. Men in uniforms can't hound her any more, she won't be forced back to the hospital against her will, she won't have to suffer another day. Eva knows Adele found what she was looking for on these walls, among the people from her past. She hopes that, in Adele's final moments, for all her failures and fabrications, her friend achieved some kind of peace.

Eva rubs the ring on her finger.

Perhaps, despite everything, she will, too?

The young woman looks once more at the women whose names she now knows. There's Gertrude, coquettish and defiant in all her poses; Vally, her deep, mournful eyes always challenging the viewer; and Edith, looking sweet and uncomfortable.

How much of themselves did they all lose?

Eva spends time in front of Schiele's paintings of sunflowers, too.

She needs a moment to calm her nerves, to settle the emotion that threatens to overtake her. The young woman sits on the bench where she'd confided in Adele. From her purse, she takes a photograph. It shows a baby boy, a few months old, his face animated with a smile. The corner of the image is torn and a spot by his arm has been rubbed away, greasy with the imprint of repeated contact. It's her son.

He died, she'd told Adele, three years ago, at six months old. He'd gone to sleep – she'd kissed his forehead and sung him a bedtime lullaby, but when she went for him in the morning, he was cold, lifeless, a replica of all he'd been just hours before. There was nothing Eva could have done, they said; it was a tragedy, she shouldn't blame herself.

But Eva does and always will do.

Eva puts her hand to her stomach and feels fresh life blossoming there. Fear and guilt have festered in her since the new pregnancy was confirmed. She has tried to push them away, bury them, but has only succeeded in killing part of herself: the part that holds the capacity for hope.

Eva looks into the eyes of Adele, the ones painted by Egon Schiele. She will try.

16 May 1968

It's a grey day. Humourless clouds do not let any shred of the sun's warmth through, despite a forecast of sunshine. The birds rattle out their song and circle against its dull blanket. The trees rustle, overladen with spring. Still, Eva is shivering.

She holds a bouquet of bright sunflowers for Adele Harms.

Eva is in the Ober-Sankt-Veit cemetery, in front of an old headstone. It shows a woman and man, hunched and stripped of their clothing, humbled, deprived of that sexual spark Eva saw so vividly in Egon Schiele's art. The bodies are yellowed with lichen and moss. There are no halos or suggestions of angelic alliances, simply creeping ivy.

They do not feel the cold.

Eva rests the sunflowers at the statues' feet. She reaches out to the sculptured shoulders, touches her fingers to the woman's hand, then warms her own. She wipes away a tear.

Egon and Edith. SCHIELE. The words are carved so solidly into the stone.

Nothing about their fates can ever change.

A coffin, with Adele's weightless body inside, is lowered into the plot. Among her letters was this request, and a receipt for the payment, made years ago.

Finally, Adele joins Egon and Edith. Blood meets blood again. Heart meets heart. Love smashed, tangled, these three souls. She is the missing piece of the puzzle, the final point of their unholy triangle; her fresh, frail bones on top of their ones, already returned to dust.

There will be no marker for Adele Harms, no date of birth, nor date of death, etched into the stone. There will be no eulogy for the woman interred here, as found on other gravestones, those tributes to much-loved mothers, beloved sisters, precious daughters. There will be nothing at all to say that Adele lived, nor to reveal that she occupies this same patch of earth, on this planet orbiting the sun, as the man she lost her heart to and the sister she betrayed. All her fierce passion, her fireworks, finally fades to black.

Adele will disappear, with so little trace. Only the works Egon Schiele made of her remain. The gravediggers pile the fresh earth back on. Eva rubs her thumb against the gold band: a gift from her friend. A reminder to forge connection, honour truth, and strive for real love and forgiveness. She'll need those lessons in the months to come.

'Adele Harms,' Eva whispers.

She is not anonymous, she is not unknown.

She told her story, to one person at least. And she shone a light on the other real women in the paintings – Gertrude Schiele, Vally Neuzil and Edith Harms.

Eva realizes it now, as never before: under all those layers of the artist's pencil and paint are wild, blazing hearts, longing to be known.

Historical Note

This book is a work of fiction, based on the limited facts I could find out about the lives of Adele and Edith Harms, Gertrude Schiele and Vally (Walburga) Neuzil. As with any work of fiction, I have at times had to invent or to 'rearrange' certain episodes for the purposes of the story – such as Edith and Egon returning to Vienna in 1918 instead of earlier in 1917. But these women were real, and below is a summary of what I gleaned about their lives.

Adele Harms

Adele Harms was born in 1890 to Johann and Josefa Harms, the elder of the sisters. She did indeed die, aged seventy-eight, penniless, unmarried and with no children, in Vienna in 1968. I was told this information by Christian Bauer at the Egon Schiele Museum in Tulln at the start of my research, and it sparked the whole thread of the opening section. I wanted to know what had happened in Adele's life for her to go from a position of affluence to one of poverty. I imagined her as a young woman, full of hopes and dreams, lofty expectations of how her life would unfold. And how she'd have been left with nothing at all once Edith and Egon died, and after the war had brought an end to the Habsburg Empire. How would she have survived those fifty lonely years? What damage did she endure?

At university in Leeds, I'd taped a postcard of *Seated Woman with Bent Knee* (1917) to the wall above my desk, and when I came to the realization, a decade later, during my research, that the woman in it was indeed Adele – that she was not the artist's wife or lover as I'd once presumed, but his sister-in-law – this sparked further avenues for fictional enquiry. Adele's blazing eyes are full of such longing – speaking of desire, disaster. I couldn't help but wonder then if she'd been in love with the artist, how she'd felt about modelling for him, if she'd once harboured hopes of her own to marry this handsome young man she'd spotted across the street.

The resulting tension between the Harms sisters is fabricated. Adele may have been very happy for Edith. She may have been perfectly comfortable, unquestioning, in the act of removing some of her clothes for her sister's husband, posing for him for hours as he painted and drew her. We will never know for certain. But I felt there were stirrings of powerful dynamics at play, ones that hadn't been fully explored in fiction related to Schiele before. The women in his story often seemed to be presented with little agency, with such a bland acceptance of their role in his life that I wanted to reclaim the narrative.

Adele Harms is buried in Ober-Sankt-Veit cemetery in Vienna, in the same plot as Egon Schiele. The adjoining plot belongs to Edith Harms, her sister, who was buried on 3 November 1918. This information had not entered the public realm. Here was this woman, fifty years after their deaths, buried in the same patch of earth as Egon. Why? How? I couldn't get an answer, but this detail spoke to such powerful unity and grief, ripe territory for an author's imagination.

It is true that there is no gravestone to mark Adele Harms' final resting place. She is buried without her name, her date of birth or date of death. I would like to see this rectified.

Gertrude Schiele

Gertrude Schiele was born in 1894 (I've used 13 April as her date of birth, but records vary) and she lived to the age of eighty-six. She died in Vienna in 1981. She is buried in the same graveyard as her brother, but not the same plot. She had a son, Anton Junior, in 1914, who lived to the age of eighty-two and died in 1997, and a daughter, Gertrude, (born in 1913) who apparently lived to the age of thirty. Gertrude's husband, Anton Peschka, died in 1940 aged fifty-five. I am not aware of any living relatives of any of the people mentioned in the novel.

It is true that Gertrude and Egon ran away to Trieste, the seaside location where their parents spent their honeymoon, and that they shared a room there. Gertrude had a very close relationship with her brother and posed for him in the nude, and when she was interviewed by the Schiele scholar Alessandra Comini in the 1970s, Gertrude spoke openly and with tenderness and pride about the intimate bond they shared.

Vally (Walburga) Neuzil

Vally Neuzil is commonly known as Wally (which is short for Walburga), but I use the softer Vally, as the name in Austria is pronounced with the V. She died, aged twenty-three, of scarlet fever on 25 December 1917 and was buried in an unmarked grave in Sinj, where she had been stationed as an army nurse. The grave was found in 2015 and restored in 2017, the centenary of her death.

It is rumoured that Vally was Gustav Klimt's model, and that that is how she met Egon, but this has never been substantiated. Schiele could have met her in a much more pedestrian way, in Park Schönbrunn, where he scouted for striking young models. Vally was the same age as

Gertrude, but had such a different start to her life. It is said that her mother, Thekla, moved with Vally and her sisters to Vienna when Vally was eleven, looking for work. It's possible she would have been able to read and write.

It was eye-opening to research the kind of work available to a young girl in those days, and the risks that would have had to be taken to put food on the table. There is no suggestion that Vally accepted money in return for sex, but removing one's clothes for an artist was tantamount to prostitution in the eyes of society at the time.

Edith Harms

Edith Harms was born in 1893 and died on 28 October 1918, aged twenty-five. She was six months pregnant with her first child. This was the detail, read at an exhibition of Schiele's work in London, that first launched the idea of writing about her in my mind. I wanted to know all about this young woman, whose life had been tragically cut short. At first, the whole book was going to be told from her perspective; that was until I discovered the other compelling, strong women in Schiele's orbit. Edith has always been presented as the sweet girl-next-door, and the more I read about Schiele's marriage to her during my initial research, the more I felt that everyone who knew the story was on 'Team Vally'.

But I had empathy for Edith right from the start. The painting of her, *Portrait of Edith Schiele, The Artist's Wife* (1915), standing in that colourful striped dress she'd reportedly made herself from a pair of old curtains, her eyes so eager to please, with her fingers touching in small circles of nervousness, moved me deeply. Schiele was said to have wanted to marry 'advantageously', and to have discarded Vally, his muse, his lover, the woman who had stood by his side. However, I wanted to depict the union between Egon and Edith as a grand love, not simply a marriage of convenience.

I was fascinated by the thought: how would the pair of them have carried the ghost of Vally into their marriage? I felt her image, those penetrating eyes, would have lingered in Edith's mind and caused ripples of friction between the newly married couple.

Edith's innocence, purity and simplicity are drawn from the portraits her husband made of her after their marriage. She is indeed portrayed like a sweet doll. Would she have been happy to be shown to the world in this way? Was she as sweet and simple as he depicted her to be? I wanted to inject Edith with an edge, with agency, her own dark side. We get a sense of her frustration in the drawing Egon made of his wife naked, 'masturbating', her face turned away from the viewer, the tension visible in the contortion of her spine. I wondered how much she must have hated being thrust into the role of model. Her reluctance, and Adele's apparent willingness, and the confidence that oozes off the artworks Schiele made of his sister-in-law, inspired the final thrust of events in the novel.

For more information, visit: sophie-haydock.com

Acknowledgements

It takes a long time to write the first word of a novel, and even longer to write the last. Throughout it all, I've been so lucky to have received encouragement from many excellent people.

First and foremost, this book is dedicated to my friend, Ali Schofield, a name I'd like to see remembered. Without her, the idea for this novel would never have entered my orbit. She was visiting London and invited me to join her at an exhibition of Egon Schiele's work at the Courtauld Gallery – an event that changed my life. I walked into that exhibition knowing I wanted to write a novel one day, and left it, my head spinning, the lines Schiele created marked in my mind. I shudder to think about the experiences I'd have missed, the people I wouldn't have spoken to and the stories I wouldn't have known about if Ali hadn't been generous enough to invite me along with her that day. Ali died at the age of thirty-four in 2018. She was a talented journalist, endlessly stylish, passionate about all the right things, and a woman who inspired me. I miss her. So, Ali, this book is for you – thank you for being all that you were, and for being the spark that led to *The Flames*.

Huge thanks to my agent, Juliet Mushens, whose enthusiasm is dizzying, for the passion you share for the women I wrote about, and the way you championed this novel at every stage. To the rest of the Mushens entertainment team: it is such a pleasure to work with you.

Thank you to my wonderful editor, Kirsty Dunseath. I was blown away when you saw potential in my novel and embraced it instantly. My respect for you has only grown during the process of taking this book to publication. It's a far better book because of you.

Thanks to the whole team at Transworld, who made me feel welcome and valued from day one, and who have worked so enthusiastically on *The Flames* – from foreign rights to audio (and to Eleanor Updegraff and Kate Samano for razor-eyed copy-edits). I particularly appreciate the excellent work of Tabitha Pelly and Lilly Cox in putting this book on people's radar. And thank you to Beci Kelly for the innovative cover design for the UK edition.

I'm grateful to the Impress Prize for New Writers, who chose an early iteration of this book's opening chapters as their winner in 2018. It was just the boost I needed to keep writing.

I'm indebted to a host of excellent writers, editors and friends who read early drafts and provided essential feedback and encouragement along the way: Rebecca F. John, Sally Orson-Jones, Melissa Fu, Jo Hamya, Esther Cann, and Aki Schilz at The Literary Consultancy.

I'm grateful to my circle of like-minded friends at the Word Factory, and Cathy Galvin for her comradeship, encouragement and her literary embrace.

The Flames is a work of historical fiction, based on the lives of real women – Adele Harms, Edith Harms, Gertrude Schiele and Walburga Neuzil – who provided inspiration to the Austrian artist Egon Schiele over the course of his brief life (1890–1918). Years of research have gone into this novel, and I am indebted to the kindness shown to me by the Egon Schiele community – including experts, scholars and enthusiasts – in the UK, Vienna and further afield. My sincere thanks go to Alessandra Comini, Jane Kallir, Deborah Feller, Gemma Blackshaw, Peter Vergo, Christian Bauer, Robert Holzbauer, Ewald Königstein, Hana Jirmusová Lazarowitz and Verena Gamper, all of whom I met or interviewed and who have been generous with their time and knowledge. I greatly enjoyed visiting and going behind the scenes at the Albertina and Leopold museums in Vienna, the Egon Schiele Art Centrum in Český Krumlov (Krumau), the Egon Schiele Museum in Tulln and the State Gallery of Lower Austria in Krems.

I've recounted many of the historical details that are known about the life and work of Schiele (although details about the women he used as models are thin), but I have taken creative licence with aspects of the story, and reimagined elements of how these women lived, what motivated them, and the tensions that may have existed between them. Any mistakes or omissions are very much my own.

Thank you to my friends, who believed in this project and listened to me talk about it, and those who celebrated the wins, big and small, along the way – including Emma Cleave, Mel Bradman, Lucy Ward, Faith Rose and Max Geller, Ruth Spedding and Jasmine F. Clark.

My mother, Pamela, read a million drafts, offered feedback, and boosted my confidence throughout every stage of this process. As a child, I remember you writing late into the night, and I'm so happy that your passion for reading and storytelling has passed on to me. To my father, Peter – printing out an early draft and reading it (perhaps the first book you'd read for decades) meant so much. How happily you highlighted my typos! And I'm grateful for the enthusiasm shown by my siblings, extended family and family-in-law. Your curiosity and care about this process have meant the world.

A gigantic thank-you to my husband, James, who fuels everything good in my world. This book couldn't exist without you, simply because I would not exist. You offered ceaseless support, elaborate sustenance and deep love at every step. I appreciate every single thing.

I also want to say how grateful I am to the followers of the Instagram account @egonschieleswomen, who are engaged, enthusiastic and enamoured with the work of Egon Schiele and the stories of his models.

Finally, thank you to you, the readers, who have picked up this book. I hope you look at the women in the frames in a new and lasting light.

Sophie Haydock is an award-winning author living in east London. *The Flames* is her debut novel. She is the winner of the Impress Prize for New Writers. Sophie trained as a journalist at City University, London, and has worked at the *Sunday Times Magazine*, *Tatler* and BBC Three, as well as freelancing for publications including the *Financial Times*, *Guardian Weekend* magazine, and organizations such as the Arts Council, Royal Academy and Sotheby's. Passionate about short stories, Sophie also works for the *Sunday Times* Short Story Award and is associate director of the Word Factory literary organization.

Her Instagram account @egonschieleswomen – dedicated to the women who posed for Egon Schiele – has a community of over 100,000 followers. For more information, visit: sophie-haydock.com.

Job Searching Fast & Easy

J. Michael Farr

THOMSON
™
DELMAR LEARNING

Australia Canada Mexico Singapore Spain
United Kingdom United States

THOMSON
DELMAR LEARNING
™

Job Searching Fast & Easy
J. Michael Farr

Vice President, Career Education Strategic Business Unit:
Dawn Gerrain

Director of Editorial:
Sherry Gomoll

Acquisitions Editor:
Martine Edwards

Developmental Editor:
Kristen Shenfield

Editorial Assistant:
Jennifer Anderson

Director of Production:
Wendy A. Troeger

Production Manager:
J. P. Henkel

Production Assistant:
Angela Iula

Technology Project Manager:
Sandy Charette

Director of Marketing:
Wendy E. Mapstone

Channel Manager:
Gerard McAvey

Marketing Coordinator:
Erica Conley

Compositor:
Stratford Publishing Services

Cover Design:
Joe Villanova

© 2006 Thomson Delmar Learning, a part of the Thomson Corporation. Thomson, the Star logo, and Delmar Learning are trademarks used herin under license.

Contents of this book and related student book and support materials are based on copyrighted materials originally published by JIST® Publishing, Inc., and used here in modified form with the permission of and under a special agreement with JIST® Publishing, Inc. The title of the original JIST® Publishing source material is *Seven Steps to Getting a Job Fast* by J. Michael Farr.

Printed in Canada
1 2 3 4 5 XXX 09 08 07 06 05

For more information contact Delmar Learning, 5 Maxwell Drive, PO Box 8007, Clifton Park, NY 12065-2919.

Or you can visit our Internet site at
http://www.delmarlearning.com

For permission to use material from the text or product, submit a request online at
http://www.thomsonrights.com

Any additional questions about permissions can be submitted by email to thomsonrights@thomson.com

Library of Congress Cataloging-in-Publication Data

Farr, Michael.
    Job searching fast & easy / J. Michael Farr.
        p. cm.
    Includes index.
    ISBN 1-4180-4272-2
    1. Job hunting. 2. Career development.
3. Resumés (Employment) 4. Employment interviewing   I. Title. Job searching fast and easy. II. Title.

HF5382.7.F373 2005
650.14—dc22

2005043999

NOTICE TO THE READER

This Book Is Short, but It May Be All You Need

Compared to many job search books, this is a short book. I set out to make it that way, by covering only those things I have found would make the most difference to you in getting a good job in less time.

You could read parts of this book in a morning and conduct a more effective job search that same afternoon. Completing the worksheets and other activities, like writing a resume, would take more time, of course—but most people should be able to complete this book in a day or less. And you may find that this is all you need. If you are using this book as part of a course or workshop, your instructor will provide you with additional resources and information.

While career planning and job search can become complicated, here are two simple truths:

1. If you will work, you might as well look for work you enjoy doing and are good at.

2. If you are going to look for a job, you might as well use methods that are likely to reduce the time it takes to find one.

These are the things I emphasize in this book. Of course, there is more to know about career planning, but this book covers the basics. If you use the techniques—not just read about them—the odds are good that you will reduce the time it takes to find your next job. And you will be more likely to find a better job than you might have otherwise.

I wish you well.

Mike Farr

Mike Farr

Table of Contents

A Brief Introduction to Using This Book   **1**

Of Course, You Can't Just Read about It... 2

So, Trust Me—Do the Worksheets 2

Why This Is a Short Book 3

Step 1: Identify Your Key Skills—and Develop a Powerful New "Skills Language" to Describe Yourself   **5**

There Are Three Types of Skills 6

Self-Management Skills. 6

Transferable Skills 9

Job-Related Skills 13

Step 2: Set a Specific Job Objective before You Go Looking   **15**

Is It Possible to Find Your Ideal Job? 19

How to Explore Specific Job Titles and Industries 20

Explore More Than 250 Specific Job Titles 20

Explore Specific Industries. 34

And, Now, We Return to Job-Related Skills 38

Step 3: Use the Most Effective Methods to Get a Better Job in Less Time   **39**

Which Job Search Methods Work Best? 40

Get the Most Out of Less-Effective Job Search Methods 40

The Two Job Search Methods That Work Best 44

Most-Effective Job Search Method #1:
Develop a Network of Contacts 45

Most-Effective Job Search Method #2:
Contact Employers Directly. 48

Use JIST Cards®—An Effective Mini-Resumé 52

The Anatomy of a JIST Card® 52

Now Write and Use Your JIST Card®. 63

Use Your JIST Card® as the Basis for an Effective Phone Script . . 64

Tips for Using the Internet in Your Job Search 65

   Ways to Increase Your Internet Effectiveness. 66

   Useful Internet Sites. 67

Step 4: Write a Simple Resumé Now and a Better One Later   69

Tips for Creating a Superior Resumé. 69

The Five Most Effective Ways to Use a Resumé 71

Chronological Resumés 72

   Tips for Writing a Simple Chronological Resume 72

   Tips for an Improved Chronological Resume. 75

Skills and Combination Resumés 77

Resumé Design and Production Tips 80

Electronic and Scannable Resumés 81

   An Electronic Resumé Should Have Lots of Key Words 81

   For an Electronic Resumé, a Simple Design Is Best. 82

   The Requirements of One Large Employer Are Typical 84

How to Write Effective Cover Letters 87

   Some Tips for Writing and Using Superior Cover Letters 87

More Sample Resumés 93

Step 5: Redefine What Counts as an Interview, Then Organize Your Time to Get Two a Day   103

Make Your Search a Full-Time Job. 104

   Decide How Much Time You Will Spend Looking for Work Each Day and Week. 104

Create a Specific Daily Job Search Schedule 105

Step 6: Dramatically Improve Your Interviewing Skills   109

Your First Impression May Be the Only One You Make 109

   A Traditional Interview Is Not a Friendly Exchange 110

How to Answer Tough Interview Questions 111

   The Three-Step Process for Answering Interview Questions . . . 111

The Most Important Interview Question of All:
"Why Should I Hire You?" 113

Tips on Negotiating Pay—How to Earn a Thousand Dollars
a Minute. 113

Close the Interview Effectively 115

Don't Say No Too Quickly 115

Step 7: Follow Up on All Job Leads — 117

Four Rules for Effective Follow-Up 117

Thank-You Notes Make a Difference 117

Develop an Organized System for Following Up. 118

In Closing. 121

Appendix A: The Essential Job Search Data Worksheet — 123

Appendix B: Sample Job Description from the *Occupational Outlook Handbook* — 135

Index — 149

A Brief Introduction to Using This Book

Why does it take some people more time than others to find a job? And what sort of job should you be looking for?

The answers to these questions will require you to learn something about career planning and job seeking. But you can't just read about getting a job. Job seeking requires action, and the most effective action is to go out and make contacts with the people who are most likely to need someone with your skills. And the best way to do *that* is to make a job out of getting a job.

This may sound simple, but doing it well requires some preparation. After many years of experience, I have identified just seven basic things that make a big difference in your job search. Each will be covered and expanded on in this book. These steps are

1. IDENTIFY YOUR KEY SKILLS.
   Most people can't explain what they are good at or what they like to do. Spending some time to clarify this will help you in so many ways, in your job search and in your life.

2. DEFINE YOUR IDEAL JOB.
   Too many people look for "a" job without knowing what "the" job would be. So I encourage you to define your ideal position, knowing you can always compromise later.

3. LEARN THE MOST EFFECTIVE JOB SEARCH METHODS.
   Once you know what you are looking for, you need to know what job search methods are most likely to help you find it.

4. WRITE A SUPERIOR RESUMÉ.
   Most people spend too much time worrying about their resumé. Instead, you will learn to write an acceptable resumé in just an hour or so and then a better one later, if you need one.

5. ORGANIZE YOUR TIME TO GET TWO INTERVIEWS A DAY.
   Yes, it's possible to get two interviews a day—if you know how to do it.

6. DRAMATICALLY IMPROVE YOUR INTERVIEWING SKILLS.
   Just an hour or so spent reading this section of the book can make a big difference in how well you handle your next

interview. What you learn could, indeed, increase your earnings a thousand dollars or more.

7. FOLLOW UP ON ALL JOB LEADS.
   Doing this well often makes the difference in who gets the job and who continues to wait for an offer.

Of Course, You Can't Just Read about It . . .

To get results in your job search, you will have to actively apply what you learn in this book. One of the biggest reasons some people stay unemployed longer than others do is that they sit at home waiting for someone to knock on their door, call them up, or make them an offer via e-mail. That passive approach too often results in their waiting and waiting, while others are out there getting the offers.

So, Trust Me— Do the Worksheets

I know you will resist completing the worksheets. But, trust me—they are worth your time. Doing them will give you a better sense of what you are good at, what you want to do, and how to go about doing it. Taking some time to learn career planning and effective job-seeking methods will likely result in your getting more interviews. And, you will present yourself better in those interviews. Is this worth giving up a night of TV? I think so.

The interesting thing is that, once you finish this book and its activities, you will have spent more time planning your career than most people do. And you will know more than the average job seeker about finding a job.

Insider Tip

Good news for those who do their homework.

Most people spend more time watching TV each week than they spend on career planning in an entire year. Fewer than 10 percent of all job seekers have even read a book on job seeking. While this lack of preparation is a big problem for them, it is good news for you. Knowing even a little more than the next person can give you a big advantage in a job search and in life.

Why This Is a Short Book

I've taught job-seeking skills for many years, and I've written longer and more detailed books than this one. Yet I have often been asked to tell someone, in a few minutes or hours, the most important things they should do in their career planning or job search. Instructors and counselors also ask the same question because they have only a short time to spend with the folks they're trying to help.

I've thought about what is most important to know, if time is short. The seven topics covered in this book are the ones I think are the most important to know. This book is short enough that you can scan it in a morning and conduct a more effective job search that afternoon. Doing all the activities would take more time but would prepare you far better. Of course, you can learn more about all of the topics covered, but this book may be all that you need.

Identify Your Key Skills—and Develop a Powerful New "Skills Language" to Describe Yourself

One employer survey found that most people interviewed by the employers did not present the skills they had to do the jobs they sought. Job applicants could not, for example, answer the basic question "Why should I hire you?"

So, if you want to do well in interviews, it is essential that you be able to describe what you are good at and why you think you can do the job. This same knowledge is important in deciding what type of job you will enjoy and do well. For these reasons,

I consider identifying your skills a necessary part of a successful career plan or job search.

There Are Three Types of Skills

Most people think of their "skills" as job-related skills, such as using a computer. But we all have other types of skills that are important for success on a job—and that are important to employers. The triangle on page 5 presents skills in three groups, and I think that this is a very useful way to consider skills for our purposes.

Let's review these three types of skills—self-management, transferable, and job-related—and identify those that are most important to you.

Self-Management Skills

Below, write three things about yourself that you think make you a good worker. Pick the first three things that come to mind.

Your "Good-Worker" Traits
1. _____
2. _____
3. _____

You just wrote what are among the most important things for an employer to know about you. They describe your basic personality and your ability to adapt to new environments. They are among the most important skills to emphasize in interviews, yet most job seekers don't realize the importance of these skills—and don't mention them.

Self-Management Skills Checklist

Review the skills list that follows and put a check mark beside each skill you have. The key self-management skills listed first are those employers find particularly important. If one or more of these key skills apply to you, mentioning them in interviews can help you greatly.

Key Self-Management Skills That Employers Value Highly

_____ accept supervision

_____ get along with coworkers

_____ get things done on time

_____ good attendance

_____ hard worker

_____ honest

_____ productive

_____ punctual

Other Self-Management Skills

_____ able to coordinate

_____ ambitious

_____ assertive

_____ capable

_____ cheerful

_____ competent

_____ complete assignments

_____ conscientious

_____ creative

_____ dependable

_____ discreet

_____ eager

_____ efficient

_____ energetic

_____ enthusiastic

_____ expressive

_____ flexible

_____ formal

_____ friendly

_____ good-natured

_____ helpful

_____ humble

_____ imaginative

_____ independent

_____ industrious

_____ informal

_____ intelligent

_____ intuitive

_____ learn quickly

_____ loyal

_____ mature

_____ methodical

_____ modest

_____ motivated

(continues)

Self-Management Skills Checklist *(continued)*

_____ natural		_____ sense of humor	
_____ open-minded		_____ sincere	
_____ optimistic		_____ solve problems	
_____ original		_____ spontaneous	
_____ patient		_____ steady	
_____ persistent		_____ tactful	
_____ physically strong		_____ take pride in work	
_____ practice new skills		_____ tenacious	
_____ reliable		_____ thrifty	
_____ resourceful		_____ trustworthy	
_____ responsible		_____ versatile	
_____ self-confident		_____ well organized	

List Your Other Self-Management Skills

_____

_____

_____

After you have completed the checklist, circle the five self-management skills you think are most important to use in your next job and list them in the box that follows.

Your Top Five Self-Management Skills

1. _____

2. _____

(continues)

3. _____

4. _____

5. _____

Transferable Skills

We all have skills that can be transferred from one job or career to another. For example, the ability to organize events could be used in a variety of jobs and might be essential for success in certain occupations. Your mission is to find a job that requires the skills you have and enjoy using.

Insider Tip

It's not bragging if it's true.

Using your new skills language may be uncomfortable at first, but employers need to learn about your skills. So, practice saying positive things about the skills you have for the job.

Transferable Skills Checklist

Put a check mark beside each of the skills you have that are listed below. You may have used them in a previous job or in some nonwork setting.

Key Transferable Skills That Employers Value Highly

_____ computer and technology skills

_____ instruct others

_____ negotiate

_____ manage money, budgets

_____ manage people

_____ meet deadlines

_____ meet the public

_____ organize/manage projects

_____ speak well in public

_____ write clearly

(continues)

Transferable Skills Checklist *(continued)*

Skills for Working with Things

_____ assemble things	_____ observe/inspect things
_____ build things	_____ operate tools, machines
_____ construct/repair things	_____ repair things
_____ drive, operate vehicles	_____ use complex equipment
_____ good with hands	_____ use computers

Skills for Working with Data

_____ analyze data	_____ investigate
_____ audit records	_____ keep financial records
_____ budget	_____ locate information
_____ calculate/compute	_____ manage money
_____ check for accuracy	_____ observe/inspect
_____ classify things	_____ record facts
_____ compare	_____ research
_____ compile	_____ set up or analyze spreadsheets
_____ count	
_____ detail-oriented	_____ synthesize
_____ evaluate	_____ take inventory
_____ find information on the Internet	_____ use database, financial, or related software

Skills for Working with People

_____ administer	_____ demonstrate
_____ advise	_____ diplomatic
_____ care for	_____ help others
_____ coach	_____ instruct
_____ confront others	_____ interview people
_____ counsel people	_____ kind

(continues)

_____ listen

_____ negotiate

_____ outgoing

_____ patient

_____ perceptive

_____ persuade

_____ pleasant

_____ sensitive

_____ sociable

_____ supervise

_____ tactful

_____ tolerant

_____ tough

_____ trusting

_____ understanding

Skills for Working with Words and Ideas

_____ articulate

_____ communicate well verbally

_____ correspond effectively with others

_____ create new ideas

_____ design

_____ edit

_____ ingenious

_____ inventive

_____ library or Internet research

_____ logical

_____ speak well in public

_____ remember information

_____ use word processing software

_____ write clearly

Leadership Skills

_____ arrange social functions

_____ competitive

_____ decisive

_____ delegate

_____ direct others

_____ explain things to others

_____ influence others

_____ initiate new tasks

_____ make decisions

_____ mediate problems

_____ motivate people

_____ negotiate agreements

_____ plan events

_____ results-oriented

_____ risk taker

_____ run meetings

(continues)

Transferable Skills Checklist *(continued)*

_____ self-confident   _____ solve problems

_____ self-motivate

Creative and Artistic Skills

_____ artistic   _____ perform, act

_____ compose music scores   _____ play musical instrument
or songs
                                 _____ present artistic ideas
_____ dance, body movement
                                 _____ use graphic design
_____ drawing, art   software

_____ expressive   _____ write fiction or creative
                                 writing

List Your Other Transferable Skills

_____

_____

_____

When you are finished, circle the five transferable skills you feel are most important for you to use in your next job and list them in the box below.

Your Top Five Transferable Skills

1. _____

2. _____

3. _____

4. _____

5. _____

Job-Related Skills

Job-related skills are those you need to do a particular occupation. A carpenter, for example, needs to know how to use various tools. Before you select your job-related skills to emphasize, you must first have a clear idea of the jobs you want. So let's put off developing your job-related skills checklist until after you have defined the job you want. That topic is covered next.

Complete the worksheet that follows after you have read "Step 2: Set a Specific Job Objective before You Go Looking."

Insider Tip

Too good to be true?

Most people say that taking inventory of their skills and activities made them feel good; some say working through the checklists was one of the best things they have ever done. If you do it right, you are telling the truth about what you are good at. It's OK to tell the truth, even if it makes you sound good. Using your new "skills language" may be uncomfortable at first, but this information is what employers need to know about you in an interview.

Your Top Five Job-Related Skills

1. _____

2. _____

3. _____

4. _____

5. _____

Set a Specific Job Objective before You Go Looking

Too many people look for a job without clearly knowing what they are looking for. So, before you go out looking for a job, you should first define exactly what you want—*the* job, not *a* job.

Most people think that a job objective is the same as a job title, but it isn't. You need to consider the other elements that make a job satisfying for you. Then, later, you can decide what that job is called—its title—and what industry it might be in.

Describe Your Current Job Objective in General Terms

In general terms, what sort of a job will you be looking for next? For example, if you are enrolled in a career education program, your next job will be related to your current training. Or your past work or other experience may give you a direction for your next job. In the space that follows, list one or more job titles and write a brief description of the job you will look for next.

_____

_____

_____

Define Your Ideal Job Now—You Can Always Compromise on It Later . . .

Let's take the general job description you just wrote and get more specific. The eight questions that follow will help you consider things that are often important in defining a position that satisfies you fully. Once you have considered your answers, your task then becomes finding a position that is as close to your ideal job as possible. Answer each question in a way that supports the general job objective you wrote above.

1. **What skills do you want to use?**
    From the skills lists in Step 1, select the top five skills that you enjoy using and most want to use in your next job.

    _____

    _____

    _____

    _____

    _____

2. **What type of special knowledge do you have?**
    Perhaps you know how to fix radios, keep accounting records, or cook food. Write down the things you know from schooling, training, hobbies, family experiences, and other sources. One or more of these knowledges could make you a very special applicant in the right setting.

    _____

    _____

    _____

    _____

    _____

(continues)

3. **With what types of people do you prefer to work?**
   Do you like to work in competition with others, or do you prefer hardworking folks, creative personalities, or some other types?

   _____

   _____

   _____

   _____

   _____

4. **What type of work environment do you prefer?**
   Do you want to work inside, outside, in a quiet place, a busy place, a clean place, or have a window with a nice view? List the types of environments that are most important to you.

   _____

   _____

   _____

   _____

   _____

5. **Where do you want your next job to be located—in what city or region?**
   Near a bus line? Close to a child-care center? Near your mom? If you are open to living and working anywhere, what would your ideal community be like?

   _____

   _____

   _____

(continues)

Define Your Ideal Job Now *(continued)*

_____

_____

6. **How much money do you hope to make in your next job?**
   Many people will take less money if they like a job in other
   ways—or if they quickly need a job to survive. You should know
   the pay range of the general type of job you want next. Think
   about the minimum you would take as well as what you would
   eventually like to earn. Your next job will probably pay somewhere in between. What benefits would you like to receive?

   _____

   _____

   _____

   _____

   _____

7. **How much and what types of responsibility are you
   willing to accept?**
   Usually, the more money you want to make, the more responsibility you must accept. Do you want to work by yourself, be
   part of a group, or be in charge? If so, at what level?

   _____

   _____

   _____

   _____

   _____

8. **What things are important or have meaning to you?**
   Do you have important values you would prefer to include as
   a basis of the work you do? For example, some people want to

(continues)

help others, clean up our environment, build things, make machines work, gain power or prestige, or care for animals or plants. Think about what is important to you and how you might include this in your next job.

_____

_____

_____

_____

_____

Is It Possible to Find Your Ideal Job?

Can you find a job that meets all the criteria you just defined? Perhaps. Some people do. The harder you look, the more likely you are to find it.

But you will likely need to compromise on some criteria, so it is useful to know what is *most* important to include in your next job. Go back over your responses to the eight questions and mark those few things that you would most like to have or include in your ideal job. Then use the general job description you wrote at the beginning of this step to write a brief outline of this ideal job in the following box. Don't worry about a specific job title, whether you have the experience, or other practical matters yet.

My Ideal Job Would Be

_____

_____

_____

_____

_____

How to Explore Specific Job Titles and Industries

Even if you are sure of the occupation you want, it may be in an industry that you're not familiar with. This combination of occupation and industry forms the basis for your job search, and you should explore a variety of options.

The jobs you could do

The industries in which these jobs exist

Your ideal job exists in the overlap of those jobs that interest you most _and_ in those industries that best meet your needs and interests!

Explore More Than 250 Specific Job Titles

Your ideal job has a variety of characteristics, but it does not yet have a job title. The reason is that some of the things you want, such as a specific work environment, can be found in many jobs and in many industries. But to conduct an effective job search, it is helpful to limit your search to a range of jobs most likely to match your ideal.

The most-often-used source of information on jobs is a book titled the *Occupational Outlook Handbook* (OOH), published by the U.S. Department of Labor. The list that follows presents 264 job titles from the *OOH,* covering more than 85 percent of the U.S. workforce.

You can simply find a job title that interests you and then get additional information on it from the OOH. The descriptions provide details on earnings, education or training required, skills and abilities needed, working conditions, related jobs, sources of additional information (including Internet sources), and other particulars.

A sample job description from the *Occupational Outlook Handbook* is included in Appendix B.

Most libraries and bookstores will have a copy of the *Occupational Outlook Handbook* or of another book with the same information, titled *America's Top 300 Jobs.* You can also get OOH job descriptions on the Internet at www.bls.gov/oco/home.htm or at www.CareerOINK.com.

A simple but effective way to explore job alternatives is to go through the list that follows and check those that you want to learn more about.

The job titles are arranged in clusters of related jobs, in the same groupings used in the *Occupational Outlook Handbook* and *America's Top 300 Jobs.* Major job groupings are identified in **bold** type, and any subgroupings are indicated in *italic* type. Job titles within the groupings are in plain type.

As you review the job titles in this list, put a check mark by those that most closely match your general job description or that would require similar skills. Then read about these jobs in the OOH.

OOH Job Clusters and Titles

Management and Business and Financial Operations Occupations

_____ Accountants and auditors

_____ Administrative services and facility managers

_____ Advertising, marketing, and public relations managers

_____ Budget analysts

_____ Claims adjusters, appraisers, examiners, and investigators

_____ Computer and information systems managers

_____ Construction managers

_____ Cost estimators

_____ Education administrators

_____ Engineering and natural sciences managers

_____ Farmers, ranchers, and agricultural managers

_____ Financial analysts and personal financial advisors

_____ Financial managers

_____ Food service managers

_____ Funeral directors

_____ Human resources, training, and labor relations managers and specialists

_____ Industrial production managers

_____ Insurance underwriters

_____ Loan counselors and officers

_____ Lodging managers

_____ Management analysts

_____ Medical and health services managers

_____ Property, real estate, and community association managers

(continues)

_____ Purchasing managers, buyers, and purchasing agents

_____ Tax examiners, collectors, and revenue agents

_____ Top executives

Professional and Related Occupations

Architects, Surveyors, and Cartographers

_____ Architects, except landscape and naval

_____ Landscape architects

_____ Surveyors, cartographers, photogrammetrists, and surveying technicians

Drafters and Engineering Technicians

_____ Drafters _____ Engineering technicians

Engineers

_____ Aerospace engineers

_____ Agricultural engineers

_____ Biomedical engineers

_____ Chemical engineers

_____ Civil engineers

_____ Computer hardware engineers

_____ Electrical and electronics engineers, except computer

_____ Environmental engineers

_____ Industrial engineers, including health and safety

_____ Materials engineers

_____ Mechanical engineers

_____ Mining and geological engineers, including mining safety engineers

_____ Nuclear engineers

_____ Petroleum engineers

(continues)

OOH Job Clusters and Titles (*continued*)

Arts and Design

_____ Artists and related workers _____ Designers

Entertainers and Performers, Sports, and Related Occupations

_____ Actors, producers, and directors

_____ Athletes, coaches, umpires, and related workers

_____ Dancers and choreographers

_____ Musicians, singers, and related workers

Media and Communications-Related Occupations

_____ Announcers

_____ Broadcast and sound engineering technicians and radio operators

_____ News analysts, reporters, and correspondents

_____ Photographers

_____ Public relations specialists

_____ Television, video, and motion picture camera operators and editors

_____ Writers and editors

Community and Social Services Occupations

_____ Clergy

   _____ Protestant ministers

   _____ Rabbis

   _____ Roman Catholic priests

_____ Counselors

_____ Probation officers and correctional treatment specialists

_____ Social and human service assistants

_____ Social workers

(continues)

Computer and Mathematical Occupations

_____ Actuaries

_____ Computer programmers

_____ Computer software engineers

_____ Computer support specialists and systems administrators

_____ Mathematicians

_____ Operations research analysts

_____ Statisticians

_____ Systems analysts, computer scientists, and database administrators

Education, Training, Library, and Museum Occupations

_____ Archivists, curators, and museum technicians

_____ Instructional coordinators

_____ Library technicians

_____ Teacher assistants

_____ Teachers—adult literacy and remedial and self-enrichment education

_____ Teachers—postsecondary

_____ Teachers—preschool, kindergarten, elementary, middle, and secondary

_____ Teachers—special education

Legal

_____ Court reporters

_____ Judges, magistrates, and other judicial workers

_____ Lawyers

_____ Paralegals and legal assistants

(continues)

OOH Job Clusters and Titles *(continued)*

Life Scientists

_____ Agricultural and food scientists

_____ Biological and medical scientists

_____ Conservation scientists and foresters

Physical Scientists

_____ Atmospheric scientists

_____ Chemists and materials scientists

_____ Environmental scientists and geoscientists

_____ Physicists and astronomers

_____ Science technicians

Social Scientists and Related Occupations

_____ Economists and market and survey researchers

_____ Psychologists

_____ Urban and regional planners

_____ Social scientists, other

Health Diagnosing and Treating Occupations

_____ Chiropractors

_____ Dentists

_____ Dietitians and nutritionists

_____ Occupational therapists

_____ Optometrists

_____ Pharmacists

_____ Physical therapists

_____ Physician assistants

_____ Physicians and surgeons

_____ Podiatrists

(continues)

_____ Recreational therapists

_____ Registered nurses

_____ Respiratory therapists

_____ Speech-language pathologists and audiologists

_____ Veterinarians

Health Technologists and Technicians

_____ Cardiovascular technologists and technicians

_____ Clinical laboratory technologists and technicians

_____ Dental hygienists

_____ Diagnostic medical sonographers

_____ Emergency medical technicians and paramedics

_____ Licensed practical and licensed vocational nurses

_____ Medical records and health information technicians

_____ Nuclear medicine technologists

_____ Occupational health and safety specialists and technicians

_____ Opticians, dispensing

_____ Pharmacy technicians

_____ Radiologic technologists and technicians

_____ Surgical technologists

Service Occupations

Building and Grounds Clearing and Maintenance Occupations

_____ Building cleaning workers

_____ Grounds maintenance workers

_____ Pest control workers

Food Preparation and Serving-Related Occupations

_____ Chefs, cooks, and food preparation workers

_____ Food and beverage serving and related workers

(continues)

OOH Job Clusters and Titles (*continued*)

Health Care Support Occupations

_____ Dental assistants

_____ Medical assistants

_____ Medical transcriptionists

_____ Nursing, psychiatric, and home health aides

_____ Occupational therapist assistants and aides

_____ Pharmacy aides

_____ Physical therapist assistants and aides

Personal Care and Service Occupations

_____ Animal care and service workers

_____ Barbers, cosmetologists, and other personal appearance workers

_____ Child-care workers

_____ Flight attendants

_____ Gaming services occupations

_____ Personal and home care aides

_____ Recreation and fitness workers

Protective Service Occupations

_____ Correctional officers

_____ Firefighting occupations

_____ Police and detectives

_____ Private detectives and investigators

_____ Security guards and gaming surveillance officers

Sales and Related Occupations

_____ Cashiers

_____ Counter and rental clerks

(continues)

_____ Demonstrators, product promoters, and models

_____ Insurance sales agents

_____ Real estate brokers and sales agents

_____ Retail salespersons

_____ Sales engineers

_____ Sales representatives, wholesale and manufacturing

_____ Sales worker supervisors

_____ Securities, commodities, and financial services sales agents

_____ Travel agents

Office and Administrative Support Occupations

_____ Communications equipment operators

_____ Computer operators

_____ Data entry and information processing workers

_____ Desktop publishers

Financial Clerks

_____ Bill and account collectors

_____ Billing and posting clerks and machine operators

_____ Bookkeeping, accounting, and auditing clerks

_____ Gaming cage workers

_____ Payroll and timekeeping clerks

_____ Procurement clerks

_____ Tellers

Information and Record Clerks

_____ Brokerage clerks

_____ Credit authorizers, checkers, and clerks

_____ Customer service representatives

(continues)

OOH Job Clusters and Titles *(continued)*

_____ File clerks

_____ Hotel, motel, and resort desk clerks

_____ Human resources assistants, except payroll and timekeeping

_____ Interviewers

_____ Library assistants, clerical

_____ Order clerks

_____ Receptionists and information clerks

_____ Reservation and transportation ticket agents and travel clerks

Material Recording, Scheduling, Dispatching, and Distributing Occupations, Except Postal Workers

_____ Cargo and freight agents

_____ Couriers and messengers

_____ Dispatchers

_____ Meter readers, utilities

_____ Production, planning, and expediting clerks

_____ Shipping, receiving, and traffic clerks

_____ Stock clerks and order fillers

_____ Weighers, measurers, checkers, and samplers, record keeping

Other Office and Administrative Support Occupations

_____ Office and administrative support worker supervisors and managers

_____ Office clerks, general

_____ Postal Service workers

_____ Secretaries and administrative assistants

(continues)

Farming, Fishing, and Forestry Occupations

_____ Agricultural workers

_____ Fishers and fishing vessel operators

_____ Forest, conservation, and logging workers

Construction Trades and Related Occupations

_____ Boilermakers

_____ Brickmasons, blockmasons, and stonemasons

_____ Carpenters

_____ Carpet, floor, and tile installers and finishers

_____ Cement masons, concrete finishers, segmental pavers, and terrazzo workers

_____ Construction and building inspectors

_____ Construction equipment operators

_____ Construction laborers

_____ Drywall installers, ceiling tile installers, and tapers

_____ Electricians

_____ Elevator installers and repairers

_____ Glaziers

_____ Hazardous materials removal workers

_____ Insulation workers

_____ Painters and paperhangers

_____ Pipe layers, plumbers, pipe fitters, and steamfitters

_____ Plasterers and stucco masons

_____ Roofers

_____ Sheet metal workers

_____ Structural and reinforcing iron- and metalworkers

(continues)

OOH Job Clusters and Titles *(continued)*

Installation, Maintenance, and Repair Occupations

Electrical and Electronic Equipment Mechanics, Installers, and Repairers

_____ Computer, automated teller, and office machine repairers

_____ Electrical and electronics installers and repairers

_____ Electronic home entertainment equipment installers and repairers

_____ Radio and telecommunications equipment installers and repairers

Vehicle and Mobile Equipment Mechanics, Installers, and Repairers

_____ Aircraft and avionics equipment mechanics and service technicians

_____ Automotive body and related repairers

_____ Automotive service technicians and mechanics

_____ Diesel service technicians and mechanics

_____ Heavy vehicle and mobile equipment service technicians and mechanics

_____ Small engine mechanics

Other Installation, Maintenance, and Repair Occupations

_____ Coin, vending, and amusement machine servicers and repairers

_____ Heating, air-conditioning, and refrigeration mechanics and installers

_____ Home appliance repairers

_____ Industrial machinery installation, repair, and maintenance workers

_____ Line installers and repairers

_____ Precision instrument and equipment repairers

(continues)

Production Occupations

_____ Assemblers and fabricators

_____ Food processing occupations

Metalworkers and Plastic Workers

_____ Computer control programmers and operators

_____ Machinists

_____ Machine setters, operators, and tenders—metal and plastic

_____ Tool and die makers

_____ Welding, soldering, and brazing workers

Plant and System Operators

_____ Power plant operators, distributors, and dispatchers

_____ Stationary engineers and boiler operators

_____ Water and liquid waste treatment plant and system operators

Printing Occupations

_____ Bookbinders and bindery workers

_____ Prepress technicians and workers

_____ Printing machine operators

Other Production Occupations

_____ Dental laboratory technicians

_____ Inspectors, testers, sorters, samplers, and weighers

_____ Jewelers and precious stone- and metalworkers

_____ Ophthalmic laboratory technicians

_____ Painting and coating workers, except construction and maintenance

(continues)

OOH Job Clusters and Titles *(continued)*

_____ Photographic process workers and processing machine operators

_____ Semiconductor processors

_____ Textile, apparel, and furnishings occupations

_____ Woodworkers

Transportation and Material Moving Occupations

Air Transportation Occupations

_____ Aircraft pilots and flight engineers

_____ Air traffic controllers

_____ Material moving occupations

Motor Vehicle Operators

_____ Busdrivers

_____ Taxi drivers and chauffeurs

_____ Truckdrivers and driver/salesworkers

Other Transportation Occupations

_____ Rail transportation occupations

_____ Water transportation occupations

_____ Job opportunities in the armed forces

Explore Specific Industries

The industry you work in can often be just as important as the occupation you select. For example, if you are interested in the medical field but are looking for a position using your accounting skills, why not consider looking for an accounting-related job in the medical industry? Some industries will simply be more interesting to you than others, so focus your job search in those industries.

Another good reason to consider various industries is that some are likely to pay more than others do, often for the same skills or jobs.

So, if the industry in which you apply your skills is not that important to you, why not look in an industry that tends to pay better?

The *Career Guide to Industries,* another book by the U.S. Department of Labor, contains very helpful reviews for each of the major industries mentioned in the following list. Organized in groups of related industries, this list covers about 70 percent of the nation's workforce.

Put a check mark by industries that interest you, and then learn more about the opportunities they present. Many libraries and bookstores carry the *Career Guide to Industries,* or you can find the information on the Internet at www.bls.gov/oco/cg/ or at www.CareerOINK.com.

Major Industries

Agriculture, Mining, and Construction
_____ Agricultural Production

_____ Agricultural Services

_____ Construction

_____ Mining and Quarrying

_____ Oil and Gas Extraction

Manufacturing
_____ Aerospace Manufacturing

_____ Apparel and Other Textile Products

_____ Chemicals Manufacturing, Except Drugs

_____ Drug Manufacturing

_____ Electronic Equipment Manufacturing

_____ Food Processing

_____ Motor Vehicle and Equipment Manufacturing

_____ Printing and Publishing

_____ Steel Manufacturing

_____ Textile Mill Products

(continues)

Major Industries (*continued*)

Transportation, Communications, and Public Utilities

_____ Air Transportation

_____ Cable and Other Pay Television Services

_____ Public Utilities

_____ Radio and Television Broadcasting

_____ Telecommunications

_____ Trucking and Warehousing

Wholesale and Retail Trade

_____ Department, Clothing, and Accessory Stores

_____ Eating and Drinking Places

_____ Grocery Stores

_____ Motor Vehicle Dealers

_____ Wholesale Trade

Finance and Insurance

_____ Banking

_____ Insurance

_____ Securities and Commodities

Services

_____ Advertising

_____ Amusement and Recreation Services

_____ Child-Care Services

_____ Computer and Data Processing

_____ Educational Services

_____ Health Services

_____ Hotels and Other Lodging Places

_____ Management and Public Relations Services

_____ Motion Picture Production and Distribution

(continues)

_____ Personnel Supply Services

_____ Social Services, Except Child Care

Government

_____ Federal Government, Excluding the Postal Service

_____ State and Local Government, Excluding Education and Hospitals

Your Top Jobs and Industries Worksheet

Go back over your lists of job titles and industries. List the jobs that interest you most. Then select the industries that interest you most and list them.

These are the jobs and industries you should research most carefully. Your ideal job is likely to be found in some combination of these jobs and industries, or in more specialized but related jobs and industries.

The Five Job Titles That Interest You Most

_____

_____

_____

_____

_____

The Industries That Interest You Most

_____

_____

_____

_____

_____

Consider the Options of Self-Employment and Starting a Business Too

About one in ten workers is self-employed or owns their own business. If these options interest you, consider them as well. Talk to people in similar roles to gather information and look for books and Web sites that provide information on options similar to those that interest you. In the space below, write your current interest in self-employment or starting a business in an area related to your general job objective.

_____

_____

_____

_____

And, Now, We Return to Job-Related Skills

Back on pages 19 and 20, I suggested that you should first define the job you want and then identify key job-related skills you have that support your ability to do it. These are the job-related skills to emphasize in interviews.

So, now that you have defined your ideal job, you can pinpoint the job-related skills it requires. Complete the Essential Job Search Data Worksheet in Appendix A.

Yes, completing the Essential Job Search Data Worksheet requires time, but doing so will help you clearly define key skills to emphasize in interviews, when what you say matters so much. So look at the worksheet now, and promise to do it tonight. Really. People who complete that worksheet will do better in their interviews than those who don't.

After you complete the Essential Job Search Data Worksheet, go back to page 13 and write in Your Top Five Job-Related Skills. Include there the job-related skills you have that you would most like to use in your next job.

Use the Most Effective Methods to Get a Better Job in Less Time

Employer surveys have found that most employers don't advertise their job openings. They most often hire people they already know, people who find out about the jobs through word of mouth, or people who happen to be in the right place at the right time. While luck plays a part, you can increase your "luck" in finding job openings.

Let's look at the job search methods that people use. The U.S. Department of Labor conducts a regular survey of unemployed people actively looking for work. The survey results follow.

Percentage of Unemployed Using Various Job Search Methods

- Contacted employer directly: 64.5%
- Sent out resumés/filled out applications: 48.3%
- Contacted public employment agency: 20.4%
- Placed or answered help wanted ads: 14.5%
- Contacted friends or relatives: 13.5%
- Contacted private employment agency: 6.6%
- Used other active search methods: 4.4%
- Contacted school employment center: 2.3%
- Checked union or professional registers: 1.5%

Source: U.S. Department of Labor, Current Population Survey

This section covers a number of job search methods. Most of the material is presented as information, with a few interactive activities. While each topic is short and reasonably interesting, taking a break now and then will help you absorb it all.

Which Job Search Methods Work Best?

The survey shows that most people use more than one job search technique. For example, one person might read want ads, fill out applications, and ask friends for job leads. Others might send out resumés, contact everyone they know from professional contacts, and sign up at employment agencies.

But the survey covered only nine job search methods and asked only whether the job seeker did or did not use each method. The survey did not cover Internet job searches, nor did it ask whether a method actually worked in getting job offers.

Unfortunately, there hasn't been much recent research on the effectiveness of various job search methods. Most of what we know is based on older research and the observations of people who work with job seekers. I'll share what we do know about the effectiveness of job search methods in the content that follows.

Get the Most Out of Less-Effective Job Search Methods

The truth is that every job search method works for someone. But experience and research show that some methods are more effective than others are. Your task in the job search is to spend more of your time using more effective methods—and increase the effectiveness of all the methods you use.

So let's start by looking at some traditional job search methods and how you can increase their effectiveness. Only about one-third of all job seekers get their jobs using one of these methods, but you should still consider using them.

Insider Tip

Your job search objective:

Almost everyone finds a job eventually, so your objective should be to find a good job in less time. The job search methods I emphasize in this book will help you do just that.

Newspaper and Internet Help Wanted Ads

Most jobs are never advertised, and only about 15 percent of all people get their jobs through the want ads. Everyone who reads the paper knows about these openings, so competition is fierce for the few advertised jobs.

The Internet also lists many job openings. But as happens with newspaper ads, enormous numbers of people view these postings. Some people do get jobs this way, so go ahead and apply. Just be sure to spend most of your time using more effective methods.

Internet job seeking is covered in more detail later in this step.

Filling Out Applications

Most employers require job seekers to complete an application form. Applications are designed to collect negative information, and employers use applications to screen people out. If, for example, your training or work history is not the best, you will often never get an interview, even if you can do the job.

Completing applications is a more-effective approach for young and entry-level job seekers. The reason is that there is a shortage of workers for the relatively low-paying jobs that less-experienced job seekers typically seek. As a result, when trying to fill those positions, employers are more willing to accept a lack of experience or job skills.

Even so, you will get better results by filling out the application, if asked to do so, and then requesting an interview with the person in charge.

When you complete an application, make it neat and error-free, and do not include anything that could get you screened out. If necessary, leave a problem section blank. It can always be explained after you get an interview.

Employment Agencies

There are three types of employment agencies. One is operated by the government and is free. The others are run as for-profit businesses and charge a fee to either you or an employer. Here are the advantages and disadvantages of using each.

The government employment service and one-stop centers. Each state has a network of local offices to pay unemployment compensation, provide job leads, and offer other services at no charge to you or to employers. The service's name varies by state. It may be called Job Service, Department of Labor, Unemployment Office, Workforce Development, or another name.

Many states also have "one-stop centers" that provide employment counseling, reference books, computerized career information, job listings, and other resources.

The Internet site www.doleta.gov/uses will give you information on the programs provided by the government employment service, plus links to other useful sites. Another Internet site, America's Job Bank at www.ajb.dni.us, allows visitors to see all jobs listed with the

Insider Tip

Whatever works is good.

I am *not* suggesting that you should *never* use less-effective techniques. Some people get very good jobs using the worst of methods, and that is fine with me. *I am* suggesting that you use *a variety* of methods, spending most of your time using techniques that work best for most people.

government employment service and to search for jobs by region and other criteria.

The government employment service lists only 5 to 10 percent of the available openings nationally, and only about 6 percent of all job seekers get their jobs there. Even so, visit your local office early in your job search. Find out if you qualify for unemployment compensation and learn more about its services. Look into it—the price is right.

Private employment agencies. Private employment agencies are businesses that charge a fee either to you or to the employer who hires you. Fees can be from less than one month's pay to 15 percent or more of your annual salary. You will often see these agencies' ads in the help wanted section of the newspaper. Many have Web sites.

Be careful about using fee-based employment agencies. Recent research indicates that more people use and benefit from fee-based agencies than in the past. However, relatively few people who register with private agencies get a job through them.

If you use a private employment agency, ask for interviews with employers who will pay the agency's fee. Do not sign an exclusive agreement or be pressured into accepting a job, and continue to actively look for your own leads. You can find these agencies in the phone book's yellow pages, and a government-run Web site at www. ajb.dni.us lists many of them as well.

Temporary agencies. Temporary agencies offer jobs lasting from several days to many months. They charge the employer a fee per hour, and then pay you a bit less and keep the difference. You pay no direct fee to the agency. Many private employment agencies now provide temporary jobs as well.

Temp agencies have grown rapidly for good reason. They provide employers with short-term help, and employers often use them to find people they may want to hire later.

Insider Tip

"Temp" while looking for long-term.

Temp agencies can help you survive between jobs and get experience in different work settings. Temp jobs provide a very good option while you look for long-term work, and you may get a job offer while working as a temp. Holding a temporary job may even lead to a regular job with the same or a similar employer.

School and Employment Services

Contacting a school employment center is one of the job search methods included in the survey presented earlier. Only a small percentage of respondents used this option. This is probably because few had the service available to them.

If you are a student or graduate, find out about these services at your school. Some schools provide free career counseling, resumé-writing help, referrals to job openings, career interest tests, reference materials, and other services.

Special career programs work with veterans, people with disabilities, welfare recipients, union members, professional groups, and many others. Check out these services and consider using them.

Mailing Resumés and Posting Them on the Internet

Many job search "experts" used to suggest that sending out lots of resumés was a great technique. That advice probably helped sell their resumé books, but mailing resumés to people you do not know was never an effective approach. Every so often this would work, but a 95 percent failure rate and few interviews were the more common outcomes, and still are.

Although mailing your resumé to strangers doesn't make much sense, posting it on the Internet might because

- It doesn't take much time.
- Many employers have the potential of finding your resumé there.

Still, job searching on the Internet has its limitations, just like other methods do.

I do believe that most job seekers should have a good resumé. How you use it to get results is the issue. I'll cover electronic resumés in more detail later and provide tips on using the Internet throughout this book.

The Two Job Search Methods That Work Best

The fact is that most jobs are not advertised. So, how do *you* find them? The same way about two-thirds of all job seekers do—

networking with people you know (which I call making *warm contacts*) and directly contacting employers (which I call making *cold contacts*). Both of these methods are based on the job search rule that you should know above all:

The Most Important Job Search Rule
Don't wait until a job is "open" before you contact the employer!

Employers fill most jobs with people they meet before a job is formally "open." So the trick is to meet people who can hire you before a job is formally available. Instead of asking, "Do you have any jobs open?" I suggest that you say, "I realize you may not have any openings now, but I would still like to talk to you about the possibility of future openings."

This simple change in how you approach the job search can make an enormous difference in your getting interviews while others wait for jobs to be advertised. They remain unemployed, while you get interviews and job offers. Here are some details on how to do this most effectively.

Most-Effective Job Search Method #1: Develop a Network of Contacts

One study found that 40 percent of all people located their jobs through a lead provided by a friend, a relative, or an acquaintance. That makes people you know the #1 source of job leads—asking their help is more effective than all other job search methods.

Five Easy Steps to Develop a Network of Contacts

Developing contacts is called *networking,* and here's how it works:

Insider Tip

Job seeking is a contact sport.

It's true. You have to know someone to get a job. I have found, though, that you can quickly get to know all sorts of new people if you go about it right. One of them often turns out to be the someone you need.

1. **Make lists of people you know.**
   Make a thorough list of anyone you are friendly with. Then make a separate list of all your relatives. These two lists alone often add up to 25 to 100

45

people or more. Next, think of other groups of people who you have something in common with, such as former coworkers or classmates, members of your social or sports groups, members of your professional association, former employers, neighbors, and other groups. You may not know many of these people personally or well, but most will help you if you ask them.

Create Your Lists of Contacts

Make a separate networking list for each group. Check any of the following groups that make sense for your situation.

_____ Friends

_____ Relatives

_____ Friends of parents

_____ Former coworkers

_____ Members of my church or religious group

_____ People who sell me things (insurance agent, real estate agent, landlord, etc.)

_____ Neighbors

_____ People I went to school with

_____ Former teachers

_____ Members of social clubs

_____ People who provide me with services (hairstylist, counselor, mechanic, etc.)

_____ Former employers

_____ Members of sports or hobby groups

_____ Members of professional organizations I belong to or can join

(continues)

Write in other groups here:

_____

_____

_____

_____

Next, list names and contact information for each person in all of the groups you listed. It may take some research to collect all the names and contact information, so start with lists of friends and relatives, whose information is easy to get. Some lists, like those from alumni associations or professional organizations, can also be obtained with a quick phone call or e-mail, or by searching a Web site.

2. **Contact them in a systematic way.**
   Contact each person on your lists. Obviously, some people will be more helpful than others are, but any one of them might help you find a job lead.

3. **Present yourself well.**
   Begin with your friends and relatives. Call and tell them you are looking for a job and need their help. Be as clear as possible about the type of employment you want and the skills and qualifications you have. Look at the sample JIST Card® and phone script later in this chapter for good presentation ideas.

4. **Ask contacts for leads.**
   It is possible that your contacts will know of a job opening that interests you. If so, get the details and get right on it! More likely, however, they will not, so you should ask each person the three magic networking questions.

The Three Magic Networking Questions

- *Do you know of any openings for a person with my skills?*
  If the answer is "No" (which it usually is), then ask . . .

- *Do you know of someone else who might know of such an opening?*
  If your contact does, get that name and ask for another one. If he or she doesn't, ask . . .

- *Do you know of anyone who might know of someone else who might know of a job opening?*
  Another good way to ask this is, "Do you know someone who knows lots of people?" If all else fails, this will usually get you a name.

5. **Contact these referrals and ask them the same questions.**
   From each person you contact, try to get two names of other people you might contact. Doing this consistently can extend your network of acquaintances by hundreds of people. Eventually, one of these people will hire you or refer you to someone who will!

If you are persistent in doing these five steps, networking may be the only job search method you need. It works.

Most-Effective Job Search Method #2: Contact Employers Directly

It takes more courage, but making direct contact with employers is a very effective job search technique. I call these *cold contacts* because people you don't know in advance will need to warm up to your inquiries. Two basic techniques for making cold contacts follow.

Insider Tip

The reason most jobs are not advertised:

Three out of four jobs are never advertised because employers don't need or want to advertise. Employers trust people referred to them by someone they know far more than they trust someone selected from a group of unknown strangers. Most jobs are filled by referrals and people whom the employer knows. This eliminates the need to advertise. So, your job search must involve more than looking at ads.

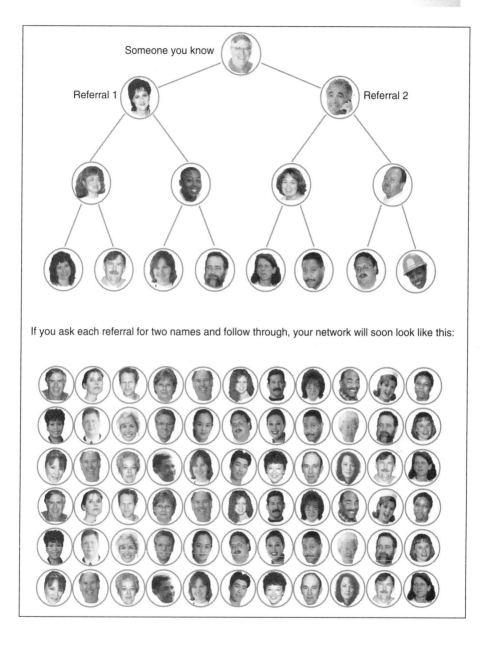

Someone you know

Referral 1

Referral 2

If you ask each referral for two names and follow through, your network will soon look like this:

Use the Yellow Pages to Find Potential Employers

Begin by looking at the index in the front of your phone book's yellow pages. For each entry, ask yourself, "Would an organization of this kind need a person with my skills?" If you answer "Yes," then that organization or business type is a possible target. You can also rate Yes entries based on your interests, writing a 1 next to those that seem very interesting, a 2 next to those that you are not sure of, and a 3 next to those that aren't interesting at all.

Here is one section of a yellow pages listing that has been marked by a person looking for a position in health care.

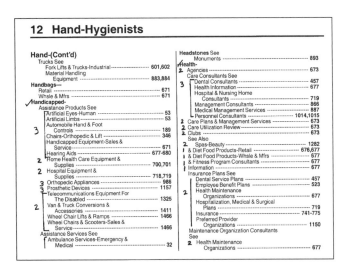

Next, select a type of organization that got a Yes response and turn to that section of the yellow pages. Call each organization listed there and ask to speak to the person who is most likely to hire or supervise you. This would typically be the manager of the business, or a department head—not the personnel manager.

You can easily adapt this approach to the Internet. Use sites such as www.yellowpages.com to get phone or e-mail contacts anywhere in the world.

A Sample Phone Contact

Here is an example of a carefully scripted phone call made to the manager of a small business. You will learn more about how to create these later in this chapter.

Hello, my name is John Kijek. I am interested in a position as an auto mechanic. I have more than three years of experience, including one year in a full-time auto mechanic's training program. I am familiar with all hand tools and electronic diagnostic equipment, and can

---

handle common auto repair tasks, such as tune-ups, brakes, exhaust systems, and electrical and mechanical repairs. I also work quickly, often completing jobs correctly in less than the standard time. I have all the tools needed to start work immediately. I can work any shift and prefer full-time work. I am also honest, reliable, and good with people. When may I come in for an interview?

Drop In without an Appointment

Another effective cold contact method is to just walk into a business or organization that interests you and ask to speak to the person in charge.

Remember to say that you realize there may not be a job opening now, but that you would like to be considered for a future opening. If your timing is inconvenient, ask for a better time to come back for an interview. Try this four or five times, and you will be surprised to find that you will often get one or two interviews.

Insider Tip

The almost perfect source of free contacts:

Your phone book's yellow pages provide the most complete and up-to-date listing of potential job search targets you can get. It even organizes them into categories that are most useful for a job seeker. Just find a category that interests you, call each listing, and ask to speak with the person who is most able to hire or likely to supervise someone with your skills.

Particularly effective in small businesses, dropping in also works surprisingly well in larger ones. Look for drop-in opportunities on your way to or from another interview.

It is an unconventional approach that can work very well, letting you see employers before they have an opening. And, if they like you and if you stay in touch, they are more likely to hire you than to advertise.

Most Jobs Are with Small Employers

Businesses and organizations with 250 or fewer employees employ about 70 percent of all U.S. workers. They are also the source for up to 80 percent of the new jobs created each year. They are simply too important to overlook in your job search! Many of them don't have personnel departments, making direct contacts even easier and more effective.

Use JIST Cards® —An Effective Mini-Resumé

Look at the sample cards that follow—they are JIST Cards®, and they get results. Computer printed or even neatly written on 3-by-5-inch cards, JIST Cards® include the essential information employers want to know.

I developed this concept years ago, and, ever since, JIST Cards® have been used by thousands of job search programs and millions of people. Employers like their direct and time-saving format, and they have been proven as an effective tool to get job leads. Attach one to your resume. Give JIST Cards® to friends, relatives, and other contacts and ask them to pass the cards along to others who might know of an opening. Enclose them in thank-you notes after an interview. Leave them with employers as a business card. However you get your JIST Cards® into circulation, you will be surprised at how well they work.

You can easily create JIST Cards® on a computer and print them on card stock you can buy at any office supply store. Or have a few hundred printed cheaply by a local quick print shop. While they are often done as 3-by-5 cards, they can be printed in any size or format. Look at the sample cards that follow for ideas on creating your own.

The Anatomy of a JIST Card®

There is more to a well-written JIST Card® than meets the eye. Look over the different sections of a JIST Card® in the sample. Additional details on each part of a JIST Card® are provided after the card.

Sample JIST Card ®

Sandra Zaremba

Home phone: (219) 555-7608
E-mail: SKZ1128@aol.com

Position: General Office/Clerical

Over two years' work experience, plus one year of training in office practices. Familiar with a variety of computer programs, including word processing, spreadsheets, accounting, and some database and graphic design programs. Am Internet literate and word process 70 wpm accurately. Can post general ledger and handle payables, receivables, and most accounting tasks. Responsible for daily deposits averaging more than $200,000 monthly. Good interpersonal skills. Can meet strict deadlines and handle pressure well.

Willing to work any hours.

Organized, honest, reliable, and hardworking.

A JIST Card® is small, so it can't contain many details. A JIST Card® should list only the information that is most important to employers. For a simple card, consider all that Sandra's sample includes:

- **Identification**

  Sandra's name is given.

- **Two ways to make contact**

  Sandra lists two ways she can be reached: a home phone number and her e-mail address. Employers want to reach you quickly, so include at least two ways you can be contacted. Because employers usually won't respond to you by letter, don't give your address. Instead, list any two of the following: a regular phone number, a cell phone number, a pager number, or an e-mail address. If you give a phone number, make sure that the phone is answered professionally by a person, voice mail, or an answering machine.

- **Position desired**

  Sandra includes a broad job objective. This encourages an employer to consider her for many jobs.

- **Length of experience**

  Sandra lists her total length of work experience. Some of this experience was in part-time and volunteer jobs, something she can explain in an interview.

- **Education and training**

  Sandra lists her total time spent in training.

- **Job-related skills, performance, and results**

  This section tells a little about what Sandra can do and how well she can do it. She describes important job-related skills for doing this work. Sandra mentions the key self-management and transferable skills she learned or used in her work and other experiences. Note that she includes several numbers. The first is "70 wpm," which means she types quickly at 70 words per minute. She states that she was responsible for $200,000 in cash deposits each month. This tells employers that she can be trusted with substantial responsibility.

- **Special conditions**

  Sandra mentions that she is willing to work any hours. This shows that she is flexible and amenable to work.

- **Good-worker traits and adaptive skills**

  Sandra lists her key personality traits and adaptive skills that would be important to an employer. (Adaptive skills are the self-management skills explored under Step 1. They describe your basic personality and your ability to adapt to new environments.)

All this on a 3-by-5-inch card that can be read in less than 30 seconds!

Following are some more sample JIST Cards®. They are for different jobs, from entry-level to those requiring more experience. Study them and use any ideas that help you write your own JIST Cards®. Although you can type or even handwrite your cards, most people use a desktop computer and laser print.

Jonathan McLaughlin
Answering machine: (509) 555-8736
Cell phone: (509) 555-0981

Objective: Electronics—installation, maintenance, and sales

Skills: Four years of work experience, plus two years advanced training in electronics. AS degree in Electronics Engineering Technology. Managed a $500,000/year business while going to school full-time, with grades in the top 25%. Familiar with all major electronics diagnostic and repair equipment.

Hands-on experience with medical, consumer, communications, business, and industrial electronics equipment and applications. Good problem-solving and communication skills. Customer service oriented.

Willing to do what it takes to get the job done.

Self-motivated, dependable, learn quickly.

Jonathan is a new graduate from a two-year technical program. He was always interested in electronics, but worked in construction jobs after high school. He then got a job helping the owner of a TV and electronics repair shop. He answered phones, kept the place clean, and handled other simple tasks. But, he also volunteered to fix items, and the owner started to show him how to do more complex repairs and encouraged him to go back to school.

Jonathan worked at the electronics shop for three years, scheduling his work time around school. Using this JIST Card®, he eventually landed a job with a circuit board design and manufacturing company, and now earns about three times more than he did previously.

Andrea Scott

Answering machine: (639) 555-9704
E-mail: andys@hotmail.com

Position Desired: Warehouse Management

Skills: Three years' experience plus two years of formal business course work. Have supervised a staff as large as eight people and warehousing operations valued at over $4,000,000. Automated inventory operations resulting in an estimated annual savings of over $25,000. Working knowledge of accounting, computer systems, and advanced inventory management systems.

Will work any hours.

Responsible, hardworking, and can solve problems.

Andrea got her work experience in the military, where she was responsible for warehouse operations for an infantry unit. Her business education includes high school courses, military training, and some college-level course she took while in the military. It was enough for her to land a job with Federal Express, where she now supervises 14 workers.

Jafar Browning

Home: (846) 555-3643
Pager: (846) 555-4525   E-mail: JMB0928@aol.com

Objective: Sales or business position requiring skills in problem solving, planning, organizing, and customer service.

Skills: Two years' experience, including course work in business, sales methods, customer service, and business software. Promoted and received several bonuses for performance. Set record for largest single sale exceeding $130,000. Consistent record of getting results. Excellent communication skills. Familiar with database, word processing, and spreadsheet programs. Internet literate. Enjoy challenges and accept responsibility.

Willing to relocate.

Results-oriented, good problem-solving skills, energetic.

Jafar does not have formal education beyond high school but is smart and very good with people. He used these adaptive and transferable skills in sales, where he could earn good pay. He landed a position selling telecommunications services to businesses and doubled his earnings.

John Harold
Home: (619) 555-0040   **E-mail: johnharold@easternair.com**

Objective: Responsible Business Management Position

Skills: Over 7 years of management experience plus a degree in Business. Managed budgets as large as $5 million. Experienced in cost control and reduction, cutting more than 20% of overhead while sales increased almost 30%. Good organizer and problem solver. Excellent communication skills.

Prefer responsible position in a medium-to-large business.

Cope well with deadline pressure, seek challenge, flexible.

John has lots of experience and great credentials. He accepted a job running a small window manufacturing company that is now growing rapidly.

The JIST Card® Worksheet

A JIST Card® is small, so it should list only the information that is most important to employers. This worksheet will help you compose your own JIST Card®. It provides tips for each section of the card. Complete each portion of the worksheet as well as you can.

Your name: _____

Tips

Keep this simple and professional. Don't use nicknames, middle names, or initials.

(continues)

The JIST Card® Worksheet *(continued)*

Contact information: _____

_____

_____

_____

Tips

Include two or more ways for an employer to contact you. Include a telephone number that will be answered all the time. Always include your area code.

If you use an answering machine or voice mail, make sure it does not have a silly greeting. If the phone is at home, make sure anyone who might answer it knows how to take accurate messages.

Include a cell phone or pager number if you have one. Including an e-mail address helps communicate that you are Internet literate.

Job objective: _____

_____

_____

_____

Tips

Don't be too narrow in your job objective. Say "General office" rather than "Receptionist" if you would consider a variety of office jobs. If you are narrower in your job objective, try to avoid a narrow job title and give other details. For example, say "Management position in an insurance-related business" or "Working with children in a medical or educational setting."

(continues)

Don't limit yourself to entry-level jobs if you have potential or interest in doing more. If you say "Office manager" instead of "Secretary," you just might get a more responsible and higher-paying job. If you are not too sure of your ability to get a higher-paying job, it is still best to keep your options open. Say "Office manager or responsible secretarial position," for example.

Your Work Experience Statement

You should take advantage of all the experience you have that supports your job objective. Depending on your situation, you can include any or all of the following as part of your work experience:

- **Paid work**
  List any work you were paid to do. The work does not have to be similar to the job you are looking for now. Babysitting and lawn-mowing jobs count. So can working in a fast-food place. If you worked part-time, estimate the total number of hours you worked. Divide this total by 160 hours to get the number of months you worked. Of course, paid work that is directly related to your job objective is the best, if you have it.

- **Volunteer work**
  You can include volunteer work as part of your total work experience. It counts, so list it if you don't have much paid work experience.

- **Informal work**
  Include work you did at home or as an unpaid hobby. It is best if this work relates to the job, but it doesn't have to. For example, if you worked on cars at home and want to be an auto mechanic, there is an obvious connection. You may have experience taking care of younger brothers or sisters, or working in the family business. This is real experience and, if it can help you, mention it.

- **Related education and training**
  If you took high school or college courses that relate to the job you want, you can count this as part of your total experience. You can also count any courses or training you received in the

(continues)

The JIST Card® Worksheet *(continued)*

military, business or technical school, or anywhere else. If they relate in some way to the job you want, they count.

Your Total Work Experience

Now, fill in the lines that follow. Write either years or months (if you don't have much experience) in the spaces beside each entry.

a. Total time paid work experience   _____

b. Total time volunteer work   + _____

c. Total time informal work   + _____

d. Total time related education or training   + _____

Total experience   = _____

Here are some tips for writing your experience statement.

- **If you have lots of work experience . . .**
  Emphasize the closest to your job objective, if you have lots of experience. For example, if you have 20 years of total experience, include just the experience that directly relates to this job. And, say "More than 15 years of experience." This keeps the employer from knowing how old you are. Your age is an advantage you will present in the interview!

- **If you don't have much paid work experience . . .**
  If you have no paid work experience related to the job you now seek, emphasize your education, training, and other work. For example, "Nearly two years of experience, including one year of advanced training in office procedures." Remember to include the total of all paid and unpaid work as part of your experience! Include all those part-time jobs and volunteer jobs by writing "More than 18 months' total work experience."

- **If your experience is in another field . . .**
  Mention that you have "Four years' work experience" without saying in what field.

- **Other points to emphasize**
  If you won promotions, raises, or have other special strengths, this is the time to say so. For example: "More than seven years

(continues)

of increasingly responsible work experience, including three years as a supervisor. Promoted twice."

Look over the sample JIST Cards® for additional ideas, and then write your own statement below.

_____

_____

_____

_____

_____

Your Education and Training Statement

If it helps, you can combine your education and training with your experience on your JIST Card®. Or you can list your education and training as a separate statement. Don't mention your education or training if it doesn't help you.

If you have a license, certification, or degree that supports your job objective, mention it here. For example, "Four years of experience plus two years of training leading to certification as an Emergency Medical Technician." If you want, you can revise your previous experience statement here to include your education and training.

_____

_____

_____

_____

_____

(continues)

The JIST Card® Worksheet *(continued)*

Your Key Skills Statement

List the things you can do to support your job objective. If appropriate, mention job-related tools or equipment you can use. Use the language of the job to describe the more important things you can do. Use some numbers to strengthen what you say and to emphasize results. For example, instead of writing "Can do word processing," say "Accurately word-process 80 words per minute and am familiar with advanced graphic and formatting capabilities of Microsoft Word and PageMaker."

Emphasize results! It is too easy to overlook the importance of what you do. Add up the number of transactions you handled, the money you were responsible for, the results you got. For example, a person with fast-food experience might write, "Have handled more than 50,000 customer contacts quickly and accurately with total sales of over $250,000." These numbers are based on a five-day workweek, 200 customers a day for one year, and an average sale of $5.

Impressive numbers, when presented in this way. The fact that this was done in a fast-food job does not have to be mentioned. These "lowly" jobs often require hard work, speed, and advanced skills that can be promoted to employers. Someone who ran a small store could say, "Responsible for business with more than $150,000 in sales per year. Increased sales by 35% within 18 months." Someone with reception, customer service, or sales experience might note her "Good appearance and pleasant telephone voice."

It is certainly OK to give numbers to support these skills, too. Think hard about your experiences and try to include numbers and results. Look over the sample JIST Cards® for ideas, and then write your own statement below.

_____

_____

_____

_____

(continues)

Special Conditions or Preferred Working Conditions Statement

This is an optional section in which you can add just a few words to let the employer know what you are willing to do. Do not limit your employment possibilities by saying "Will only work days" or "No travel wanted." Look at the sample JIST Cards® for ideas, and then write your own statement below.

_____

_____

_____

Your Good-Worker Traits and Skills Statement

Refer to Step 1, then list three or four of your key adaptive (self-management) skills below. Choose skills that are most important in the job you are seeking.

_____

_____

_____

_____

Now Write and Use Your JIST Card®

You will have to revise the content from the worksheet you just completed so that all your information fits onto a 3-by-5-inch card. To do so, make every word count. Get rid of anything that does not directly support your job objective. Use short phrases; you don't have to use complete sentences. Add more information if your JIST Card® is too short, but add things only if they make your statements stronger. Get rid of anything that does not present you in a positive way.

Handwrite or print your content on a 3-by-5-inch card to help you see if you have included too much or too little information. Edit it again as needed to make it fit. Reading your JIST Card® out loud will help you to know how it sounds and may give you additional ideas to improve it. Ask someone else to help you with the final version so that it has no grammar or spelling errors.

Once you have your final content, you'll want to put lots of your JIST Cards® in circulation. While you can type or even handwrite individual JIST Cards®, it is best to have them printed in quantities of at least 100 to 500. You can print your own JIST Cards® on a computer or have them done at most print shops for a modest fee.

You can fit five copies of a JIST Card® on one standard sheet of 8½-by-11-inch light card stock (available at most office supply stores and printers). You will need to cut the sheets down to the correct size of the individual cards. Office supply stores may also sell "micro-perforated" sheets that easily can be torn into 3-by-5-inch cards. This lets you produce the cards on your own printer without having to divide the sheets yourself.

Use Your JIST Card® as the Basis for an Effective Phone Script

Once you have created your JIST Card®, you can use it as the basis for a phone script to make warm or cold calls. Revise your JIST Card® content so that it sounds natural when spoken, and then edit it until you can read it out loud in about 30 seconds. The sample phone script that follows is based on the content of a JIST Card®. Use it to help you modify your own JIST Card® into a phone script.

> *Hello, my name is Pam Nykanen. I am interested in a position in hotel management. I have four years' experience in sales, catering, and accounting with a 300-room hotel. I also have an associate degree in hotel management, plus one year of experience with the Bradey Culinary Institute. During my employment, I helped double revenues from meetings and conferences and increased bar revenues by 46 percent. I have good problem-solving skills and am good with people. I am also well organized, hardworking, and detail oriented. When may I come in for an interview?*

Once you have your script, make some practice calls to warm or cold contacts. If making cold calls, contact the person most likely to supervise you. Then present your script just as you practiced it, without stopping.

Making cold calls takes guts, but job search programs find that most people can get one or more interviews an hour using cold calls. Start by calling people you know and the people they refer you to. Then try calls to businesses that don't sound very interesting. As you get better, call more desirable targets. Hey, what's the worst that could happen?

While the sample script assumes that you are calling someone you don't know, it can be changed to address warm contacts and referrals. Making cold calls takes courage—but works very well for many who are willing to do it.

Tips for Using the Internet in Your Job Search

I provide Internet-related tips throughout this book, but it deserves a separate section, so here it is.

The Internet has limitations as a job search tool. While many have used it to get job leads, it has not worked well for far more. Too many assume they can simply add their resumé to resumé databases, and employers will line up to hire them. Just as with the older approach of sending out lots of resumés, good things sometimes happen, but not often.

Insider Tip

Dialing for dollars:

The phone is an essential job search tool that can get you more interviews per hour than any other job search tool. But it won't work unless you use it actively throughout your job search!

I recommend two points of view that apply to all job search methods, including the Internet:

Remember . . .
It is unwise to rely on just one or two methods in conducting your job search. It is essential that you use an active rather than a passive approach in your job search.

Ways to Increase Your Internet Effectiveness

I encourage you to use the Internet in your job search but suggest that you use it along with other techniques, including direct contacts with employers. The following suggestions can increase the effectiveness of using the Internet in your job search:

- **Be as specific as possible in identifying the job you seek.**
  This is important in using any job search method and even more so in looking for jobs on the Internet. The Internet is enormous, so it is essential to be as focused as possible in what you are searching for. Narrow your job title or titles to be as specific as possible. Limit your search to specific industries or areas of specialization.

- **Have reasonable expectations.**
  Success on the Internet is more likely if you understand its limitations. For example, employers trying to find someone with skills in high demand, such as network engineers or nurses, are more likely to use the Internet to recruit job candidates.

- **Limit your geographic options.**
  If you don't want to move, or would move but only to certain areas, state this preference on your resumé and restrict your search to those areas. Many Internet sites allow you to view only those jobs that meet your location criteria.

- **Create an electronic resumé.**
  With few exceptions, resumés submitted on the Internet end up as simple text files with no graphic elements. Employers search databases of many resumés for those that include key words or meet other searchable criteria. So create a simple text resumé for Internet use and include on it words likely to be used by employers searching for someone with your abilities.

- **Get your resumé into the major resumé databases.**
  Most Internet employment sites let you add your resumé for free, and then charge employers to advertise openings or to search for candidates. These easy-to-use sites often provide all sorts of useful information for job seekers.

- **Make direct contacts.**
  Visit Web sites of organizations that interest you and learn more about them. Some will post openings, allow you to apply online, or even provide access to staff who can answer your questions. Even if they don't, you can always e-mail a request for the name of the person in charge of the work that interests you and then communicate with that person directly.

- **Network.**
  You can network online, too, finding names and e-mail addresses of potential employer contacts or of other people who might know someone with job openings. Look at interest groups, professional association sites, alumni sites, chat rooms, and employer sites—these are just some of the many creative ways to network and interact with people via the Internet.

Useful Internet Sites

Thousands of Internet sites provide information on careers or education. Many have links to other sites that they recommend. Service providers such as America Online (www.aol.com) and the Microsoft Network (www.msn.com) have career information and job listings, plus links to other sites. Larger portal sites offer links to recommended career-related sites. Alta Vista (www.altavista.com), Lycos (www.lycos.com), and Yahoo! (www.yahoo.com) are just a few of these portals.

These major career-specific sites can get you started:

- The Riley Guide—www.rileyguide.com—Good information and lots of links to other career sites.
- America's Job Bank—www.ajb.dni.us—Run by the U.S. Department of Labor, lists job openings across the country.
- The JIST® site—www.jist.com—Free career information, links to other career sites, and resources.
- Monster.com—www.monster.com—A major source of employer job postings.
- Careerbuilder—www.careerbuilder.com—Another major site listing job openings by employers.
- Career OINK—www.CareerOINK.com—Provides descriptions for thousands of job titles and other good information.

Write a Simple Resumé Now and a Better One Later

You've already learned that sending out paper resumés and waiting for responses is passive and not an effective job-seeking technique. Posting your resumé on one or more Internet sites is also passive but can make sense if you use more active approaches, too.

The fact is that many employers *will* ask you for a paper or Internet resumé, so a resumé can be a useful tool in your job search. Unfortunately, too many people spend weeks working on their resumé when they should be out getting interviews instead.

So I suggest you begin with a simple resumé you can complete quickly and start using today. If you want a "better" resumé, you can work on it on weekends and evenings.

Tips for Creating a Superior Resumé

The following are some basic tips that make sense for any resumé format, paper or electronic.

Write It Yourself

It's okay to look at other resumés for ideas, but write yours yourself. It will force you to organize your thoughts and background.

Make It Error-Free

One spelling or grammar error will create a negative impressionist (see what I mean?). Get someone else to review your final draft for any errors. Then review it again because these rascals have a way of slipping in.

Make It Look Good

Poor copy quality, cheap paper, bad type quality, or anything else that creates a poor appearance will turn off employers to even the best resumé content. Internet resumés have format rules of their own, and you will need to make them look presentable in that format.

Get professional help with design and printing, if necessary. Many professional resumé writers and even print shops offer writing and desktop design services.

Be Brief; Be Relevant

Many good resumés fit on one page, and few justify more than two. Include only the most important points. Use short sentences and action words.

If it doesn't relate to and support the job objective, cut it!

Be Honest

Don't overstate your qualifications. If you end up getting a job you can't handle, who does it help? And a lie can result in your being fired later.

Be Positive

Emphasize your accomplishments and results. A resumé is no place to be too humble or to display your faults.

Be Specific

Instead of saying "I am good with people," you can say, "I supervised four people in the warehouse and increased productivity by 30 percent." Use numbers whenever possible, such as the number of people served, the dollars saved, or the percentage by which sales increased.

Insider Tip

Avoid the resumé pile.

Resumé experts often suggest that a "dynamite" resumé will jump out of the pile. This is old-fashioned advice. It assumes that you are applying to large organizations and for advertised jobs. Today, most jobs are with small employers and are not advertised. My advice is to avoid joining that stack of resumés in the first place, by looking for openings that others overlook.

You should also know that everyone feels that he or she is a resumé expert. Whatever you do, someone will tell you that it's wrong.

Remember that a resumé is simply a job search tool. You should never delay or slow down your job search because your resumé is not "good enough." The best approach is to create a simple and acceptable resumé as quickly as possible and then use it. As time permits, create a better one if you feel you must.

The Five Most Effective Ways to Use a Resumé

Even an excellent resumé won't get you talking with an employer unless you use it effectively. These five tips suggest how to use your resumé to get more interviews:

1. **Get the interview first.**
   It is always better to contact employers by phone, e-mail, or in person *before* you send a resumé. If possible, get a referral from someone you know. Or make a cold contact directly with the employer. In either case, ask for an interview. If no opening is available now, ask whether you can come in and discuss the possibility of future openings.

2. **Then, send your resumé.**
   Whenever possible, send or e-mail your resumé after you schedule an interview, so that the employer can read about you before your meeting. Valuable interview time can then be spent discussing your skills rather than details that are best presented in a resumé.

3. **Follow up with a JIST Card® and thank-you note.**
   Immediately after an interview, send a thank-you note. Even if you use e-mail to communicate with employers, most appreciate a mailed thank-you note. And mailing the note allows you to enclose your JIST Card® or another copy of your resumé.

4. **Send your resumé and JIST Card® to everyone in your growing job search network.**
   This is an excellent way for people in your network to help you find unadvertised leads. They can pass or e-mail information to others who might be interested in a person with your skills.

5. **Send your resumé in the traditional way if you can't make direct contact.**
   In some situations, you can't easily make contact with an employer. This is true, for example, if you want to post your resumé on the Internet. Another example is when responding to a want ad that gives only a box number. Go ahead and do these things; just plan on using more active job search methods, too.

Chronological Resumés

Most resumés use a chronological format in which the most recent experience is listed first, followed by each previous job. This arrangement works fine for someone with work experience in several similar jobs, but not as well for those with limited experience or for career changers.

Look at the following two resumés for Judith Jones. Both use the chronological approach. The first resumé would work fine for most job search needs—and it could be completed in about an hour. Notice that the second one includes some improvements. The first resumé is good, but most employers would like the additional positive information in the improved resumé.

Tips for Writing a Simple Chronological Resumé

Follow these tips for writing a basic chronological resumé.

Name

Use your formal name rather than a nickname if the formal name sounds more professional—for example, Judith Jones, rather than Judy Jones.

Address and Contact Information

Avoid abbreviations in your address and include your ZIP code. If you may move soon, use a friend's address or include a forwarding address.

Most employers will not write to you, so you must provide reliable phone numbers, e-mail addresses, or other contact options. Always include your area code in your phone number because you never know where your resumé might travel. If you don't have an answering machine, get one—and leave it on whenever you leave home. Make sure your voice message presents you in a professional way.

Include alternative ways to reach you, like through a cell phone or pager number and an e-mail address.

Basic Chronological Resumé

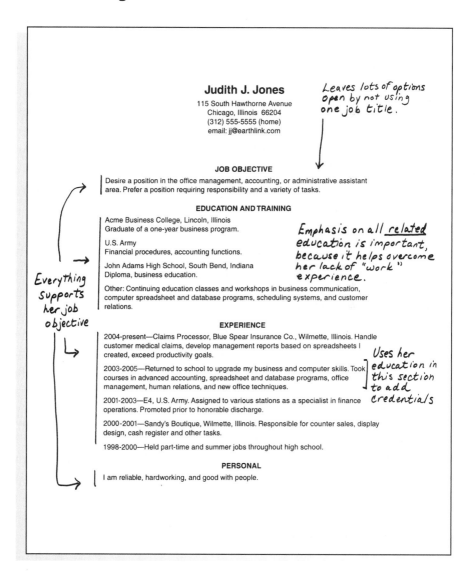

Job Objective

You should almost always have a job objective, even if it is general.

In the sample resumés, notice how Judith kept her options open with her broad job objective. Writing "secretary" or "clerical" might keep her from being considered for other jobs she might accept.

Education and Training

Include any training or education you've had that supports your job objective. If you did not finish a formal degree or program, list what you did complete and emphasize accomplishments. If your experience is not strong, include details that do support your job objective, such as related courses and extracurricular activities.

In the two examples, Judith put her business schooling in both the Education and Experience sections. Doing this filled a job gap and allowed her to present her training as equal to work experience.

Previous Experience

Include the basics such as employer name, job title, dates employed, and responsibilities. Emphasize things such as specific skills, results, accomplishments, and superior performance.

Personal Data

Do not include irrelevant details like height, weight, and marital status—doing so is considered very old-fashioned. But you can include information like hobbies or leisure activities in a special section if these directly support your job objective.

Judith Jones's basic resumé includes a Personal section, in which she listed some of her strengths, traits that often aren't mentioned in a resumé.

References

You do not need to list references. Employers will ask for references if they want them. If your references are particularly good, you can mention this somewhere—the last section of your resumé is often a good place.

List your references on a separate page and give it to employers who ask. Ask your references what they will say about you and, if it is positive, ask them to write a letter of recommendation that you can give to employers.

Improved Chronological Resumé

Judith J. Jones

115 South Hawthorne Avenue • Chicago, Illinois 66204
(312) 555-5555 (home)
email: jj@earthlink.com

Adds lots of details to reinforce skills throughout.

More details here.

JOB OBJECTIVE

Seeking position requiring excellent business management skills in an office environment. Position should require a variety of tasks, including office management, word processing, and spreadsheet and database program use.

EDUCATION AND TRAINING

Acme Business College, Lincoln, Illinois.
Completed one-year program in Professional Office Management. Grades in top 30 percent of my class. Courses included word processing, accounting theory and systems, advanced spreadsheet and database programs, time management, and basic supervision.

John Adams High School, South Bend, Indiana.
Graduated with emphasis on business courses. Excellent grades in all business topics and won top award for word processing speed and accuracy.

Other: Continuing education programs at my own expense, including business communications, customer relations, computer applications, sales techniques, and others. *Uses numbers to reinforce results.*

EXPERIENCE

2004-present—Claims Processor, Blue Spear Insurance Company, Wilmette, Illinois. Handle 50 complex medical insurance claims per day, almost 20 percent above department average. Created a spreadsheet report process that decreased department labor costs by over $30,000 a year (one position). Received two merit raises for performance.

2003-2005—Returned to business school to gain advanced skills in accounting, office management, sales and human resources. Computer courses included word processing and graphics design, accounting and spreadsheet software, and database and networking applications. Grades in top 30 percent of class.

2001-2003—Finance Specialist (E4), U.S. Army. Responsible for the systematic processing of over 200 invoices per day from commercial vendors. Trained and supervised eight employees. Devised internal system allowing 15 percent increase in invoices processed with a decrease in personnel. Managed department with a budget equivalent of over $350,000 a year. Honorable discharge.

2000-2001—Sales Associate promoted to Assistant Manager, Sandy's Boutique, Wilmette, Illinois. Made direct sales and supervised four employees. Managed daily cash balances and deposits, made purchasing and inventory decisions, and handled all management functions during owner's absence. Sales increased 26 percent and profits doubled during my tenure.

1998-2000—Held various part-time and summer jobs through high school while maintaining good grades. Earned enough to pay all personal expenses, including car and car insurance. Learned to deal with customers, meet deadlines, work hard, handle multiple priorities, and develop other skills.

SPECIAL SKILLS AND ABILITIES

Quickly learn new computer applications and am experienced with a number of business software applications. Have excellent interpersonal, written, and oral communication and math skills. Accept supervision well, am able to supervise others, and work well as a team member. Like to get things done and have an excellent attendance record.

Tips for an Improved Chronological Resumé

Once you have a simple, errorless, and eye-pleasing resumé, get on with your job search. There is no reason to delay! If you want to create a better resumé in your spare time (evenings or weekends), try these additional tips.

Job Objective

A poorly written job objective can limit the jobs that an employer might consider you for. Think of the skills you have and the types of jobs you want to do; describe them in general terms. Instead of using a narrow job title such as "Restaurant manager," you might write "Manage a small to midsized business."

Education and Training

New graduates should emphasize their recent training and education more than those with a few years of related work experience would. A more detailed description of education and training might mention specific courses you took, and activities or accomplishments that support your job objective or reinforce your key skills.

Include other details that reflect how hard you work, such as working your way through school or handling family responsibilities.

Skills and Accomplishments

Include things that support your ability to do well in the job you seek now. Even small things count. Maybe your attendance was perfect, you met a tight deadline, or you did the work of others during vacations. Be specific and include numbers—even if you have to estimate them.

The improved chronological resumé example features a Special Skills and Abilities section and more accomplishments and skills. Notice how numbers can reinforce results.

Job Titles

Past job titles may not accurately reflect what you did. For example, your job title may have been "Cashier," but you also opened the store, trained new staff, and covered for the boss on vacations. Perhaps "Head cashier and assistant manager" would be more accurate.

Check with your previous employer if you are not sure.

Promotions

If you were promoted or received good evaluations, say so— "Cashier, promoted to assistant manager," for example. A promo-

---

tion to a more responsible job can be handled as a separate job, if doing so results in a stronger resumé.

Gaps in Employment and Other Problem Areas

Employee turnover is expensive, so few employers want to hire people who won't stay or work out. Gaps in employment, jobs held for short periods, or a lack of direction in the jobs you've held are all things that concern employers.

So consider your situation and try to give an explanation of a problem area. Here are a few examples:

2004—Continued my education at . . .

2004—Traveled extensively throughout the United States.

2005 to present—Self-employed barn painter and widget maker.

2003—Had first child, took year off before returning to work.

Date your employment using entire years to avoid displaying an employment gap you can't explain easily. For example "2004 to 2005" can cover a few months of unemployment at the beginning of 2004.

Skills and Combination Resumés

The functional, or "skills," resumé emphasizes your most important skills, supported by specific examples of how you have used them. This approach allows you to use any part of your life history to support your ability to do the job you want.

A skills resumé can be very effective, though creating one requires some work. And some employers don't like skills resumés because they can hide a job seeker's faults (such as job gaps, lack of formal education, or little related work experience) better than a chronological resumé. Still, a skills resumé may make sense for you.

Look over the sample resumé that follows for ideas. Notice that it includes elements of a skills *and* a chronological resumé. This so-called combination resumé makes sense if your previous job history or education and training are positive. More combination examples follow at the end of this chapter.

Combination Resumé

This sample for a recent college graduate emphasizes applicable education and skills as real experience and relates all sections back to the applicant's job objective. Key adaptive and transferable skills are highlighted throughout.

A two-page combination format for a soon-to-graduate student.

Emphasizes what he can do and not just what he wants!

Jonathan McLaughlin

6926 Mapleton Court   (602) 555-5555 cell phone

Phoenix, AZ 85009   jafar@quickwit.com e-mail

JOB OBJECTIVE

Position in the electronics industry requiring skills in the design, sale, installation, maintenance, or repair of computer, audio, video, and other advanced electronics. Prefer tasks needing creative problem-solving skills and customer contact.

EDUCATION

PHOENIX TECHNICAL INSTITUTE
Phoenix, AZ, Graduating in June with AS Degree in Electronics Engineering Technology, top 25% of class.

Completing a comprehensive, two-year curriculum, including over 1,000 hours of classroom instruction and advanced laboratory experience. Theoretical, practical, and hands-on knowledge of audio and RF amplifiers, AM/FM transmitter-receiver circuits, circuit board theory and practice, PC and network systems and maintenance, microwave and radar communications, digital circuits, and much more. Excellent attendance while working two jobs to pay tuition.

These statements show he is responsible, hard working, motivated.

PLAINS JUNIOR COLLEGE
Phoenix, AZ

Courses included digital electronics, programming, computer software applications, and business topics. Worked full time and maintained a B+ average.

DESERT VIEW HIGH SCHOOL
College prep courses, including advanced math, business, marketing, merchandising, computer software applications, and computer programming. Very active in varsity sports and National Honor Society for two years.

Gives lots of emphasis to recent and past education, including specific things he learned that relate to his job objective.

This section allows him to emphasize the skills from school, work, and life that support his job objective.

↓

SKILLS

PROBLEM-SOLVING: Familiar with the underlying theory of most electronic systems and am particularly good at isolating problems by using logic and persistence. I enjoy the challenge of solving complex problems and will work long hours, if necessary, to meet a deadline.

Explains important adaptive skills ↑

INTERPERSONAL: Have supervised five staff and trained many more. Comfortable with one-to-one and small group communications. Can explain technical issues simply to staff and customers of varying levels of sophistication. Had over 10,000 customer contacts and several written commendations.

TECHNICAL: Background in a variety of technical areas, including medical equipment, consumer electronics, computers, automated cash registers, photocopiers, and standard office and computer equipment and peripherals. Have designed special applications using sequential logic circuits and TTL logic. Constructed a microprocessor and wrote several machine language programs for this system. Can diagnose and repair problems in digital and analog circuits.

ORGANIZATIONAL: Have set up and run my own small business and worked in another responsible job while going to school full-time. Earned enough money to live independently and pay all school expenses during this time. I can work with minimal supervision and have learned to use my time efficiently.

→ *While 2 of his 3 jobs are not related to his current objective, he uses them to support skills that will help him do his next job.*

EXPERIENCE

BANDLER'S INN: 2004-present. Waiter, promoted to night manager. Complete responsibility for all operations of a shift grossing over $500,000 in sales per year. Supervised five full-time and three part-time staff. Business increased during my employment by 35% and profits by 42%, much of it due to word-of-mouth advertising of satisfied customers. *Uses numbers to reinforce his skills.*

FRANKLIN HOSPITAL: 2003-present. Electronic Service Technician Assistant. Work in General Medicine, Diagnostic Labs, and radiology departments. Assisted technicians in routine service and maintenance of a variety of hospital equipment. Left to attend school full time but continue to work weekends while attending school.

JON'S YARD SERVICE: 2000-2003. Set up a small business while in school. Worked part-time and summers doing yard work. Made enough money to buy a car and save for tuition.

More examples of his willingness to work hard and meet goals.

Resumé Design and Production Tips

Insider Tip

Skip the negatives.

Remember that a resumé can get you screened out, but it is up to you to get the interview and the job. So, cut out *anything* negative in your resumé!

What you say in your resumé is very important. How you present it is just as important. Here are some brief tips that will help you create a superior resumé after the writing is done.

Make Your Resumé Look Good

Make sure that your resumé looks good. Word processing software and laser printers allow you to create a professional-looking resumé. All major word processors have resumé-writing templates and "wizards" that make designing your resumé simple.

If you are not experienced in using word processing software, composing your resumé is not the time to learn. Trust me on this.

If you don't have access to a computer and a high-quality printer, most small print shops and resumé-writing services can produce a professional-looking resumé for a modest cost. Unless you get their help in writing your resumé, these shops should charge no more than $50 to format a one- or two-page resumé.

Get Lots of Copies

Earlier in this book, you learned how you can develop hundreds of job leads through networking and cold contacts. It is to your advantage to give each contact one or more copies of your resumé. Plan on having lots of copies available. You may go through several hundred before you land your job.

If you have access to a computer and a good laser printer, you can print excellent quality copies. If you don't have regular access to a computer system, you can get good photocopies made at most quick print shops. Look in the yellow pages for listings.

Use Good Paper and Matching Envelopes

Most office supply stores and print shops have good-quality papers and matching envelopes for resumés and cover letters. The best papers have a rich look and texture. They cost more but are worth every penny. Ivory, white, and off-white are conservative colors that look professional.

Electronic and Scannable Resumés

A traditional resumé is printed on paper. The Internet and other technology now often require resumés to be in electronic form.

If you plan to use the Internet in your job search, you will need to submit your resumé in electronic form. Once you do so, your resumé is entered into a database that might be searched by many employers.

Even if you don't plan on using the Internet, you need to understand how electronic resumés work. More and more employers are scanning the resumés they receive.

Scanners are machines that convert your resumé into electronic text. This allows employers to use a computer to quickly search hundreds or thousands of resumés to find qualified applicants. The computers look for key words in the resumés—usually qualifications and skills that match the criteria needed for the open positions—and sort out the resumés with the most "hits."

Many larger employers use scanning technology. Your paper resumé is likely to be scanned into a database without your knowing it.

Because electronic resumés are used differently than those on paper, it is important to understand how you can increase their effectiveness and their "readability" by a machine.

An Electronic Resumé Should Have Lots of Key Words

Employers using electronic databases search for key words in resumés. So, the more key words you include, the more likely your resumé will be selected. Key words are words and phrases specific to the job you want. Here are some ways to find and present key words on your resumé:

- **Add a key word section.**
  A simple technique is to add a section to your resumé titled "Key Skills." You can then add key words not included elsewhere in your resumé.

- **Include all your important skill words.**
  If you completed the worksheets in Steps 1 and 2, include the key skills documented there.
- **Think like a prospective employer.**
  List the jobs you want. Then think of the key words employers are likely to use when searching a database.
- **Review job descriptions.**
  Carefully review descriptions for jobs you seek in major print references like the *Occupational Outlook Handbook* and the *O*NET Dictionary of Occupational Titles*. Most large Web sites that list job openings have lots of employer job postings and job descriptions to review. Corporate Web sites often post information on job openings, another source of key words. Make a list of key words in descriptions of interest and include them in your resumé.
- **Be specific.**
  List certifications and licenses, name any software and machines you can operate, and include special language and abbreviations used in your field.

Insider Tip

A resumé is not the most effective tool for getting interviews.

A better approach is to make direct contact with those who hire or supervise people with your skills and ask them for an interview, even if no openings exist now. *Then* send a resumé.

For an Electronic Resumé, a Simple Design Is Best

The databases that your resumé goes into want only text, not design. Scanners introduce fewer errors when the text is simple. What this means is that your resumé's carefully done format and design elements need to be taken out, and your resumé reduced to the simplest text format. Follow these guidelines:

- No graphics
- No lines
- No bold, italic, or other text variations
- Only one easy-to-scan font
- No tab indentations
- No line or paragraph indents
- No centering; align text to the left

This may be discouraging, but it's the way it is.

Electronic Resumé

The sample resumé has been rewritten from a traditional "on-paper" format to one for scanning or e-mail submission. It has a plain look that is easily read by scanners and key words that increase its chances of being selected in a search.

RICHARD JONES

3456 Generic Street

Potomac MD 11721

Format to be scanned or e-mailed. No bold, bullets, or italics.

Phone messages: (301) 555-5555

E-mail: richj@generic.com

Lots of key words to help get selected by computer searches by employers.

SUMMARY OF SKILLS

Rigger, maintenance mechanic (carpentry, electrical, plumbing, painting), work leader. Read schematic diagrams. Flooring (wood, linoleum, carpet, ceramic and vinyl tile). Plumbing (pipes, fixtures, fire systems). Certified crane and forklift operator, work planner, inspector.

+++

EXPERIENCE *Includes results statements and numbers below*

Total of nine years in the trades—apprentice to work leader.

* MAINTENANCE MECHANIC LEADER, Smithsonian Institution, Washington, DC, April 2004 to present: Promoted to supervise nine staff in all trades, including plumbing, painting, electrical, carpentry, drywall, flooring. Prioritize and schedule work. Inspect and approve completed jobs. Responsible for annual budget of $750,000 and assuring that all work done to museum standards and building codes.

* RIGGER / MAINTENANCE MECHANIC, Smithsonian Institution, February 2001 to April 2003: Built and set up exhibits. Operated cranes, rollers, forklifts, and rigged mechanical and hydraulic systems to safely move huge, priceless museum exhibits. Worked with other trades in carpentry, plumbing, painting, electrical and flooring to construct exhibits.

* RIGGER APPRENTICE, Portsmouth Naval Shipyard, Portsmouth, NH, August 2000 to January 2001: Qualified signalman for cranes. Moved and positioned heavy machines and structural parts for shipbuilding. Responsible for safe operation of over $2,000,000 of equipment on a daily basis, with no injury or accidents. Used cranes, skids, rollers, jacks, forklifts and other equipment.

+++

TRAINING AND EDUCATION

HS graduate, top 50% of class.

Additional training in residential electricity, drywall, HV/AC, and refrigeration systems. Certified in heavy crane operation, forklift, regulated waste disposal, industrial blueprints.

The Requirements of One Large Employer Are Typical

Employers want resumés in electronic or scannable form to save time. It's not practical to look through hundreds or thousands of paper resumés. For this reason, Internet resumé sites and many employers require you to submit your resumé in a way that can be easily put into their databases. To show you how this works, I have included the following instructions from one large employer's Web site on how to submit a resumé (see page 85). I've deleted references to the specific employer.

While these instructions aren't friendly, the reason for submitting a resumé this way is pretty clear: No matter how you send your resumé to the company, the company will convert the resumé into a simple text file, and a machine will probably read it before a human being does.

Quick Tips to Reformat Your Paper Resumé

Fortunately, you can easily take your existing resumé and reformat it for electronic submission. Here are some quick tips for doing so:

- Copy and paste your resumé text into a new file in your word processor.
- Eliminate any graphic elements, such as lines or images.
- Set your margins so that text is no more than 65 characters wide.
- Use one easy-to-scan font, such as Courier, Arial, Helvetica, or Times Roman. Eliminate bold, italic, and other font styles.
- Introduce major sections with words in all uppercase letters, rather than in bold or a different font.
- Keep all text aligned to the left and eliminate centering, unless you use the space key to do so.
- Use a standard keyboard character, such as the asterisk, instead of using special symbols as bullets.
- Use the space key to indent, instead of using the tab key or paragraph indents.
- When done, click the File menu, choose the Save As command, and select the Plain Text, ASCII (American Standard Code for Information Interchange), or Text Only option.

Instructions from a Large Employer on How to Submit Your Resumé

We are employing a new electronic applicant tracking system that uses the latest in document-imaging/scanning technology. The system allows us to receive your resumé by e-mail, direct line fax, or hard copy. This system will enhance your exposure to a wider variety of employment opportunities at all sites within our company. The one-time submission of your resumé makes you eligible for consideration of any openings for which you meet the minimum qualifications.

As your resumé is input into our system, you receive an acknowledgment and your resumé is kept active in our database for one year. As openings occur, our recruiters search the database for individuals whose qualifications and skills match the criteria needed for the open positions. If a match occurs, you receive further notification regarding the specific opening.

To increase the effectiveness of your resumé, be sure to clearly state your skills and experiences, educational background, work history, and specific salary information. In addition, please follow these directions when preparing your resumé:

- Prepare your resumé on white or light-colored 8½-by-11 paper (hard copy or faxing).
- Please use a standard paper weight so that the system will produce a quality image (if hard copy or faxing).
- Avoid fancy treatments such as italics, underlining, and shadowing. Bold-faced type and capital letters are acceptable.
- Place your name at the top of the page on its own line, use a standard address format below your name, and list each phone number on a separate line.

You may submit your resumé by one of the following methods:

- **Electronic mail.** The e-mail address is resumé@bigcompany.com. You must put the word *resumé* in the subject or reference line when e-mailing and submit it in ASCII text format. All information must be contained in the body of the message. We cannot accept attachments into this system.
- **Fax.** You may fax your information to 866-555-3325. Please fax in fine mode.
- **Postal mail.** You may mail a hard copy of your resumé to Corporate Recruitment, Big Company, Corporate Center, Big City, TX 90214.

- Name the file and click Save or OK.
- Reopen the file to see how it looks. Make additional format changes as needed.

While this reformatting may undermine your creative side, think of it as mashed potatoes: It can be very good if you do it right.

A Few Final Words on Resumés

Before you write and use your resumé, here is some advice that applies to both paper and electronic resumés:

- **Even the best of resumés will not get you a job.**
  You have to do that yourself. To do so, you have to get interviews and do well in them. Interviews are where the job search action is, not resumés.

- **Don't listen to resumé experts.**
  If you ask ten people for advice on your resumé, they will all be willing to give it—yet no two will agree. You have to make up your own mind about your resumé. Feel free to break any "rules," if you have a good reason.

- **Don't avoid the job search by worrying about your resumé.**
  Write a simple and error-free resumé, and then go out and get lots of interviews. Later, you can write a better resumé—if you want or need to.

- **Look over the sample resumés.**
  I include several sample resumés at the end of this chapter. Some break "rules," and none are perfect. However, all are based on real resumés written by real people, although the names and other details have been changed. So look them over, learn from them, and then write your own.

How to Write Effective Cover Letters

A cover letter is sent with and "covers" a resumé. Different situations need different types of letters. When sending your resumé via e-mail, adapt the tips here so that you include carefully written e-mail text along with your resumé. As always, make certain that your correspondence makes a good impression.

You may find that you don't need to send many formal cover letters. Job seekers using the approaches I recommend get by with informal thank-you notes sent with resumés and JIST Cards®. But certain types of jobs and some organizations require a more formal approach. Use your judgment.

The sample cover letters that follow deal with a variety of typical situations. Look them over for ideas to use when writing your own letters.

Some Tips for Writing and Using Superior Cover Letters

Here are some suggestions to help you create and use superior cover letters.

Target Your Letter

Typical reasons for sending a cover letter include responding to an ad, preparing an employer for an interview (the best reason!), and following up after a phone call or interview. Each of these letters is different.

Samples for each situation are included with the sample letters.

Send It to Someone by Name

Get the name of the person who is most likely to supervise you. Call first to get an interview. Then send your letter and resumé.

Get It Right

Make sure you get the person's name, organization name, and address right. Include the person's correct job title. Make sure that your letter does not contain grammar and other errors; this creates a poor impression.

Be Clear about What You Want

If you want an interview, ask for it. If you are interested in the organization, say so. Give clear reasons why the company should consider you.

Be Friendly and Professional

A professional, informal style is usually best. Avoid a hard-sell "Hire-me-now!" approach. No one likes to be pushed.

Make It Look Good

Just like a resumé, correspondence to an employer must look good. Use good-quality paper and matching envelopes. A standard business format is good for most letters.

Follow Up

Remember that contacting an employer directly is much more effective than sending a letter. Don't expect letters to get you many interviews. They are best used to follow up after you have contacted the employer.

Cover Letter for a Specific Opening

This new graduate called first and arranged an interview—the best approach of all. She mentions specifically how she changed procedures for a business and saved money. Note how she includes skills such as working hard and dealing with deadline pressure.

113 S. Meridian Street
Greenwich, Connecticut 11721

March 10, 20XX

Ms. Willa Hines
New England Power and Light Company
604 Waterway Boulevard
Parien, Connecticut 11716

Dear Ms. Hines:

I am following up on the brief chat we had today by phone. After getting the details on the position you have open, I am certain that it is the kind of job I have been looking for. A copy of my resume is enclosed providing more details of my background. I hope you have a chance to review it before we meet next week.

My special interest has long been in the large-volume order processing systems that your organization has developed so well. While in school I researched the flow of order processing work for a large corporation as part of a class assignment. With some simple and inexpensive procedural changes I recommended, check-processing time was reduced by an average of three days. For the number of checks and dollars involved, this one change resulted in an estimated increase in interest revenues of over $135,000 per year.

While I have recently graduated from business school, I have considerable experience for a person of my age. I have worked in a variety of jobs dealing with large numbers of people and deadline pressure. My studies have also been far more hands-on and practical than those of most schools, so I have a good working knowledge of current business systems and procedures. This includes a good understanding of various computer spreadsheet and application programs, the use of automation, and experience with cutting costs and increasing profits. I am also a hard worker and realize I will need to apply myself to get established in my career.

I am most interested in the position you have available and am excited about the potential it offers. I look forward to seeing you next week.

Sincerely,

Wendy Presson

Cover Letter after an Interview

The writer uncovered a problem during an interview and afterward offers to solve the problem when no job exists. Many job seekers never think of scheduling an interview when there is no job opening, but many jobs are created this way to accommodate a good person.

Sandra A. Zaremba

115 South Hawthorn Drive
Dunwoody, Georgia 21599

April 10, XXXX

Ms. Christine Massey
Import Distributors, Inc.
417 East Main Street
Atlanta, Georgia 21649

Dear Ms. Massey:

I know you have a busy schedule so I was pleasantly surprised when you arranged a time for me to see you. While you don't have a position open now, your organization is just the sort of place I would like to work. As we discussed, I like to be busy with a variety of duties and the active pace I saw at your company is what I seek.

Your ideas on increasing business sound creative. I've thought about the customer service problem and would like to discuss a possible solution. It would involve the use of a simple system of color-coded files that would prioritize correspondence to give older requests priority status. The handling of complaints could also be speeded up through the use of simple form letters similar to those you mentioned. I have some thoughts on how this might be done too, and I will work out a draft of procedures and sample letters if you are interested. It can be done on the computers your staff already uses and would not require any additional cost to implement.

Whether or not you have a position for me in the future, I appreciate the time you have given me. An extra copy of my resume is enclosed for your files—or to pass on to someone else.

Let me know if you want to discuss the ideas I presented earlier in this letter. I can be reached at any time on my cell phone at (942) 267-1103. I will call you next week, as you suggested, to keep you informed of my progress.

Sincerely,

Sandra A. Zaremba

Cover Letter from a Network Contact

The person uses names from a professional association to conduct a long-distance job search. He explains the end of his old job, indicates certain skills, and mentions the availability of positive references. He also requests an interview even though no job may be open.

July 10, XXXX

Mr. Paul Resley
Operations Manager
Rollem Trucking Co.
I-70 Freeway Drive
Kansas City, Missouri 78401

Mr. Resley:

    I obtained your name from the membership directory of the Affiliated Trucking Association. I have been a member for over 10 years, and I am very active in the Southeast Region. The reason I am writing is to ask for your help. The firm I had been employed with has been bought by a larger corporation. The operations here have been disbanded, leaving me unemployed.

    While I like where I live, I know that finding a position at the level of responsibility I seek may require a move. As a center of the transportation business, your city is one I have targeted for special attention. A copy of my resume is enclosed for your use. I'd like you to review it and consider where a person with my background would get a good reception in Kansas City. Perhaps you could think of a specific person for me to contact?

    I have specialized in fast-growing organizations or ones that have experienced rapid change. My particular strength is in bringing things under control, then increasing profits. While my resume does not state this, I have excellent references from my former employer and would have stayed if a similar position existed at its new location.

    As a member of the association, I hoped that you would provide some special attention to my request for assistance. I plan on coming to Kansas City on a job-hunting trip within the next six weeks. Prior to my trip I will call you for advice on who I might contact for interviews. Even if they have no jobs open for me now, perhaps they will know of someone else who does.

    My enclosed resume lists my phone number and other contact information should you want to reach me before I call you. Thanks in advance for your help on this.

Sincerely,

John B. Goode
Treasurer, Southeast Region
Affiliated Trucking Association

John B. Goode

312 Smokie Way   Nashville, Tennessee 31201

Cover Letter Following Up on a Cold Call

This person made contact with the office manager by phone and set up an interview for his upcoming visit to the area.

1768 South Carrollton Street
Nashville, Tennessee 96050
May 26, XXXX

Ms. Karen Miller
Office Manager
Lendon, Lendon, and Sears
Suite 101, Landmark Building
Summit, New Jersey 11736

Dear Ms. Miller:

Enclosed is a copy of my resume that describes my work experience as a legal assistant. I hope this information will be helpful as background for our interview next Monday at 4 p.m.

I appreciate your taking time to describe your requirements so fully. This sounds like a position that could develop into a satisfying career. And my training in accounting—along with experience using a variety of computer programs—seems to match your needs.

Lendon, Lendon, and Sears is a highly respected name in New Jersey. I am excited about this opportunity and I look forward to meeting with you.

Sincerely,

Richard Wittenberg

More Sample Resumés

The sample resumés that follow give you content, style, and format ideas. Space limited the number of samples I could include. The ones I do include use pretty simple formats. Professional resumé writers created some of these resumés, and their names are noted at the bottom of those examples. You can find professional resumé writers in your area through the Professional Association of Résumé Writers and Career Coaches at www.parw.com and the National Résumé Writers' Association at www.nrwa.com.

If you want to see more resumés, many good books and Web sites provide samples. JIST® publishes excellent resumé collections written by professional resumé writers. And I've written several resumé books that provide lots of examples.

Insider Tip

Keep competitive with two resumés.

As use of electronic resumés and scanning increases, it makes sense to have two resumés: one on paper that looks good to humans and another that scans and e-mails well. Having both, for use in different situations, gives you a competitive edge.

Chronological Resumé Stresses Technical Credentials

This resumé emphasizes Jack's technical qualifications. The Additional Qualifications section highlights statements that do not fit into a traditional chronological form.

Chronological resume with some nice features that make it very effective.

Simple but attractive use of bold, centering, and lines.

Jack B. Harris

12 Browertown Road	Little Falls, NJ 07424	Messages: (201) 555-5555
	e-mail: Jbquick@net.com	

Class A Automotive Mechanic
Specializing in complete engine overhaul and front end repair work

Education & Training

Graduate of Rockford Community College, 1998
Basic and Advanced Automotive Technology courses. Top 20% of class.
ASE Certified in repair of:

- ✔ Engines
- ✔ Suspensions
- ✔ Steering
- ✔ Cooling systems
- ✔ Brakes
- ✔ Electrical systems

GM training on the job:
- ✔ Use of computerized engine analyzers and other electronic test devices.
- ✔ Diagnostics and service to electronic fuel injection, ignition, and emission control components.

Additional Qualifications *This section includes details that would not be easy to list in a typical chronological format.*

- ✔ Experience with foreign and domestic late model cars, vans and light trucks.
- ✔ Stay current on new technology; understand and act on instructions from repair manuals and manufacturers' bulletins.
- ✔ Very service oriented, hard working and cooperative.
- ✔ Own power and hand tools for most applications; able to do heavy lifting.

Strong, direct words emphasize effectiveness and results.

Work Experience

2003–Present   **Master Automotive Technician**
                                  DRISCOLL CHEVROLET, South Caldwell, NJ

- ✔ Attained highest status at dealership employing 12 technicians because of ability to quickly diagnose troubles and make accurate repairs.
- ✔ Kept track of recurring problems in certain models for manufacturer notification. Shared information with other mechanics.
- ✔ Increased department profitability by consistently performing most services in 10-20% less time than allowed by industry standards.
- ✔ Contributed to 29% increase in customer satisfaction levels over the last year.

Numbers support his results and skills.

2000–2003   **Automotive Mechanic**
                            SEARS AUTO CENTER, Clairmont, NJ

- ✔ Started with basic tune-ups and tire service, advancing after 2 months to brake, general repair, radiator and air conditioning repairs.
- ✔ Was often assigned to customers with complaints of unsatisfactory original service. Corrected problems and maintained good relationships.
- ✔ Trained 6 newly hired mechanics in shop procedures.

Chronological section - notice the use of check marks. Much better than a paragraph of text!

Submitted by Melanie A. Noonan

Chronological Resumé Emphasizes Results

A simple format emphasizes Maria's accomplishments through the use of numbers. While her resumé does not say so, it is obvious that she works hard and that she gets results.

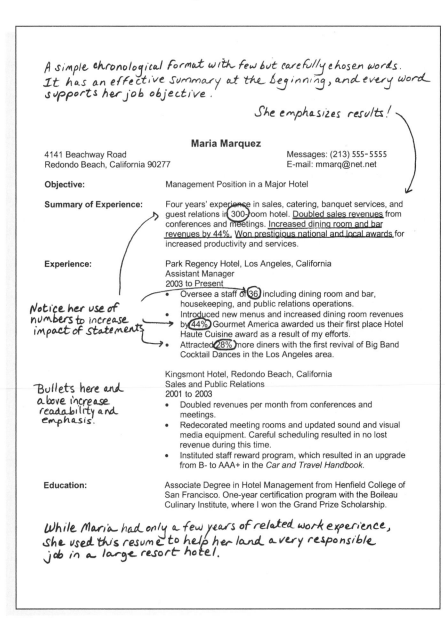

A simple chronological format with few but carefully chosen words. It has an effective summary at the beginning, and every word supports her job objective.

She emphasizes results!

Maria Marquez

4141 Beachway Road
Redondo Beach, California 90277

Messages: (213) 555-5555
E-mail: mmarq@net.net

Objective: Management Position in a Major Hotel

Summary of Experience: Four years' experience in sales, catering, banquet services, and guest relations in 300-room hotel. Doubled sales revenues from conferences and meetings. Increased dining room and bar revenues by 44%. Won prestigious national and local awards for increased productivity and services.

Experience: Park Regency Hotel, Los Angeles, California
Assistant Manager
2003 to Present

- Oversee a staff of 36 including dining room and bar, housekeeping, and public relations operations.
- Introduced new menus and increased dining room revenues by 44%. Gourmet America awarded us their first place Hotel Haute Cuisine award as a result of my efforts.
- Attracted 28% more diners with the first revival of Big Band Cocktail Dances in the Los Angeles area.

Notice her use of numbers to increase impact of statements

Kingsmont Hotel, Redondo Beach, California
Sales and Public Relations
2001 to 2003

- Doubled revenues per month from conferences and meetings.
- Redecorated meeting rooms and updated sound and visual media equipment. Careful scheduling resulted in no lost revenue during this time.
- Instituted staff reward program, which resulted in an upgrade from B- to AAA+ in the *Car and Travel Handbook*.

Bullets here and above increase readability and emphasis.

Education: Associate Degree in Hotel Management from Henfield College of San Francisco. One-year certification program with the Boileau Culinary Institute, where I won the Grand Prize Scholarship.

While Maria had only a few years of related work experience, she used this resume to help her land a very responsible job in a large resort hotel.

Skills Resumé for Someone with Limited Work Experience

This resumé is for a recent high school graduate whose only paid work experience was at a fast-food restaurant.

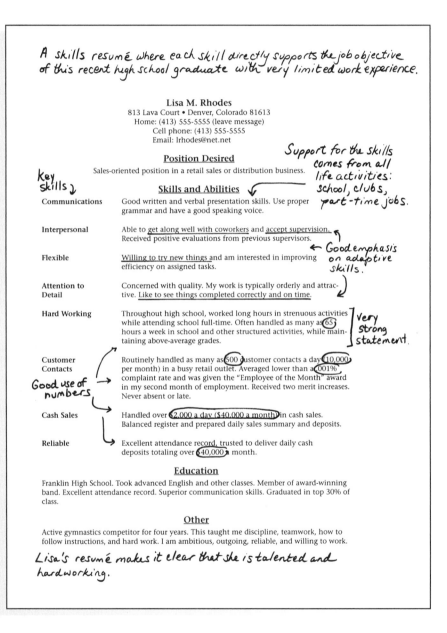

A skills resumé where each skill directly supports the job objective of this recent high school graduate with very limited work experience.

Lisa M. Rhodes
813 Lava Court • Denver, Colorado 81613
Home: (413) 555-5555 (leave message)
Cell phone: (413) 555-5555
Email: lrhodes@net.net

Position Desired

Sales-oriented position in a retail sales or distribution business.

Support for the skills comes from all life activities: school, clubs, part-time jobs.

Skills and Abilities

key skills

Communications Good written and verbal presentation skills. Use proper grammar and have a good speaking voice.

Interpersonal Able to get along well with coworkers and accept supervision. Received positive evaluations from previous supervisors.

← Good emphasis on adaptive skills.

Flexible Willing to try new things and am interested in improving efficiency on assigned tasks.

Attention to Detail Concerned with quality. My work is typically orderly and attractive. Like to see things completed correctly and on time.

Hard Working Throughout high school, worked long hours in strenuous activities while attending school full-time. Often handled as many as 65 hours a week in school and other structured activities, while maintaining above-average grades.

Very strong statement.

Customer Contacts Routinely handled as many as 500 customer contacts a day (10,000 per month) in a busy retail outlet. Averaged lower than a .001% complaint rate and was given the "Employee of the Month" award in my second month of employment. Received two merit increases. Never absent or late.

Good use of numbers →

Cash Sales Handled over $2,000 a day ($40,000 a month) in cash sales. Balanced register and prepared daily sales summary and deposits.

Reliable Excellent attendance record, trusted to deliver daily cash deposits totaling over $40,000 a month.

Education

Franklin High School. Took advanced English and other classes. Member of award-winning band. Excellent attendance record. Superior communication skills. Graduated in top 30% of class.

Other

Active gymnastics competitor for four years. This taught me discipline, teamwork, how to follow instructions, and hard work. I am ambitious, outgoing, reliable, and willing to work.

Lisa's resumé makes it clear that she is talented and hardworking.

Combination Resumé for a Career Changer

Because this job seeker has no work experience in the computer programming field, this resumé focuses on her relevant education and transferable skills.

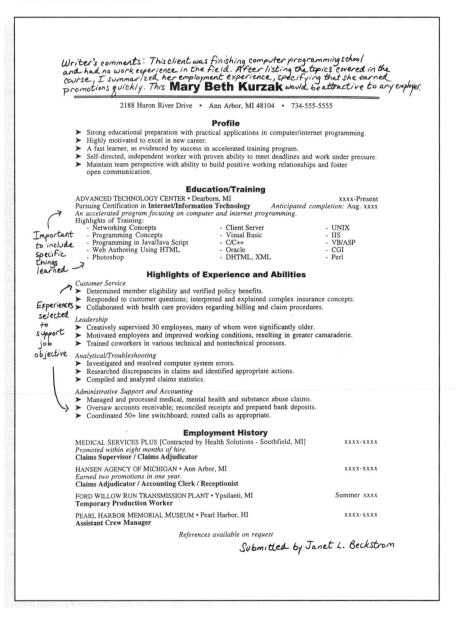

Writer's comments: This client was finishing computer programming school and had no work experience in the field. After listing the topics covered in the course, I summarized her employment experience, specifying that she earned promotions quickly. This Mary Beth Kurzak would be attractive to any employer.

Mary Beth Kurzak

2188 Huron River Drive • Ann Arbor, MI 48104 • 734-555-5555

Profile

➤ Strong educational preparation with practical applications in computer/internet programming.
➤ Highly motivated to excel in new career.
➤ A fast learner, as evidenced by success in accelerated training program.
➤ Self-directed, independent worker with proven ability to meet deadlines and work under pressure.
➤ Maintain team perspective with ability to build positive working relationships and foster open communication.

Education/Training

ADVANCED TECHNOLOGY CENTER • Dearborn, MI   xxxx-Present
Pursuing Certification in **Internet/Information Technology**   *Anticipated completion:* Aug. xxxx
An accelerated program focusing on computer and internet programming.
Highlights of Training:

Important to include specific things learned →

- Networking Concepts	- Client Server	- UNIX
- Programming Concepts	- Visual Basic	- IIS
- Programming in Java/Java Script	- C/C++	- VB/ASP
- Web Authoring Using HTML	- Oracle	- CGI
- Photoshop	- DHTML, XML	- Perl

Highlights of Experience and Abilities

Experiences selected to support job objective

Customer Service
➤ Determined member eligibility and verified policy benefits.
➤ Responded to customer questions; interpreted and explained complex insurance concepts.
➤ Collaborated with health care providers regarding billing and claim procedures.

Leadership
➤ Creatively supervised 30 employees, many of whom were significantly older.
➤ Motivated employees and improved working conditions, resulting in greater camaraderie.
➤ Trained coworkers in various technical and nontechnical processes.

Analytical/Troubleshooting
➤ Investigated and resolved computer system errors.
➤ Researched discrepancies in claims and identified appropriate actions.
➤ Compiled and analyzed claims statistics.

Administrative Support and Accounting
➤ Managed and processed medical, mental health and substance abuse claims.
➤ Oversaw accounts receivable; reconciled receipts and prepared bank deposits.
➤ Coordinated 50+ line switchboard; routed calls as appropriate.

Employment History

MEDICAL SERVICES PLUS [Contracted by Health Solutions - Southfield, MI]   xxxx-xxxx
Promoted within eight months of hire.
Claims Supervisor / Claims Adjudicator

HANSEN AGENCY OF MICHIGAN • Ann Arbor, MI   xxxx-xxxx
Earned two promotions in one year.
Claims Adjudicator / Accounting Clerk / Receptionist

FORD WILLOW RUN TRANSMISSION PLANT • Ypsilanti, MI   Summer xxxx
Temporary Production Worker

PEARL HARBOR MEMORIAL MUSEUM • Pearl Harbor, HI   xxxx-xxxx
Assistant Crew Manager

References available on request

Submitted by Janet L. Beckstrom

Combination Resumé with Matching JIST Card®

This resumé showcases the job seeker's substantial work experience. He emphasizes skills related to his job objective in the first section and then includes his work history in chronological form later. Peter's JIST Card® shows how these two job search tools can relate to each other effectively.

Carefully written combination resumé includes both skills and chronological sections.

Peter Neely

203 Evergreen Road
Houston, Texas 39127
Messages: (237) 555-XXXX   Pager: (237) 555-XXXX

POSITION DESIRED: Short- or Long-Distance Truck Driver

Summary of Work Experience:	Over fifteen years of stable work history, including substantial experience with diesel engines, electrical systems, and driving all sorts of trucks and heavy equipment.

Skills format allows him to stress experiences that are important for the job

SKILLS ←

Driving Record/ Licenses:	Have current Commercial Driving License and Chauffeur's License and am qualified and able to drive anything that rolls. No traffic citations or accidents for over 20 years.
Vehicle Maintenance:	I maintain correct maintenance schedules and avoid most breakdowns as a result. Substantial mechanical and electrical systems training and experience permit many breakdowns to be repaired immediately and avoid towing.
Record Keeping:	Excellent attention to detail. Familiar with recording procedures and submit required records on a timely basis.
Routing:	Thorough knowledge of most major interstate routes, with good map reading and route planning skills. I tend to get there on time and without incident.
Other:	Not afraid of hard work, flexible, get along well with others, meet deadlines, excellent attendance, responsible.

Lots of emphasis on reliability and results.

Key adaptive skills

WORK EXPERIENCE

Short chronological listings reinforce his good work history

2003—Present	CAPITAL TRUCK CENTER, Houston, Texas Pick up and deliver all types of commercial vehicles from across the United States. Am trusted with handling large sums of money and handling complex truck purchasing transactions.
2001—2003	QUALITY PLATING CO., Houston, Texas Promoted from production to Quality Control. Developed numerous production improvements resulting in substantial cost savings.
1999—2001	BLUE CROSS MANUFACTURING, Houston, Texas Received several increases in salary and responsibility before leaving for a more challenging position.
Prior to 1999	Truck delivery of food products to destinations throughout the South. Also responsible for up to 12 drivers and equipment maintenance personnel.

Summarizes "old" experience

OTHER

No dates on older military experience, but emphasizes related skills.

Four years' experience in the U.S. Air Force, driving and operating truck-mounted diesel power plants. Responsible for monitoring and maintenance on a rigid 24-hour schedule. Stationed in Alaska, California, Wyoming, and other states. Honorable discharge.

High school graduate plus training in diesel engines and electrical systems. Excellent health, love the outdoors, stable family life, nonsmoker and nondrinker.

Peter Neely   Messages: (237) 555-1234
                                                        Pager: (237) 555-9876

Position: Short- or Long-Distance Truck Driver

Background and Skills: Over fifteen years of stable work history including no traffic citations or accidents. Formal training in diesel mechanics and electrical systems. Familiar with most major destinations and have excellent map-reading and problem-solving abilities. I can handle responsibility and have a track record of getting things done.

Excellent health, good work history, dependable.

Chronological Resumés with Unique Graphic Touches

These two resumés show how simple graphic images can convey a job objective and make a resumé stand out in a crowd. Both also feature lots of white space for easy reading.

Writer's comments: Skip has limited broadcasting experience, so the challenge was to demonstrate his potential for success. The resume emphasizes Skip's production and on-air experience, stressing high-quality production, audience appeal and broad knowledge of many kinds of music. The graphic and fonts gave the resume the desired funky look.

Daniel "Skip" Norton

44 Buckingham Road • Allston, MA 02132 • (617) 555–5555

Summary

Over 5 years in broadcasting, including production, engineering, and on-air experience. Knowledge of extensive variety of music with appeal to broad range of listeners. Expertise in state-of-the art technology, including 24-track recording and digital editing. Ability to work well under pressure. Commitment to high standards of quality.

Related Experience

WZZX 92.9 FM Boston, MA   xxxx–present
Host, Producer, Engineer of six-hour weekly show called Daydream. Freeform format consisting of music from station's playlist and from extensive personal library and combining alternative and popular material.

- Expanded audience size by encouraging and increasing listener feedback.
- Successfully modified format to appeal to broader audience.
- Serve as substitute host for other shows, as needed.
- Maintain consistent, high standards of production by reviewing program tapes and responding to listener feedback.
- Introduce and feature new local artists.
- Produce promotional spots.

A very clean format with good use of white space

Boston Audio, Allston, MA   xxxx–present
Producer, Manager of my own project studio.

- Archive rare and odd records.
- Record material for promotions, including sound effects and music.
- Produce and record local artists for demos and release material.

Other Experience

Head Barista, Coffee Brewers, Newton, MA   xxxx–present
Assistant Manager, Coffee Specialties, Needham, MA   xxxx–xxxx

Education

Full Sail Center for the Recording Arts, Winter Park, FL   xxxx
Associate's Degree in Audio Engineering

Submitted by Wendy Gelberg

Writer's comments: The graphic tells you that this trim resumé is about food — the serving or preparation of it — before you have a chance to read one word.

François J. Boudreau

88 Harbor Place
Rock Cove, ME 00000

(207) 555-5555

Objective:

Assistant or Sous Chef

Good design, lots of white space, and few but well-chosen words make this an effective resumé

Summary of Qualifications:

- ✦ Associate's Degree in Culinary Arts with training in American and International Cuisines
- ✦ Restaurant experience has included broiler, grill, sauté, fryer, expo, breakfast and salads
- ✦ Able to handle a multitude of tasks at once, meeting deadlines under pressure
- ✦ Demonstrates ability to respond with speed and accuracy in a highly productive setting
- ✦ Works cooperatively and harmoniously with coworkers and supervisors
- ✦ Dedicated to quality in service and product

Experience:

Broiler/Prep Cook | Jacques Restaurant, West Cove, Maine (9/03 to Present)
200-seat Four Diamond restaurant featuring an extensive menu of French and American cuisine

Fry Cook | The Lobster Net, Port Hancock, Maine (2001–2003)
Indoor and outdoor dining, specializing in fresh lobsters and seafood; take-out and banquet service

Fry/Prep Cook | The Weathervane, Rocky Coast, Maine (2000–2001)
Traditional New England seafood served in a casual setting

Education:

Associate's Degree in Culinary Arts – Newbury College, Brookline, Massachusetts (2000)
Curriculum and Training included:

- ✧ Soup, Stock and Sauces
- ✧ Breads and Rolls
- ✧ Desserts
- ✧ Classical Bakeshop

- ✧ American Cuisine
- ✧ International Cuisine
- ✧ Yarde Manger
- ✧ Sanitation and Dining Room

Submitted by Becky J. Davis

Redefine What Counts as an Interview, Then Organize Your Time to Get Two a Day

The average job seeker gets about 5 interviews a month—fewer than 2 a week. Yet many job seekers use the methods in this book to get 2 interviews a day. Getting 2 interviews a day equals 10 a week and 40 a month. That's 800 percent more interviews than the average job seeker gets.

Who do you think will get a job more quickly?

However, getting 2 interviews a day is nearly impossible unless you redefine what counts as an interview. If you consider an interview in a different way, getting 2 a day is quite possible.

The New Definition of an Interview

An interview is any face-to-face contact with someone who has the authority to hire or supervise a person with your skills—even if no opening exists at the time when you interview.

If you use this new definition, it becomes *much* easier to get interviews. You can now interview with all sorts of potential employers, not just those who have job openings now. While most other job seekers look for advertised or actual openings, you can get interviews before a job opens up or before it is advertised and widely known. You will be considered for jobs that may soon be created but that others will not know about. And, of course, you can also interview for existing openings as everyone else does.

Spending as much time as possible on your job search and setting a job search schedule are important parts of Step 5. If you are a student or are working now, set aside what time you can for job seeking. Later, when you can look full-time, plan in advance to spend more time looking for your next job.

Make Your Search a Full-Time Job

Job seekers average fewer than 15 hours a week looking for work. On average, unemployment lasts three or more months, with some people out of work far longer (e.g., older workers and higher earners).

My many years of experience researching job seekers indicates that the more time you spend on your job search each week, the less time you will likely remain unemployed.

Of course, using the more effective job search methods presented in this book also helps. Many job search programs that teach job seekers my basic approach of using more effective methods and spending more time looking have proven that these seekers often find a job in half the average time. More importantly, many job seekers also find better jobs using these methods.

So, if you are unemployed and looking for a full-time job, you should plan to look on a full-time basis. It just makes sense to do so, although many do not, or they start out well but quickly get discouraged. Most job seekers simply don't have a structured plan—they have no idea what they are going to do next Thursday. The plan that follows will show you how to structure your job search like a job.

Decide How Much Time You Will Spend Looking for Work Each Day and Week

First and most importantly, decide how many hours you are willing to spend each week on your job search. You should spend a minimum of 25 hours a week on hard-core job search activities with no goofing around. Let me walk you through a simple but effective process to set a week's job search schedule.

Plan Your Job Search Week

1. How many hours are you willing to spend each week looking for a job? _____

   _____

2. Which days of the week will you spend looking for a job?

   _____

   _____

   _____

3. How many hours will you look each day?

   _____

   _____

4. At what times will you begin and end your job search on each of these days? _____

   _____

   _____

   _____

Create a Specific Daily Job Search Schedule

Having a specific daily schedule is essential because most job seekers find it hard to stay productive each day. The sample daily schedule that follows is the result of years of research into what schedule gets the best results. I tested many schedules in job search programs I ran, and this particular schedule worked best.

You can review the sample daily schedule for ideas on creating your own, but I urge you to consider using one like this.

Insider Tip

Time is money.

The daily schedule you see on this page is based on my years of managing results-oriented job search programs. As simple as it seems, keeping a schedule like this will cut your job search time. Many thousands have used it as a basis for their daily job search plan, and it does work.

A Sample Daily Schedule That Works

Time	Activity
7 A.M.	Get up, shower, dress, eat breakfast.
8–8:15 A.M.	Organize work space; review schedule for today's interviews and promised follow-ups; update schedule as needed.
8:15–9 A.M.	Review old leads for follow-up needed today; develop new leads from want ads, yellow pages, the Internet, warm contact lists, and other sources; complete daily contact list.
9–10 A.M.	Make phone calls and set up interviews.
10–10:15 A.M.	Take a break.
10:15–11 A.M.	Make more phone calls, set up more interviews.
11 A.M.–Noon	Send follow-up notes and do other "office" activities as needed.
Noon–1 P.M.	Lunch break, relax.
1–3 P.M.	Go on interviews, make cold contacts in the field.
Evening	Read job search books, make calls to warm contacts not reachable during the day, work on a "better" resumé, spend time with friends and family, exercise, relax.

Do It Now: Get a Daily Planner and Create a Specific Daily Schedule
If you are not accustomed to using a daily schedule book or electronic planner, promise yourself to get a good one tomorrow.

Choose one that allows plenty of space for each day's plan on an hourly basis, plus room for daily to-do lists. Write in your daily schedule in advance, and then add interviews as they come. Get used to carrying it with you and use it!

There are a variety of computer programs that can be used to help organize your job search. And pocket-sized schedulers can be very helpful. If you have these resources, adapt the advice I have provided in this step to use these tools. If you don't use electronic tools, a simple schedule book and other paper systems will work just fine.

Dramatically Improve Your Interviewing Skills

Interviews are where the job search action is. You have to get them; then you have to do well in them. According to surveys of employers, most job seekers do not effectively present the skills they have to do the job. Even worse, most job seekers can't answer one or more problem questions. This lack of performance in interviews is one reason why employers will often hire a job seeker who does well in the interview instead of someone with better credentials.

The good news is that you can do simple things to dramatically improve your interviewing skills. This section will emphasize interviewing tips and techniques that make the most difference.

Your First Impression May Be the Only One You Make

Some research suggests that if the interviewer forms a negative impression in the first five minutes of an interview, your chances of getting a job offer approach zero. I know from experience that many job seekers can create a lasting negative impression in seconds.

A positive first impression is so important—here are some suggestions to help you get off to a good start:

- **Dress and groom like the interviewer is likely to be dressed—but cleaner!**

  Employer surveys find that almost half of all people's dress or grooming create an initial negative impression. So this is a *big* problem. If necessary, get advice on your interviewing outfits from someone who dresses well. Pay close attention to your grooming, too. Little things do count.

- **Be early.**

  Leave in plenty of time to be a few minutes early to an interview.

- **Be friendly and respectful with the receptionist.**

  Doing otherwise will often get back to the interviewer and result in a quick rejection.

- **Follow the interviewer's lead in the first few minutes.**

  It's often informal small talk but very important for that person to see how you interact. This is a good time to make a positive comment on the organization or even something you see in the office.

- **Do some homework on the organization before you go.**

  You can often get information on a business and on industry trends from the Internet or a library.

- **Make a good impression before you arrive.**

  Your resumé, e-mails, applications, and other written correspondence create an impression before the interview, so make them professional and error free.

A Traditional Interview Is Not a Friendly Exchange

In a traditional interview situation, there is a job opening, and you will be one of several who've applied for it. In this setting, the employer's task is to eliminate all applicants but one. The interviewer's questions are designed to elicit information that can be used to screen you out. And your objective is to avoid getting screened out. It's hardly an open and honest interaction, is it?

This illustrates yet another advantage of setting up interviews before an opening exists. This eliminates the stress of a traditional interview. Employers are not trying to screen you out, and you are not trying to keep them from finding out stuff about you.

Having said that, knowing how to answer questions that might be asked in a traditional interview is good preparation for any interview you face.

How to Answer Tough Interview Questions

Your answers to a few key problem questions may determine if you get a job offer. There are simply too many possible interview questions to cover one by one. Instead, the ten basic questions that follow cover variations of most other interview questions. So, if you can learn to answer these ten questions well, you will know how to answer most others.

Top Ten Problem Interview Questions

1. Why should I hire you?
2. Why don't you tell me about yourself?
3. What are your major strengths?
4. What are your major weaknesses?
5. What sort of pay do you expect to receive?
6. How does your previous experience relate to the jobs we have here?
7. What are your plans for the future?
8. What will your former employer (or references) say about you?
9. Why are you looking for this type of position, and why here?
10. Why don't you tell me about your personal situation?

The Three-Step Process for Answering Interview Questions

I know this might seem too simple, but the three-step process is easy to remember and can help you create a good answer to most interview questions. The technique has worked for thousands of people, so consider trying it. The three steps are

1. Understand what is really being asked.
2. Answer the question briefly.
3. Answer the real concern.

Step 1. Understand what is really being asked.

Most questions are designed to find out about your self-management skills and personality, but interviewers are rarely this blunt. The employer's *real* question is often one or more of the following:

> *Can I depend on you?*
>
> *Are you easy to get along with?*
>
> *Are you a good worker?*
>
> *Do you have the experience and training to do the job if we hire you?*
>
> *Are you likely to stay on the job for a reasonable period of time and be productive?*

Ultimately, if you don't convince the employer that you will stay and be a good worker, it won't matter if you have the best credentials— he or she won't hire you.

Step 2. Answer the question briefly.

Present the facts of your particular work experience, but . . . *present them as advantages, not disadvantages.*

Many interview questions encourage you to provide negative information. One classic question I included in my list of Top Ten Problem Interview Questions was, "What are your major weaknesses?" This is obviously a trick question, and many people are just not prepared for it.

A good response is to mention something that is not very damaging, such as *"I have been told that I am a perfectionist, sometimes not delegating as effectively as I might."*

However, your answer is not complete until you continue with Step 3.

Step 3. Answer the real concern by presenting your related skills.

Base your answer on the key skills you have that support the job, and give examples to support these skills.

In the previous example (about failing to delegate as a weakness), a good skills statement that addresses the interviewer's real concern might be the following:

112

I've been working on this problem and have learned to let my staff do more, making sure that they have good training and supervision. I've found that their performance improves, and it frees me up to do other things.

In another scenario, an employer might say to a recent graduate, "We were looking for someone with more experience in this field. Why should we consider you?" Here is one possible answer:

I'm sure there are people who have more experience, but I do have more than six years of work experience including three years of advanced training and hands-on experience using the latest methods and techniques. Because my training is recent, I am open to new ideas and am used to working hard and learning quickly.

Whatever your situation, learn to answer questions that present you well. It's essential to communicate your skills during an interview, and the three-step process can help you answer problem questions and dramatically improve your responses. It works!

The Most Important Interview Question of All: "Why Should I Hire You?"

This is the most important question to answer well. Do you have a convincing argument why someone should hire you over someone else? If you don't, you probably won't get that job you really want. So think carefully about why someone *should* hire you and practice your response. Then, make sure you communicate this in the interview, even if the interviewer never asks the question in a clear way.

Tips on Negotiating Pay—How to Earn a Thousand Dollars a Minute

The following statements are *not* recommended ways to start negotiating for pay:

I can't even discuss the job before I know if you'll meet my price range.

I really don't care about money . . .

What do you think I'm worth?

My bottom line is $45,000, plus an expense account.

Well, I'd like $3 billion, but you probably can't afford me. Ha, ha . . .

I made $30,000 a year in my last job. Can you match that?

I'll work for any amount. I just need a job.

When it comes time to negotiate your pay, the above tactics won't work. Instead, remember these few essential ideas:

The only time to negotiate is after you have been offered the job.

Employers want to know how much you want to be paid so that they can eliminate you from consideration. They figure, if you want too much, you won't be happy with their job and won't stay. And, if you will take too little, they may think you don't have enough experience. So *never* discuss your salary expectations until an employer offers you the job.

If pressed, speak in terms of wide pay ranges.

If you are pushed to reveal your pay expectations early in an interview, ask the interviewer what the normal pay range is for this job. Interviewers will often tell you, and you can say that you would consider offers in this range.

If you are forced to be more specific, speak in terms of a wide pay range. For example, if you figure that the company will likely pay from $20,000 to $25,000 a year, say that you would consider "any fair offer in the low to mid-twenties." This statement covers the employer's range *and goes a bit higher.* If all else fails, tell the interviewer that you would consider any reasonable offer.

For this to work, you must know in advance what the job is likely to pay. You can get this information by asking people who do similar work, or from a variety of books and Internet sources of career information.

Salary Negotiation Rule
The one who names a specific number first, loses.

Close the Interview Effectively

Most interviews simply end with a fizzle, but there are some things you can do while an interview is ending that can make a difference. Even if you are not certain you want this job, it is wise to go after a job offer—you can always turn it down later. And it is quite possible that there are other jobs with the same employer, if the interviewer likes you.

- **Emphasize your key skills.**

  Tell the interviewer why they should hire you over someone else by reviewing the skills you have to do this job.
- **Ask for the job.**

  If you do want the job, say so. Employers want to hire people who are enthusiastic about doing the sort of work they need done.
- **Arrange to call back.**

  Ask for a specific time and date to call the employer back and ask questions or learn of your status.

Don't Say No Too Quickly

Never, ever turn down a job offer during an interview! Instead, thank the interviewer for the offer and ask to consider the offer overnight. You can turn it down tomorrow, saying how much you appreciate the offer and asking to be considered for other jobs that pay better or whatever.

But, this is no time to be playing games. If you want the job, you should say so. And it is okay to ask for additional pay or other concessions. But if you simply can't accept the offer, say why and ask the interviewer to keep you in mind for future opportunities. You just never know.

Follow Up on All Job Leads

It's a fact: People who follow up with potential employers and with others in their network get jobs faster than those who do not. Here are a few rules to guide you in your job search.

Four Rules for Effective Follow-Up

1. Send a thank-you note or e-mail to every person who helps you in your job search.

2. Send the note within 24 hours after speaking with the person.

3. Enclose JIST Cards® with thank-you notes and all other correspondence.

4. Develop a system to keep following up with good contacts.

Thank-You Notes Make a Difference

While thank-you notes can be e-mailed, most people appreciate and are more impressed by a mailed note. Here are some tips about mailed thank-you notes that you can easily adapt to e-mail use.

Thank-you notes can be handwritten or typed on quality paper and matching envelopes. Keep them simple, neat, and error free. And make sure to include a few copies of your JIST Cards®. An example of a simple thank-you note follows.

Sample Thank-You Note

2244 Riverwood Avenue
Philadelphia, PA 17963
April 16, XXXX

Ms. Helen A. Colcord
Henderson & Associates, Inc.
1801 Washington Blvd., Suite 1201
Philadelphia, PA 17993

Dear Ms. Colcord:

Thank you for sharing your time with me so generously today. I really appreciated seeing your state-of-the-art computer equipment.

Your advice has already proved helpful. I have an appointment to meet with Mr. Robert Hopper on Friday. As you anticipated, he does intend to add more computer operators in the next few months.

In case you think of someone else who might need a person like me, I'm enclosing another JIST Card. I will let you know how the interview with Mr. Hopper goes.

Sincerely,

William Henderson

William Henderson

Develop an Organized System for Following Up

If you use contact management software, use it to schedule follow-up activities. Pocket schedulers and organizers can also be very helpful to remind you of interviews and things to do. A simple paper system can work very well also or can be adapted for setting up your contact management software.

Following are a few ideas to help you follow up more effectively.

Use Job Lead Cards

By using the job search methods you have learned in this book, you can develop hundreds of contacts. Keeping track of them is more than any person's memory can handle.

Look at the following sample job lead card. It shows the kind of information you can keep about each person who helps you in your job search. (If desired, you can list the same kind of information in a computer database.)

To start such a system, buy a few hundred 3-by-5-inch cards. Create one job lead card for every person who gives you a referral or who is a possible employer. Keep brief notes each time you talk with that person, to help you remember important details for your next contact. Notice that the notes on the sample card are short, but they contain enough data to help the job seeker remember what happened and when to follow up.

Organization: _Mutual Health Insurance_

Contact person: _Anna Tomey_

Phone number: _(555) 555-2211_

Source of lead: _Aunt Ruth_

Notes: _4/10 called. Anna on vacation. Call back 4/15. 4/15 Interview set 4/20 at 1:30. 4/20 Anna showed me around. They use the same computers we used in school. Sent thank-you note and JIST Card. Call back 5/1. 5/1 Second interview 5/8 at 9 a.m._

Maintain a Job Search Follow-Up Box

As you contact more and more people in your job search, the number of job lead cards you create for future follow-up will increase. You will get more and more new leads as you follow up with people you've contacted one or more times in the past. You need a way to organize all those job lead cards.

Most department and office supply stores sell small file boxes for 3-by-5-inch cards, as well as tabbed dividers for these boxes. Everything you need will cost about $10.

Set up file box dividers for each day of the month, numbering them 1 through 31. Then, file each completed job lead card under the date when you want to follow up on it.

Every Monday, simply review all the job lead cards filed for the week. On your weekly schedule, list any interviews or follow-up calls you promised to make at a particular date and time. At the start of each day, pull the job lead cards filed under that date. List appointments and calls on your Daily Job Search Contact Sheet (described in the next section).

Keep Trying

Here are some other ways you can use this simple follow-up system to get results:

- You get the name of a person to call, but you can't reach this person right away. Create a job lead card and file it under tomorrow's date.
- You call someone from a yellow pages listing, but she is busy this week. She asks you to call back in two weeks. You file this job lead card under the date for two weeks in the future.
- You get an interview with a person who doesn't have any openings now. He gives you the name of someone who might have an opening. After you send a thank-you note and JIST Card® to the original contact, you file his name under a date a few weeks in the future, so that you can check for any future openings.

Following up with past contacts is one of the most effective ways of getting a job! The job search follow-up box is a simple, inexpensive system that works very well. You can do the same thing with computer scheduling software, but it doesn't work any better than the box.

Insider Tip

Is a computer or PDA better than 3-by-5-inch cards?

Maybe not. If you already use a PDA or scheduling or time management software, go ahead and use it to manage your job search contacts. If you don't use such software now, you will probably be better off trying the card system I suggest. The reason is simple—it works. Instead of spending your time messing with new software, you can go right to work making contacts and getting results.

Daily Job Search Contact Sheet

If you do what I suggest, you will try each day to set up two interviews. To get this done, you will have to contact a lot of people. Some you will contact for the first time; others you will follow up with from earlier contacts.

To get you started, I suggest that you begin each day by completing a Daily Job Search Contact Sheet. Use it to list at least 20 people or organizations to call. Use any sources to get these leads, including people you know, referrals, yellow pages leads, Internet leads, and want ads. An example of a contact sheet follows.

Sample Daily Job Search Contact Sheet

Contact Name/ Organization	Referral Source	Job Lead Card?	Phone Number/ E-Mail Address
1. Manager/The Flower Show	Yellow pages	Yes	555-6041
2. Manager/Rainbow Flowers	Listed on Rainbow's Web site	Yes	admin@rainbow flowers.com
3. Joyce Wilson/ Hartley Nurseries	John Lee	Yes	555-2224
4. John Mullahy/ Roses, Etc.	Uncle Jim	Yes	555-4226
5. None/Plants to Go	Want Ad	Yes	555-7016

In Closing

This is a short book, but it may be all you need to get a better job in less time. I hope this will be true for you and wish you well in your search.

Do remember that you won't get a job offer because someone knocks on your door and offers one. Job seeking does involve luck, but you are more likely to get lucky if you are out getting interviews.

I'll close this book with a few final tips:

- **Approach your job search as if it were a job itself.**
  Create and stick to a daily schedule, and spend at least 25 hours a week looking.
- **Follow up on each lead you generate and ask each contact for referrals.**
- **Set out each day to schedule at least two interviews.**
  Use the new definition of an interview, which includes talking to businesses that don't have an opening now.
- **Send out lots of thank-you notes and JIST Cards®.**
- **When you want the job, tell the employer that you want it and why the company should hire you over someone else.**

Don't get discouraged. There are lots of jobs out there, and someone needs an employee with your skills—your job is to find that someone.

I wish you luck in your job search and in your life.

The Essential Job Search Data Worksheet

Take some time to complete this worksheet carefully. It will help you write your resumé and answer interview questions. You can also tear it out and take it with you to help complete applications and as a reference throughout your job search.

Use an erasable pen or pencil to allow for corrections. Whenever possible, emphasize skills and accomplishments that support your ability to do the job you want. Use extra sheets as needed.

Essential Job Search Data Worksheet

Your name _____

Date completed _____

Job objective _____

_____

_____

_____

(continues)

Essential Job Search Data Worksheet *(continued)*

Key Accomplishments

List three accomplishments that best prove your ability to do the kind of job you want.

1. _____

2. _____

3. _____

Education and Training

Name of high school(s); years attended _____

_____

_____

Subjects related to job objective _____

_____

_____

_____

_____

Related extracurricular activities/hobbies/leisure activities

_____

_____

_____

_____

_____

(continues)

Accomplishments/things you did well _____

_____

_____

_____

_____

Specific things you can do as a result _____

_____

_____

_____

_____

Schools you attended after high school;
years attended; degrees/certificates earned _____

_____

_____

_____

_____

Courses related to job objective _____

_____

_____

_____

_____

(continues)

Essential Job Search Data Worksheet *(continued)*

Related extracurricular activities/hobbies/leisure activities

_____

_____

_____

_____

Accomplishments/things you did well _____

_____

_____

_____

Specific things you can do as a result _____

_____

_____

_____

Other Training

Include formal or informal learning, workshops, military training, things you learned on-the-job or from hobbies—anything that will help support your job objective. Include specific dates, certificates earned, or other details as needed.

_____

_____

(continues)

_____

_____

Work and Volunteer History

List your most recent job first, followed by each previous job. Military experience, unpaid or volunteer work, and work in a family business should be included here, too. If needed, use additional sheets to cover *all* significant paid or unpaid work experiences.

Emphasize details that will help support your new job objective! Include numbers to support what you did: number of people served over one or more years, number of transactions processed, percentage of sales increased, total inventory value you were responsible for, payroll of the staff you supervised, total budget responsible for, and so on.

Emphasize results you achieved, using numbers to support them whenever possible. Mentioning these things on your resumé and in an interview will help you get the job you want!

Job 1

Dates employed _____

_____

Name of organization _____

_____

Supervisor's name and job title _____

_____

Address _____

_____

_____

_____

(continues)

Essential Job Search Data Worksheet *(continued)*

Phone number/e-mail address/Web site _____

_____

_____

What did you accomplish and do well? _____

_____

_____

_____

Things you learned, skills you developed or used _____

_____

_____

_____

Raises, promotions, positive evaluations, awards _____

_____

_____

_____

_____

Computer software, hardware, and other equipment you used

_____

_____

_____

_____

(continues)

Other details that might support your job objective _____

_____

_____

_____

Job 2

Dates employed _____

_____

Name of organization _____

_____

Supervisor's name and job title _____

_____

Address _____

_____

_____

_____

Phone number/e-mail address/Web site _____

_____

_____

What did you accomplish and do well? _____

_____

_____

_____

(continues)

Essential Job Search Data Worksheet *(continued)*

Things you learned, skills you developed or used _____

_____

_____

_____

Raises, promotions, positive evaluations, awards _____

_____

_____

_____

Computer software, hardware, and other equipment you used

_____

_____

_____

Other details that might support your job objective _____

_____

_____

_____

(continues)

Job 3

Dates employed _____

_____

Name of organization _____

_____

Supervisor's name and job title _____

_____

Address _____

_____

_____

_____

Phone number/e-mail address/Web site _____

_____

_____

What did you accomplish and do well? _____

_____

_____

_____

Things you learned, skills you developed or used _____

_____

_____

_____

(continues)

Essential Job Search Data Worksheet *(continued)*

Raises, promotions, positive evaluations, awards _____

_____

_____

_____

_____

Computer software, hardware, and other equipment you used

_____

_____

_____

Other details that might support your job objective _____

_____

_____

_____

_____

References

Think of people who know your work well and will say positive things about your work and character. Past supervisors are best.

Contact them and tell them what type of job you want and your qualifications, and ask what they will say about you if contacted by a potential employer. Some employers will not provide references by phone, so ask them for a letter of reference for you in advance.

(continues)

If a past employer may say negative things, negotiate what they will say or get written references from others you worked with there.

Reference name _____

_____

Position or title _____

_____

Relationship to you _____

_____

Contact information (complete
address, phone number, e-mail address) _____

_____

_____

_____

_____

Reference name _____

_____

Position or title _____

_____

Relationship to you _____

_____

(continues)

Essential Job Search Data Worksheet *(continued)*

Contact information (complete
address, phone number, e-mail address) _____

_____

_____

_____

_____

_____

Reference name _____

_____

Position or title _____

_____

Relationship to you _____

_____

Contact information (complete
address, phone number, e-mail address) _____

_____

_____

_____

_____

_____

Sample Job Description from the *Occupational Outlook Handbook*

The following is an example of one of the many job descriptions that can be found in the *Occupational Outlook Handbook* (OOH), compiled by the U.S. Department of Labor. Reviewing OOH job descriptions will help you match your skills to jobs that interest you and will introduce you to the powerful skills language that draws employers' attention.

The OOH can be found in most libraries, as well as on the Internet at the Web site www.stats.bls.gov/oco/home.htm. The OOH is updated every two years, so make sure you are using a current edition so that you get the most recent information available.

Accountants and Auditors

Related O*NET Occupations: 13-2011.01 *Accountants*; 13-2011.02 *Auditors*

Significant Points

- Most jobs require at least a bachelor's degree in accounting or a related field.
- Overall job opportunities should be favorable, although job seekers who obtain professional recognition through certification or licensure, a master's degree, proficiency in accounting and auditing computer software, or specialized expertise will have an advantage.
- An increase in the number of businesses, changing financial laws and regulations, and increased scrutiny of company finances will drive growth of accountants and auditors.

Nature of the Work

Accountants and auditors help to ensure that the Nation's firms are run efficiently, its public records kept accurately, and its taxes paid properly and on time. They perform these vital functions by offering an increasingly wide array of business and accounting services to their clients. These services include public, management, and government accounting, as well as internal auditing. Beyond the fundamental tasks of the occupation—preparing, analyzing, and verifying financial documents in order to provide information to clients—many accountants now are required to possess a wide range of knowledge and skills. Accountants and auditors are broadening the services they offer to include budget analysis, financial and investment planning, information technology consulting, and limited legal services.

Specific job duties vary widely among the four major fields of accounting: public, management, government, and internal.

Public accountants perform a broad range of accounting, auditing, tax, and consulting activities for their clients, who may be corporations, governments, nonprofit organizations, or individuals. For example, some public accountants concentrate on tax matters, such as advising companies of the tax advantages and disadvantages of certain business decisions and preparing individual income tax returns. Others offer advice in areas such as compensation or employee healthcare benefits, the design of accounting and data-processing systems, and the selection of controls to safeguard assets. Still others audit clients' financial statements and report to investors and authorities that the statements have been correctly prepared and reported. Public accountants, many of whom are Certified Public Accountants (CPAs), generally have their own businesses or work for public accounting firms.

Some public accountants specialize in forensic accounting—investigating and interpreting white collar crimes such as securities fraud and embezzlement, bankruptcies and contract disputes, and other complex and possibly criminal financial transactions, such as money laundering by organized criminals. Forensic accountants combine their knowledge of accounting and finance with law and investigative techniques in order to determine if illegal activity is going on. Many forensic accountants work closely with law enforcement personnel and lawyers during investigations and often appear as expert witnesses during trials.

In response to the recent accounting scandals, new Federal legislation restricts the nonauditing services that public accountants can provide to clients. If an accounting firm audits a client's financial statements, that same firm cannot provide advice in the areas of human resources, technology, investment banking, or legal matters, although accountants may still advise on tax issues, such as establishing a tax shelter. Accountants may still advise other clients in these areas, or may provide advice within their own firm.

Management accountants—also called cost, managerial, industrial, corporate, or private accountants—record and analyze the financial information of the companies for which they work. Other responsibilities include budgeting, performance evaluation, cost management, and asset management. Usually, management accountants are part of executive teams involved in strategic planning or new-product development. They analyze and interpret the financial information that corporate executives need to make sound business decisions. They also prepare financial reports for nonmanagement groups, including stockholders, creditors, regulatory agencies, and tax authorities. Within accounting departments, they may work in various areas, including financial analysis, planning and budgeting, and cost accounting.

Government accountants and auditors work in the public sector, maintaining and examining the records of government agencies and auditing private businesses and individuals whose activities are subject to government regulations or taxation. Accountants employed by Federal, State, and local governments guarantee that revenues are received and expenditures are made in accordance with laws and regulations. Those who are employed by the Federal Government may work as Internal Revenue Service agents or in financial management, financial institution examination, or budget analysis and administration.

Internal auditors verify the accuracy of their organization's internal records and check for mismanagement, waste, or fraud. Internal auditing is an increasingly important area of accounting and auditing. Internal auditors examine and evaluate their firms' financial and information systems, management procedures, and internal controls to ensure that records are accurate and controls are adequate to protect against fraud and waste. They also review company operations—evaluating their efficiency, effectiveness, and compliance with corporate policies and procedures, laws, and government regulations. There are many types of highly specialized auditors, such as electronic data-processing, environmental, engineering, legal, insurance premium, bank, and healthcare auditors. As computer systems make information timelier, internal auditors help managers to base their decisions on actual data, rather than personal observation. Internal auditors also may recommend controls for their organization's computer system to ensure the reliability of the system and the integrity of the data.

Computers are rapidly changing the nature of the work for most accountants and auditors. With the aid of special software packages, accountants summarize transactions in standard formats for financial records and organize data in special formats for financial analysis. These accounting packages greatly reduce the amount of tedious manual work associated with data management and record keeping. Computers enable accountants and auditors to be more mobile and to use their clients' computer systems to extract information from databases and the Internet. As a result, a growing number of accountants and auditors with extensive computer skills specialize in correcting problems with software or in developing software to meet unique data management and analytical needs. Accountants also are beginning to perform more technical duties, such as implementing, controlling, and auditing systems and networks, and developing technology plans and budgets.

Increasingly, accountants also are assuming the role of a personal financial advisor. They not only provide clients with accounting and tax help, but also help them develop personal budgets, manage assets and investments, plan for retirement, and recognize and reduce exposure to risks. This role is a response to client demands for a single trustworthy individual or firm to meet all of their financial needs. However, accountants are restricted from providing these services to clients whose financial statements they also prepare. (See financial analysts and personal financial advisors elsewhere.)

Working Conditions

Most accountants and auditors work in a typical office setting. Self-employed accountants may be able to do part of their work at home. Accountants and auditors employed by public accounting firms and government agencies may travel frequently to perform audits at branches of their firm, clients' places of business, or government facilities.

Most accountants and auditors generally work a standard 40-hour week, but many work longer hours, particularly if they are self-employed and have numerous clients. Tax specialists often work long hours during the tax season.

Employment

Accountants and auditors held about 1.1 million jobs in 2002. They worked throughout private industry and government, but 1 out of 5 wage and salary accountants worked for accounting, tax preparation, bookkeeping, and payroll services firms. Approximately 1 out of 10 accountants or auditors were self-employed.

Many accountants and auditors are unlicensed management accountants, internal auditors, or government accountants and auditors; however, a large number are licensed Certified Public Accountants. Most accountants and auditors work in urban areas, where public accounting firms and central or regional offices of businesses are concentrated.

Some individuals with backgrounds in accounting and auditing are full-time college and university faculty; others teach part time while working as self-employed accountants or employed as accountants for private industry or government. (See teachers—postsecondary.)

Training and Other Requirements

Most accountant and auditor positions require at least a bachelor's degree in accounting or a related field. Beginning accounting and auditing positions in the Federal Government, for example, usually require 4 years of college (including 24 semester hours in accounting or auditing) or an equivalent combination of education and experience. Some employers prefer applicants with a master's degree in accounting, or with a master's degree in business administration with a concentration in accounting.

Previous experience in accounting or auditing can help an applicant get a job. Many colleges offer students an opportunity to gain experience through summer or part-time internship programs conducted by public accounting or business firms. In addition, practical knowledge of computers and their applications in accounting and internal auditing is a great asset for jobseekers in the accounting field.

Professional recognition through certification or licensure provides a distinct advantage in the job market. CPAs are licensed by a State Board of Accountancy. The vast majority of States require CPA candidates to be college graduates, but a few States substitute a number of years of public accounting experience for a college degree. As of early 2003, based on recommendations made by the American Institute of Certified Public Accountants (AICPA), 42 States and the District of Columbia required CPA candidates to complete 150 semester hours of college course work—an additional 30 hours beyond the usual 4-year bachelor's degree. Another five States—Arizona, Minnesota, New Mexico, New York, and Virginia— have adopted similar legislation that will become effective between 2004 and 2009. Colorado, Delaware, New Hampshire, and Vermont are the only States that do not require 150 semester hours. Many schools have altered their curricula accordingly with most programs offering masters degrees as part of the 150 hours, and prospective accounting majors should carefully research accounting curricula and the requirements of any States in which they hope to become licensed.

All States use the four-part Uniform CPA Examination prepared by the AICPA. The 2-day CPA examination is rigorous, and only about one-quarter of those who take it each year passes every part they attempt. Candidates are not required to pass all four parts at once, but most States require candidates to pass at least two parts for partial credit and to complete all four sections within a certain period. Most States also require applicants for a CPA certificate to have some accounting experience. In May 2004, the CPA exam will become computerized and offered quarterly at various testing centers throughout the United States.

The AICPA also offers members with valid CPA certificates the option to receive the Accredited in Business Valuation (ABV), Certified Information Technology Professional (CITP), or Personal Financial Specialist (PFS) designations. The addition of these designations to the CPA distinguishes those accountants with a certain level of expertise in the nontraditional areas in which accountants are practicing more frequently. The ABV designation requires a written exam, as well as completion of a minimum of 10 business valuation projects that demonstrate a candidate's experience and competence. The CITP requires payment of a fee, a written statement of intent, and the achievement of a set number of points awarded for business experience and education. Those who do not meet the required number of points may substitute a written exam.

Candidates for the PFS designation also must achieve a certain level of points, based on experience and education, and must pass a written exam and submit references.

Nearly all States require CPAs and other public accountants to complete a certain number of hours of continuing professional education before their licenses can be renewed. The professional associations representing accountants sponsor numerous courses, seminars, group study programs, and other forms of continuing education.

Accountants and auditors also can seek to obtain other forms of credentials from professional societies on a voluntary basis. Voluntary certification can attest to professional competence in a specialized field of accounting and auditing. It also can certify that a recognized level of professional competence has been achieved by accountants and auditors who have acquired some skills on the job, without the formal education or public accounting work experience needed to meet the rigorous standards required to take the CPA examination.

The Institute of Management Accountants (IMA) confers the Certified Management Accountant (CMA) designation upon applicants who complete a bachelor's degree or attain a minimum score on specified graduate school entrance exams. Applicants, who must have worked at least 2 years in management accounting, also must pass a four-part examination, agree to meet continuing education requirements, and comply with standards of professional conduct. The CMA program is administered by the Institute of Certified Management Accountants, an affiliate of the IMA.

Graduates from accredited colleges and universities who have worked for 2 years as internal auditors and have passed a four-part examination may earn the Certified Internal Auditor (CIA) designation from the Institute of Internal Auditors (IIA). The IIA recently implemented three new specialty designations—Certification in Control Self-Assessment (CCSA), Certified Government Auditing Professional (CGAP), and Certified Financial Services Auditor (CFSA). Requirements are similar to those of the CIA. The Information Systems Audit and Control Association confers the Certified Information Systems Auditor (CISA) designation upon candidates who pass an examination and have 5 years of experience in auditing information systems. Auditing or data-processing experience and a college education may be substituted for up to 2 years of work experience in this program. For instance, an internal auditor might be a CPA, CIA, and CISA.

The Accreditation Council for Accountancy and Taxation, a satellite organization of the National Society of Public Accountants, confers three designations—Accredited Business Accountant (ABA), Accredited Tax Advisor (ATA), and Accredited Tax Preparer (ATP)—on accountants specializing in tax preparation for small- and medium-sized businesses. Candidates for the ABA must pass an exam, while candidates for the ATA and ATP must complete the required coursework and pass an exam. Often, a practitioner will hold multiple licenses and designations.

The Association of Government Accountants grants the Certified Government Financial Manager (CGFM) designation for accountants, auditors, and other government financial personnel at the Federal, State, and local levels. Candidates must have a minimum of a bachelor's degree, 24 hours of study in financial management, and 2 years' experience in government, and must pass a series of three exams. The exams cover topics in governmental environment; governmental accounting, financial reporting, and budgeting; and financial management and control.

Persons planning a career in accounting should have an aptitude for mathematics and be able to analyze, compare, and interpret facts and figures quickly. They must be able to clearly communicate both written and verbally the results of their work to clients and managers. Accountants and auditors must be good at working with people, as well as with business systems and computers. At a minimum, accountants should be familiar with basic accounting software packages. Because financial decisions are made based on their statements and services, accountants and auditors should have high standards of integrity.

Job Outlook

Employment of accountants and auditors is expected to grow about as fast as the average for all occupations through the year 2012. An increase in the number of businesses, changing financial laws and regulations, and increased scrutiny of company finances will drive growth. In addition to openings resulting from growth, the need to replace accountants and auditors who retire or transfer to other occupations will produce numerous job openings in this large occupation.

As the economy grows, the number of business establishments will increase, requiring more accountants and auditors to set up books, prepare taxes, and provide management advice. As these businesses grow, the volume and complexity of information developed by accountants and auditors regarding costs, expenditures, and taxes will increase as well. Increased need for accountants and auditors will arise from changes in legislation related to taxes, financial reporting standards, business investments, mergers, and other financial matters. The growth of international business also has led to more demand for accounting expertise and services related to international trade and accounting rules, as well as to international mergers and acquisitions. These trends should create more jobs for accountants and auditors.

As a result of the recent accounting scandals, Federal legislation was enacted to increase penalties, and make company executives personally responsible for falsely reporting financial information. These changes should lead to increased scrutiny of company finances and accounting procedures, and should create opportunities for accountants and auditors, particularly Certified Public Accountants, to more thoroughly audit financial records. In order to ensure finances comply with the law before public accountants conduct audits, management accountants and internal auditors will increasingly be needed to discover and eliminate fraud. And, in an effort to make government agencies more efficient and accountable, demand for government accountants should increase.

Increased awareness of financial crimes such as embezzlement, bribery, and securities fraud will also increase the demand for forensic accountants to detect illegal financial activity by individuals, companies, and organized crime rings. Computer technology has made these crimes easier to commit, and it is on the rise. But, development of new computer software and electronic surveillance technology has also made tracking down financial criminals easier, thus increasing the ease and likelihood that forensic accountants will discover their crimes. As success rates of investigations grow, demand will also grow for forensic accountants.

The changing role of accountants and auditors also will spur job growth, although this growth will be limited as a result of financial scandals. In response to demand, some accountants were offering more financial management and consulting services as they assumed a greater advisory role and developed more sophisticated accounting systems. Since Federal legislation now prohibits accountants from providing nontraditional services to clients whose books they audit, opportunities for accountants to do non-audit work could be limited. However, accountants will still be able to advise on other financial matters for clients that are not publicly traded companies, and for nonaudit clients, but growth in these areas will be slower than in the past. Also, due to the increasing popularity of tax preparation firms and computer software, accountants will shift away from tax preparation. As computer programs continue to simplify some accounting-related tasks, clerical staff will increasingly handle many routine calculations.

Overall, job opportunities for accountants and auditors should be favorable. After most States instituted the 150-hour rule for CPAs, enrollment in accounting programs declined; however, enrollment is slowly beginning to grow again as more students are attracted to the profession because of the attention from the accounting scandals. Those who pursue a CPA should have excellent job prospects. However, many accounting graduates are instead pursuing other certifications such as the CMA and CIA, so competition could be greater in management accounting and internal auditing than in public accounting. Regardless of specialty, accountants and auditors who have earned professional recognition through certification or licensure should have the best job prospects. Applicants with a master's degree in accounting, or a master's degree in business administration with a concentration in accounting, also will have an advantage. In the aftermath of the accounting scandals, professional certification is even more important in order to ensure that accountants' credentials and ethics are sound.

Proficiency in accounting and auditing computer software, or expertise in specialized areas such as international business, specific industries, or current legislation, may be helpful in landing certain accounting and auditing jobs. In addition, employers increasingly seek applicants with strong interpersonal and communication skills. Because many accountants work on teams with others from different backgrounds, they must be able to communicate accounting and financial information clearly and concisely. Regardless of one's qualifications, however, competition will remain keen for the most prestigious jobs in major accounting and business firms.

Advancement

Capable accountants and auditors may advance rapidly; those having inadequate academic preparation may be assigned routine jobs and find promotion difficult. Many graduates of junior colleges and business and correspondence schools, as well as bookkeepers and accounting clerks who meet the education and experience requirements set by their employers, can obtain junior accounting positions and advance to positions with more responsibilities by demonstrating their accounting skills on the job.

Beginning public accountants usually start by assisting with work for several clients. They may advance to positions with more responsibility in 1 or 2 years, and to senior positions within another few years. Those who excel may become supervisors, managers, or partners; open their own public accounting firm; or transfer to executive positions in management accounting or internal auditing in private firms.

Management accountants often start as cost accountants, junior internal auditors, or trainees for other accounting positions. As they rise through the organization, they may advance to accounting manager, chief cost accountant, budget director, or manager of internal auditing. Some become controllers, treasurers, financial vice presidents, chief financial officers, or corporation presidents. Many senior corporation executives have a background in accounting, internal auditing, or finance.

In general, public accountants, management accountants, and internal auditors have much occupational mobility. Practitioners often shift into management accounting or internal auditing from public accounting, or between internal auditing and management accounting. However, it is less common for accountants and auditors to move from either management accounting or internal auditing into public accounting.

Earnings

In 2002, the median wage and salary annual earnings of accountants and auditors were $47,000. The middle half of the occupation earned between $37,210 and $61,630. The top 10 percent of accountants and auditors earned more than $82,730, and the bottom 10 percent earned less than $30,320. In 2002, median annual earnings in the industries employing the largest numbers of accountants and auditors were:

Federal Government—$51,070

Accounting, tax preparation, bookkeeping, and payroll services—$49,520

Management of companies and enterprises—$49,110

Local government—$44,690

State government—$42,680

According to a salary survey conducted by the National Association of Colleges and Employers, bachelor's degree candidates in accounting received starting offers averaging $40,647 a year in 2003; master's degree candidates in accounting were initially offered $42,241.

According to a 2003 salary survey conducted by Robert Half International, a staffing services firm specializing in accounting and finance, accountants and auditors with up to 1 year of experience earned between $29,500 and $40,500. Those with 1 to 3 years of experience earned between $34,000 and $49,500. Senior accountants and auditors earned between $41,000 and $61,500; managers earned between $47,500 and $78,750; and directors of accounting and auditing earned between $66,750 and $197,500 a year. The variation in salaries reflects differences in size of firm, location, level of education, and professional credentials.

In the Federal Government, the starting annual salary for junior accountants and auditors was $23,442 in 2003. Candidates who had a superior academic record might start at $29,037, while applicants with a master's degree or 2 years of professional experience usually began at $35,519. Beginning salaries were slightly higher in selected areas where the prevailing local pay level was higher. Accountants employed by the Federal Government in nonsupervisory, supervisory, and managerial positions averaged $69,370 a year in 2003; auditors averaged $73,247.

Related Occupations

Accountants and auditors design internal control systems and analyze financial data. Others for whom training in accounting is valuable include budget analysts; cost estimators; loan officers; financial analysts and personal financial advisors; tax examiners, collectors, and revenue agents; bill and account collectors; and bookkeeping, accounting, and auditing clerks. Recently, accountants have assumed the role of management analysts and are involved in the design, implementation, and maintenance of accounting software systems. Others who perform similar work include computer programmers, computer software engineers, and computer support specialists and systems administrators.

Sources of Additional Information

Information on accredited accounting programs can be obtained from:

> AACSB International—Association to Advance Collegiate Schools of Business, 600 Emerson Rd., Suite 300, St. Louis, MO 63141. Internet: http://www.aacsb.edu/accreditation/AccreditedMembers.asp

Information about careers in certified public accounting and CPA standards and examinations may be obtained from:

> American Institute of Certified Public Accountants, 1211 Avenue of the Americas, New York, NY 10036. Internet: http://www.aicpa.org

Information on CPA licensure requirements by State may be obtained from:

> National Association of State Boards of Accountancy, 150 Fourth Ave. North, Suite 700, Nashville, TN 37219-2417. Internet: http://www.nasba.org

Information on careers in management accounting and the CMA designation may be obtained from:

> Institute of Management Accountants, 10 Paragon Dr., Montvale, NJ 07645-1760. Internet: http://www.imanet.org

Information on the Accredited in Accountancy, Accredited Business Accountant, Accredited Tax Advisor, or Accredited Tax Preparer designations may be obtained from:

> Accreditation Council for Accountancy and Taxation, 1010 North Fairfax St., Alexandria, VA 22314. Internet: http://www.acatcredentials.org

Information on careers in internal auditing and the CIA designation may be obtained from:

The Institute of Internal Auditors, 247 Maitland Ave., Altamonte Springs, FL 32701-4201. Internet: http://www.theiia.org

Information on careers in information systems auditing and the CISA designation may be obtained from:

Information Systems Audit and Control Association, 3701 Algonquin Rd., Suite 1010, Rolling Meadows, IL 60008. Internet: http://www.isaca.org

Information on careers in government accounting and the CGFM designation may be obtained from:

Association of Government Accountants, 2208 Mount Vernon Ave., Alexandria, VA 22301. Internet: http://www.agacgfm.org

Information on obtaining an accounting or auditing position with the Federal Government is available from the U.S. Office of Personnel Management (OPM) through a telephone-based system. Consult your telephone directory under U.S. Government for a local number or call (703) 724-1850; Federal Relay Service: (800) 877-8339. The first number is not toll-free, and charges may result. Information also is available from the OPM Internet site: http://www. usajobs.opm.gov.

Index

A

Administrative support occupations, OOH, 29–30
Agricultural industry, 35
Air transportation occupations, 34
America's Job Bank, 67
America's Top 300 Jobs, 21
Applications, process of filling out, 41–42
Architects, 23
Artistic skills, 12
Arts and design occupations, 24

B

Basic chronological resumé, 73
Building and grounds clearing and maintenance occupations, 27
Business occupations, OOH, 22–23

C

Careerbuilder, 67
Career Guide to Industries, 34
Career OINK, 35, 67
Cartographers, 23
Checklists
    self-management skills, 7–8
    transferable skills, 9–12
Chronological resumé
    basic, 73
    emphasizing results, 95
    improved, 75–77
    stressing technical credentials, 94
    tips for improved, 75–77
    tips for writing simple, 72–74

with unique graphic touches, 100–101
Cold contacting. *See* Direct contacts with employers
Combination resumé, 77
    for career changer, 97
    with matching JIST Card®, 98–99
    sample, 78–79
Communication industry, 36
Communication-related occupations, 24
Community occupations, 24
Computer occupations, 25
Construction industry, 35
Construction trades and related occupations, OOH, 31
Contacts. *See* Networking
Cover letters, 87
    after an interview, 90
    following up on a cold call, 92
    from network contact, 91
    for specific opening, 89
    tips for writing superior, 87–88
Creative skills, 12

D

Daily job search contact sheet, 121
Databases, resumé, 66
Design occupations, 24
Direct contacts with employers, 48
    dropping in without an appointment, 51
    phone script, 50–51
    Web sites for making, 67

Direct contacts with employers
(*cont.*)
yellow pages to find potential
employers, 49–50
Dispatching occupations, 30
Distributing occupations, 30
Drafters, 23
Dress and grooming, 109

E

Education occupations, 25
Electrical and electronic equipment
mechanic occupations, 32
Electronic and scannable resumés,
81
design considerations, 82
key words, 81–82
needs of large employers, 84–86
sample, 83
tips for reformatting, 84, 86
Electronic resumés, 66
Employers
direct contacts with. *see* Direct
contacts with employers
resumé requirements of large,
84–86
small, 51
yellow pages to find potential,
49–50
Employment agencies, 42–43
Engineering occupations, 23

F

Farming, fishing, and forestry
occupations, OOH, 31
Finance industry, 36
Financial clerks, 29
Financial operations occupations,
OOH, 22–23
First impressions made by job
applicants, 109–110
Follow-up techniques
rules for effective follow up, 117

system for follow up, 118–121
thank-you notes, 117–118
Food preparation and service-
related occupations, 27
Functional resumé, 77
for person with limited work
experience, 96

G

Gaps in employment, chronological
resumé handling of, 77
Geographic location of job,
consideration of, 66
Good-worker traits, 6
Government employment agencies,
42–43
Government industry, 37
Grooming, 109

H

Health care support occupations, 28
Health diagnosing and treating
occupations, 26–27
Health technologist and technician
occupations, 27

I

Ideal job, finding, 19–20
Improved chronological resumé,
75–77
Information and record clerks,
29–30
Installation occupations, OOH, 32
Installers, 32
Insurance industry, 36
Internet
job search methods and, 65–67
tips for increasing effectiveness
on, 66–67
useful sites, 67
Interview(s)
closing the interview, 115

defined, 103
first impressions, 109–110
grooming for, 109
negotiating salary, 113–115
problem questions. *See* Problem
    interview questions
purpose of, 110
questions. *See* Problem
    interview questions
redefining what counts as an,
    103–104
top ten tough and most
    frequently asked questions,
    111
turning down job during, 115
two a day, 103–104

J

JIST Cards®
    anatomy of, 52–54
    as basis for effective phone
        script, 64–65
    combination resumé with
        matching, 98–99
    contents of, 53–54
    sample, 53, 55–57
    uses for, 52, 71
    worksheet, 57–63
    writing and using, 63–64
JIST® site, 67
Job clusters and titles, OOH, 22–34
Job lead cards, 118–119
Job leads, follow up on. *See*
    Follow-up techniques
Job objective, defining preliminary,
    15–19
Job-related skills, 13
Jobs, finding ideal, 19–20
Job search
    deciding on time spent on,
        104–105
    as full-time job, 104
    methods. *See* Job search
        methods

most important rule for, 45
schedule, 105–107
Job search contact sheet, daily, 121
Job search data worksheet,
    123–134
Job search follow-up box, setting
    up and using, 119–120
Job search methods
    application process, 41–42
    direct contacts with employers.
        See Direct contacts with
        employers
    employment agencies, 42–43
    Internet and, 65–67
    less-effective, 40–44
    most-effective, 40, 44–51
    networking, 45–48
    newspaper help wanted ads, 41
    percentage of types used, 39
    school employment center, 44
    sending out and posting
        resumés, 44
Job titles, exploring, 20–34

L

Large employers, resumé
    requirements of, 84–86
Leadership skills, 11–12
Legal occupations, 25
Library occupations, 25
Life scientist occupations, 26

M

Maintenance occupations, OOH,
    32
Management occupations, OOH,
    22–23
Manufacturing industry, 35
Material moving occupations,
    OOH, 34
Material recording occupations,
    30
Mathematical occupations, 25

Media and communication-related occupations, 24
Metalworker occupations, 33
Mining industry, 35
Mini-resumé. *See* JIST Cards®
Monster.com, 67
Motor vehicle operator occupations, 34
Museum occupations, 25

N
National Resumé Writers' Association, 93
Negotiating salary, 113–115
Networking
methods of, 45–48
online, 67
three magic questions, 48
Newspaper help-wanted ads, 41

O
Occupational Outlook Handbook (OOH), 21
job clusters and titles, 22–34
sample job description, 135–148
Office and administrative support occupations,
OOH,rrsid10638908 29–30
One-Stop Centers, 42
O*NET Dictionary of Occupational Titles, 82
Online networking, 67
OOH. *See Occupational Outlook Handbook* (OOH)

P
Personal care and service occupations, 28
Phone script
JIST Card® as basis for effective, 64–65
sample, 50–51
Physical scientist occupations, 26

Plant and system operator occupations, 33
Plastic worker occupations, 33
Postal service occupations, 30
Printing occupations, 33
Private employment agencies, 43
Problem interview questions
answering, 111–113
answer real concern by presenting your skills, 112–113
brief and nondamaging answers, 112
three steps to answering, 111–113
top ten tough and most frequently asked interview questions, 111
understanding what is being asked, 112
"why should I hire you?", 113
Production occupations, 33–34
Production occupations, OOH, 33–34
Professional and related occupations, OOH, 23–27
Professional Association of Resumé Writers and Career Coaches, 93
Protective service occupations, 28
Public utilities industry, 36

Q
Questions
problem interview questions. *See* Problem interview questions
top ten tough and most frequently asked interview questions, 111

R
Repairers, 32

Repair occupations, OOH, 32
Resumés
    advice for, 86
    appearance of, 70, 80
    chronological. *See* Chronological resumé
    combination. *See* Combination resumé
    content of, 70–71
    creation of electronic, 66
    databases for, 66
    design and production tips, 80–81
    electronic and scannable. *See* Electronic and scannable resumé
    errors in, 69–70
    five most effective ways to use, 71–72
    functional, 77, 96
    mini-resumé. *See* JIST Cards®
    samples, 73, 75, 78–79, 83, 93–101
    scannable. *See* Electronic and scannable resumés
    sending out and posting, 44
    skills, 77, 96
    tips for creating superior, 69–71
    tips for reformatting, 84, 86
    writing, 69
Retail trade industry, 36
Riley Guide, 67

S

Salary negotiations, 113–115
Sales and related occupations, OOH, 28–29
Scannable resumés. *See* Electronic and scannable resumés
Scheduling occupations, 30
School employment center, 44
Science-based occupations, 26
Search engines, 67
Self-employment, 38
Self-management skills, 6–9

Service occupations, OOH, 27–28
Services industry, 36–37
Simple chronological resumé, tips for writing, 72–74
Skills
    job-related, 13
    self-management, 6–9
    transferable, 9–12
    types of, 6–13
Skills resumé, 77
    for person with limited work experience, 96
Skills triad, 5
Small employers, 51
Social scientist occupations, 26
Social services occupations, 24
Specific industries, exploring, 34–38
Superior cover letters, tips for writing, 87–88
Superior resumés, tips for creating, 69–71
Surveyors, 23

T

Telephone contacts, phone script for
    JIST Card® as basis for effective, 64–65
    sample, 50–51
Temporary employment agencies, 43
Thank-you notes, 71, 117–118
Top jobs and industries worksheet, 37
Top ten tough and most frequently asked interview questions, 111
Training occupations, 25
Transferable skills, 9–12
Transportation and material moving occupations, OOH, 34
Transportation industry, 36
Transportation occupations, 34

V

Vehicle and mobile equipment
    mechanic occupations, 32

W

Warm contacts. *See* Networking
Wholesale trade industry, 36
Worksheets
    JIST Card®, 57–63

job search data, 123–134
top jobs and industries, 37
World Wide Web (WWW). *See*
    Internet

Y

Yellow pages to find potential
    employers, 49–50